THE

PARIS

APARTMENT

"Kelly Bowen has crafted a story of deep humanity and re-demption, demonstrating the stunning beauty that can emerge from the darkest places. A true work of art."

—Erika Robuck, bestselling author of *The Invisible Woman*

"A moving story of danger and intrigue, love and loss, set against the glamour of the Paris Ritz. Like the artworks so beautifully portrayed in this novel, *The Paris Apartment* is a treasure."

—Christine Wells, author of *Sisters of the Resistance*

"An intriguing mix of high art and espionage, *The Paris Apartment* is a thrilling read from beginning to end!"

—Celia Rees, author of *Miss Graham's Cold War Cookbook*

"Expertly weaving together history, suspense, and mystery, Bowen has produced a novel that's both exciting and profound, driven by compelling characters and stunning twists. A page-turner from start to finish."

—Imogen Kealey, author of *Liberation*

Acclaim for Kelly Bowen and
The Paris Apartment

"Kelly Bowen's *The Paris Apartment* is a compelling story of two women navigating the dangers of occupied Paris with bravery and compassion. Bowen paints a richly layered picture of glamour, intrigue, and sacrifice that is at once heartbreaking and hopeful."

—Julia Kelly, international bestselling author of
The Light Over London

"A dual timeline connects past and present; a painting of a house, two matching pendants, and old photographs of a woman act as pivotal clues that bridge between the two; and fine works of art and a heartfelt love story between two people who were destined to meet brings the story full circle. A lovely *aha* moment at the end and the reminder to make one's life count will make this book and its characters linger long after the last page is turned."

—Karen White, *New York Times* bestselling author of
The Last Night in London

"A breathtaking, page-turning WWII tale of courage, espionage, and true love. Kelly Bowen's engaging characters will take you on an unforgettable journey of adventure and discovery. You won't want to put the book down for even a moment!"

—Genevieve Graham, international bestselling author of
Letters Across the Sea

THE

PARIS
APARTMENT

KELLY
BOWEN

FOREVER

New York   Boston

Copyright © 2021 by Kelly Bowen
Reading group guide copyright © 2021 by Kelly Bowen and Hachette Book Group, Inc.

Cover design by Daniela Medina. Cover photography © Trevillion; Shutterstock. Cover copyright © 2021 by Hachette Book Group, Inc.

Forever
Hachette Book Group
1290 Avenue of the Americas, New York, NY 10104
read-forever.com
twitter.com/readforeverpub

First Edition: April 2021

Forever is an imprint of Grand Central Publishing. The Forever name and logo are trademarks of Hachette Book Group, Inc.

The publisher is not responsible for websites (or their content) that are not owned by the publisher.

The Hachette Speakers Bureau provides a wide range of authors for speaking events. To find out more, go to www.hachettespeakersbureau.com or call (866) 376-6591.

Print book interior design by Tom Louie.

Library of Congress Cataloging-in-Publication Data

Names: Bowen, Kelly (Romance fiction writer), author.
Title: The Paris apartment / Kelly Bowen.
Description: First edition. | New York, NY : Forever, 2021.
Identifiers: LCCN 2020053579 | ISBN 9781538718155 (trade paperback) | ISBN 9781538718148 (ebook)
Subjects: LCSH: World War, 1939-1945--Underground movements--France--Fiction. | GSAFD: Historical fiction.
Classification: LCC PR9199.4.B68523 P37 2021 | DDC 813/.6--dc23
LC record available at https://lccn.loc.gov/2020053579

ISBNs: 978-1-5387-1815-5 (trade paperback), 978-1-5387-1814-8 (ebook)

Printed in the United States of America

LSC-C

Printing 1, 2021

*To the unsung heroes who fought hatred and
persecution with uncommon courage and strength.
Your sacrifice and efforts will not be forgotten.*

CHAPTER

1

Aurelia

PARIS, FRANCE
10 JUNE 2017

The woman was nude.

Painted in a swirl of angry scarlets and oranges, the woman's arms were flung over her head, her hands outstretched, her hair a cloud of midnight floating behind her. Caught in the shaft of light that fell through the open apartment door, she gazed out with dark eyes from her canvas, angry and accusing, as if she resented the intrusion into her space and privacy. Lia froze in the open doorway, one hand clutching the heavy key and the other gripping the packet of neatly organized legal papers that said she had every right to be here.

And that this unknown apartment, along with all its contents, now belonged to her.

It is an incredibly valuable property, the lawyers had assured her. *Your grandmother must have adored you*, the administrative assistant had said enviously as she had examined the printed address. And Lia hadn't replied to any of them because Grandmère's motives in death were as murky as they had been in life, and Lia couldn't be sure that adoration had figured in either.

"Utilities should be on," the building's concierge said from the top of the stairs behind Lia. The property caretaker was a surprisingly young woman with a close-cropped pink bob and a quick smile who had introduced herself simply as Celeste. Lia had liked her immediately. "I'm not often in the office but I'm always around if you need anything else. Just ring me."

"Thank you," Lia replied faintly, slipping the key into her pocket.

"You said on the phone this place was your grandmother's?" Celeste leaned casually on the stair railing.

"Yes. She left it to me when she passed." Or at least that was what the lawyers had said when they had summoned her to their offices and laid a steady stream of documents before her. And while the flat had been paid for and maintained from an account with Grandmère's name on it, as far as Lia knew, Estelle Allard had never lived anywhere other than Marseille.

"Ah." The woman's expression softened. "My condolences on her passing."

"Thank you. It wasn't unexpected. Though this apartment was a...shock."

"Not a bad one as shocks go, I think?" Celeste remarked. "We should all be so lucky."

"True," Lia acknowledged, playing with the enameled pendant at her throat. Until this morning, the antique necklace had been the only gift Grandmère had ever given her, presented without fuss on her eighteenth birthday. She considered the concierge. "How long have you worked here?"

"Six years."

"I don't suppose you know anything about this apartment? Or my grandmother? Estelle Allard?"

Celeste shook her head. "I'm sorry, I don't. While I'm familiar with most of the tenants in the building, in truth, I had no idea who owned this apartment, only that it's been unoccupied since I started."

On impulse, Lia jammed the packet of paper under her arm and unzipped her portfolio bag. From inside, she withdrew a small painting, about the size of a legal document. It was a vivid, if somewhat clumsy, painting of a manor house surrounded by clumps of emerald trees and silhouetted against a cobalt sky. Along with the key to this apartment, the painting had been the only other thing her grandmother had specifically left her.

"What about the name Seymour? William Seymour? Does that sound familiar?" Lia asked, holding the painting toward Celeste.

Celeste shook her head again. "No. May I ask who he was?"

"No clue. Other than the artist who signed this painting."

"Oh." Celeste looked intrigued. "Were you thinking that he was once a tenant here?"

"I have no idea." Lia sighed, sliding the little painting back into her bag. She hadn't really expected an answer but she had nothing to lose by asking.

"I can check the building's records for you if you like," Celeste offered. "We have archives going back a lot of years. If a William Seymour lived here at one point in time, I might be able to find out."

Lia was touched by the kindness of the offer. "No, that's all right." She didn't want to waste this woman's time. At least until she had done a little research of her own.

"Sure. But if you reconsider, just let me know."

"Thank you. I will."

Celeste seemed to hesitate. "Are you planning to live here?" she finally asked.

Lia opened her mouth to answer and then closed it. The simple answer was yes, at least temporarily. But beyond temporarily? Lia had no simple answer for that.

"None of my business." The woman ducked her head. "Sorry."

"Don't be." Lia smiled. "I haven't made a decision yet."

"I hope you stay," Celeste said sincerely. "It would be nice to have—"

The sound of a lock being released, accompanied by a brief torrent of hysterical barking, made Lia turn. An elderly woman emerged from the apartment across the landing and shuffled toward her. A small bundle of writhing white fur was clamped under one arm, a pointy cane clutched in her other hand. She was dressed like a model from a midcentury American advert peddling soap or vacuums, in a wide-skirted floral dress with a pinched waist and a string of heavy pearls at her throat. Her white hair was curled around a liberally powdered face, her lipstick an angry crimson. Color had bled into the deep lines that tracked outward from her lips, and the whole effect was rather macabre. Unbidden, Aurelia could almost hear Grandmère *tsk* in disapproval.

One should never notice your cosmetics, Lia. Unless, of course, you only wish to be noticed but not seen.

At the time, an adolescent, lip-gloss-loving Lia remembered being annoyed by the cryptic, critical comment. Now, Lia couldn't say Grandmère had been wrong.

Lia's neighbour was now shuffling across the marble floor,

her eyes fixed beyond Lia at the tall, nude painting propped up inside the apartment and visible in the meagre light. She looked as shocked as Lia had felt when she had first opened the door, though that shock was fading into clear condemnation. Lia pasted on a smile and stepped more fully into her doorway, blocking the view inside.

The woman scowled and craned her neck, trying to peer past.

"Good afternoon," Lia said politely, her ingrained boarding-school manners demanding that she make some sort of greeting.

In response, the dog resumed its frantic tirade, the shrill noise bouncing mercilessly off the marble floor and plaster walls. The woman's face soured further, and she produced a piece of sausage from somewhere in the folds of her dress. That silenced the barking, two beady eyes now fixed not on Lia but on the prize held in clawlike fingers.

"You own this apartment?" the woman asked into the ensuing quiet with a voice like sandpaper.

"Yes." A fact that was still so new and novel that it was hard to answer with conviction.

"I've lived here my entire life. Since 1943," the woman said, her eyes narrowing.

Lia's smile was slipping. "Um. That's a long time—"

"I know everything that goes on in this building. And in all that time, no one has ever gone in or come out of that apartment. Until now."

"Mmm." Lia made some noncommittal sound. She wasn't sure if that was a question, a statement, or an accusation. She adjusted her grip on the legal envelope, pressing it against her chest.

"You living here by yourself?" Her gaze shifted to Lia's left hand.

"I beg your pardon?" Lia resisted the urge to shove her hand in her pocket.

"You seem old to not have a husband. Too late now, I suppose. Unfortunate."

Lia blinked, uncertain she had heard right. "I'm sorry?"

"I know your type," Lia's neighbour sniffed, her eyes lingering first on Lia's heavy backpack and the portfolio bag, and finally on her bare shoulders and the straps of her red sundress tied around her neck.

"My type?" Lia's patience was wearing thin, and irritation was starting to creep in.

"I don't want to hear your music. No drugs or booze or parties. No strange men prowling around my door at all hours of the night looking for you."

"I'll try to keep the men confined to daylight hours," Lia replied pleasantly, unable to help herself.

Celeste, who had remained silent through the entire exchange, snorted in laughter before trying to cover it up with a fit of coughing.

The woman's head snapped around.

"Good afternoon, Ms. Hoffmann." Celeste composed herself. "How are you doing today?"

Madame Hoffmann gave the woman's pink hair a hard look, scarlet lips twisting into a sneer. "Degenerate," she muttered.

Celeste's phone chimed, and she glanced down at the screen. "Duty calls," she said, shooting Lia an apologetic glance. "Let me know if you need anything. And welcome to the building." She pushed herself off the railing and vanished down the stairs, triggering another hysterical tirade of barking.

Lia used the distraction to retreat into her apartment and close the door behind her, abruptly enveloping herself in a stuffy darkness but saving herself from further conversation.

"No wonder you're angry," she muttered in the direction of the nude canvas that rested somewhere in front of her. "I'd be angry, too, if I'd lived across from a neighbour like that since 1943."

She didn't get an answer.

The air in the apartment was thick with the scent of age and dust, suggesting that the apartment had been unoccupied far longer than the six years Celeste knew about. Lia set her belongings down and let her eyes adjust to the gloom. Deeper in the apartment, on the side that would face the wide, sunny street, faint lines of light were seeping around what Lia surmised must be heavy curtains covering the windows. Enough light to give the suggestion of shapes but not enough for her to see anything clearly.

Carefully, Lia inched forward out of the foyer, past the dim outline of the canvas, and made her way toward the windows. The floor beneath her creaked with each step as if it, too, resented her intrusion. She reached the curtained wall and extended her hand, the tips of her fingers colliding with a heavy fabric that felt like damask. So far, so good. Nothing had jumped out or fallen on her head or run over her toes. She found the edge of the curtain, rings rattling on their rod somewhere above. Without hesitating, she pulled the curtain back.

And regretted it immediately.

As blinding sunlight spilled through the antique panes, thick, choking clouds of dust billowed around her. Lia gagged and coughed, her eyes instantly watering. She fumbled frantically with the latch on the window, relieved beyond measure when it reluctantly gave way. She pushed one of the leaded-glass panels open a crack, ignoring the groan of protest from the hinges, and pressed her face out into the fresh air.

She stayed that way for a good minute, her head stuck out the window, gasping and hacking and trying not to imagine how ridiculous she must look to people passing by down below. Perhaps she should have just left the apartment door wide open. Perhaps she should have sent the charming Madame Hoffmann in first.

Her coughing finally subsiding, Lia took a deep, fortifying breath and straightened, bracing herself for what she might find. She turned slowly away from the window. And discovered that, upon her death, Grandmère had not left Lia an apartment after all.

She'd left Lia a museum.

Dust still swirled but the brilliant light illuminated walls covered in patterned wallpaper the grey-blue of a stormy sky. Dozens of painted landscapes and seascapes in gilded frames were hung on the wall opposite the windows, some capturing images of bucolic country scenes, others freezing ships forever in their quest across the horizon, and each one bursting with saturated color.

In the center of the room, upholstered Louis XV sofas in dust-covered turquoise faced off against each other across a wide Persian rug. A long writing desk bridged the ends of the sofas closest to Lia, and it was against the desk that the tall, nude canvas had been propped, facing the door to greet anyone who entered.

On the back wall adjacent to the windows, an elaborate marble mantelpiece swept over an empty hearth. A bracket had been mounted to the wall high above the fireplace, suggesting that a piece of art had once hung in the tall space, although whatever was once there wasn't now. And above her head, a chandelier hung in the center of the room, its dripping, dazzling crystals muted only partially by dust.

On unfeeling legs, Lia headed deeper into the apartment. She stopped at a dainty side table at the far end of a sofa and examined a collection of framed photos. With care, she picked up the first and wiped the glass. A young woman had been captured leaning against a light post in front of a jazz club, wearing a silky, beaded dress that clung to each and every curve like a second skin, a fur stole draped carelessly over her shoulders. She held a cigarette holder in one hand, eyes meeting the camera's lens with smoky, sensual indifference. Lia turned it over. *Estelle Allard, Montmartre, 1938* was written in pencil across the back.

Lia swallowed hard.

Though she had been told repeatedly by the estate lawyers that this apartment was the domain of Estelle Allard, Lia realized that she hadn't truly believed it until right now. She hadn't truly believed that her grandmother, who had not once in her life mentioned that she had ever travelled to Paris, much less lived here, had kept a secret of this magnitude for this long.

And Lia couldn't even begin to imagine why she would have done so.

She set the photo back down and examined the second. In this one, the beautiful Estelle was behind the wheel of a low-slung Mercedes, leaning out the window and laughing at the photographer. Her hair was loose over her shoulders, a jaunty hat cocked over one eye. Lia blinked, trying to reconcile these sultry, fearless images with the rigid, reserved woman Lia had known. She failed miserably.

She turned her attention to the last of the photos and frowned. A German officer stared back at her, unsmiling and severe. From his uniform, it was clear that it was an image from the First World War. Lia frowned and turned it over but there was nothing written on the back. She set the photo down and glanced at a pile of magazines stacked beside it.

She slid the top one to the side. The issue beneath, devoid of dust, was easy to read. *Signal* blazed from the upper left corner in bold red text, the cover beneath dominated by an image of a Nazi soldier with an intense expression. A strip of the same bold red color ran down the spine of the magazine, *September 1942* easily visible at the top. Lia snatched her hand away.

"This is not happening," she said into the silence, as if saying it out loud would make it true. Because she already knew without opening the magazine what she'd find. German propaganda and glossy pro-Nazi photos, all published at a time when Nazis had overrun and occupied this very city.

Lia stared again at a young Estelle Allard laughing from her Mercedes and the nameless German officer before she turned away from the photos and the magazines and all their ominous implications. With a queasy dread settling into her gut, she made her way past the ornate hearth mantel and around the corner. Here, the space narrowed into a formal dining room. The center was dominated by a rosewood table surrounded by eight matching chairs. On the wall to her right, a cabinet taller than she was filled the space, rows of crystal, silver, and porcelain dinnerware displayed on the shelves.

On the wall opposite the cabinet was another collection of paintings, striking and arresting portraits of men and women in clothing from centuries past. Lia bit her lip hard enough to hurt as the dread intensified. Art had been a desirable souvenir for the Nazis during the occupation, entire collections stolen—

"Stop it, Lia." She shook her head, not caring how foolish she sounded, talking to no one. "Don't be absurd."

Yes, there was Nazi propaganda in the apartment. But a single photo and a handful of magazines did not mean that the paintings on these walls had been stolen or otherwise illicitly obtained. It did not mean that her grandmother had deliberately kept this collection here, in this apartment, for any reason other than that she had liked art when she had been younger. Conjuring conspiracy theories was best left to Hollywood. And radical zealots.

Lia tore her gaze from the paintings and continued through the dining room, stepping into a hallway. On her right, a doorway opened up into a kitchen with a tiny stove, a small refrigerator, and a deep sink set into a countertop free of clutter, save for a single crystal tumbler.

Just to her left, a set of French doors stood open, the dim outline of a four-poster bed identifying this last space as a bedroom. As in the living room, lines of sunlight from tall windows were visible on the far wall. Lia entered the room, skirted the bed, and, with a great deal more care than she had taken earlier, eased the heavy curtains open.

In the light, the room was a decidedly feminine space, the walls papered in a shade of rose, the edges near the ceiling only slightly yellowed and discolored. The room consisted of a double bed, a dressing table and chair, and an enormous wardrobe, all carved with a provincial flair. The bed was neatly made, and the linens, once washed, would likely be the same rose hue as the walls.

The room was impeccably tidy save for a garment that had

been tossed carelessly on top of the smooth coverlet, crumpled and forgotten and dulled by dust. It was an evening gown, Lia realized, moving to lift it by its thin straps. A stunning creation of lemon-yellow chiffon and crepe, beaded with crystals, and something that would have been obscenely expensive no matter what century it had been purchased in. Not something one would toss aside like an old pair of socks.

Bewildered, she let the dress drop back to the bed and eyed the narrow, arched doorway in the corner beside the wardrobe. It led into what looked like a modern walk-in closet. A dressing room, Lia guessed, though there was almost no space to walk in. On both sides, dresses and gowns and furs and coats hung crammed together, spilling out on top of one another in such numbers that Lia couldn't even see the back wall. Shoes lined the floor, dozens and dozens of pairs, and along a shelf at the top, hat boxes were stacked. Smaller jewelry boxes, some of them covered in leather and satin, were piled in front.

"Good Lord," Lia mumbled, the excess hard to comprehend.

She backed away and cautiously opened the wardrobe next, expecting to be inundated with another jumble of extravagance. But the wardrobe was almost empty, the cavernous interior yielding only a half-dozen gowns.

These gowns, protected from the years of dust, were a collection of couture silks and satins, each one exquisitely embroidered, appliquéd, and detailed. Lia ran her fingers along the length of a sapphire-colored skirt before pulling her hand back, afraid that she would soil the fabric. She closed the wardrobe and rested her forehead against the double doors. The gowns, the shoes, the furs—there was a fortune in clothing here. Just like there was a fortune in fine furnishings and fine art.

All of it hidden for over seventy years.

Lia had fallen down a rabbit hole. An overwhelming, insane rabbit hole that made a jump to abhorrent conclusions far too easy. She lifted her head and took a steadying breath. Assumptions never ended well—a career dedicated to science had taught her that. She would give her grandmother the benefit of the doubt. She would not believe the worst until such time as she was presented with irrefutable proof.

For right now, she would put conjecture aside. Instead, she would make a list of things that needed to be done, tasks that required her attention immediately. Lists were made of numbers and needs, and not speculations and suppositions. Lists were ordered and rational, and they had always helped her focus on what she could control when presented with disorder and uncertainty. Yes, a carefully curated collection of lists was exactly what she needed right now.

Feeling a little better, Lia headed back toward the bedroom doors but stopped abruptly as she caught sight of her reflection. A little tarnished and spotted, the mirror mounted above the dressing table nonetheless revealed the troubled lines that still suffused Lia's features. Almost involuntarily, she sank onto the little chair, ignoring the dust, not taking her eyes off her reflection. Had her grandmother been the last to be reflected in this mirror? And if Lia could go back in time, what would she have seen? Whom would she have seen?

Her eyes dropped to the surface of the dressing table. A collection of decorative glass bottles huddled in the center. A pair of women's gloves lay discarded beside them, abandoned where they had been dropped. Beside the gloves, propped up against the bottom of the mirror, was a small card. A postcard of some sort, Lia thought as she reached for it.

It was a black-and-white photo of a long, looming building, a row of Roman columns lining the entire façade like an ancient temple. An impressive display of architecture, marred only by the Nazi flag snapping proudly in the wind in the foreground. Dread returned and manifested into something far more sinister. Very slowly, Lia turned the postcard over.

For the lovely Estelle, it read in scrawled, faded ink. *With thanks, Hermann Göring.*

Lia dropped the postcard as though it had bitten her and stumbled to her feet, knocking the little chair to the side. Despair warred with revulsion, leaving her nauseated. She was such a fool. Only a fool would have clung to hope. Only a delusional fool would have refused to truly accept the evidence scattered all over this apartment. As far as irrefutable proof went, Lia couldn't imagine anything more damning.

She still had no idea why her grandmother had chosen to leave her this apartment but the reason that she had kept its existence a secret was abundantly clear. Because her grandmother, a woman who had hung the French flag out every May in celebration, a woman who had repeatedly declared her love for her country, hadn't been a patriotic citizen at all. Her grandmother had been a liar and a traitor and a fraud.

Her grandmother had been a Nazi collaborator.

CHAPTER

2

Sophie

S ophie Seymour had been eight years old when she'd first
heard someone refer to her as unnatural.

It had been at Heloise Postlewaithe's birthday party, an event
that Sophie had attended only because Mrs. Postlewaithe had
invited the entirety of her daughter's summer Sunday school
class. The party had been an affair marked by fancy frocks
with copious ruffles, rich cakes and tepid tea, and games that
had bored Sophie to death, quite frankly. She'd wandered away
from the shrill fracas of musical chairs and pass the parcel without anyone noticing and made her way to the Postlewaithes'
library that was up on the first floor.

The Postlewaithes' country manor was impressive, their
library equally so. Here, amid the blessed silence and the soft
afternoon light, Sophie had found a Latin primer, no doubt
a leftover from a previous Postlewaithe's Eton days. At eight,
Sophie was already fluent in French, Spanish, and Italian,

though she'd never seen the root language from which all of those had been derived. She'd been instantly captivated and settled down in a warm corner of the room to read.

As absorbed in her newfound study and tucked away upstairs as she was, she hadn't heard the discovery of her absence. She hadn't been aware of the uproar and panic when it was finally discerned that an eight-year-old girl was missing or hearkened to the fears that, as the initial search had turned up nothing, she might have fallen into one of the manor's ponds and drowned.

It wasn't until a frantic Mrs. Postlewaithe had finally discovered Sophie in the library an hour later that Sophie had any indication that anything was wrong. She'd yanked Sophie to her feet, relief dissolving into fury, and snatched the primer out of Sophie's hands.

"What is wrong with you?" she'd demanded, her face flushed an alarming shade beneath a stylish coiffure that was still perfectly in place.

"Nothing," Sophie replied, blinking with incomprehension.

"You left the party."

"The noise was hurting my ears," Sophie explained, trying to be polite.

"You ruined Heloise's party," the woman hissed. "Ruined it all."

"I don't understand."

"We all had to look for you. We thought you'd drowned."

Sophie shook her head. "I know how to swim," she tried to reassure her hostess. "My mum made both my brother and me take lessons before we were allowed to go exploring on our own."

The woman's lips curled in disgust. "Perhaps your mum

should have also taught you that stealing is rude. Taking things that aren't yours."

"I wasn't stealing," Sophie told her. "I was just reading. And I was going to put it back when I was done."

Mrs. Postlewaithe looked down at the Latin primer. "And you're a liar too," she sneered. "You can't read this."

"I can." Sophie had never been called a liar by a grown-up before. It made her stomach feel awful. "It's just Latin," she tried to explain. "And this book starts with basic grammar in tables and uses that to build up more complex sentences. It's not that hard. I could show you."

"I don't need you to show me anything. I know my place in this world. You need to learn yours."

Mrs. Postlewaithe stared at Sophie and Sophie had stared back.

"You are an unnatural creature," the woman continued, her expression as hard and cold as the diamonds that hung from her neck. "No one will ever want you. There is something wrong with you."

That conversation had been thirteen years ago, but Sophie had never forgotten it.

"Am I unnatural?" Sophie asked, staring up at the ceiling.

Beside her, Piotr rolled over in bed. His dark hair was thoroughly tousled, eyes the color of the Baltic Sea thoroughly amused. "Is this a trick question? A test for new husbands?" He propped his head up on his hand.

"You're laughing at me."

"You deserve it with questions like that." He reached over and stroked her bare shoulder. "You're not having regrets, are you?"

"I regret we did not do this sooner."

"That makes two of us." Piotr Kowalski was smiling as he said it. "If I had known that you would have said yes, I would have asked you to marry me the day you ran me over with your bicycle."

"I did not run you over. I avoided you and hit a tree. Mostly."

"No, I think you ran me over on purpose. You couldn't help yourself," he teased.

"I ran you over because I was late for work. And you should know that I did my best not to fall in love with you."

"Mmm." Piotr leaned forward and kissed her with a thoroughness that curled her toes. "You never stood a chance, wife."

Sophie managed to nod because he was right. Love had been wearing the green-brown uniform of a Polish cavalry officer and had not cursed or seethed when he'd been sent sprawling by her inattention and haste. Instead, love had gently helped her stagger to her feet, her hose torn and beyond salvage, her knee scraped and throbbing, and her lip split and bleeding. He'd righted her bicycle with easy motions before turning back to her, concern stamped across his features.

She'd made a cake of herself after that, in the face of his kindness and his devastatingly vivid blue eyes, babbling apologies and stammering something about needing to get back to the embassy. He had only wet a linen kerchief with his canteen and wiped the blood from her lip with a tenderness that had suddenly made her want to burst into tears. She'd fled, clambering back on her bicycle and pedaling away, realizing only when she'd reached the embassy that she was clutching his kerchief, now stained and crushed.

She'd locked herself in the loo and unsteadily put herself back together as best she could, thoroughly mortified. The practical part of her knew she'd likely never see the kind blue-eyed officer again but instead of relief, she'd felt an intense regret.

"Why did you come back that day?" she asked suddenly. "To the embassy?"

"Because the extraordinary, beautiful blond girl who kept apologizing in at least four languages stole my only kerchief, and I wanted it back."

"You brought flowers."

"Because she had also stolen my heart. Though I never got that back, nor do I want it returned. That will be yours forever, *moja kochana*."

Sophie glanced down at the band around her finger. In the long rays of the sun that was beginning its descent over the roofs and spires of the city, the ruby and tiny pearls gleamed with a lustrous glow. "You, Piotr Kowalski, are a shameless romantic."

"Guilty." He flashed her a roguish grin. "It's why you love me."

"I love you because you are kind and brave and honourable. Because you are patient and gentle and smart."

"What about handsome?"

"The most handsome man of all." Sophie smiled.

"Indeed. Do go on. What else do you love about me?"

"Now you're just fishing for flattery."

"Yes. You can have a turn later. I promise I'll make it worth your while."

Sophie laughed before sobering. "I love you because the day I told you that I would become a professor of languages at Oxford, you asked why I hadn't already applied. And where we would live."

"Perfectly reasonable questions."

Sophie toyed with the edge of the sheet. "Most men wouldn't think so."

Piotr caught her hand. "And I am not most men. Where is this coming from?"

"Childhood insecurities," Sophie mumbled. "I'm sorry. This is embarrassing and not at all a romantic topic on our wedding night."

Piotr sat up, the hotel bed protesting the movement. He slid an arm under her shoulders and hauled her up against him. "Any man who would wish to extinguish the fire that burns so bright in you is no man at all. Whatever dreams you wish to chase, I will chase them with you."

"I am the luckiest girl in the world right now," she whispered, looking up at him.

"Careful," he replied, his eyes dancing. "You might be accused of being a shameless romantic."

"I'll have you know that the women in my family are not romantics, shameless or otherwise," she sniffed. "We leave that to our menfolk."

"I can't wait to meet them."

"You will."

"They will not be angry? That I married their daughter without even meeting them?"

Sophie bit her lip. For as long as she could remember, marriage had ever been an enemy to her ambitions and dreams and an adversary to her independence and freedom. Her antipathy toward the institution had increased each time some meddling matriarch told Sophie that it was well past time that she abandon her frivolous studies and do what was natural—marry well and settle down.

A thousand times she had sworn to her family that she

would never fall in love. Never marry. A thousand times she had sat down at her writing desk to tell her family that she'd been a liar. And each time, the words hadn't come. She would remedy that as soon as she got back to Warsaw tomorrow.

"They will love you," she told him. That was the truth.

"I wish my parents were still alive and could have known you," he said, his finger tracing patterns along the top of her arm. "Though they would have been appalled that I did not marry you in front of a hundred people, in a church filled with flowers, with a brass ensemble to serenade us out. Or that I did not take you to Paris or Vienna for our honeymoon and sleep on silk sheets."

"That all sounds complicated." Sophie squeezed his hand with hers, twining her fingers through his. "This world is complicated enough."

"I didn't even manage a proper photographer."

"I didn't particularly want to marry a proper photographer."

"Very funny."

"I love you," she said simply, those words seemingly inadequate for the storm of emotion that was constricting her chest.

He glanced over at her, holding her eyes with his own, the smile slipping from his lips, his expression intense. "I love you too," he replied.

"I wish your leave wasn't so short. I wish you didn't have to go back to your regiment tomorrow. I don't want to lose you again so quickly—"

"This was the best leave of my life." He cut her off. "And you can't lose me. You're stuck with me for good. Your last name is now the same as mine. You are wearing my grandmother's ring. I'm well and truly yours."

Sophie closed her eyes and listened to the steady beat of his heart beneath her ear.

"The answer to your question is yes," he said presently. "You are unnatural." His lips found the hollow behind her ear. "Unnaturally brilliant, unnaturally beautiful." His hand slid under the sheet over her hip. "And most of all," he whispered, "unnaturally bewitching."

Sophie opened her eyes. "Show me," she said.

And he did.

Sophie wasn't sure what had woken her.

She lay in the bed, listening intently, but nothing disturbed the stillness aside from Piotr's steady breathing. Her husband had indeed had more than a few ideas on how best to spend what little time they had left before he was required to report back, but then so had she. Both had finally fallen into an exhausted, sated sleep sometime in the small hours before dawn.

She crept from the bed with care and opened her small suitcase as quietly as possible, feeling for her clothes.

"Leaving me already?" Piotr's sleepy voice mumbled out of the dark.

"Just to watch the sunrise," she said, pulling a simple frock over her head. "Go back to sleep."

"Not a chance. This is the first dawn of the first day of our life together. I'm coming with you." The bed creaked, and a light flickered on.

Sophie buttoned the collar of her dress and slipped on her shoes. Piotr joined her a moment later, and they exited the old stone building and stepped out in front. Turning away from the empty street that led back in the direction of the town center, they circled the hotel and found themselves in a deserted, grassy expanse. Based on the long, dilapidated building that sagged forgotten on the south side of the space, Sophie guessed that, in a century past, the expanse might once have been a carriage yard.

Dawn was pushing at the horizon, a soft gold glow layered below the bruised purples of a retreating night. The air was cool, sharp edges of an encroaching autumn lurking on the breeze. Sophie caught Piotr's hand and tugged him along a well-trodden path that crossed the yard to end near a pasture gate, dew making the toes of her shoes wet where they brushed the grass.

They reached the gate, and she leaned over the rail. The wood was rough beneath her arms but she paid little attention, delighted to find that the fenced enclosure was home to a dappled mare and her foal, both appearing like apparitions in the watery light. With fingers of mist swirling through the tall grass and an ever-lightening sky behind them, the horses looked like they might be posing for a postcard, the sort of photograph of the Polish countryside that was sold in the streets of Warsaw. The beauty of the scene made her sigh. She wanted to fix this moment in her memory forever.

"Isn't it lovely?" she breathed happily.

"He is a handsome little fellow," Piotr replied. "I like his shoulders and legs already."

Sophie made a face at her husband. "The landscape, dear," she said dryly.

He kissed her. "That too."

In the pasture, the copper-colored colt pranced and bucked before nearly toppling sideways.

Sophie laughed. "I think he's trying to impress you. Angling for a cavalry job, maybe."

"Perhaps." He ducked through the rails and held out his hand. "Come," he said, grinning. "Let's go make friends."

Sophie followed him and took his hand. She'd never ridden as a child—her parents hadn't kept horses at the family's Norfolk estate—but Piotr had taken her often. It was not long before his deep love for the noble creatures became hers as well.

The mare whickered a greeting and turned toward them, approaching as the colt continued to prance beyond. The mare stopped beside Piotr and blew gently against his arm. He reached up and scratched between its ears, murmuring something that Sophie couldn't hear. The horse lowered its head.

"You've cast a spell on her." Sophie joined him, watching the way his hands moved over the horse. She'd always loved Piotr's hands, strong, rough, callused, and yet infinitely gentle. Even the most nervous of mounts seemed to settle under his touch.

"I have done no such thing," he said softly. "Merely introduced myself. The colt will come when he's ready."

Sophie watched the colt circle Piotr and the mare, tossing its head. Finally, it inched closer, its nose almost touching Piotr's shirt. Piotr didn't move, merely continued to stroke the mare's neck, speaking quiet words. The colt moved closer still, and Piotr shifted his hand from the mare to the colt. It shied away. Piotr returned his attention to the mare.

"He's skittish," Sophie said.

"No," Piotr murmured. "Trust needs to be earned. He is only reminding me of that fact."

The colt came back toward Piotr. This time it didn't shy when Piotr lifted his hand. He rested his palm on the colt's withers for only a few seconds before removing it. The colt lowered its head and took another step closer.

"There you are," Piotr breathed. He ran a hand along the back of the colt with slow, gentle movements. "Trust cannot be a single-sided affair. One day, this horse might be asked to do the impossible. Charge into a situation when every instinct he possesses is telling him to flee the opposite way. But he will do what you've asked because you have earned his trust. Trust is everything."

He dropped his hand and stepped away from both the mare and the colt to join Sophie and slip an arm around her.

She laid her head on his shoulder, a quiet ache constricting her heart. She wished that she could stay in this perfect moment forever but she could feel time slipping away from her. From them. "I wish you didn't have to go," she whispered.

"You're the one who stole a car from the Foreign Office and needs to return it before they come looking."

"I didn't steal it, I borrowed it. I'll have it back before they even know it's gone. And what I do with my days off are my business. Don't change the subject."

He squeezed her shoulder. "My regiment isn't even mobilized."

Sophie grimaced. "But they were."

"Everyone was, for a day. And now we're not. It seems it is just a great deal of hurry-up-and-waiting for something that might never happen. Most of the boys in the squadron don't think we will see action."

"Most of the boys in your squadron haven't heard what I've heard in the embassy," Sophie muttered.

"Hitler is ambitious and arrogant, yes, but he is not stupid. I have to believe that he will not risk war with Britain and France by pushing into Poland."

"I'm not so sure, Piotr. I'm worried."

Piotr turned to face her. "I know. I am too."

Sophie sighed and watched the mare and her colt wander away a few paces. "I'm sorry. We agreed that we wouldn't talk of politics and war in what little time we have here—"

"Don't apologize." He tucked a loose strand of her hair behind her ear. "Maybe we should. Maybe we need to talk about what should happen if the Germans do decide to do something stupid."

She frowned.

"I think you should leave Poland."

"What? No."

"Just until things settle—"

"And go where?"

"To France, at least. From there you'd still be able to get back to England in case—"

"No. My home is where you are."

"I want you safe."

"I will be safe. I'll be in Warsaw. Where I'm needed. Where, in my own small way, I can still contribute to whatever diplomatic efforts are being made to avoid disaster." She stepped forward and slipped her hands around his waist. "I will not run, and you will not send me away. We are in this together, come what may."

"But if the worst happens—if there is war—I need to know you are all right."

"I'll be fine—"

"Promise me that you will do the smart thing when the time comes, Sophie. That you will take care of yourself and not do anything foolish."

"Piotr—"

"Promise me." His demand was urgent.

Sophie bit her lip. "I promise."

"Thank you." Piotr rested his forehead against hers. "I didn't really think you'd agree to go."

"Good. I'm glad we got that settled." The breeze gusted, and she shivered.

"May I at least take you inside and warm you up?" he asked.

"Mmm. I like that idea much better."

Arm in arm, they started back toward the hotel. The dappled mare was cropping grass just ahead, her colt dancing in playful circles around her.

Sophie's stomach growled. "What do you think the chances are we might find something to eat—"

The mare's head came up abruptly, her ears pricked, her attention riveted in the direction of the hotel.

Sophie stopped, Piotr along with her, but she could see nothing in the shadowed carriage yard that might have alarmed the mare. In the street beyond, a dog started barking incessantly, joined by a handful more. Sophie frowned. The mare snorted and backed away, head high and nostrils flaring, before breaking into a canter toward the end of the pasture, her foal at her heels. And as the sound of the mare's pounding hooves faded, Sophie heard the engines.

She didn't understand where they were coming from at first. Her mind did not immediately register the high-pitched whine of rapidly descending planes until a flash of light in the southwestern sky caught her attention. She stared dumbly as the spots became larger and louder, approaching the village.

"Are those ours?" she whispered.

"No," Piotr croaked.

The first bomb detonated somewhere in the center of the village, the muffled thump and roar followed by a series of explosions. Smoke and dust billowed into the air and still the planes came, the white-and-black crosses painted on the undersides of the wings now visible. More explosions followed, a never-ending string of destruction that shook the ground. And through that, the chilling sounds of rapid gunfire.

"They're strafing the streets," Piotr shouted, yanking Sophie forward. "We need to find cover."

They ran from the pasture, Sophie's heart in her throat and terror clawing at her insides. She scrambled through the pasture gate, scraping her hands on the wood. The hem of her dress snagged on a nail as the planes screamed their approach. Desperately, she yanked herself free and pushed herself away from the gate, breathing hard. Piotr was beside her, urging her to run faster. She had taken only two steps forward when the hotel abruptly disintegrated before her eyes. Stone was hurled into the air, and the force of the explosion threw her back against the gate and then to the ground.

The breath was knocked from her, and as she gasped for air a cloud of roiling dust enveloped her, filling her mouth and her nose and making her gag. She turned onto her stomach, ignoring the searing pain in her ribs, and dragged herself farther back into the pasture, past splinters of railings and posts. Disoriented, she pushed herself to her knees, and then to her feet, pressing her hands to her ears. The world had gone strangely silent, a distant ringing replacing the shriek of the planes.

The dust was clearing, though flames and smoke still billowed heavenward, smears of horror against what once promised to be a perfect September sky. The space where the hotel had been was just a pile of scattered brick and timbers, only the northern wall jutting up like a broken tooth. Sophie staggered forward. Where was Piotr?

She tripped over a pile of broken brick, a woman's shoe sticking out incongruously from the mound. Beside it, the matching purse lay, papers spilling from the inside and fluttering back and forth. Around her, people appeared, covered in dust and blood and looking like ghostly spectres. Most were running blindly while some wandered aimlessly, and a few simply cowered on the ground. None were Piotr.

A shadow passed over her head and then another. The ground seemed to vibrate under her feet. To her left, small puffs of smoke and dust were erupting, the bodies of those who had run by her jerking awkwardly and then crumpling to the ground. A pair of hands grabbed her and spun her around. She found herself looking into brilliant blue eyes, and she almost wept with relief.

Piotr was shouting something at her as he pointed toward the dilapidated carriage house, which was still standing. He pushed her toward the building, and Sophie fought to make her legs work, the sensation that she was running underwater making her feel slow and sluggish. The ringing in her ears was starting to dissipate, replaced again by the roaring and shrieking of engines. Behind Sophie, a woman's scream was abruptly silenced.

Hidden by the wall of swirling smoke that rose from the remnants of the hotel, another plane was approaching unseen, its high-pitched whine filling the air. A thump reverberated through the ground followed by the rattle of more guns. Sophie stumbled as she ran on, panic making her clumsy. Piotr steadied her, urging her faster toward the darkened doorway that had long since lost its door.

They had almost reached the carriage house when the plane burst through the veil of smoke and flame over the hotel.

Clods of earth exploded as the gunner shredded the ground beneath him. Piotr shoved her forward, and Sophie landed hard halfway through the doorway of the carriage house. His weight came down on top of her as the plane roared past, punching the air from her lungs and driving her chin into the ground. She squeezed her eyes closed, the coppery taste of blood in her mouth. She tried to move but Piotr's weight still had her pinned.

"Piotr?" she rasped.

He didn't answer.

"Piotr?" she asked again, a new sort of terror surging through her. Sophie shoved herself to her elbows, Piotr's weight shifting slowly from her back. She made a sound she didn't recognize and struggled feverishly out from under her husband, dread giving her a strength she didn't know she possessed.

"No, no, no, no, no." She was on her knees beside him now, afraid to touch him, afraid not to.

He had rolled onto his back, and his dark lashes lay still against dust-caked cheeks. Blood bloomed across his chest, mottling his once white shirt with a macabre pattern of red.

He was breathing, but barely. With shaking fingers, Sophie used the torn hem of her dress to wipe a smear of blood from his lips with as much care as she could manage.

His eyes fluttered open.

"Did you ... run me over ... with your bicycle again?" he managed roughly.

Sophie swallowed a sob. "Not quite."

"Didn't ... think so."

"You're going to be all right," she told him. "If you survived me, you can survive this."

He might have smiled but his eyes fluttered closed again. "Don't cry." His words were barely audible.

She dashed away the tears that had escaped and tucked her hand in his. His fingers were cold. So very cold.

"Look in my...front shirt pocket," he whispered.

Sophie did as he bid, her hand shaking. In the pocket of his shirt she found a photo, a black-and-white image of her mounted bareback on a big-boned gelding. She was grinning triumphantly at the camera, her hair tumbled around her shoulders, her clothing muddy at the elbows and knees. Sophie recognized it instantly.

"You took this picture the first day you took me riding."

"Yes."

"I lost count of how many times I slid off that poor horse."

"Yet you kept...getting back up." Bright blue eyes opened again to meet hers. "You need to get up again today."

She shook her head, her breath catching on a sob. "Not without you."

"Make it count, Sophie. Every day after this one. Make it all count."

"I love you." Her tears were falling unchecked now.

A new, distant thunder was approaching, and Sophie crouched over Piotr, as if she could protect him from whatever new threat was coming. Out of the corner of her eye, hooves flashed as the mare galloped wildly past, the copper-colored foal nowhere to be seen.

Sophie straightened and pressed a soft kiss to her husband's lips.

And fourteen hours after she had become a wife, Sophie became a widow.

CHAPTER

3

Estelle

Twenty-two widows.

Twenty-two was the number of men wearing wedding bands who died before Estelle Allard could get them to the field hospital in her ambulance. And it was barely past noon.

She wasn't entirely sure when she had started noticing that detail or why it seemed to matter so much to her. Each one of the men she transported from the front lines was a loved one to somebody, married or not. Perhaps it was because she had always wondered what it might be like to love and be loved with the entirety that a marriage suggested. To have someone simply accept your flaws and love you despite them. Or maybe for them. To love so deeply and so completely that you couldn't imagine a future without that person.

The thought of a love like that was as terrifying as it was enviable because it could be lost in a second. As it had been for the twenty-two women who were waiting for a love who would never come home again.

Estelle's ambulance bounced over the deep ruts across the field, and she shifted down to bring the battered vehicle to a shuddering halt, eyeing the rows of men waiting on stretchers. Rows of writhing, screaming, and bleeding men and still more who were simply lying in ominous silence. So many. Too many.

"What the hell took you so long, Allard?" a haggard medic barked at her as she shoved her door open and slid down from the hard bench.

She swayed slightly as her feet hit the ground. "And it's good to see you're still alive too, Jerome."

"You were gone too long." Jerome de Colbert ignored her greeting, kneeling beside one of the prone figures on the ground. "You need to be faster."

"There's no fuel," she replied dully. It was always the fuel that slowed her down. That slowed all the drivers down. The little that was in the ambulance's tank had come from a newly abandoned farmyard a mile south, the inhabitants terrified enough to have left everything behind in the face of the invading Germans.

"Rachel driving behind you somewhere?" he asked, standing.

"Maybe?" The truth of the matter was that she hadn't seen her dearest friend since dawn, and then only as they had driven past each other in the farmyard being used as a field hospital. Estelle had tried very hard all day not to think about all the awful things that might have befallen her. Tried very hard not to imagine Rachel wounded or dead, her ambulance crippled or obliterated by the steady shelling.

Even now, the ceaseless guns roared and rattled, almost

drowning out the screams and moans of the wounded and dying awaiting transport. The air was stagnant and gritty, and the stench of gunpowder and smoke mingled with the sharp scent of blood and urine. Estelle put a hand on the ambulance door for a moment to steady herself before she hurried forward toward the next group of wounded men waiting to get to the field hospital.

She crouched beside a soldier lying motionless on his stretcher, his arm flung to the side, his entire head swathed in blood-and-dirt-caked rags.

"Leave that one," Jerome said gruffly. "He didn't make it. See if the one beside him is still alive. I'll be right back to help you load."

She reached for the soldier's lifeless hand and rested it gently on his chest. The gold of a wedding band glinted in the sunlight filtering through the haze.

Twenty-three widows.

She touched the band. A Hebrew word had been engraved in a familiar—

"No." Estelle froze for a fraction of a second before she fumbled for his tags. She pulled them from beneath his stained uniform. They were sticky with congealing blood but were still legible. *Alain Wyler.*

Estelle dropped the tags and lurched away from the body as if that would make what she already knew less real. Her throat constricted, and she fought the urge to simply collapse and weep, because that would accomplish nothing in the face of so much suffering and death and loss. Instead, she struggled to her feet, though her vision seemed to waver and the ground tilted precariously beneath her. She found herself on her hands and knees, nausea roiling through her.

"Jesus, Allard, when did you last eat?" Jerome was back, crouching beside her, one of his hands resting on her shoulder.

"Yesterday?" It was hard to remember. It was harder still to keep the days separate.

Jerome grunted. "Here." What looked like a piece of dried sausage was thrust in front of her face. "Eat this. I've got enough casualties without adding you to the goddamn list."

Estelle sat back on her heels and did as she was told. She accepted the additional offer of a canteen and took careful sips of tepid water.

"Have you slept?"

"Enough." An hour or so sometime between midnight and two. There wasn't time for sleeping.

The spots before her eyes were clearing, and the nausea receding, though the tightness in her throat was still there along with a chronic, aching sadness that seemed to have settled deep in her chest. She put a hand over Alain's for the last time.

"You knew him?" Jerome was watching her with reddened, tired eyes, unnaturally bright against the dark smudges of soot and mud that covered his face.

"Yes," Estelle managed.

"Who was he?"

"Rachel's brother." *My brother*, she wanted to say. Because he was just that, in every way but blood. Though in Estelle's experience, blood didn't count for much when it came to family. "He has a wife. Hannah. And a three-year-old daughter. Aviva."

"Goddammit." Jerome dropped his head. "Goddammit," he repeated.

"I should be the one to tell Rachel."

"Yes," he mumbled. "I'm so sorry, Allard."

Estelle handed the canteen back to him. "Me too."

Jerome stood and held out his hand, helping her to her feet. He had kind eyes, Estelle thought numbly as she took his hand. The color of melted caramel, steady and—

The ground in the field beyond Estelle's ambulance suddenly erupted. She dove to the ground, soil and debris flung into the air like a geyser raining down on them and the patients. Something stung the skin near her temple but Estelle ignored it.

"Goddamn Boches," Jerome was screaming in the direction of the front lines. "Goddamn stop for a goddamn minute so I can do my goddamn job!"

Estelle clambered back to her feet. Something warm trickled down the side of her face, and she brushed at it angrily with her sleeve.

Jerome turned and thrust an empty tin at her. "I need you to drive," he said, hoarse from shouting. Bits of debris fell from his shoulders. "And bring back more bandages. We're stripping corpses to use their goddamn uniforms for wraps. I can't keep up."

Estelle took the box and tossed it in the front of the ambulance. She returned to help load those who were still living into the back.

"Hurry back," Jerome panted as he slammed the back shut. "Please."

"Yes," she said. "Don't die on me in the meantime."

"Likewise, Allard."

Estelle swung back into her ambulance and stomped on the clutch, jamming it into gear. The vehicle gave a tortured groan and then rolled forward, jolting mercilessly. A soldier in the back shrieked in pain. She maneuvered the ambulance onto the uneven road and accelerated over the rise, driving as fast as she dared. She'd gone only perhaps a half mile when she was forced to slow to a crawl. In front of her, the road was clogged with people fleeing away from the front lines that were continuously inching closer. Most were walking, many with small children in their arms. Some had wheelbarrows or dog carts. The lucky ones had horse- or ox-drawn carts or bicycles, and there was even a tractor farther up, belching black clouds of exhaust. But all had fatigue and fear etched deeply into their faces.

She stayed on the road for long minutes before she veered away from the crowds and bounced into a pasture, following a rutted track that had once been a livestock trail. She burst through a hedgerow and found herself almost at the newest field hospital that had been set up yesterday in a modest manor house abandoned by its previous tenants. Surgeries were being conducted in the kitchen and what had once been a parlour. In the rest of the rooms, men were laid wherever there was space, waiting. Waiting to die, waiting to live.

Uniformed men came out to meet Estelle as the ambulance coughed and jerked past the barn and empty livestock pens. They unloaded the patients from the back, but instead of turning toward the manor, they headed for the barn.

"Stop," she protested. "These men need to go to the manor. They need a doctor."

"No room," one of the men mumbled, adjusting his grip on the stretcher. "Manor's full. An' they all need a damn doctor."

Estelle stared after them and sank down on the back edge of the ambulance, the doors still hanging ajar. She rested her head in her hands, her palms pressing hard against her eyes. She was tired. So very tired.

She forced herself to sit up. She had never been a quitter, and she would not quit now, not when men like Alain had sacrificed everything for her and for their country. She returned to the cab of her vehicle and checked the fuel gauge. She would not make it to the front lines and back with the fuel she had left.

Estelle stood. Perhaps in the last hour someone had secured more fuel or perhaps a cache had been brought up from—

"Estelle!" The sound of her name had her spinning, and she saw Rachel running toward her. Most of her dark hair had escaped its bindings and spilled across her shoulders in a tangled mess, and her uniform, like her face, was filthy.

The immediate relief at seeing her friend alive and whole was snuffed violently by a suffocating wave of grief. She swallowed hard.

"Estelle," Rachel said again as she reached her and enveloped her in a hug. "I was so worried. The men coming back said that some of the shells were reaching beyond the lines and—" She stopped and pulled back. "You're hurt." Rachel reached up to touch Estelle's temple, and her fingers were bloody when she withdrew them.

"I'm fine," Estelle whispered. She realized that the tears she hadn't shed with Jerome were now running freely down her cheeks.

"What's wrong? What's happened?"

Estelle tried to speak but couldn't seem to make the words come out.

Rachel backed up a step. "Alain."

Estelle nodded.

Her friend put a hand out and grasped the ambulance door.

"Is he—" She couldn't seem to say it either. As if neither of them saying what they both knew would make it not true.

"I'm sorry, Rachel," Estelle said. "I'm so sorry."

Rachel staggered and sat down hard on the back of the ambulance. She didn't speak, didn't move, and Estelle had no idea what to do. Or what to say.

After a moment, Rachel stood and approached Estelle. "How much fuel do you have left?"

"What?" Estelle shook her head, not understanding.

"How much fuel do you have? My ambulance isn't drivable anymore; the front axle broke when I—"

"Rachel." Estelle cut her off. "What are you doing?"

"I'm doing what Alain would have wanted us to do," she said, her voice shaking. "There are men out there he would have considered friends, men he fought beside, men who are still fighting. Men who need our help. He would not want us to fall apart now." She took Estelle's hand and squeezed it tight.

"Rachel—"

"I won't cry now," she said, and the pressure on Estelle's hand increased. "Because if I do, I won't be able to stop. And that helps no one. We need to find some fuel."

"Yes."

Rachel let go of Estelle's hands. "We need to get back to Jerome."

The two women started across the yard, skirting the smallest of the outbuildings. Estelle hadn't gone more than a dozen steps before she stopped, abruptly aware of the stillness of the yard. Vehicles sat unattended, posts had seemingly been deserted. Out of the corner of her eye, she saw a young soldier running toward the barn.

"What's happening?" she called out.

"A radio address," he replied without slowing down. "From our government."

Estelle exchanged a look with Rachel, and for the first time in a long while, hope surfaced. Estelle started forward, daring to believe that this would be the announcement they had been waiting for. That somehow, some way, more troops and more help would be coming. That the goddamn Boches would indeed be driven back to where they had come from and their seemingly unchecked aggression halted before it was too late.

The barn doors had been propped open, and Estelle and Rachel stepped into the cavernous space. Along the wall to Estelle's right, a dozen patients languished on beds of straw. The one closest to her was moaning and mumbling, an empty space where his lower left leg should have been beneath his thin blanket. The others lay motionless, a handful watching her with haunted eyes shadowed by pain and exhaustion.

At the far end of the barn, a radio had been set up on a barrel, the long antenna snaking up through the hayloft and out the roof. A knot of men in various uniforms was crowded around. Estelle picked up her pace, anxious to hear what was being said. Rachel was on her heels. But as they got to the end, someone reached up and turned off the radio, the silence in the space unnerving and absolute. Only the whimpers of the patient by the door could be heard.

Estelle faltered. The expressions on each face ranged from grave to dismayed, furious to forlorn. One aging soldier, old enough that he had likely fought the Germans twenty years ago, was crying openly.

She grabbed the arm of a nearby medic. "What has happened?"

"We've surrendered."

Estelle stared at him, not comprehending. "I don't understand."

"Reynaud has resigned, Pétain has taken power, and his first action as premier has been to ask the Germans to let France surrender."

"That's not possible." Because that would mean everything in these last months had been for nothing. That all this suffering and death and sacrifice had been for nothing.

That Alain's sacrifice had been for nothing.

"It's done." The medic pulled his arm from Estelle and stalked away.

Rachel made a tortured sound in her throat and sank to the ground on one knee, her hand over her mouth.

The others who had been listening to the radio were dispersing. Estelle and Rachel were left alone, staring at the space the crowd had just occupied. Dust motes danced in the light streaming down from the open loft door above, disturbed by their movements.

The generals in resplendent uniforms and the politicians in tailored suits had assured Estelle and everyone else that France was prepared for Germany. They'd asserted that France would crush any hostile overtures the Germans might dare to make. They'd proclaimed that the Maginot Line, with all its tunnels and troops and arms, was indestructible and impenetrable. And they'd affirmed that there was no tactical way an army could invade through the Ardennes or navigate the River Meuse. France would never fall.

They had all been liars.

CHAPTER

4

Gabriel

PARIS, FRANCE
28 JUNE 2017

Gabriel Seymour was turning into a liar.

When the woman emailed him yesterday, insisting she had found a painting that belonged to his family—a painting executed by his grandfather, no less—he almost deleted the message out of hand. But before he could swipe the communication out of existence, a pixelated photo attachment popped up on his screen, and Gabriel found himself looking at a rendition of Millbrook Hall, his family's estate in Norfolk. The painting in the photo was executed in the same flat colors that were characteristic of his grandfather's work, but the composition itself exhibited a hopeful quality, as though any shortcomings could be eclipsed by the sheer enthusiasm of its creator. It was a style that was as familiar to Gabriel as his own face after a lifetime of seeing dozens of similar paintings that still lined the walls of his ancestral home.

In her message, the woman—Aurelia Leclaire—indicated

that she was emptying out an apartment that had once belonged to a deceased relative. Ms. Leclaire asked if Gabriel had any idea how the painting might have made its way to Paris, or if the name Estelle Allard meant anything to him. She further wondered if the painting might be valuable—she was unfamiliar with the artist, she said, and did not know if the market for his work was at all significant. Ms. Leclaire made it clear that she did not intend to keep the painting either way; she was determined to return the work to Gabriel's family, its rightful owners, free of cost. She concluded her message by inviting him to Paris to view it.

The message communicated several things to Gabriel right away. First, its author had plenty of her own money. Too much, probably, to care about potentially adding to an existing fortune. And, second, whoever this woman was, she knew absolutely nothing about art. This last realization was further substantiated when Gabriel noticed the second canvas that was visible in the photo attachment, hiding just behind the optimistic little landscape.

A nude woman glared out of that second canvas, the bold style and deliberate colors obvious even considering the poor quality of the photo. Gabriel nearly dropped his phone when he saw it, the thrill of discovery running like lightning through his veins. Within seconds, he was booking a Eurostar ticket from London to Paris for the first train out the following morning. Years of experience had taught him that no matter how certain he might be about identifying a particular artist and their work, a careful and thorough examination needed to be done in person before making grand pronouncements. Offering a client false hope about a piece in their possession never ended well for anyone. And so he told Ms. Leclaire only that he wanted to come get a better look at the plain little landscape.

He'd lied. Without regret. Because if that nude canvas turned out to be what he suspected it might be…

Gabriel double-checked the address on his phone as he made his way up the steady incline of the street. He'd always liked the energy of the ninth arrondissement with its array of bustling commercial and multinational businesses, all arranged in ordered beauty down the wide, grand boulevards. The legacy of Baron Haussmann's nineteenth-century redevelopment work had turned the dark, cluttered labyrinth of old Paris into a community of splendour and light that was evident everywhere, its crown jewel the soaring Opéra Garnier that Gabriel had visited more than once. The building Ms. Leclaire lived in was also one of Haussmann's designs, a beautiful, Lutetian limestone structure, its creamy three-story façade adorned with uniform windows and perfectly aligned balconies.

Gabriel shifted the bag slung over his shoulder as he entered the building and headed up the stairs, a familiar anticipation winding through him. Much of his job could be tedious, careful work, but moments like these made him feel a little like Indiana Jones hunting down the next great buried treasure.

He reached the landing and raised his hand to lift the brass knocker on Ms. Leclaire's apartment door but the sound of a door opening behind him, accompanied by a brief cacophony of high-pitched barking, made him turn. An elderly woman wearing an alarming shade of lipstick and dressed in a floral outfit that would not have been out of place a half century earlier was standing on the other side of the landing. One hand grasped the head of a cane and the other a small, struggling dog.

"What do you want?" she demanded in French.

Gabriel blinked. "I beg your pardon?"

"I can't get a moment's peace." She narrowed her eyes, the heavy liner making them look like angry black slashes. "What business do you have here?"

"None of yours," he replied pleasantly.

The dog growled and resumed its frantic barking. Gabriel winced.

"I suppose you're here to see the girl." The woman had to raise her voice over the barking.

"Yes, he is." A new voice cut through the din from behind Gabriel. He turned to find a woman in a bright red sundress, long chestnut hair scraped back into a careless ponytail, a smile playing at the corners of her lips.

"Ms. Leclaire?" he blurted. Somehow, in their brief correspondence, he'd had a vision fixed in his mind of a dutiful, dour matron looking after estate business.

"Guilty," she replied. "I'm Aurelia. But everyone calls me Lia. You must be Mr. Seymour."

"Yes. But Gabriel, please." He realized he was staring and averted his gaze, proper manners reasserting themselves. He held out a hand. "A pleasure."

Lia shook it, her hand firm and warm in his. He released it with a peculiar sense of reluctance.

"And this is Madame Hoffmann. My neighbour."

Gabriel inclined his head. "Also a pleasure," he managed.

The old woman rapped her cane on the floor. "I know your type," she snapped. She eyed his shaggy hair and the ink on his arms. "And you're not wanted here. This is a building for upstanding citizens. Not a hovel for degenerate artists and drug addicts."

"That's quite a...leap," Gabriel remarked, not sure if he was amused or irritated by the woman's hostility.

"You don't know the half of it," Lia murmured beside him in English. "If a winged monkey appears, I suggest you run."

"You think we can outrun a winged monkey?" he whispered back.

"I only have to outrun you."

Gabriel laughed, and the sound sent the writhing dog into a renewed frenzy.

"Please come in," Lia repeated loudly, switching back to French and stepping aside to usher Gabriel in.

He wasted no time ducking through the doorway into her apartment. The dog snarled and snapped behind him.

Lia sighed. "Have a good afternoon, Madame—"

"I can have you evicted, don't think I can't." Lia's neighbour wasn't done yet. "I know people—"

"Good afternoon, Madame Hoffmann," Lia said again, and then simply closed the door after them.

"She's charming," Gabriel commented. He could still hear muffled barking on the other side of the door.

"I'm quite sure she's harmless. Lonely, maybe. My grand-mère used to say, 'Only beware the man who does not talk and the dog that does not bark.'" She slipped by him, a light scent of jasmine following in her wake.

"I haven't heard that one before." He glanced around at the small foyer with wainscoted walls.

"An American proverb, as it turns out."

"Your grandmother was an American?"

"No." Lia frowned briefly but did not elaborate. Then her expression cleared. "I appreciate you coming so quickly. I hope I didn't inconvenience you."

"Not at all." Gabriel set down his bag. "I was intrigued." Just not by what she thought.

"The painting is here." She bent to retrieve the little landscape that had been propped up against the wall near the door. Of the bold, nude canvas there was no sign.

Lia handed it to him. "Do you recognize it?"

Gabriel examined the painting. It looked even more desperate to please up close than it had in the photo, but the subject matter was easily identifiable. *William Seymour* was signed with a flourish in the bottom right-hand corner. "This is a painting of Millbrook Hall, a property my family has owned for generations. That is my grandfather's signature. He painted dozens and dozens of landscapes featuring Millbrook."

"He was an artist?"

"He was a wealthy landowner with a lot of free time on his hands who loved art," he allowed. "He always dreamed of exhibiting his work."

"And did he?"

"Only in the manor dining room, despite his wife's vehement objections." He glanced up with a wry smile. "Or so the story goes."

Lia smiled back.

Gabriel turned the painting over. Nothing was written on the back that would give any indication as to how it had ended up here.

Lia seemed to read his mind. "It belonged to my grandmother. I still have no idea how she got it."

"Huh." Gabriel righted the painting.

"And you're sure the name Estelle means nothing to you? Estelle Allard?"

He shook his head. "No, I'm sorry. I called my father before I left, and he hadn't heard the name either. He's going to ask my grandfather at his first opportunity."

"He's still alive? The William who painted this?"

"Yes. And ninety-eight years might have taken their toll physically, but they have done nothing to dull his mind. Perhaps he will have an answer." He looked up at her. "I assume Estelle Allard was your grandmother?"

"Yes. She was the same age when she passed away. Ninety-eight."

"Were you close with her?"

Lia exhaled and played with a small oval pendant that hung at her throat. The three tiny red stones set into the enameled surface glittered as she twisted it. "I thought so. I mean, as close as one could get to a woman who wasn't much of a people person..." She trailed off, suddenly looking distinctly uncomfortable. "I thought I knew her. But now, it seems I didn't know her at all."

Gabriel wasn't sure what to say to that.

"I'm sorry. Never mind my ramblings. Do you think your family would like the painting returned?" she asked. "Perhaps it has some sentimental value?"

"I appreciate the gesture, but this obviously belonged to your grandmother. It is yours to do with as you wish." He handed the little landscape back to her, wondering how best to broach the subject of the nude painting. Because he was damned if he was leaving here without taking a good look at it. "May I ask how you found me?"

"Your website." Intelligent hazel eyes considered him. "You're an art appraiser."

"Yes. For over a decade. I also specialize in restoration work." If she had read his website, she would know that too.

"Of paintings," she confirmed. "Early modernist works are your specialty."

"Yes. But I have experience with works dating from the fifteenth century onward. I also do mosaics and murals, though I usually recommend a specialist to my clients for more valuable pieces. I know enough to know what I don't know."

"Mmm. Tell me about your clients."

Gabriel was suddenly revising his original assessment of what this woman might or might not know about art. Because this conversation was starting to sound less like a conversation and more and more like an interview.

"Insurance agencies. Auction houses. Museums." He crossed his arms. "Do you wish to call any of them for a reference?" he asked dryly.

She clasped her hands in front of her and looked down. "I, um, kind of already did."

He hadn't expected that. "Which one?"

"All of them."

"Oh." He hadn't expected that either.

"You come very highly recommended. And I'm reasonably sure you're not a serial killer."

"Thank you, I think."

"I have a confession."

"A confession?"

She set the little landscape back down. "I didn't really ask you here to look at your grandfather's painting. Not entirely."

The irony of that confession nearly made him laugh out loud.

"I did search for your name at the beginning," Lia continued, looking back up. "Because, strangely enough, this particular landscape was kept in a safety deposit box I knew nothing about until after my grandmère's death. And I have no idea why. No offense meant to your grandfather," she added hastily.

"None taken."

"In her will, she specifically directed that this painting go to me."

"I see." He didn't know what else to say.

"Searching out your family seemed like a good first step in my search for answers. I have so many questions, and I thought maybe one of you could help me fill in some blanks. But then when I saw what you did for a living, it seemed like fate, and I thought that maybe—" She stopped. "There are others. I'm trying to identify them and catalogue them but I—" She took a deep breath. "I'm not making sense. Let me start over. I know enough to know what I don't know." She stole his words. "I have a number of paintings that need to be appraised. I was hoping that I might be able to hire you to do so."

Gabriel tried to temper the elation that bubbled up. He was positively desperate to take a better look at the nude—would have looked at that canvas for free—but the idea of being paid to do so was almost too good to believe. "Why not take these paintings to an appraiser in Paris?" he asked reasonably, trying to understand exactly what was going on here. "Not," he added, "that I'm not happy to be here."

"I can't really take them anywhere. Not easily."

"I don't understand."

She gave him a funny look. "I think I just need to show you."

"All right."

"Follow me." Lia led him into the apartment.

Except it wasn't so much an apartment as a dazzling time capsule from a different century. It was a residence straight out of a history book, filled with luxury and opulence, and meant to impress. The exquisite furnishings and rugs were of the quality that was currently in demand at high-end auctions. At the far end of the room, over a wide hearth, a marble mantel was lined with antique jade sculpture. The hearth itself was flanked by two towering bookcases that rose all the way to the ceiling. The light caught the gilded print on the leather spines, and Gabriel couldn't help but wonder how many first editions existed in the ordered rows.

And on almost every wall, there was art.

"This is..." He struggled for a word, taking in the space, all awash in sunlight and tiny rainbows cast by the chandelier above their heads.

"Overwhelming?"

"That's an understatement."

"I found it like this," she told him. "It was, of course, significantly dustier and mustier, but the curtains had been drawn and nothing had faded much. I've cleaned since then. Carefully and extensively. But I haven't touched the paintings. This is the first group that I need appraised."

Gabriel moved toward the collection of landscapes and sea-scapes on the wall opposite the windows. His practiced eye easily picked out two compositions that had all the hallmarks that had made John Constable so famous. There was likely a significant fortune hanging on this wall alone.

"What do you mean you found it like this?" he asked, her words finally registering.

"I inherited this apartment," she explained. "Grandmère willed it to me. It seems she lived here during the late twenties, throughout the thirties, and into the early forties. I found correspondence dated up until 1943."

"And no one in your family has lived here since?"

"No one in my family knew it existed," she corrected. She swiped an errant hair away from her face and tucked it behind her ear. "Until recently, I believed Grandmère had lived in Marseille her entire life."

"I see," Gabriel said again, not seeing anything at all.

"This is her." Lia moved away from him and picked up a photo from a carved table, holding it out to Gabriel. "Estelle Allard."

Gabriel reluctantly left the paintings and took the photo from her, examining the image. He'd seen old movie posters of film stars like Olivia de Havilland or Ingrid Bergman, and they had nothing on the woman in this photo leaning against a lamppost.

"She was stunning," he said honestly.

"She was," her granddaughter agreed with little enthusiasm.

There were other photos of Estelle Allard. One had her in the driver's seat of a low-slung car, another mounted on a sleek horse.

"Looks as though she was quite the daredevil too," Gabriel remarked.

"No," Lia mumbled. "She wasn't. The Grandmère I knew grew lilies, fed the feral cats in the park across the way, and walked the same stretch of beach alone every morning. All of her neighbours played bocce ball on the last Tuesday of every month, but she always declined their invitations. She said she didn't need the company, and aside from that, she found the noise intolerable. She didn't drive, she didn't smoke, she didn't drink. She was in bed by eight p.m. sharp. She favoured high collars, sensible shoes, and polyester slacks."

"This picture was taken a long time ago," Gabriel said, handing the photo back. "People can change."

Lia made a funny sound.

"Who is this?" Gabriel picked up a photo of an officer in an old German uniform.

"I have no idea. There was nothing written on the back."
She winced. "I think..." She trailed off, her hands twisting
in front of her.

"You think what?" Gabriel prompted.

"I think my grandmother was a Nazi collaborator during
the war."

Given what he still held in his hands, Gabriel wasn't
completely surprised by her words. "Because of this?"

"Partially. There were also pro-Nazi magazines. Receipts
from the bars at the Paris Ritz Hotel. A postcard signed by
Göring himself."

He set the photo down. "I'm not sure you should jump
to conclusions just yet," he ventured. "There could be other
explanations."

"That's kind of you to say, and it's what I tried to tell myself.
But experience has taught me that when one hears hooves,
one does not generally look for zebras." She tried to smile and
failed. "The evidence is pretty convincing. And I think that
this was why she kept this—this apartment, and everything in
it—all hidden. Who in their right mind would want to admit
to being a collaborator?"

A silence fell.

"And there's more." Lia sounded distinctly uncomfortable.
"Art, that is."

"Why don't you show me?"

She nodded and led him deeper into the apartment, stopping in a formal dining room. She gestured wordlessly at the
long wall covered in framed canvases.

Gabriel maneuvered himself past her to examine this
collection. The portraits were extensive, an assortment of
nineteenth- and twentieth-century compositions peppered by

a handful that were far older. John Singer Sargent was represented for certain, along with at least two works that appeared to be the product of Henry Fuseli's artistic brilliance. Gabriel didn't even want to dare guess at the rest without proper examination.

"If these were stolen, would you be able to determine from where? And from whom?" Lia asked.

Gabriel glanced at her, trying to think of something reassuring to say. He settled on the truth. "If they were stolen—and that's a big if—I can't guarantee I'd be completely successful. Entire families perished during those years. Establishing rightful ownership in the cases where there is no next of kin can often prove impossible. But I would certainly try."

"Good." It was barely audible.

"If it makes you feel better, I haven't yet seen anything on these walls that I recognize from lists of missing or stolen works. I'm not an authority but I'm familiar with the art world's Most Wanted."

Lia offered a weak smile. "I suppose that is something."

"Are there any more paintings?" Gabriel prompted. He still hadn't seen the nude.

"One more. It's different from the rest."

Gabriel tried to keep his expression neutral. "Is it here?"

Lia nodded and led him to a set of French doors, pulling them wide. Sheer, gauzy curtains let in a dreamy, diffuse light through two long windows. Gabriel had a vague impression of a wide bed and a large wardrobe opposite. But what made him freeze where he stood was the canvas that had brought him here.

And the only thing that ran through Gabriel's mind was that, like Indiana Jones, he had found the Holy Grail.

CHAPTER

5

Lia

Lia didn't have to be an art expert to feel the emotion that had gone into each bold brushstroke. Every time she looked at this painting, she saw something new—an elusive nuance or a subtle detail previously missed. And she had spent a great deal of time looking at this painting and wondering what the woman who glared back at her might have seen in this apartment.

For now, Lia simply leaned against the wall, studying the expert who was, in turn, studying the painting. Gabriel Seymour had gone eerily still just inside the bedroom door as he had caught sight of the canvas, and Lia wasn't even sure he was still breathing.

He was not what she had been expecting when she had sent her original message. Given the long list of degrees and scholarly accomplishments documented on his website and the impeccable, enthusiastic references she'd gotten from places like Christie's and Sotheby's, she'd been expecting someone older. Someone who looked more...academic. Buttoned-up. Maybe even garnished with a bow tie. The man who was currently getting down on his hands and knees in front of the evocative painting looked more like the drummer of an indie band.

"Holy shit," he said from the floor before he seemed to catch himself. "I beg your pardon."

"Don't apologize," Lia said. "Just agree to work for me. Help me identify these paintings."

"Yes," he breathed. "God, yes. At the risk of sounding like a serial killer, you'd require an armed tactical team to drag me out of here now." His eyes swept the length of the painting. "I think this is a Munch."

"I agree. His initials appear in the lower left. Though I haven't been able to find any provenance or records for it. Or any of them, for that matter," she muttered.

His head snapped up. "What did you say you did for a living?"

"I didn't." She tipped her head. "But since you asked, I'm a chemical engineer."

"Who is well versed in art history?"

"Hardly. I'm much better at math than modernism. But the internet can be helpful from time to time," she said. "Still, my Googling abilities certainly do not make me an expert on anything. Which is why I really contacted you. And why, I suspect, you got here as quickly as you did."

Grey eyes pinned her where she stood. "You put this painting in the background of the picture you sent me on purpose."

"Of course I did."

"That was positively diabolical."

"I've been accused of worse. It worked, didn't it?"

"It did."

"I need to know if this painting, like the rest, could be stolen."

"I understand." Gabriel remained crouched in front of the painting. "If you are agreeable, I'd like to make arrangements to take the entire collection back to my studio in London," he said.

"But there are so many."

"That's no problem. I've arranged for transport of much larger collections before. I'll be able to establish authenticity there and get second opinions, if need be. I'd prefer to have them stored securely until they've been processed and identified. At the very least, they should be insured."

"Of course." Lia hadn't thought of that.

"I'd like for you to visit my studio once the paintings are there. So that we can go over exactly what I'll be doing with each piece. There will be significant paperwork involved, and if possible, I'd like to cover that with you in person. Will you have time to come to London?"

"Yes," Lia said. "I just finished out my last contracted position, and there is a new posting in Seville that I intend to chase but interviews don't start for a few weeks yet. With the death of my grandmother, I didn't try to find work in between. Which, it seems, was just as well."

"Seville?" Gabriel lifted an eyebrow.

"I'm in consulting. Which means I go wherever the work is and stay as long as the job lasts. I don't spend a lot of time here in Paris."

"Well, this might make it easier for you to pick and choose your jobs. You know that if this proves to be an authentic

Munch, and you wish to sell, it'll be worth a fortune." He ran a finger along the edge of the frame.

"It might not be mine to sell." Her words were quiet. "And if that's the case, I want it returned to its rightful owner."

"Let's cross that bridge if and when we come to it," Gabriel said, straightening. "It's strange though," he mused, his eyes lingering on the canvas.

"What is?"

"That this is the only piece composed by an Expressionist. It certainly doesn't fit with the rest of the collection in the apartment." He turned back to her. "You didn't find any others like this?"

Lia lifted her hands helplessly. "No."

He turned in a slow circle. "There was no art in this room?"

"Not the painted kind. But there was an obscene amount of vintage couture clothing. Most of which I've donated to the Palais Galliera and the Museum of Decorative Arts." She gestured at the arched entrance beside the wardrobe. "That dressing room was overflowing."

Gabriel left the painting and ducked into the tiny space. "Mmm."

"What does 'mmm' mean?" Lia followed him and stopped at the opening.

Gabriel was peering at the walls of the now-empty dressing room. "Artists like Munch were labeled as degenerate by the Nazis. Which didn't prevent some Nazis from stealing their work, of course, but most works were either auctioned internationally or destroyed. Over the years, I've personally appraised and restored a half-dozen paintings that were found hidden from the Nazis in attics and cellars and barns." He had his phone out now and was running the beam of the flashlight toward the back.

Lia frowned. He couldn't possibly be suggesting what she thought he was. "I don't have an attic or cellar or barn."

"No. But you have an oddly short dressing room."

"What?"

"This dressing room's back wall is not plaster. It's painted wood."

"So?"

"Come here." Without turning, he gestured for her to join him.

Lia did as he asked. He was examining a gap between the floor and the back wall.

"This wall was added," he said. He ran his light up the wall to reveal a seam that divided the back wall into two equal panels. "I don't know when, but it's not original."

"You're seriously suggesting that there's a hidden space behind this wall?"

"It's likely." He said it like she had simply asked him if he thought it might rain later on.

"For what?" she asked incredulously.

"I don't know. Would you like to find out?"

"Um."

He caught her hand in his and pressed his phone into her palm. "Let me fetch my tools." He didn't give her time to answer but simply ducked back out of the dressing room and reappeared a half minute later with his bag.

"Hold the light over my shoulder," he instructed as he got down on his hands and knees to study the gap along the floor.

"Does this sort of thing happen to you often?" Lia asked weakly. "Secret rooms and whatnot?"

"First time." His answer was muffled as he worked a flat bar beneath the left panel.

She crouched down beside him, feeling the warmth of his body against her bare arms. His presence was comforting. "What if—"

There was a quiet snap, and the edge of the panel abruptly released. "Ah. It just slides."

They both got to their feet, and Gabriel slipped his fingers under the seam. He glanced at Lia with an unspoken question, waiting until she nodded before he pulled the panel free.

Lia put a hand out to steady herself, and her stomach plummeted as the beam of the flashlight exposed a hidden space—an extension of the dressing room—just as Gabriel had suggested. And inside, stacked upright on the floor and on a single shelf above that spanned the space, were dozens of paintings in a wide range of sizes. These had been removed from their frames, apparently for storage. Parts of the larger canvases were visible, and Lia could see that they were Expressionist and Impressionist works. A complete departure from what hung on the apartment walls.

Gabriel slid the second panel free and set it down behind them with the first. In the additional light, the hoard looked even more extensive.

"Oh God, Grandmère, what did you do?" Lia whispered.

"Don't think the worst," Gabriel said quietly, rejoining her.

"How can I not?" She looked up at him, the backs of her eyes burning. "Why else would a woman who received a god-damn thank-you note from Hermann Göring have a hidden hoard of art if it wasn't stolen?" She thrust the phone back at Gabriel and spun, hurrying out of the dressing room and every horrible secret in it. She stopped in front of the wardrobe, trying to settle the despair and distress that were constricting her chest and making it hard to breathe.

"Lia."

She hadn't heard him follow her out. "I'm sorry. This is all...it's just..." She tried to put her thoughts in order. "It's horrifying. And unforgivable."

"Hey." He caught her hand in his for the second time and gently pulled her around. "Whatever this is, whatever your grandmother may or may not have done, it has nothing to do with you. You did not do this. If the worst turns out to be the truth, it is not your fault. Do you understand?"

Lia nodded miserably, looking down to where their fingers joined. "I'm sorry."

"Please don't be. This is a lot. For anyone."

"I'm glad you're here." The words slipped out before she could stop them. It was the truth but not something she should be saying to a man she had only just met.

"Me too." If he found her confession inappropriate or strange, he hid it well. "We'll figure this out."

Lia nodded again and withdrew her hand from his, trying to regain her composure.

Gabriel seemed to hesitate. "Is there anyone else...is anyone else helping you? Sibling? Parents?"

"No siblings," Lia told him. "And when I told my parents about the apartment, they were more relieved that they were not required to return to France than interested in what it might contain. This is my problem." She looked up at him and made an effort not to embarrass herself further. "Honestly, I'll be fine. I'm used to dealing with things on my own."

"You're not on your own." He held her gaze, his grey eyes giving none of his thoughts away. "Whatever side your grandmother may have been on, we'll figure out the truth together."

CHAPTER

6

Estelle

The Ritz Hotel had been divided into two when the Germans had marched into Paris. In truth, it was already two edifices long before the red-and-black flags had unfurled over the city but the physical had also become the social when the Nazis commandeered the Parisian landmark. The Ritz went from simply a catch basin for the wealthy and the royal, the artistic and the intellectual, to the official headquarters of the Luftwaffe.

The side of the hotel that had once been the residence of princes and dukes, facing the stately Place Vendôme, was now the residence of high-ranking German officers, including the head of the Luftwaffe, Hermann Göring. On the other side of the palatial hotel, facing rue Cambon and separated by a corridor filled with shops that boasted the most expensive, most luxurious, and most unusual wares that might be purchased in Paris, lived the civilians. Or at least those civilians carefully approved by the Third Reich.

The appropriation of the hotel by the Luftwaffe did not come without its inconveniences for the longtime residents who were evicted to smaller, less glamourous rooms. Some patrons left and didn't return at all. Those who stayed endured the frantic renovations that preceded the Luftwaffe's occupation, the greatest of which were the changes to the Imperial Suite that Göring had selected for his own use. Though if any of the civilian residents had complaints, they did not share those in front of Estelle. Or the Luftwaffe.

At the same time, Estelle Allard was also completing renovations to her own apartment. The work was carried out with the same sort of urgency but that was where the similarities stopped. In Estelle's apartment, the alterations had been completed surreptitiously by a single individual aside from herself, a small space annexed from the existing layout and cleverly concealed. In the Ritz's Imperial Suite, with its multiple salons and bedrooms, its maids' quarters and formal dining room, crews had worked tirelessly to improve the palatial atmosphere and meet the demands of its new occupant.

The men on the crews, when questioned discreetly once the work had been completed, had described the extraordinarily large bathtub Göring had ordered. The hotel staff, when questioned guilelessly after the Reichsmarschall had taken up residence, had described a great deal more. The tub, they said, on their way to the suite with stacks of towels and trays upon trays of food, was part of a cure for the Luftwaffe general's addiction to morphine. A doctor came, they said, to submerge the man in water, give him a series of injections, and then submerge him again. But in a hotel where the staff was long used to providing unflappable, unquestioning service to exacting, difficult guests, these changes and demands seemed to be taken in stride.

That type of service, coupled with the hotel's lavishness, had made the Ritz as popular with the occupying Germans as it had always been with its preceding clientele. Estelle's own parents had favoured the Ritz, especially when they wished to host a soiree while staying in Paris. They liked being at the center of the social elite, and the Allard fortune, having the benefit of being both French and vast, had always been welcomed warmly, as had their daughter. Estelle, in fact, had celebrated her eighteenth birthday in the Ritz's grand dining room, on one of the rare occasions her parents were in Paris on her birthday. They had thrown a party for their friends, treated Estelle to caviar, given her a necklace with eighteen glittering emeralds set in gold, and presented her with a dark green Mercedes roadster to match. At the end of the evening, they had toasted her with champagne, careful to ensure that a photographer for the *Paris-Soir* captured the moment. Appearances, after all, were paramount.

So the return of Estelle Allard, heiress, socialite, and patron of the Parisian art landscape, to the dining rooms and bars of the Ritz Hotel that September did not raise eyebrows. It was not at all remarkable that she had not been in Paris prior to the Germans' arrival—even Coco Chanel had fled south before returning—and one could not be faulted for being prudent. And the newly installed inhabitants of the Ritz Hotel were delighted when the young Frenchwoman drifted gracefully through the grand salons. Beautiful Frenchwomen were always appreciated by the officers of the Luftwaffe.

Estelle was the recipient of that appreciation now. At the

enthusiastic and insistent request of the officers crowded into the room, she stood by the piano and sang Rina Ketty's *"J'attendrai,"* which never failed to please her audience. It was probably a nod to the glamour and extravagance of the hotel, or perhaps it was the lyrics or the melody, but the moment she began, all conversations stopped and every eye was upon her.

Including those of the man who sat in a chair just off to the side, as if holding himself apart from the other officers. At this distance, in the soft light, it was difficult to see the insignias on his dark uniform but the way he was looking at her made her uneasy. He was wiry in build, his face thin, his eyes close-set beneath well-coifed blond hair. While the other men generally gazed at her with expressions that ranged from admiration to lust, enchantment to indifference, this man was looking at her with what only could be described as suspicion.

It unsettled her more than she cared to admit.

Estelle finished her song to a warm round of applause, aware that the officer's eyes had not left her. She ignored him and withdrew to the bar, taking herself out of the spotlight and away from the attention of the solitary man. Perhaps she would not linger tonight. Perhaps it would be best if she slipped away and came back another time—

"One wonders why such a beautiful woman is all alone."

Estelle should have moved faster. Slowly she turned, pasting a blank expression on her face.

"Good evening," she said with a vacuous smile. After letting the seconds tick away, she allowed her smile to slip. "I'm sorry, I don't speak German," she lied. "I don't know what you just said."

"I said I enjoyed your song." The officer switched to French.

"Oh. Well, thank you." She tipped her head flirtatiously as she noted the Gestapo uniform, the strip of black at his shoulder, and the SS runes at his collar. A sergeant, perhaps, given the absence of any sort of braid.

"I am Scharführer Schwarz," he said, confirming her guess. "And you are?" Cold blue eyes bored into hers.

"Estelle Allard," she replied, wondering if this was simply a lonely officer's attempt to make conversation. She was used to the overtures of Luftwaffe officers but she found advances from those associated with the Gestapo unnerving in their intensity and directness. The Gestapo were not so easily manipulated or deflected.

"You live here? In this hotel?" he asked, leaning toward her.

She forced a gay laugh. "Alas, no."

"Then why are you here?" He wasn't smiling.

"I don't understand. Why does anyone come here if not for a good time?" She giggled. "And to admire such handsome men in uniform."

The sergeant didn't smile. "How often do you come to the hotel?"

"Whenever I fancy putting on a pretty dress." She cringed inwardly at such a deliberately superficial reply but it earned the reaction she had hoped for.

He scoffed with obvious disparagement but his scorn didn't stop his questions. "And you sing each time you come?" he pressed.

Uneasily, Estelle blinked and put a hand to her chest, hating how she could feel her pulse pounding beneath her fingers. She toyed with the emerald necklace that rested against her skin. "Well, not every time. Whenever I'm asked."

Schwarz's eyes had followed the movement of her hand, and he was openly sneering now. "By whom?"

"Why are you asking me so many questions?" She let petulance creep into her tone.

"Because it's my duty."

"It's not your duty to harass beautiful women, Scharführer Schwarz." A new voice cut into the conversation, saving her from a reply.

Estelle turned to find a Luftwaffe officer standing behind her, holding two glasses of champagne. He wasn't looking at Estelle. Instead, he was glaring at the sergeant.

"Colonel Meyer." The sergeant took a half step back.

"I can't imagine that you were doing anything other than complimenting Mademoiselle Allard on her captivating performance." The colonel put the glasses of champagne on the polished mahogany surface of the bar. His movements were casual but the edge to his voice was anything but. "The Luftwaffe is, after all, quite selective about who we let in to this establishment. Do you understand, Scharführer Schwarz?"

Schwarz took another half step back, his jaw clenched. "Of course."

"Excellent. You are dismissed."

The sergeant gave Estelle one last hard look and spun, stalking away.

"Heavens, what an unpleasant man," Estelle breathed. Her heart was only beginning to slow.

"Apologies, Mademoiselle. Please pay him no mind. The Gestapo can be a disagreeable lot, Scharführer Schwarz more so than others." He snorted derisively. "Ambitious bastard, never pleased with anything."

That information did not reassure Estelle at all. Instead, her unease intensified.

"If he made you feel uncomfortable in any way, I can have a further word with him—"

"Oh, no, that is not necessary," Estelle hastened to assure him. To draw additional attention to herself from the Gestapo was the last thing she wanted. "Please do not trouble yourself. In fact, I was just getting ready to leave."

"Leave? You can't possibly." He pushed one of the champagne glasses toward her. "You must sing for us again later this evening. None of us knew we had such a songbird in our midst. The Reichsmarschall was particularly taken with you the other night."

"I'm flattered." Estelle hoped she sounded sincere. "But I'm afraid I must depart. Curfew comes early."

"Nonsense," the smooth-talking Meyer scoffed, brushing at the immaculate sleeve of his uniform. "You are welcome to stay at the hotel. Spend the night as my guest, and I will see you to your home tomorrow morning."

"That is generous, truly." She really should have moved faster. Retreated far beyond the bar and the reach of these men and into the safety of the night. "Yet I must decline."

"Pity. But of course, I will not insist." He patted her hand reassuringly. "But you have only to ask if you change your mind."

She looked up at the colonel beneath her lashes. He was probably in his forties, with a pleasant face and a ready smile. A perfectly ordinary-looking man in a different time and place, but anything but ordinary in the here and now.

She wrapped her fingers around her glass and raised it to her lips, pretending to take a sip. Out of the corner of her eye, she could see the bartender in his white bar coat casually mixing a drink. She was reasonably convinced that he harboured anti-Nazi sentiments, but she couldn't be sure. She was, however, quite sure that he was listening to their conversation, so she chose her words with care.

"There is, actually, a different matter that I wished to speak to you about," she said in a low voice.

"Oh?" Meyer removed his spectacles and then polished the lenses.

Estelle set her drink back on the gleaming bar top and undid the necklace that hung at her throat. "The Reichsmarschall might have been taken with my songs, but I believe he was taken with these emeralds more," she said, laying the necklace on the bar. In the light, the gems pulsed with an unearthly glow.

"He does covet such treasures," Meyer agreed.

"At the time, he expressed his desire to possess them," she continued, ignoring the shudder that rose at the memory of his sausagelike fingers at her throat. "I confess that I declined his offer. They were a gift from my parents." Her words were ridiculous, really, because what Hermann Göring wanted, Hermann Göring took. It was only a matter of time before the emeralds disappeared into his burgeoning collection of gems pillaged from all over Paris. Estelle figured she might as well extract an advantage while she could.

She slid the necklace toward him. "I know how hard you work to keep operations here running smoothly and the Reichsmarschall appeased. I thought that perhaps you should offer these jewels to him. I suspect such a gesture would be well regarded."

The colonel replaced his spectacles and regarded her

curiously. "Why would you do that? Why not offer them to him yourself?"

Estelle shrugged, her fur wrap sliding off her shoulder. "I was hoping you might be able to do something for me in return."

"Such as?"

"I cannot eat emeralds." She leaned in and dropped her voice. "And I do not wish to spend my days queuing for rations that always seem to run out."

"That's why you should move into the hotel," Meyer protested. "Join Arletty and Coco. Inga and Daisy. Their every need is met, as would yours be. You'd not want for anything. I would personally see to it."

"It's tempting," Estelle lied. "But I find great comfort in my own home. A failing on my part, I suppose."

"Not a failing. One must admire a woman who takes pride in her home. Perhaps you will share it with a husband and family of your own soon?"

"That is my fondest wish." Estelle schooled her expression into one of wistfulness. She knew exactly what role the Reich expected their women to play.

Meyer nodded his approval. "I will instruct the kitchens that you may have whatever you need. A woman such as yourself should not concern herself over such trifling matters."

As if Paris starving was a trifling matter, Estelle thought despairingly. There were not enough emeralds in the world to keep the city from starving but at least the gems on the bar in front of her would keep those who were already depending on her from perishing.

"I am much relieved," she said, pressing her hand to her chest. "Thank you."

"No, it is I who should thank you." He picked up the necklace and examined it before putting it back down. "But I, in turn, have a request for you to make our arrangement final."

"Oh?" Estelle tried to sound interested when all she wanted to do was escape the clouds of smoke and heavy scent of too many bodies and too much perfume.

"One more song." He held up his hand as she opened her mouth to protest. "And I will escort you home myself. You do not need to worry about curfew."

All hope of a quiet escape slipped away as she reminded herself that there was more at stake than her feelings. "Very well."

Meyer clasped his hands together. "Wonderful. I cannot think of a better finish to such a successful day for the Luftwaffe and all of its fine people. Almost like a grand finale, as it were."

"Oh?" Estelle gathered her wrap around her. "And what is it that I should be celebrating?"

Meyer glanced about. "I probably shouldn't say anything but you'll read about it in the papers in the next few days anyway, so I can't see the harm."

The bartender had moved away and was now pouring for a loud group of patrons.

Estelle leaned closer to the colonel as if hanging on his every word. Which, she supposed, she was. Just not for the reasons he thought.

Estelle wasn't sure if any of the information she collected in this hotel was at all useful to the network to which she reported or what, if anything, they were able to do with such knowledge. It had been the field medic whom she had worked with for months, Jerome de Colbert, who had set up the initial meetings—his cousin Vivienne being the resistance operative Estelle met with most often. Half the time, Estelle felt ridiculous passing on details like the number and identities of the Luftwaffe officers who had taken up residence in the hotel, the names of the women who warmed their beds, or the fragments of conversations she overheard at the bars and in the salons. But all of it was absorbed with grave intensity. And solemn encouragement to keep watching and listening.

Like she was doing now.

"We've destroyed Britain's air force." Meyer clenched his fist and then opened it like he was mimicking a bomb detonating. "Utterly routed them. There is nothing left."

"Nothing?" Estelle remarked, attempting to sound impressed. Inside she was shaking. With anger or despair, she wasn't sure.

"We pulverized them," he said with relish.

Estelle only nodded.

"The Reichsmarschall has now ordered the annihilation of London. Without a challenge, we will all be able to celebrate Göring's brilliance and Churchill's surrender right here in this beautiful city. This war will be over quickly, of this I am sure. Days, perhaps, weeks at worst." He picked up his glass, raised it in a silent toast, drained it with gusto, and signalled the barman for another. "And I'm also sure we would all like to hear you sing to mark the occasion."

I'd rather die, Estelle thought but, as always, she kept her smile firmly upon her lips. She managed another nod, already trying to determine if there was any logical way that she might get this information to Vivienne before tomorrow morning. Though for all Estelle knew, the Luftwaffe was already dropping explosives on London as the RAF sat in ruins and she sat sipping fine champagne at a Paris bar.

Estelle knew that Vivienne or the others in her network were in contact with London sporadically because they brought news of what was happening beyond the borders of France. Perhaps, at the very least, Estelle might be assured that Meyer's comments were nothing more than a cog in the machine that was Nazi propaganda. Perhaps the Germans had underestimated the air force on the other side of the channel. Perhaps the RAF was merely biding its time.

Or perhaps the horrific red-and-black flags shrouding every building and monument in Paris would soon similarly hang from London's edifices.

The barkeep had set a drink down in front of the colonel and nodded in Estelle's direction. The lenses of his pince-nez perched on the bridge of his nose reflected the light from above and hid his eyes and his thoughts. Another reminder of things she didn't know.

She drew her own glass across the smooth wood surface of the bar. "Shall I—"

"Colonel." A harried officer who looked as if he'd just run a Roman mile approached Meyer, speaking in rapid German. "I was told I could find you in here."

"What do you want from me?"

"I've come from Saint-Germain-en-Laye. I have a message for the Reichsmarschall."

Meyer waved his hand in exasperation. "Then give it to him."

"I can't find him, sir. Do you know where he is?" He held a folded paper in his hand.

"I do not." Meyer looked mildly annoyed. "If not in the dining room or one of the salons or one of the bars, he will most likely be in his suite. If that is the case, he will not appreciate disturbances."

Estelle kept her face perfectly blank and put her handbag beside her drink, releasing the clasp.

The man shifted from foot to foot. "But it is imperative I speak with him."

"Whatever the meddling field marshal wants, I'm sure it can wait."

"But the message is from the Führer himself."

The colonel stilled. "From the Führer?"

"Sent directly from Berlin. And the Führer demands an immediate answer from the Reichsmarschall. I'm to wait for a response and return with a reply for encryption."

"It's ridiculous that we are running messages back and forth across this damn country like rats scurrying about," Meyer growled at the hapless officer. "Not only is the inefficiency of this process an affront to the entire Luftwaffe, it's dangerous."

"The mobile unit in Saint-Germain is well secured, Colonel. The location is changed regularly."

"They are trucks," Meyer snarled. "Vulnerable to anyone who can drive one."

"I can assure you that we—"

The colonel banged his fist on the surface of the bar. "The field marshal has been promising the Luftwaffe its own communication equipment that has thus far failed to materialize. Can you explain that?"

The beleaguered officer cleared his throat. "I'm quite sure that everything possible is being done—"

"The Kriegsmarine does not seem to suffer such delays receiving their encryption devices." The colonel still sounded furious.

"Those devices are not nearly as secure and sophisticated as the ones at Saint-Germain. The one that is being delivered here."

Meyer didn't seem impressed. "I have a teleprinter already installed that is sitting idle and useless, waiting to be connected, and the men who are supposed to be operating the system sitting just as idle and useless. Did von Rundstedt at least tell you when we might expect delivery of this sophisticated encryption unit?" He practically spat the word *sophisticated* back at the officer.

"I-I'm not sure, sir. Days, I think. They are waiting for a part of the machine from Berlin. It's shipped in pieces, as I understand. For security purposes."

Meyer cursed under his breath.

"Is something wrong?" Estelle looked up from her handbag with wide eyes.

"No, no," he assured her in French. "Just a small matter." He turned to the officer and switched back to German, visibly composing himself. "Give the message to me. I will take it to the Reichsmarschall."

"Very good, sir." The younger officer sounded relieved. "I will wait for a response."

The colonel held out his hand, and the officer placed the paper in his waiting palm.

"You can also tell von Rundstedt that he is trying my patience. And that of the Reichsmarschall."

"Sir?"

"Never mind." Meyer waved the officer away impatiently.

"Is that important?" Estelle asked, gesturing at the paper.

"A message from Berlin," Meyer told her. "And something I must deal with, I'm afraid." He picked up the emeralds still lying on the polished bar and weighed them in his palm. "On second thought, perhaps you may reconsider your offer?"

"My offer?"

"To sing tonight, of course."

"Of course." This man had a way of twisting words.

"Come with me to the Reichsmarschall's suite. If I must disturb him, he will take such an inconvenience more gracefully if it is accompanied by a welcome distraction such as yourself. He would enjoy a private audience with his favourite songbird, I think, and even more so should she come bearing gifts."

Estelle stilled. "I don't think that would—"

"We are exchanging favours here, are we not, Mademoiselle Allard?" Meyer put the emeralds on the table in front of her.

Estelle took another tiny sip of champagne that now tasted like poison. She set her glass back down and picked up the necklace. "It would be my honour," she lied.

"Excellent." Meyer gestured toward the entrance to the bar. "Shall we?"

Estelle followed the colonel from the bar, through the grand salons, and up to the étage noble. In all of her pampered, monied life, she had never actually been inside the Imperial Suite. There was a guard standing outside the suite's door, and he stepped smartly aside as the colonel approached. Estelle could feel the guard's eyes on her, and she turned to meet his stare boldly. He dropped his gaze.

Meyer knocked twice, loudly, and almost immediately the door was opened by another man within. An aide, Estelle guessed, taking in the crisp creases of his uniform, the polished black leather of his boots, and the haughty, smug expression he wore above it all. She'd seen that sort of expression her entire life on the faces of people who believed themselves superior because they were part of an elite inner circle.

"Colonel Meyer to see the Reichsmarschall," Meyer said loudly, though for whose benefit Estelle wasn't sure.

"All due respect, it's rather late, don't you think, Colonel?" the aide grunted before his eyes slipped to Estelle. "And he certainly did not request a whore this evening, no matter how beautiful she might be." He was speaking in German.

Estelle adopted a bright, pleasing smile, looking back and forth between the men in uncomprehending question.

"Mademoiselle Allard is favoured for her voice," Meyer emphasized with biting condescension, "and for the treasures she brings him. You would be wise to remember that in the future, Hesse."

The aide called Hesse didn't look convinced. Or cowed. "Hmph."

"Further, I have a message from the Führer that demands immediate response. But by all means, continue to make imprudent comments about matters you know little about."

Hesse's features tightened. "Göring is currently resting, but I will advise him that you are here." He led them into a grand salon. "Wait in this room," he said before disappearing through two tall, narrow doors.

Here, in the salon, the ceilings soared overhead, crystal chandeliers spaced throughout. Windows taller than two men reached up and away, framed by elegant draperies caught neatly on each side. Antique chairs and chaises and tables were arranged in intimate groupings, as if waiting for their occupants to return to resume intimate discussions.

Except Estelle only registered all of this distantly. Because filling the space in between, propped up against walls, and resting on chairs and tabletops, was a collection of paintings, drawings, sculptures, and tapestries that would dwarf those of some museums.

"Quite an assortment, isn't it?" Meyer murmured. "He's got more at the Jeu de Paume. I don't understand art much myself but the Reichsmarschall is making great efforts to assemble the finest pieces in all of Europe. Everything you see here will all be moved shortly."

"To where?" Estelle asked, trying to sound merely curious and not horrified.

"As I understand, the collection is officially destined for the grand Führermuseum that will be a cultural showcase for the Reich. Unofficially, of course, I think the Reichsmarschall may have taken a more personal interest in some of the pieces. He has a weakness for beautiful things." The colonel winked at Estelle. "You're a bit of a collector yourself, are you not?"

"I am." The words seemed to stick in her throat.

"Then you'll appreciate all this more so than I."

Slowly, Estelle turned in a circle, trying to control and conceal the emotion that was bubbling up. Fury, hatred, help-lessness, horror. This wasn't a collection, she thought clearly. This was a desecration. The theft and pillaging of history and culture, and, standing in this room, she couldn't begin to imagine how any of it might be saved. She thought of the art hidden behind her walls at the Wylers' request, because they had all heard the rumours of Nazis seizing personal collections. But she hadn't truly appreciated the scope of the devastation and exploitation until this moment.

"Colonel Meyer."

Estelle's head snapped around to find the aide standing before them once again.

"The Reichsmarschall will see you now. But only you, Colonel. The mademoiselle is to wait here."

The colonel grunted and strode toward the doors, yanking them open with little fanfare. Through them, Estelle glimpsed a massive bed, framed and draped like something out of Marie Antoinette's boudoir. On the bed, a man lay reposing, clad in what looked like a burgundy silk robe, trimmed in fur and belted around his substantial girth. Two lavender-clad legs stuck out from beneath the hem.

The aide turned his attention to Estelle. "The Reichsmarschall is not in the mood to be ... entertained this evening." His French was heavily accented but precise. "He will not grant an audience but he is curious what you have brought him."

"Of course." Estelle handed him the emeralds.

The aide took them without comment and followed Meyer into the bedroom. The doors snapped shut behind him.

Estelle stood motionless in the center of the room before she forced herself to move. She circled the art, tipping a few paintings to look for anything that might tell her where they had come from or where they might be going. There were Flemish, French, Italian, and English paintings, some, she was sure, from the years marking the Renaissance. Pieces that were irreplaceable and priceless. She had nothing with which to make a list but maybe she could—

"Looking for something in particular?" Hesse was back, a hard look on his narrow face. He was holding a gauzy mass of lemon-yellow fabric that cascaded over his arm.

"Oh, no," Estelle breathed. "I've just never seen so many lovely pieces in one spot before. It's like a ... like a grand museum. And I do so adore museums."

"Of course you do." Clear antipathy made his lips curl

unpleasantly. "Here. You're to put this on." He thrust his arm and the bundle of yellow fabric in Estelle's direction.

"I beg your pardon?"

"Reichsmarschall Göring was very pleased with your gift. He would like to extend a thank-you. You are to wear this the next time you...sing."

His inflection made it clear that he still believed that she was a whore. Estelle didn't bother to correct him. She stepped toward him and took the garment from his outstretched arm. It was a dress of lightweight crepe, lined with silk, the straps beaded with crystal. The irrational part of her wanted to throw it back at the German. The rational part of her wondered if she would be able to sell it and, if so, for how much.

"He also asked me to give you this." He handed Estelle a rectangular card.

A postcard, Estelle realized as she took it. The front depicted a long, columned building adorned by a Nazi flag. She turned it over. *For the lovely Estelle, With thanks, Hermann Göring.* Her stomach churned.

"He would like you to try the dress on now," Hesse said. "While he sees to Reich business with the colonel."

Estelle found herself unable to reply, fighting the urge to simply turn and run.

"You really are as stupid as you seem, aren't you?" the aide muttered irritably in German.

"I don't understand what you said." She forced herself to focus and slipped the postcard into her handbag.

"The Reichsmarschall would like me to ensure that you are pleased with your dress before you go," the aide prompted with clear contempt, slowing down his speech as if Estelle were a half-wit.

"Is it couture?" she asked, grasping for the single most self-absorbed comment she might make in this moment.

Hesse sneered. Hell, Estelle was sneering at herself, standing as she was in the middle of such desolation that she could do nothing about. Accommodating a morphine-riddled general who was destroying everything she knew and loved. And for what? For the chance that she might overhear something that would make a difference?

God, London might already be on fire, and she had heard nothing until it was a fait accompli. What was she even doing here? Did anything she might hear or see even matter?

"Lanvin, I'm told," the man said derisively. "I'm sure it will satisfy your...impeccable taste."

Estelle lifted her chin and looked down her nose at the man as imperiously as possible. "I demand you show me to a suite where I might change."

The aide shook his head in disgust. He glanced back at the doors that were still tightly closed on Meyer and Göring and then smirked. "Yes. For you, I have the perfect place." He indicated that Estelle should follow him.

He led them across the salon, weaving between the piles and stacks of stolen art, to the far side of the room. On their left, a set of ornate doors was open, and what looked like a luxuriously appointed dining room sat in shadows beyond. Just in front of them, another door existed, though this one was camouflaged as part of the wall itself, like the secret doors in the bedchambers of Versailles.

A closet? Estelle wondered, thinking of the many cleverly concealed cupboards and storage spaces César Ritz had built into his hotel. Or a servants' entrance? Or possibly a portal by which guests could arrive and leave with secrecy and discretion? Hesse released a catch near the wainscoting, and a thick, heavy door swung silently inward. He stepped forward and reached above his head, switching on a light.

"I think this will be suitable for you." He was enjoying this.

Estelle let him. It suited her to be underestimated. Better yet, dismissed. "A closet? I refuse."

"One does not refuse the Reichsmarschall, Mademoiselle," the aide said. "Do let me know if you require further assistance." He finished with an unmistakable leer before stepping back and closing the door behind him.

Estelle looked around the space, lit only by the bare bulb over her head. It was indeed a closet. A drafty, somewhat dusty broom closet, and she did not doubt for a second that he had put her in here to humiliate her. There was a small latch on the inside of the door, and Estelle slid the bolt across. At least Hesse wouldn't be able to humiliate her further. She knew his type. The sort who could feel big only if they could make those beside them feel small.

The closet had clearly been part of the renovation in some manner, given the scent of newly cut lumber that lingered in the air and the wisps of sawdust beneath her feet. Against the wall to her right, a set of narrow shelves housed a collection of tins. Furniture polish, Estelle discovered, set beside a small stack of cloths. She put her handbag on the shelf next to them.

To her left, in the back corner, three brooms of varying sizes were propped together, a dusty toolbox at their base. Above them, a twist of what looked like heavy wires emerged. They were newly installed, Estelle judged, based on the shiny, gleaming tacks that secured them. The wires climbed the wall, ran across the ceiling, and then vanished into the opposite corner closest to the lightbulb. Estelle frowned. What was the purpose of having a nearly empty closet in the Imperial Suite that housed a few tins of furniture polish and brooms, other than to humiliate would-be whores?

She turned, the yellow dress slipping from her arm before she could catch it. It landed at her feet, creating clouds of dust that swirled around the floor at her feet. The dust rose, only to be sucked to the back of the closet by a draft, vanishing under the back wall. Estelle kicked off her shoes and, in three steps, crossed to the rear of the closet. Here, she could feel the draft tickling her bare toes and instantly recognized what that meant. The back wall was not a wall at all but a door. Something she would never have been able to identify had she not just finished a similar renovation in her own apartment. How very ironic.

Estelle ran her fingers around the edges of the wall. It took her only seconds to find the latch, and seconds more before she was able to release it. The back of the closet swung silently inward on well-oiled hinges. Beyond, a narrow, wooden staircase vanished down into darkness.

She had minutes, she knew, before the German aide would start to wonder what was taking her so long. But those were minutes she could use. Without stopping to consider what she was doing, Estelle started down the stairs. A hiding place for more stolen art, she guessed, keeping her hands along the uneven plaster of the wall as she descended. Or maybe a place to secrete the most valuable of all Paris's treasures.

Or maybe a dungeon where they kept assumed whores too curious for their own good.

The air became cooler as she reached the bottom of the stairs, and she guessed she was somewhere at the level of the Ritz cellars. Here, the light from above was losing its battle against the shadows. The scent of newly cut lumber was as strong as it had been above, mingled with the oily, metallic aroma of machinery. Someone had recently been working down here, though she could see nothing in the space beyond. She lifted her hand over her head and was not at all surprised to find a light cord identical to the one in the closet. The Germans were nothing if not predictably efficient.

She wrapped her fingers around the cord and tugged, flooding the room with a bright glare.

The space down here was far bigger than the closet above and closer to the size of her bedroom at home. Fresh lumber had been used to construct a heavy bench that ran the length of the room. On it, at the far end, sat a machine that looked like a bulky typewriter. Next to it, close to the center of the table, was an empty space, save for an array of disconnected cords coiled and resting at the rear. Closest to Estelle, stacks of what looked like rolls of paper ribbon were lined up in neat rows, and bundles of plain paper and boxes of pens and ink were set out in ordered groupings. Beside that, small canisters of what might have been oil were gathered next to a toolbox. Four wooden chairs were tucked in under the bench, waiting, presumably, for operators.

Not a hidden room for stolen art at all, Estelle understood. This looked like a radio communications station of some sort. The familiar, twisting collection of wires that she'd first seen secured in the closet above ran down the side of the room here and seemed to end somewhere behind the bench. Estelle had never seen a teleprinter before but she guessed that the machine that looked like a typewriter was exactly that. Waiting idly beside an empty space for the sophisticated encryption device that Meyer was expecting, though there was nothing on the bench that suggested what that device might look like.

A file cabinet stood just to her right inside the door. She crept forward and pulled the handle on the top drawer. Locked. As were the next two drawers. She knew she did not have the time to try to open them.

Instead she looked hard at the room one more time, trying to memorize its contents, and then snapped off the light. Hustling quietly up the stairs in her bare feet, she heard pounding on the door above.

"Is all to your satisfaction, Mademoiselle?" the aide's muffled, mocking voice filtered down.

She closed the hidden door, the click of the latch sounding overly loud.

"Mademoiselle?"

Estelle deliberately knocked two tins off the shelf with a deafening clatter. "This space is not to my satisfaction at all," she snapped loudly as she yanked her dress off. She tossed it aside and retrieved the yellow confection from where it still lay on the floor. She pulled it hastily over her head. "It is filthy."

On the other side of the door, the German laughed.

The yellow dress was a good fit, the cut beautiful, the fabrics luxurious, and the color, she knew, would flatter her complexion. She hated everything about it.

The closet door rattled. "Mademoiselle?"

Estelle retrieved her own dress and jammed her feet into her shoes. She snatched her handbag from the shelf, unlatched the door, and pulled it open.

"A horrid room," she complained. "Not even a mirror."

Hesse only smirked. "Whores do not need mirrors."

"I am not a whore." She tried to sound suitably indignant.

"You are all whores," he spat in German. "An entire city full of entitled, weak women."

Estelle crossed her arms. "Is Colonel Meyer done yet?" she demanded.

"Shortly, I'm sure."

"Then you may tell him that I will wait at the bar," Estelle said with as much haughty arrogance as she could manage. She needed to get away. Needed to get out of these rooms. Needed to gather the information that was swirling around in her head into a logical, clear list that could be passed on to London.

Provided London still existed.

"And you may tell the Reichsmarschall that his gift has left me speechless," Estelle continued.

The aide's expression was sour. "Of course."

"And you can also tell him that, one day soon, I hope I can repay him for what he has done."

In the end, it hadn't been Colonel Meyer who had seen Estelle back to her apartment. He had sent his regrets along with a wrapped parcel from the kitchens and a driver and car to escort her home. The ride had been almost intolerable, the big, black car rolling through the carcass of a once vibrant city. Instead of neighbourhood streets filled with throngs of evening revelers, the boulevards and avenues were now silent and empty, a bleak warren devoid of life. Windows and doors that once blazed with warm, welcoming light were now sealed and shuttered, adding to the sense that the entire city had been abandoned.

Perhaps, Estelle mused as the car slipped through the suffocating darkness, this was a little like how it might feel to be buried alive.

The Citroën had barely stopped before Estelle was out, slipping into her building with both a profound sense of relief and an overwhelming feeling of exhaustion. Every moment she spent in the web of the Reich bled the soul something terrible. She reached the stairs and put a hand on the bannister, a mere suggestion in the gloom, and hurried up toward her apartment. She reached her door and unlocked it by feel, closing it silently behind her as if a wooden barrier could insulate her from the misery outside. She took a single step into her darkened apartment before she stilled, the hairs on the back of her neck rising. There was something that wasn't quite right—

A hand covered her mouth.

"Don't scream, Allard," a rough voice whispered from behind her. "It's me."

"Jerome." Estelle twisted her head, and the pressure against her lips fell away. At her back was a solid, warm presence, a steadying arm at her waist. For a moment, she had an insane urge to simply lean against that strength and close her eyes and pretend that none of this was happening. Which was indeed insane because no amount of pretending would end this nightmare. She pulled away from him and took a deep breath, trying to steady her pounding heart.

"*Merde.*" Estelle turned toward the man standing before her in the darkness, unable to make out his features. "How did you get in here?"

"You keep a spare key above the door. You're lucky it was I who found it." His words were an accusation, and one she deserved.

"I'll remedy that."

"You should."

"How long have you been here?"

"Long enough to watch the sun go down waiting for you."

"Are you all right? Has something happened?" Estelle asked, still whispering.

"No. I'm fine."

She ran a hand through her hair. "You scared the life out of me."

"I'm sorry." He didn't sound sorry.

"Do you know what they would do if they caught you out at this time?" The idea of Jerome shot or hanged in the streets turned Estelle's stomach.

"I know exactly what they'd do." His voice was hard. "I've seen exactly what they do. Though you seem to have found a way around such injustice."

"I beg your pardon?"

"From the window, I saw you get out of that car a few minutes ago. I didn't expect you to have your own personal Nazi driver."

"I was at the Ritz," Estelle said, feeling defensive. "And accepted the ride home that was offered because the alternative is dangerous."

"You could have spent the night. I'm sure you would have been welcomed."

Estelle frowned at the harshness of his tone. She moved away from him and felt her way cautiously around the writing desk. She dumped the wrapped package on its surface, left her handbag and fur wrap on a sofa, and made her way to the windows, ensuring that they were tightly covered before returning.

She switched on the small lamp that sat on the corner of the desk. "Why are you here, Jerome?" she asked abruptly.

The medic hadn't moved but stood perfectly still. He was bareheaded and dressed simply, his thick hair longer than she remembered and falling over his forehead. He looked thinner, too, his face leaner and his cheekbones sharper. He was watching her now with those caramel-colored eyes that, tonight, seemed more critical than kind. "I came because Vivienne said she hadn't spoken to you in a while. She was worried something was wrong."

"I haven't had anything of significance to report," Estelle told him. "But tonight I—

"This apartment is something else," he said, interrupting her.

"I beg your pardon?"

"So many losing so much, and yet here you live alone amid such opulence, untouched and unscathed."

"I've lived here alone my entire life. With the exception of the rotating series of nannies, au pairs, and tutors my parents hired to oversee the raising of their daughter." She stopped, regretting her words. She sounded like the spoiled, entitled heiress she had sworn never to be. Jerome was right. She was lucky to be surrounded by luxury. "I'm sorry. That wasn't how I wanted that to come out."

Jerome finally moved and made his way over to the small table at the end of one of her sofas. He picked up the copy of *Signal* that was lying on its surface and examined it carefully. "Your subscription seems to be up to date," he said coldly without looking at her. He dropped the magazine and lifted the framed black-and-white photo of a German officer from the previous war. "A relative of yours?"

Estelle felt her jaw slacken. Surely, he couldn't possibly think that she—

"Doesn't matter," he said before she could reply. He set it

back on the table carelessly and watched it wobble and then topple facedown. He left it where it lay and wandered over to the hearth, gazing up at the painting that hung above. "Is this painting supposed to represent betrayal?"

Estelle blinked at the abrupt question before she came to stand beside him and considered the image. It depicted a beautiful maiden with flowing auburn locks, arms outstretched, her bosom bare above a tunic of cobalt blue, her expression one of sorrowful resignation. A soldier had her restrained while another stood just behind her shoulder, ready to plunge the dagger he held into her heart. On the farthest edge of the painting, an older woman reached desperately for her daughter, trying to stop the inevitable.

"Not betrayal, exactly. It's called *The Sacrifice of Polyxena* by Charles Le Brun," she told Jerome. "She's being sacrificed to appease the ghost of Achilles. The artist, Le Brun, became the official painter for Louis XIV. Which, I think, is the only reason why my mother bought it and had it hung—"

"I understand that we all need to make our own choices when it comes to surviving this war, but I thought you were better than this, Allard," he said quietly, interrupting her again. "I thought that, after everything, you were with us."

"What?"

He still hadn't looked at her. "At least promise me that you will not betray Vivienne."

Estelle recoiled. "Jesus. You think I'm one of them."

"Aren't you?"

"No." It came out as a raw whisper. "You can't believe that."

"What am I supposed to believe, given everything I've found in this apartment? You can't play both sides and expect to win, Allard."

Estelle stared at him, a growing fury pounding through her veins in time with her pulse. "Let me show you something." She turned on her heel and strode toward her bedroom, not waiting for Jerome.

Once in the bedroom, she similarly went to the windows to ensure that the curtains were closed in this room as well. Only then did she turn on the lamp.

Jerome had appeared in the doorway.

"Come in," she demanded. "And tell me what you see."

Jerome gave her a long look but did as she asked. He circled the room, sticking his head into the dressing room before stopping in front of the wardrobe. "A woman with more clothes than she would ever need in her life."

"True," she agreed, and that admission seemed to take him aback.

He turned slowly, reexamining his surroundings. "What is it that you want me to see in here, Allard?" Now he sounded impatient.

Estelle crossed her arms, still seething. "Nothing."

"What is that supposed to mean?"

"Exactly that. Nothing."

Jerome threw up his hands.

"Let me tell you what you don't see. At the rear of that dressing room, hidden by a false wall, is a space that currently houses the entirety of Rachel's family's art collection," Estelle told him in clipped tones. "An easy alteration, and conveniently hidden by more clothes than I will ever need in my lifetime."

Jerome frowned.

"Rachel's father, Serge Wyler, has been an avid Impressionist and Expressionist collector for most of his life. He feared that he would lose his collection to the thieving Nazis, so he asked me to hide it. He helped me build the false wall," she added.

"I don't—"

"I'm not done," she snapped.

Jerome fell silent.

"Serge also helped me build this." Estelle moved to the wardrobe and pulled the doors wide. She leaned in, released a hidden catch in the top corner, and pushed open the back of the wardrobe. "When I was a child, this small room was the room used by whatever au pair or governess lived with me at the time. We simply modified and moved this wardrobe to conceal it."

Jerome was staring at the space beyond, the bedroom light casting shadows onto the narrow bed and table inside. "I've never seen anything like it," he murmured.

"There was an American widow who used to live at the Ritz in the Imperial Suite before the Luftwaffe moved in and Göring appropriated the suite for himself. Her name was Laura Mae, and when the Germans came, she had an extensive collection of furs that she feared would be similarly appropriated. So she hid them in one of the Ritz's built-in cupboards and moved a massive antique armoire in front of it to hide the door. It's where I got the idea."

"How do you know this?" Jerome asked, his head deep inside the wardrobe. "What she did?"

"She told me. I thought it rather clever."

"What happened to her? The American?"

"She sold everything else she owned to the Nazis—the most impressive of her jewels went to Göring, and some things even went to Hitler, I heard—and left Paris. I don't know where she went. Though her furs, I must assume, are still behind the walls of the Ritz."

Jerome turned toward her. "What is this room for?" He had the grace to sound somewhat abashed.

"Did you know that Serge is a doctor?"

Jerome nodded slowly. "I think Rachel mentioned that once."

"He lost his practice," Estelle said. "He is restricted to seeing only Jewish patients, in their homes or in his. So long as people only get sick during the hours before curfew."

Jerome said nothing.

"This room is here just in case he needs it. If his patients need it. Because while the Nazis might suspect a Jewish doctor of hiding Jewish patients, they will not search the apartment of the Parisian socialite who lives across the hall. But one can never be too careful. So, yes, I keep my subscription to *Signal* renewed, and, yes, I display the photo of a German soldier that I found in my German primer ten years ago, and, yes, I linger at the Ritz when asked. But, no, I am not one of them, and, no, I will never betray Vivienne, and, no, I will never betray you." She was breathing hard when she finished speaking.

Jerome looked down at his boots. "I'm so sorry, Allard" was all he said.

Estelle ducked back into the wardrobe and pulled the hidden door closed, her anger draining and leaving nothing but exhaustion in its wake. "Me too."

"Will you ever be able to forgive me?"

"Yes. You are not my enemy, Jerome."

She sank down onto the edge of her bed. Neither of them spoke for a long minute.

"Meyer told me tonight that the Luftwaffe had destroyed the

British air force." It was Estelle who broke the silence. "Said that unopposed, London would be obliterated within days."

"Meyer is full of shit."

"How do you know that?"

Jerome looked away. "All Nazis are full of shit."

"I need to talk to Vivienne. Soon. I want to ask her about it. London, that is. And there is radio equipment in the cellar of the Ritz. I think they are putting some sort of special encryption device down there for Göring. It might be important."

He looked back at her. "I'll see what I can do."

"Thank you." She smoothed her hand over the lemon-yellow skirt and looked up to find Jerome staring at her intently with a peculiar expression on his face.

"Do I have something in my teeth?" Estelle asked him. "Or is there something else you want to accuse me of?"

He seemed to start. "No." He jammed his hands into his pockets. "It's just I've never seen . . . that is to say I . . . you look different," he finished awkwardly.

"Different?"

"That's not—" He stopped. "You look really pretty, Allard."

Estelle glanced down at the couture dress. She couldn't bring herself to acknowledge the compliment. If Jerome wasn't standing in the middle of her bedroom, she would have yanked the dress off right there. "Do you know that there is an entire suite at the Ritz full of stolen paintings and drawings and sculpture?" she asked instead. "I saw them tonight."

Jerome exhaled. "All due respect, Allard, but those are just things. There are bigger problems at hand than art."

"I know. But I looked at all of those pieces in that room, and I wondered how much tragedy was attached to each of those objects. What the acquisition of each of those pieces cost. What I saw in that room was a great mass of lives torn apart, stacked up, awaiting shipment to some vague destination from which they won't return." She leaned her head against one of the bedposts. "How much history will a family or a country lose when they lose the things that unite them? That tell the stories of their pasts?"

Jerome came and sat down carefully beside her, the mattress dipping farther under his weight.

"I am not an Allied general with troops and tanks and guns at my disposal," Estelle whispered. "I don't even have an ambulance anymore." She wrapped her hands around her middle. "I am a single woman with fancy clothes, a high-born pedigree that opens any door in society that I damn well please, and a carefully crafted reputation that makes my willingness to dance and drink this war away expected. Those are the only weapons I have."

"They are formidable weapons. After all, you fooled me, a man with no excuse not to have known better."

"Are they? Because it doesn't feel like it. I endure the officers who fill up the cabarets and hotels every night, giggle at their jokes, keep my lipstick bright, and try to avoid being touched. I sing when they ask me to and play dumb when they speak to each other in German. And I wait. And hope. For those moments when inebriation or just plain arrogance loosens tongues enough to compromise discretion. All the while knowing that the little crumbs of information that I collect might not make any difference in the end."

"Everything makes a difference. Everything. You never know what crumb might turn a tide."

"Crumbs aren't enough anymore, Jerome. I need to do more."

"How much more?"

Estelle twisted in surprise at the gravity of his question. "What do you mean?"

He held her eyes with his. "How much would you be willing to risk?"

"Anything. Tell me what else I can do."

He tipped his head toward the wardrobe. "There are . . . opportunities that would require you to hide people from time to time. But it would be dangerous. More dangerous than hiding an occasional patient."

"You do remember where I met you, do you not?"

Jerome lifted his hand as though he might take hers but then let it drop to his thigh. "I remember. But this is different than driving an ambulance across a battlefield, Allard. I need to make sure you understand that. I need to make sure that you think your answer through before you agree to anything."

Estelle considered her next words carefully. "When Rachel and I were young, Serge would often have what he liked to call salons in his home. Artists, writers, intellectuals, all debating, or sharing, or teaching. No subject matter was taboo, no opinions censored. We were probably not more than eleven or twelve when we first started attending, and we continued to do so right up until we left to join the service. The point, he said, was not to learn what other people thought, but to learn to think for yourself. And in learning that, he said, you will learn who you are."

"He sounds like a very smart man."

"He is." Estelle studied Jerome's fingers where they were splayed over the fabric of his thigh. They were strong and callused yet capable of the most delicate of touches when it came to his patients. They were the hands of a man who had always seemed to know just what to do and had never wavered.

"In this city," she said, "I am surrounded by people who look the other way and pretend that they don't see what is happening. Nights like tonight, I am surrounded by even more people who don't seem to care, so long as they are not inconvenienced or, even worse, can use it to their own advantage. They disgust me. Make me feel filthy."

"Estelle—"

"You asked me to think my answer through?" she interrupted. "Then here it is. If I am not fighting—if I am not doing everything I am capable of—then I am complicit in every atrocity that has happened and will continue to happen. This I know with every fiber of my being."

"Then just know this, too, Allard." Without warning, Jerome leaned forward and brushed his lips across her cheek before pulling back. "Know that you are not alone in your fight."

Estelle let the warmth of his touch seep into the cold and empty places deep inside her. "I'll try," she whispered.

CHAPTER

7

Sophie

S ophie stared at the work on her desk and tried to remember that she was still fighting.

The document in front of her was written in German, one of hundreds decoded and needing translation today. One of hundreds that she would translate and pass on. One of hundreds that would probably be too late to make any difference to the Allied men on the fronts and on the seas. Men who, unlike Piotr, still breathed and hoped—and fought and bled for what and whom they loved.

Her grief had been coupled with a numbing terror in the months after Piotr's death, which, in retrospect, had probably been for the best. It had been the terror that had driven her onward, that had kept her from simply tumbling over the edge and into an empty abyss of grief. It had been pervasive fear that had helped her evade the Wehrmacht that flooded Poland with their tanks and troops and the Luftwaffe that rained bombs from the sky.

By the time she had made her way back to Warsaw, she found the city burning, entire sections reduced to rubble or skeletal forests of blackened timbers and jagged brick. The staff at the embassy were long gone, and Sophie hadn't spent time looking for familiar faces. The north side of her own residence had been hit, though her south side flat was still partially intact. She was able to salvage her winter coat, the small wooden box of money that she'd hidden under a floorboard next to her bed, and a photograph of Millbrook that had survived in its broken frame. And then she had fled Poland.

It had taken her thirteen months to get home. Thirteen months that she had woken up each morning wondering if she would survive the day. Wondering if her wits would be enough to overcome the fear that threatened to paralyze her and the grief that refused to lessen its grip. When she had finally set foot on English soil, she had gone directly to London, emotionally and physically spent.

And discovered that she was too late. The Luftwaffe had taken the family Sophie had left.

The moment she'd stood in front of the crater and rubble that had once been her family's London home, the grief she'd carried with her from Poland had detonated. The mass of sorrow had splintered and shattered, leaving her soul nothing but an empty shell, not unlike the devastation before her.

But in the days and weeks and months that had followed, the empty space started to fill. White-hot rage drifted and curled through the vacuum like smoke. Anguish and abhorrence thrashed and howled at the edges. And, most of all, a burning sense of impotency pulsed and writhed, robbing her of sleep.

The need to do something—anything—to fight those who had taken everything from her gnawed at her relentlessly.

Bletchley Park was supposed to have salved that enraging impotence. The knowledge that Sophie was doing something to help the war effort and not standing idly by was supposed to have eased the inescapable fury. Instead, it only seemed to hone it. Because her efforts were accompanied by the knowledge that the decoded messages she translated were often too late to save the men dying on the fronts and on the seas.

She didn't know how much longer she could do this without going mad—

"Sophie Kowalski?"

Sophie turned toward the door. A tall, thin man sporting a neatly trimmed beard and dressed in unremarkable clothes was standing in the doorway, a paper held in his hands. She stood.

"Yes?"

His eyes narrowed, assessing her appearance without apology. "You are Sophie Kowalski?"

Sophie bit back the retort on her tongue. "Yes," she repeated.

"Come with me, please." It wasn't so much a request as a command.

Sophie followed the man, ignoring the stares of the other men and women. She frowned as he led her away from the bustle of the huts and deep into the gardens, brilliant with the color of summer growth. Here, they were far away from anyone who might hear their conversation.

The man stopped on a gravel path surrounded by bushes badly in need of a pruning.

"I am told you are good at languages," the man said in flawless French without preamble.

"I am competent," she replied in the same, her curiosity piqued. "If I wasn't, I would not have found work here."

"You speak French with a Parisian accent."

"I lived there for two years."

"Hmm." The man stroked his beard and continued to study her with unremarkable brown eyes.

He was not physically threatening but there was something about him that put her on edge. As if somewhere behind his tidy, contained appearance lurked a dangerous man. Sophie stared back, refusing to be intimidated.

"Where else have you lived?" He had switched to German, his dialect one that would be found in the high country.

"Geneva for a year. Warsaw for three." She answered him in German.

"Not Berlin?"

"No."

"You speak like a native of the city."

"My tutor was." And she had been stern and unforgiving and terrifying in her instruction.

"Ah." He brushed at a fly that had landed on his sleeve. "So you are not a German?"

"I beg your pardon?"

"Do you have an affiliation to the Nazi Party?"

Sophie's curiosity was abruptly snuffed by the icy rivulet of unease that slithered down her spine. "What? No."

He made a vague gesture with his hand in her direction. "You look like a German."

"I look like a German?" Sophie repeated as evenly as she could. "And what, pray tell, does a German look like these days?"

The man shrugged carelessly. "Tall, blond, blue-eyed—"

"You just described a quarter of the men who work here,"

Sophie snapped. "If Allied intelligence has resorted to using blond hair and blue eyes to identify Germans, we'll all be dead or speaking this language within a year."

He didn't seem fazed. "How long have you worked at Bletchley Park?"

"A year and a half. Maybe a little more."

"And what do you do in Hut Three, Sophie?"

"Work." She didn't elaborate, nor did she like the casual use of her first name. This man was not her friend.

"For whom?"

Sophie knew she should be terrified at the implications of that question but fear took a backseat to the fury that stirred. She let that fury strengthen. "State your accusation plainly."

"To the point. I like that."

"Then get to yours." If this man was going to accuse her of using her position at Bletchley to assist the Nazis, or spying, or sabotaging—

"Do you like what you do here, Sophie?" Her adversary abruptly switched back to French.

"What?" She had steeled herself for a much different question.

"Answer me in French."

Sophie blinked, thoroughly lost.

"You've expressed a desire to your supervisor more than once to do more to help the war effort," the man continued. "I'd like to know what you meant."

"I don't know, exactly. Just . . . more."

"Mmm," he mused, as if he had expected that answer. He tapped his fingers along the edge of the paper in his hand. "Your linguistic talents have identified you as a person of interest to a number of people in London."

"Who?"

"People."

Sophie tipped her head. "This conversation is some sort of test, isn't it?"

"They said you were intuitive."

"They?"

"Also that you were clever with numbers, organized, punctual, polite, but socially reticent." He ignored her question. "'Standoffish' might have been used."

"I didn't come to Bletchley for the taverns and ale. I came to fight the only way I know how."

He didn't seem offended at her tone. "You applied to Bletchley as Sophie Kowalski."

"Yes."

The brown-haired man plucked a leaf from the bush nearest him and twirled it between his fingers. "Kowalski is a Polish name, is it not?"

"Yes."

"You were married."

"Yes."

"Ah. So you are a widow. I wasn't entirely sure."

She clenched her fist, Piotr's ring cutting hard into her finger, but kept her face a mask of impassivity. He had tricked her into admitting something that she had told no one here.

"Why not apply as Sophie Seymour?"

Sophie stared at him in shock.

"Ah." He chuckled. "You didn't expect me to know your name."

She shrugged, unwilling to give him the satisfaction of an answer.

"Someone recognized you here," he continued, sounding amused. "As Sophie Seymour. Late of Warsaw, Poland."

She relaxed her hand where it was still clenched at her side. In hindsight, she supposed that it had probably only been a matter of time. At the beginning, she hadn't deliberately set out to hide that information but then it had simply become far easier to avoid questions that would inevitably become probing. And painful.

"You used to work at the Foreign Office," he continued. "As a very talented linguist."

"My past employment has no bearing on what I do now at Bletchley."

"See, now I might disagree. You concealed important information."

"I took all the required tests and filled out all the required forms related to this job. I was hired as a translator, and no one has had cause to complain about my work. So you can save your accusations. Or put them in my file and let me get back to work."

The man exhaled in what might have been amusement. "Ah, yes, your file. I've read it, even if no one else has. And then I went and tracked down the file the Foreign Office has for you—when you were still Sophie Seymour. And there were curious things that were not in that file. The Foreign Office had no travel records for you. No marriage records. No records at all after August of 'thirty-nine. In fact, Sophie Seymour was written up as deserting her post and then, later, presumed dead."

Sophie had died. Just not how this man meant. "Paper records have never fared well under German bombs."

"Neither did your family, as I understand."

The words were gentle but it was like he had punched her. The air whooshed out of her lungs, and she nearly doubled over.

"Your parents are recorded as having perished in the raids last year. Your twin brother, a pilot with the RAF, shot down on a bombing run before that."

"My brother is missing, not dead," she managed roughly.

The leaf fell from his fingers, spiralling to the ground. "I admire your optimism."

"I will mourn my brother when there is a body."

"How pragmatic of you."

Sophie didn't reply.

"Aside from the London address in your Foreign Office file—the address that, regrettably, no longer exists—there was a Norfolk address. My lieutenant, when tasked with investigating, discovered that the staff in your family's employ at that address currently believes you to be dead."

Sophie looked down.

"I'm not judging," the man said. "Merely curious as to your motivations."

"Motivations?" she asked dully.

"To remain here, anonymous."

"I will return when my brother returns," Sophie mumbled. "And then I won't have to explain why I was the only one of my family who deserved to live." Or face the crushing guilt that came with that acknowledgement.

"Mmm." The man considered her for an uncomfortably long minute. "For what it's worth, I'm sorry," he finally said. "For the loss of your family."

"Everyone here has lost someone."

"Yes," the man agreed, and there was a genuine note of weary sadness to his reply. He extended his hand. "Major James Reed. I'm here on behalf of Colonel Maurice Buckmaster, from London. Forgive my lack of introduction earlier.

As well as any offense I might have inferred regarding your loyalties."

"Don't be coy. You fully intended offense." Sophie looked up and shook his hand briefly. "It was part of your test."

"Perhaps." Reed was still studying her. "Tell me about Poland."

"What about Poland?"

"Tell me how you got out."

"Is this another part of your test?"

"Perhaps," he said again.

Sophie suddenly felt exhausted, trying to find the words that wouldn't betray the terror and grief that had accompanied her every step of the way. "North. Gdynia to Copenhagen. Then to Gothenburg. Then Edinburgh. Then London."

Reed studied her. "You make it sound easy."

"It wasn't," Sophie replied flatly. "It was months of waiting for opportunity. It was lying constantly, pretending to be a more believable persona whenever necessary. It was depending on people for generosity or stealing from them when you couldn't. It was accepting that desperation always trumped morals. It was putting trust into strangers and their homes and barns and trucks and fishing boats, knowing at any moment you might be betrayed and that there was little you could do to stop it."

The major was still watching her keenly. "Indeed" was all he said.

"There are a great many people who loathe the Nazis and everything they stand for. They just don't say it out loud and instead let their actions speak for them. The trick is to find them."

"And you did. You found your way back."

Sophie looked up at the sky, buoyant white clouds dotting the blue expanse. "Not in time."

The major didn't offer platitudes this time. Instead he only regarded her with an intense expression. "Mmm."

Sophie suddenly wanted this conversation to end. It was everything she could do not to simply bolt from the over-grown garden. "Did I pass your test, Major? Can I get back to my work? Unless you know something I don't, there is still a war to be fought, and I intend to keep fighting."

Reed might have smiled. "Tell me, Sophie, would you be willing to go back to France? Or even Poland?"

Sophie felt her jaw slacken. This conversation had taken an abrupt turn that she had seemingly missed. "What? Now?"

"No. There would be matters to be sorted first. Many phases of training that you would be required to undergo. Many more tests for you to pass."

"You mean here? At Bletchley?"

Reed shook his head. "Not here."

"Then where?"

"Surrey to start. Hampshire eventually, if you make it that far."

"That tells me nothing," Sophie said in frustration.

"That is rather the point."

"Why me?"

Major Reed glanced down at the paper he still held in his hand but didn't answer her question. "I think, Sophie Kowalski, that you are fighting the wrong battle in this war," he said.

"I am only a translator. I don't have any other special skills," she blurted.

The major's lips twisted. "I disagree."

"But I can't just leave my position at Bletchley."

"You can." He looked at her and handed her the paper. "You'll stay on at Bletchley for a bit but, once the wheels are in motion, you won't be back."

Sophie glanced down at it. *Inter-Services Research Bureau* was neatly printed across the top. She'd never heard of the bureau. "What is this?"

Major James Reed did smile then. "An opportunity to do more."

CHAPTER

8

Estelle

Estelle watched the travellers as they exited the train station, each moving with a grim swiftness that she had never seen before the war had started, because in the cheerful morning sunshine, the Gare du Nord was a terrifying place. It was a locale where the grey blight converged, a morass of Wehrmacht, SS, and Gestapo uniforms, all peppered with black spots of police. It was a place where tragedy and casual violence struck when one least expected it.

To avoid attention, those who flowed around the occupiers were careful to keep their gaze on the ground, answered questions with single syllables only when necessary, and had their papers in a place from which they could be produced without delay. Only misfortune came from lingering in and around a Paris train station these days.

Estelle adjusted the bright red flowers affixed to her hat and glanced casually at her watch as she did so. She strolled along the pavement in front of the station, her heels clacking unhurriedly, scanning the thinning crowd. There. Right on time. A familiar man in a threadbare suit, emerging from the station and walking deliberately toward her, a paper folded under his arm. A discreet distance behind him would be the airman.

Estelle slowed even further as he approached. Jerome walked by her, meeting her eyes for only a fraction of a second with his own. Estelle stopped and opened her handbag, pulling out her compact as though she was fixing her hair. In the mirror, she saw Jerome veer off toward the row of makeshift cabs that lined the street.

No more than five feet in front of her, another man in another threadbare suit had emerged, an identically folded paper under his arm. He stopped and glanced up, blue eyes clashing with hers before he looked away almost as quickly as Jerome had. Estelle frowned. Beneath the battered hat he wore, his face was ashen, his expression strained, bruised shadows under his eyes. He was ill. Or, more likely, injured. Unfortunately, there was nothing she could do about it now. He had survived the train journey from Belgium—he would need to survive just a little longer, and then she could deal with whatever ailed him.

Estelle resumed her unhurried walk, angling west, away from the station and toward the streets. She checked her lipstick one last time, the reflection in her mirror confirming that the man with the bright blue eyes was walking behind her. She dropped her compact back into her handbag and picked up her pace. Every minute that she was exposed with a man who likely did not speak a word of French was a minute too long.

She wound her way through the streets, Sacré-Coeur

intermittently looming up on its hill to the north between buildings. Here, away from the train station and in the labyrinth of streets lined with apartments and shops and cafés, Estelle relaxed fractionally. This close to her flat, each corner was familiar.

At the boulangerie on the corner, the queue was already long, hunger and weariness etched on each face. A Jewish family passed her, the yellow stars bright against their clothing. People on bicycles wove through the street, dodging the occasional pony cart. It wasn't often she saw vehicles anymore, unless they were military, and the little red-and-black flags affixed to each were a constant reminder of the evil that had consumed her city.

Estelle continued walking, and her stomach rumbled as the scent of baked bread broke through the heavier smells of horse manure and dust. She had eaten last night but nerves had kept her from dipping into her dwindling rations this morning. This was far from the first time she had collected an Allied fugitive, but the fear of discovery never went away. If anything, she'd become more anxious over time, though she supposed that wasn't a bad thing. It had kept her alert and careful, and she was still here when others had ominously vanished.

Estelle entered her building, glancing behind her as she pulled open the door. Blue-eyes was still behind her, though his gait was decidedly uneven. She would need to get him upstairs as quickly as possible. She paused at the bottom of the stairs to listen for the sound of footsteps but only silence met her. She was always cognizant of those who came and went— one could never become too comfortable, even here.

A minute later, the door swung open again, and the airman

staggered through. His face was tight with pain, his breathing shallow.

"Can you make it up the stairs?" she asked in French but got only a blank look in response. She asked again in English.

He nodded, gripping the railing hard enough that his knuckles were white.

"There are three flights."

"I'm fine."

"Yes, I can see that." Estelle put an arm around his waist.

The pilot resisted and tried to pull away.

"Save the heroics for when you're back in the air, yes?" she whispered harshly. "I can do a lot of things but carrying you up the stairs if you fall is not one of them."

He nodded, leaning on her shoulder. They navigated the stairs up to her apartment, and she maneuvered them inside, closing the door firmly behind them. "This way. Almost there."

She led him through the living area and all its ostentatious furnishings, around the long dining table, and into her bedroom. She opened the wardrobe and released the catch at the back. "Through here."

The hidden door swung open to reveal the concealed room.

"You'll stay here and rest until the next portion of your journey," she told him, helping him step up into the wardrobe and into the diminutive space.

Lately, too many of the network's agents had had their private, barricaded apartments raided and their fugitives caught with nowhere to hide. Since she had started smuggling Allied airmen, Estelle had done the opposite and made a point to invite people in at carefully selected intervals—acquaintances, Vichy officials, and once even a Wehrmacht officer who had insisted on walking her home so that, if ever questioned, they would all say the same thing. Mademoiselle Estelle Allard was merely an endearing ingenue surrounded by the spoils of old money, a vapid product of constant indulgence and flattery. She had nothing to hide from anyone.

And the Gestapo couldn't take what they couldn't find.

"It's cramped, I know, but you will be safe here," she told the airman.

He collapsed on the bed, breathing hard as she lit a small lantern.

"Ill or injured?" she asked, bending to retrieve his hat.

The man gestured vaguely at his left hip. "Shrapnel wound. Not quite healed yet."

"May I see?"

He hesitated. "Are you a nurse?"

"At the moment, I am everything you need me to be. Beggars can't be choosers, yes?"

The pilot closed his eyes and nodded. With practiced hands, Estelle removed the man's coat. She felt for his papers in his coat pocket and retrieved them, holding them up toward the light. They were good, she acknowledged. Whoever was putting together the papers on the Belgian end these days was talented. Blue-eyes had been assigned the name of Jean-Phillipe Brossoit, born in Bruges. And they'd used proper Belgian photos this time, not the photos that the Allied air forces provided their pilots with. The Nazis were getting smarter about details like that.

"Where are you from?" she asked, setting his papers and coat aside.

"Nova Scotia. Canada."

Estelle gently pulled the hem of his shirt from the waistband of his trousers and frowned. The bottom of his shirt, along with the side of his trousers, was soaked in blood. She shoved his shirt up his torso. He'd been bandaged crudely, a length of linen wrapped around his hips, and blood had saturated the entire side. She loosened the waistband of his trousers and peeled the bandage to the side.

"Jesus."

"That bad?" The airman tried to sit up.

She pushed him back down, still frowning. What had Jerome been thinking? The wound was deep, and blood seeped from a tangle of torn stitches that looked as though they had been executed by a child. More blood had run down his leg and soaked into his trousers, and only the dark color had prevented her from noticing earlier. There was very likely damage to one or more of the significant vessels that ran through his groin and into his leg. He needed a doctor. A real one. "This is a mess."

"You should see the plane," he joked feebly.

"You're not ready to travel. The journey from here to the Spanish border only gets worse."

Again, she wondered what had happened that had made Jerome feel like he had no choice but to travel with a wounded airman. With Jerome back and forth between Belgium and France, she barely saw him anymore, other than brief glimpses like the one just outside the train station. There was little chance she'd get any sort of explanation, but she'd have to let the network know that the man in her apartment would not be ready for further travel for a while. Provided he didn't die on her first.

Estelle was certainly adept at basic first aid but this was beyond her. A wound like this if not dealt with properly . . . infection or gangrene would be quick to follow if he didn't simply bleed to death first.

"Did they say anything to you? Before you got on the train for Paris?" she asked.

He grimaced. "I didn't understand much of what was being said, but there seemed to be a rush to leave Brussels. I couldn't stay." He looked up at her. "Can you fix it?"

"I don't know." She snatched a clean towel from the table and folded it square, pressing it to the wound. "Hold that there. Firmly."

"I need you to fix it." His other hand gripped the side of the bed. "Please."

Estelle made a decision and ducked through the little door. "I'll be back. Wait here."

"Where are you going?"

She paused. "Save your breath. I will never answer that question. You will never know where I am or when I might be back. You can't tell what you don't know. It is safer that way. Now wait here."

Estelle pulled her hat from her head and tossed it on the bed. She retraced her steps back through her apartment, stopping to place a potted geranium in the first window. The bright red flowers were easily seen from below and would communicate to Jerome that the airman was safely concealed. From there, she headed out across the landing and tapped on the door across from hers.

A moment later, it was opened by her beautiful dark-haired friend, an equally beautiful dark-haired little girl peering out from behind her skirt. Estelle stepped into the apartment and closed the door behind her.

"Good morning, Rachel." Estelle smiled and then bent down in front of the child. "And good morning to you, Aviva."

Five-year-old Aviva Wyler dashed toward Estelle and threw

her arms around her neck. "Ellie," she squealed with delight, using the nickname she had given Estelle when she had first started speaking. "Are you here for my birthday?"

"Your birthday?" Estelle pretended to be puzzled. "You have a birthday today?"

"Aunt Rachel and me both have a birthday tomorrow," Aviva told her earnestly. "We have the same birthday."

"You know, I think your aunt might have mentioned that." Estelle tapped her chin in thought.

"We're making a cake today. Aunt Rachel got all the ingredients. Even two eggs. You can have some when it's done."

"That is very kind of you. I would love to have some birthday cake." She dropped her voice into a conspiratorial whisper. "I might even have a birthday surprise for you."

"Is it a dog?" The little girl's eyes grew round. "Aunt Rachel says when I'm older we can get a dog. And I'm old tomorrow."

Over Aviva's head, Rachel gave her a sad smile. Aviva loved all animals, but especially dogs.

"It's not a dog," Estelle said. "Six is very old, I agree, but I think it would be best to wait just a few more years."

"That's what Aunt Rachel says too."

"Your aunt's very smart. But," Estelle added, "she doesn't know what my surprise is."

"Is it dancing shoes? Because when I get older, I am going to be a ballerina, even if I don't have a dog. Just like the dancers in the pictures," Aviva proclaimed. "I miss those pictures," she added gravely.

"In the pictures?" Estelle sent a questioning look at Rachel.

"The Degas paintings that used to hang in the hall," her friend whispered.

"Ah." The paintings that now languished behind Estelle's dressing room wall. "Well, I can tell you, it's not dancing shoes either."

"Well, if I can't be a ballerina, then I'm going to be a doctor like Saba," Aviva stated very matter-of-factly. "Though I'd like to listen to dancing music when I fix people."

Estelle laughed. "I think that you would make a very excellent doctor," she said. "And I think that you would be a wonderful ballerina as well." She dropped her voice. "In fact, I think that you should be both when you grow up."

Aviva's eyes lit up. "Yes," she said. "I will be both." She clasped her small hands together. "But you still haven't told me what the surprise is."

"No." Estelle pretended to button her lips shut.

Aviva glanced at Rachel and then beamed at Estelle. "Then it will be a surprise for everyone tomorrow."

"Yes." Estelle gave her a kiss on the forehead. "I have it all wrapped up, and I'll leave it with your aunt after you go to bed. It will be waiting for you in the morning."

Aviva grinned.

"Why don't you go and put your apron on?" Rachel asked her niece. "And then we can get started on your cake right away." She watched as Aviva skipped away before turning back to Estelle. "You have no idea how happy you've made her."

"Aviva has already lost so much of her childhood. I'm not letting her lose this birthday. I'll bring her gift over tonight."

"You're still really going to give her your violin?"

"Yes," Estelle said firmly.

"It's too much. She's a child."

"It's not too much. I was five when I first learned to play. Honestly, I think the gift is more for me than her. I can't wait to teach her."

"I'm not sure if Hannah will want—"

"I don't really care what Hannah wants," Estelle interrupted.

Rachel winced. "She is Aviva's mother."

"Who lives in your home and has all but abandoned her daughter into your and your father's care."

"Estelle—"

"Fine. Let's ask her if she has any objections to her daughter learning to play the violin. Where is she?"

"Sleeping."

"Again?"

Rachel looked away. "Yes."

Estelle rubbed her temples, self-reproach pricking at her conscience. "I shouldn't judge. I'm sorry."

"So am I. But I'm most sorry for Aviva that her mother has withdrawn from her. And that makes me angry, and then I feel guilty that I'm angry, and then I feel angry that I feel guilty." She pushed her hair from her forehead. "But I lost a brother when Hannah lost a husband. And so did you."

Estelle reached for her hand and squeezed it. "But I haven't lost you. Or Aviva. Or Serge. All we can do is hold on to what we have."

Rachel nodded and looked back at Estelle. "Speaking of having things, you should be keeping more of the food you're giving us—"

"Stop. You're barely allowed to buy food as it is. I have no intention of watching your family starve."

"But eggs? Sugar? I'm almost afraid to ask how you managed to find them."

"Then don't ask."

Rachel frowned. "You were out again last night."

"Yes."

"Spying." It was an accusation.

"We're not having this conversation again."

"Estelle, what if you're caught?"

"Then you can have my apartment. All your art is in there anyway."

"That's not funny."

"None of this is funny, Rachel. But I can't just do nothing."

"How much of what you see and learn from drunken Nazis is actually helpful?" Rachel demanded.

"You never know what crumb might turn a tide." Jerome's words.

Rachel frowned. "And that's worth the risk? Crumbs? What if they kill you—"

"And what if we all starve to death before this damn war is over?" Estelle released her hand. "At the very least, being there gets me access to the kitchens, and access to a lot more than crumbs." And those extra rations helped not only the Wylers but also the extra mouths Estelle fed in her own apartment.

Rachel's forehead creased in worry. "I wish you would stop—"

"I will. When the war is over."

"You should go south," Rachel said. "Or stay with your parents. Are they still in Portugal?"

Estelle snorted. "They are. In fact, my parents' solicitor sent me another letter. To inform me that my parents will not be returning to France during this—what did he call it? Ah, yes, during this troubling time," she finished, trying not to sound bitter. Estelle wondered why her parents' utter disinterest could still sting at moments such as these.

"They're still your family," Rachel chided.

"No, they're not. They've been benevolent spectators of

my life, happiest when they're able to do so from a distance. You're my family."

"But I can't get you to Portugal. Or anywhere else where it would be safer for you, Estelle."

"It's not my safety that concerns me, Rachel. It's yours. What your family has already endured—it's getting worse. As are the rumours. Of Jewish deportations in Poland that no one comes back from."

"I know what you've told me. And I'm not sure where you even hear things like that. But regardless if it's true or not, that's Poland, not Paris."

"For now. I'm afraid it's only a matter of time before—"

"Estelle." Rachel gave her a quick hug. "This will all end eventually," she whispered. "We'll be fine. We'll get our lives back. I have to believe that because it's hope that gets us all out of bed every morning."

Estelle nodded and pulled away. "I have a favour to ask," she said carefully.

"Anything."

"I need to speak with your father."

Rachel's eyes filled with worry. "Are you all right? Are you ill?"

"I'm fine," Estelle told her with perfect honesty. She hated keeping things from the woman she loved as a sister but, like she had told the airman, ignorance was safer for everyone.

Rachel gave her a long look. "Very well." She squeezed Estelle's hand. "Come tomorrow afternoon for cake."

"I wouldn't miss it for the world."

Rachel vanished back in the direction of the kitchen, and a moment later, Serge Wyler appeared.

"Estelle," he greeted her warmly, "I hear you are coming

to our little party tomorrow. With a surprise, according to my granddaughter." He was a distinguished-looking man with greying hair, round spectacles, and the kind, calm demeanor that Estelle had always loved.

"I am. I can't wait."

His intelligent eyes appraised her. "Rachel says you needed to speak with me. What about?"

"It's about the project you helped me with." Estelle spoke quietly.

"Ah. Where you've kindly hidden so many of our treasures. And an occasional patient."

"Yes. And um . . ." She trailed off, hesitating. Once she said what she was about to say, there was no unsaying it.

Serge took his spectacles off and polished them slowly with an embroidered handkerchief he drew from his pocket. "You're hiding more than that, aren't you Estelle?" It was more of a statement than a question.

Silently, she nodded.

"I could pretend to be surprised but I'm not." He replaced the spectacles. "What do you need?"

"A doctor. To provide the sort of help that, if discovered, would result in your own arrest." She met his eyes directly. "You can refuse because you have two daughters and a grand-daughter who need you and love you very much. I will understand, and from this moment, we will never speak of it again. This conversation never happened."

"Someone is hurt?"

"Yes."

"Then I cannot say no, can I?" There was such kindness in his eyes that it unexpectedly made Estelle want to cry. "Let me get my bag."

★ ★ ★

The shouts of men from outside and the thunder of pounding feet on the stairs had Estelle bolting upright in her bed, her heart hammering so hard in her chest that she thought it might crash through her ribs.

She sat paralyzed in the anemic light of early dawn, disbelief warring with a sense of fatalistic resignation. This is how it would end, then. She would be arrested with an injured airman hidden behind her wall, and all her efforts at subterfuge, all her attempts at capricious coquetry and genteel eccentricity, would not save her from the fate that was charging up the stairs from below.

She sucked in a ragged breath and forced herself from her bed, pulling on a robe. Pointless that she should wish to preserve some sort of modesty given what she would face. She glanced at the wardrobe but made no move to open it. The airman was under strict orders to stay where he was no matter what he heard. Once they took Estelle away, provided they didn't find him, there was at least a chance for him to escape when she was gone. Someone in the network would know that he was with Estelle and come looking once news of her arrest got out—

Fists hammered on the door. Estelle stood immobile outside her bedroom, trying to understand what was happening. Because it wasn't her door they were pounding on. It sounded like the noise was coming from the floor below her, echoing loudly up the staircase. Swiftly, she made her way through her apartment to her front door and cracked it open. The chaos from the floor below continued, and now the shrieks of women and the wailing of children added to the din.

Across the hall, the Wylers' door suddenly flew open, a rumpled Rachel dragging a sleepy Aviva by the hand.

"Rachel? What is happening?" Estelle croaked.

"They've come to take us."

"Take who?"

"Jews." Rachel's face was pale.

"Who, Serge?"

"And the women and children too. I need you to hide Aviva. Where you've hidden our paintings."

"What?"

"Hide her." Rachel shoved Aviva through Estelle's door. "Promise me you'll take care of her."

"What?" Estelle grasped Aviva's hand tightly in hers. The little girl's face crumpled as she looked up at her aunt.

"Promise me you won't let them find her. I'll come back when I can to get her. But I need you to promise me you'll take care of her until then."

"Yes," Estelle whispered. "Of course. I promise."

Rachel nodded and, without another word, turned and fled back across the hall. Estelle closed her apartment door as Aviva started to cry. Estelle crouched down. "Be brave," she said to the little girl. "Can you do that for me?"

Aviva looked up at her with tearful eyes. "I'm scared," she whispered.

Something shattered below, followed by the terrifying thunder of more boots coming up the stairs.

"Come with me." Estelle hauled Aviva up into her arms and headed back toward her bedroom. "I'm going to introduce you to my friend," she whispered. "He's hurt. And he's sometimes scared too. Do you think you could make him feel better?" she asked. "You could practice being a doctor."

"Yes," she replied in a small voice. "Does he have a dog?"

"I don't know," Estelle told her, opening the wardrobe and shoving the dresses aside. "You can ask him."

Aviva clung to her neck as Estelle pushed the back of the wardrobe in. The airman was sitting on the edge of the bed, his knuckles white where they clutched the sheets, obviously woken by the commotion. "What is happening?" he asked hoarsely. "Are they here for me?"

"No. It's not you they are after this time. You're safe for now. So long as you stay here. But I need to make sure that this little girl is safe too."

The airman met her gaze and nodded. "I understand."

Estelle set Aviva down inside the little room and crouched in front of her. "This is my friend," she said. "His name is Jean-Phillipe. He has a hurt leg. You're going to stay with him for a little bit until I can find out what is happening. Do you think you can look after him if he gets frightened?"

"I would like that," Jean-Phillipe said quietly to Aviva.

Aviva looked at the airman with an uncertain expression. "Do you have a dog?"

"I do." He smiled at her. "At home, I have four dogs. And five sisters, the youngest one who is just about your age. Would you like me to tell you about them?"

Aviva nodded and climbed onto the bed beside the airman.

Outside her apartment, fists pounded on Rachel's door, followed by angry shouts.

"You'll have to be very quiet," Estelle told her, trying hard to keep her voice from shaking. "And whatever you hear, don't come out until I come to get you."

She didn't wait for either to respond but pulled the hidden door shut, shifted the dresses back, and closed the wardrobe.

Loud shouts echoed on the landing, and now Estelle could hear Rachel's voice. Outside, three stories below, more voices, punctuated by cries of children, drifted up through the open window in the living area. Estelle stumbled to the window to find a swarm of French police herding a ragged group comprising mostly women and children and elderly down the street below. Many of the group had small suitcases in their hands. A bus was parked at the end of the street, more policemen ushering people aboard. Estelle swallowed against a rising tide of panicked nausea.

She hurried across the living room and yanked the door to her apartment open. A policeman was waiting in the landing like a hulking spectre in his black uniform and square hat, tapping a baton impatiently against the palm of his hand. He turned to stare at Estelle.

"What is this?" she demanded. "What is going on?"

"We're here to collect the Jews," he said, leering at Estelle's attire. "They're being relocated."

She pulled her robe more tightly around her as her eyes flew to Rachel's door. It was wide open. "Where?"

"What difference does it make to you? Go back inside. This doesn't concern you."

"Those are my neighbours." Her family.

"And they are Jews," he spat. "Stay out of it unless you want me to arrest you." He cracked the baton against Rachel's doorframe. "Hurry up!"

Rachel appeared, her lip split and swelling.

"Where is the child?" Another policeman was behind her, consulting what looked like a long list of names on a clipboard.

"Died," said Rachel. "Two weeks ago. Of a fever. There was no medicine."

"There is a child's bed and things in the apartment," the second policeman said.

"Because I can't bear to put them away yet," Rachel hissed at him.

The man in the landing cracked his baton against the door-frame again, loudly enough to make Estelle jump. "Watch your tone," he barked. "Or you can join the dead child."

Serge appeared in the doorway. He had a long laceration across his temple that was bleeding profusely, blood dripping down the side of his face and splattering onto the rug at the entrance of their apartment. His spectacles were gone, though he carried his doctor's bag in one hand, his other arm across Hannah's shoulder. Hannah was staring at the floor and seemed oblivious to everything going on around her. He met Estelle's frantic gaze and shook his head slightly, warning her away.

Horror and helplessness ripped through Estelle. "You can't do this. You are a Frenchman, same as they are. They have done nothing wrong," she cried.

Estelle didn't see the blow coming. She reeled back against the wall, her ears ringing, the side of her face numb.

"They exist, and that is enough," the policeman barked. "And they are nothing like we are. Get back inside." He shoved Estelle back through her apartment door, and she fell, her head striking the tiled floor.

Everything swam before her eyes, dark spots crowding her vision.

"Search in here too!" the policeman bellowed, his voice sounding like it was coming from a distance. Estelle was aware of boots thumping past her into her apartment. She tried to sit up, but dark spots danced across her vision, threatening to obliterate it completely.

The boots returned. "No one else in here," someone reported, and then abruptly, she was left alone.

Estelle wasn't sure how long she lay there—it could have been seconds or hours as she tried to catch her breath and regain her bearings. She managed to get to her hands and knees, and then to her feet. She lurched out into the deserted landing. An eerie silence had settled over the building, and only the muffled sounds of engines floated up to where she stood.

Estelle stumbled down the stairs, an intense dizziness making her want to retch. In the stairway near the ground floor, the elderly concierge was sitting on a step, his head in his hands, staring wretchedly at the floor.

He looked up at Estelle as she went by. "I didn't know they were coming," he said, his voice breaking. "I didn't know. I didn't know."

Estelle banged through the front door and out into the street, enveloped instantly by a cloud of noxious exhaust. But Rachel and her family were already gone. The street was deserted save for an assortment of boxes and bundles that had been lost and left behind.

Two policemen were picking through them like scavenging crows, tossing larger items to the side and pocketing smaller ones. Near Estelle's feet, a doll lay forlorn and abandoned. Overhead, shutters rattled as someone drew them closed, as if that would ever block out what had just happened. What was still happening.

Thieving bastards, she wanted to scream. *Collaborating cowards*, she wanted to rail at the men in the street. But she did none of those things. Instead, Estelle slipped back into her building, trying to control the sob that she could feel gathering somewhere deep in her chest.

There was nothing to be done right now, she told herself as she staggered back up the stairs, leaning on the railing, her head throbbing. She would find out where Rachel and Serge and Hannah had been taken once she had controlled her emotions. She would make inquiries in a practical, intelligent manner that would not bring unwanted attention to herself. Because Aviva and the airman in her apartment could not afford that sort of attention.

Estelle reached her landing, pausing in front of Rachel's open door. Without meaning to, she wandered into the empty apartment, stepping around the books and clothes that had been scattered in haste. She stopped in the little kitchen, a perfectly browned cake sitting in the center of the table. A stub of a candle had been pressed into the center of the cake, waiting to be lit.

Plates had been swept to the floor and lay in broken shards beneath the table, and off to the side, a violin case had been opened and upturned. The shattered remains of the violin lay beside it, a pink ribbon still tied around the neck. With unfeeling hands, she picked up the broken instrument and tucked the pieces back into the case, latching it securely. She placed it on the surface of the table and then bent again to retrieve a small wooden box, also tied with a pink ribbon.

She slipped the ribbon from the box and opened it. Two small, enameled pendants nestled on a cushion of velvet cloth. Both were oval in shape, three tiny red stones forming a bright row down the center. To RACHEL AND AVIVA, the tag on the box read. LOVE, ESTELLE.

Estelle's legs abruptly gave out, and she sat down on a kitchen chair, the sob that she had tried to suppress escaping.

She folded her arms on the table and put her head down, trying to breathe through the hysteria that was hollowing out her stomach and filling her chest. She could have hidden Rachel too. She could have hidden Serge and Hannah but it was too late now. Too late. Too late.

She should have known this was coming. The buses, the clipboards of names—all of this had been planned a long time ago. She should have heard something. All that time she had spent amongst the Nazi officers and their minions and she had heard nothing. What good were her efforts if they couldn't save the people she considered family?

Estelle bent over, weeping as if she might never stop. Great, heaving sobs wracked her body and blurred her vision. Yet as the minutes passed and she continued to cry, something new germinated deep within her, radiating through her limbs and calming her mind.

She thought she'd already known what hate felt like. She'd heard people say that unbridled hate clouded one's mind and judgement, but for Estelle, the hate, or whatever it was that was coursing through her, was so pure and consuming that it brought everything around her into sharper focus. Colors seemed brighter, noises sharper, details more distinct. What also became clear was the absolute certainty that she would die before she let the Nazis who had already taken so much from her get to the souls hidden in her apartment.

She closed the little box and slid it into the pocket of her robe and picked up the violin case. On unsteady legs, she stood. From the corner of the kitchen, she fetched the large woven basket Rachel had once used at the markets. Moving quickly and quietly, she went through the apartment, adding items to the basket. A collection of books with bright illustrations and covers. A carved wooden dog, a knit doll, and as many items of Aviva's clothing as she could fit.

Returning to the front of the flat, she searched the gaping, jumbled drawers of Serge's desk but could find no papers for any of the family. Someone had gone through the contents in a hurry. Whether it had been Serge or the police was impossible to tell. But whatever documents they'd found had clearly been taken or destroyed.

She listened for noises or voices, but the building seemed to have descended into an unnatural hush. Estelle picked her way back to the doorway but stopped just short of it to retrieve a stray photo that lay creased near the door. It was a photo of Rachel and Aviva that had probably been taken just before the war, her friend sitting on the sofa, the little girl in her lap, both laughing at the camera.

She slipped the photo into her pocket, next to the little box, and then left the Wylers' apartment, closing the door noiselessly behind her. Estelle didn't fool herself into thinking that they wouldn't be back. The French police or the Nazis or maybe both. All of them scavenging vultures, looking to seize what treasures might have been left behind. Looking for opportunities to destroy more lives. And she wouldn't be able to stop them.

But they would never take the lives and the secrets concealed in her apartment.

CHAPTER

9

Gabriel

The collection that Gabriel and Lia pulled out of the concealed space at the rear of the dressing room was humbling. And thrilling and astonishing, and Gabriel was quite sure he would never in his life see anything like it again.

He had no way of knowing if the paintings now arrayed in the bedroom had belonged to a single individual but if they had, that person had had an eye for brilliance. Currently, there was a Pissarro leaning up against the foot of the bed and a Morisot languishing beside it. There was a work by Kirchner resting on the dressing table and what Gabriel suspected would prove to be a Heckel propped below on the chair.

Gabriel glanced at the woman standing in the center of the bedroom, looking around her with an expression that was difficult to read. Worry, maybe. Apprehension, perhaps. Both of which no doubt were making it impossible for Lia to share the thrill of discovery that was still buzzing through his veins.

"Again, I see nothing here that is ringing any alarm bells," he told her, straightening from where he had been crouched in front of the Pissarro. "Nothing that I'm aware has been reported stolen or looted."

"Thanks. But you don't have to keep trying to make me feel better."

Gabriel exhaled. "Focus on the positive, Lia. No matter where these paintings came from, your grandmother kept them safe when so many others were destroyed." He gestured to the painting on the dressing table. "Kirchner had hundreds upon hundreds of his works destroyed after being labelled a degenerate artist. Works that are gone forever. This one has been saved."

Lia leaned back against the wardrobe, looking unconvinced.

"None of these paintings prove your grandmother was a collaborator," he said. "Though if you happened to have found the *Portrait of a Young Man* by Raphael in that wardrobe behind you, I might have questions."

"Very funny."

"No *Painter on the Road* by Van Gogh inside? Caravaggio's *Portrait of a Courtesan* wasn't left behind?"

Lia rolled her eyes but at least she was smiling now. "There was almost nothing in this wardrobe except a half-dozen couture gowns."

That stopped Gabriel short. "The dressing room was filled to overflowing but the wardrobe was almost empty?"

"Yes."

"Don't you think that's unusual?"

"I've been thinking a lot of things as of late," Lia mumbled. "None of them good, most of them unusual."

"May I take a look?"

Lia shrugged and pushed herself away from the wardrobe. "I'm telling you, there was nothing in it except the dresses."

"I believe you." Gabriel swung the wardrobe doors open wide and stepped into the interior, stooping awkwardly.

"If you fall in, say hello to the White Witch for me. And maybe ask her about the paintings."

He chuckled, the sound bouncing around the wooden interior. He ran his fingers along the interior edges, not really expecting to find anything. But given the hoard of paintings in the bedroom, it was worth a shot. "Three years ago in Limoges, a colleague of mine found a Chagall hidden behind the false back of a wardrobe similar to this one," he said over his shoulder. "Also a work that had disappeared during the war—"

A loud click made him freeze.

"What was that?" Lia asked from behind him.

Gabriel withdrew from the wardrobe. "It opens," he said to Lia.

"What?"

"The back of the wardrobe opens."

Lia followed his gaze. The back of the wardrobe was actually a hinged door that opened, revealing an unseen space beyond. The wall behind the wardrobe was not a wall at all.

"I don't know if I can do this again. I don't know if I want any more of my grandmother's treachery on my hands."

"We can wait."

Lia laughed, a humourless sound. "For what?"

"Until you're ready. These secrets have all been here for over seventy years. They're not going anywhere."

Lia pressed her hands to her temples. "There is probably just more art behind there."

"Probably," Gabriel agreed.

"I'm being ridiculous."

"You're being human."

Lia let her arms drop. "And you're being kind."

"Human," Gabriel corrected with a gentle nudge.

"You're right."

"About?"

"That whatever secrets lie beyond are not going anywhere. Standing here and procrastinating is stupid. The sooner I know what I'm dealing with the sooner I can start making reparations."

"Whenever you're ready, then. I'm not going anywhere either."

Slowly, Lia stepped forward, reached into the wardrobe, and pushed the door open.

The light flooding in from the bedroom revealed a small room with a single bed that ran the length of one side, a narrow table that lined the long wall opposite, and a chair positioned against the back wall between the two. Wool blankets were folded neatly on one end of the bed, pillows on the other. And on the wall above the bed, three paintings hung, all of ballerinas.

"The painter of dancing girls," Gabriel remarked, not knowing what else to say, gesturing at the paintings on the wall. They were all depictions of ballerinas at rehearsal, all looking as though they might dance right off the wall in their glorious costumes. And Gabriel would bet the entire collection of art in this apartment that they would prove to be genuine Degas.

"I'm sorry?"

"It's what Edgar Degas called himself. Ironically, it wasn't the girls themselves who interested him insomuch as subject matter, but their movement and clothes."

Lia blinked at him. "What?"

"The paintings in here," he said. "A first-year art student standing where I am would be able to identify the artist. When I take them to London, I will confirm that they were painted by Degas. They will also be worth an utter fortune."

"Um." Lia looked back into the small room.

"A peculiar décor choice for a hidden room."

"Yes," Lia replied faintly.

"Are you going in?"

"Yes," she said again.

Gabriel nodded and moved to the side so Lia could step up into the wardrobe. She ducked and stepped down into the small room and motioned for Gabriel to join her.

They both stood in the center of the room and gazed around.

On the far edge of the table was an oil lamp beside a tall stack of books. A pad of paper that looked like an artist's sketch pad leaned against the books, a collection of pencil stubs at its base. A small, hand-carved wooden dog sat next to those. On the end of the table nearest to them was a porcelain washbasin, a mirror, and a men's shaving kit. A steamer trunk had been shoved beneath the table, securely latched.

"Grandmère was hiding people," Lia croaked.

Gabriel couldn't tell if that was a question but he answered anyway. "Yes. Looks like it."

"She wasn't a collaborator." She sounded like she was going to cry.

"No. I think that everything out in that apartment was put there to make you think that."

"God." Lia leaned forward and put her hands on her knees like she had just run a marathon. "I've spent every waking moment of these last weeks full of shame and guilt and revulsion because I believed the worst about her." Her head dropped. "What does that say about me?"

"That you are human?"

"Why are you still being so kind? I'm a wretched grand-daughter. I really believed my grandmother helped the Nazis for her own gain."

"That's what she wanted anyone who walked in here to think. And if you were such a wretched granddaughter, I can't imagine she would have entrusted these secrets to you to unravel."

Lia lifted her head. "Then perhaps the art isn't stolen."

"I would suggest that the pieces hidden behind the dressing room may, in fact, belong to your grandmother. Alternatively, it's entirely possible she might have hidden them on someone's behalf." Gabriel's gaze fell on the books stacked on the table. "May I take a look at these?"

Lia nodded and straightened.

He reached for the volume on top, picking it up and turning it carefully in his hands. It was an English copy of *The Murder at the Vicarage*, well read, judging from the cracked spine and dog-eared pages. He set it aside and picked up the second volume, this one a copy of *Mystery Mile*. The third novel was a French publication, *La Voie Royale*, but the fourth was written in what looked like Polish.

"I think she might have been hiding Allied soldiers or airmen," Gabriel mused. "That might explain the books. And the shaving kit."

"But it doesn't explain these." Lia had picked up the sketchbook and was flipping through it.

Gabriel peered over her shoulder to find a collection of child-like drawings, most of them of dogs of some sort. At the rear of the thick pad, someone had drawn lines across the page and written the alphabet in neat letters. In the pages that followed, simple French words had been printed with the same neat efficiency, traced by a less steady hand. *Aviva* had been written many times across the last page.

"Doesn't explain these either." Gabriel set the novels aside and sorted through the books that had been stacked beneath. There was a copy of *The Sword in the Stone*, its tattered cover making the print barely legible, along with a collection of French picture books, brightly illustrated with animals and objects.

"There was a child here at some point," Lia said.

"Agreed." Gabriel picked up the last of the books. *Winnie-the-Pooh* by A. A. Milne. And judging by the worn condition, just as well loved as the novels.

"Are there any names in the books?" Lia asked.

Gabriel went through each carefully but came up empty. "No. But perhaps the name Aviva written in the sketchbook was someone important? Perhaps the child herself?"

"Or a sister? Or mother? Or aunt?"

"What about the trunk? Maybe there is something in there that will give you answers?"

Lia crouched down and lifted a small padlock. "It's locked," she said.

Gabriel joined her. "May I have a go?"

"At the lock?"

"It's a pretty rudimentary lock. It wouldn't be hard to open, I don't think."

"This is something they teach you in art school? Breaking and entering?"

"This is something that they teach all little brothers who want to read their big sister's diary."

"You didn't."

Gabriel winced. "I did."

"So there are some advantages to being an only child."

"My sister almost became one that day when she found out what I had done."

Lia laughed. "Then by all means, do your worst. Again."

Gabriel ducked out of the hidden room and fetched a leather-bound tool kit from his bag, returning quickly. He unrolled it, ignoring the neat row of brushes, spatulas, and tweezers, and selected the two rake picks from the end.

"You seriously carry around lock picks?"

"Useful every once in a while in my line of business. These won't steal the crown jewels, if that is what you're worried about. But they do provide access to places long forgotten on occasion."

"The crown jewels are about the least of my concern at the moment."

Gabriel bent to his task. The padlock was old and bulky but protected from the elements and free from rust. It gave way fairly easily.

He opened the trunk and shuffled to the side so that Lia could have access.

On top were a few sets of what appeared to be men's clothes—pants, shirts, socks, and even underwear. A thread-bare coat had been neatly folded alongside, the fabric faded to a mousy brown. Lia took out each item of clothing with care, placing them all on the bed behind her. Beneath the clothes was an old rifle, gleaming and free from the usual signs of age. Beside that rested a square biscuit tin. Lia pulled that out, set it on the floor, and levered the lid off. Inside was a stack of what appeared to be identity cards. She examined each one and then passed them to Gabriel. There were Belgian and French papers, battered and covered with stamps and ink, all with black-and-white images of unsmiling men.

"Any of these names familiar to you?" Gabriel asked. He peered at a set of Belgian papers proclaiming the unfamiliar image to be Jacques Brunet of Charleroi.

"No. None of these names mean anything to me."

They tucked the papers back into the tin and continued to search the trunk. With a small gasp, Lia withdrew a violin case.

"You recognize that?" Gabriel asked as she set it down.

"Not this one in particular. But Grandmère played the violin, and she—" Her words died as she opened the case.

Inside rested the ruins of what had once been a beautiful instrument. The body of the violin was splintered into three pieces, the neck sheared at the base. A length of pink satin ribbon had been tied sadly around the top.

Lia touched it gingerly. "Grandmère would have been beside herself if this was hers."

"Maybe it belonged to someone else?"

"Why keep it, then?"

Gabriel shrugged, at a complete loss.

Lia snapped the lid shut as if she couldn't stand to look at it any longer. "What else is left in the trunk?"

Gabriel reached inside and withdrew a leather-bound tool kit remarkably similar to his. With deft movements, he un-rolled it to reveal not tools but a set of four wicked-looking blades that gleamed in the light, ranging from a long-bladed stiletto to a stubby knife no longer than his middle finger. A cord with loops at the end had been coiled and secured against the leather.

"This looks like a set of James Bond assassination tools," Gabriel said, examining the blunt end of the small thumb dagger. "All of these weapons could be concealed in a pocket or a lapel or a handbag." He gestured to the ringed cord. "Including the garrote. Do you think they might have belonged to your grandmother?"

"I don't see how," Lia mumbled. "She would leave the room if I was watching TV with any sort of violence. She hated it."

"Perhaps this set belonged to one of the men she was hiding, then. Look." He pointed to the lower corner of the leather sheathing. "There is an initial. *S.*"

"Are you suggesting that my grandmother hid an assassin?" Lia asked dubiously. "After what I just said about her abhorring violence?"

Gabriel sat back on his heels and stared at the array of items. "More likely is the possibility that one of the men she might have hidden was a special agent," he suggested, warming to the idea. "There were people all over Paris who helped Allied intelligence."

"If this was true—if she had helped the Allies during the war—why wouldn't she have said something? Told her story?"

"Perhaps she was trying to forget?"

"Forget what?" She shook her head. "I just don't understand. Any of this."

Gabriel pushed himself to his feet and stepped toward the opening, running his fingers along the edge of the wardrobe's false back where it had been cleverly cut.

"My grandfather," he said after a moment, "the one who painted that little landscape, was an RAF pilot during the war. He spent almost five years in a POW camp after his plane was shot down. He has never spoken of those years—of the war and everything and everyone it cost him—to me. Ever." He turned and leaned back against the wall. "Perhaps your grandmother was no different. Perhaps the cost of whatever she endured was too painful."

"Perhaps."

"Would it have changed anything?" he asked. "Between you and your grandmother if you had known about all of this?"

"Maybe." Lia looked up at him. "I admit that I was a little afraid of her as a child. My parents left me with her every summer while they travelled, and she always seemed so severe. Distant. Though as I got older, she seemed less distant and just more . . . alone. Does that make sense?"

"Yes," he replied.

"And maybe that was part of the reason that I still visited her every summer on my own accord as I got older." She made a soft noise. "I'm not sure who was more surprised by that, her or me." She sighed. "I don't know what might have happened here or why she never came back but maybe, if she had shared some of it, I might have understood her more."

"Maybe this is your chance. She chose you, after all, to find this part of her life."

Lia smoothed the flyaway strands of hair back from her face. "I think I would have preferred to find it with her and not alone."

"You're not alone. I'm with you." Gabriel could have bitten his tongue. That was the second time he had made that sort of declaration. He edged away a little more so he would not embarrass them both further with an uncomfortable lack of professionalism. "What's in the envelope?" he asked, grasping for a distraction.

"Envelope?"

"At the bottom of the trunk." He could see a thick yellowed envelope that was wedged in the bottom corner of the trunk, as if it had slid down the side amidst the contents.

Lia retrieved it and stood, emptying the contents out onto the table next to the stack of novels.

"More pictures, ration cards, and a railway pass. It seems my grandmother hid women as well," she said on a breath.

Gabriel left his post and joined her at the table, still careful to keep a respectful space between them. On top was a twelve-month rail pass for one Sophie Beaufort, of Marseille, France, dated and stamped January 17, 1943. The black-and-white photo on the left side of the pass depicted an unsmiling woman with the cheekbones of a supermodel and the fair hair and pale eyes of a Nordic fairy-tale princess.

Lia handed it to Gabriel, who took it from her, careful to hold it at the edges. He studied the photo, frowning as a sense of familiarity nagged at the edges of his mind.

"Whoever this woman was, she was beautiful," Lia murmured beside him.

He tore his eyes from the rail pass to see that Lia had spread out a half-dozen photos, all of the same woman. Only in these photos, Sophie Beaufort was laughing, smiling, or looking at the camera over her shoulder with a sultry expression. Each of the photos was a headshot, her hair expertly styled, cosmetics applied to her lips, eyes, and cheeks with the sort of professional precision that put Gabriel in mind of glossy fashion adverts.

He reached for the closest one, holding it up to the light.

"That's impossible," he muttered.

"What is?"

"The woman in this photo. I know her."

Lia laughed with a snort of disbelief. "I think you're about seventy years too late to know her."

"This is my great-aunt. Sophie Seymour. I'm sure of it."

"And she was from Marseille?" Lia asked skeptically.

"No."

"Well, this woman was. And her name isn't Sophie Seymour."

"There's a photo—a portrait of her—that hangs on the walls at Millbrook," Gabriel said. "I've seen it a thousand times. And my grandfather has a photo of the two of them together on his bedside table. They were always very close until she—" He stopped.

"Until?" Lia prompted.

"Um." Gabriel ran a hand through his hair self-consciously. "Never mind. Forget I said anything."

"Come on," Lia said. "You can't leave me hanging. What happened to her?"

Gabriel winced. "She was working for the Foreign Office as a translator in Warsaw. She disappeared—died—when the Germans bombed the city in 1939."

"Which one was it? Disappeared? Or died?" To her credit, Lia wasn't laughing at him.

"The records say she fled her post before Warsaw was bombed. But she vanished without a trace in the carnage that followed. Hundreds of thousands of civilians were killed in that initial invasion. She was one of them."

"Well," Lia said dryly, her lips twitching, "she looks pretty good for a dead person given that the pass is dated 1943."

"Do you think we might just pretend I didn't say anything so that I can preserve whatever shreds of dignity I have left?"

"They say everyone in the world has a doppelgänger," Lia offered. "We just happened to have found hers."

"Now who's being kind?" Gabriel muttered.

"I think I owe you a little kindness," she replied with a grin. She picked up one of the glossy headshots. "Whoever she was, she looks bold and daring. Like the way my grandmère looks in the photos out in the apartment. I wonder if they were friends."

"Hard to say. It's possible."

"I'm trying to imagine what a girls' night out for these two might have looked like in Paris before the war. Like a *Thelma and Louise* meets Moulin Rouge. Less the car off the cliff, of course, though they probably kept Brad Pitt for fun." She laughed lightly and stole a glance at him. "Think your great-aunt might have joined them?"

"God, no. Sophie Seymour was nothing like that," Gabriel told her, thankful that Lia could find the humour in his idiocy. "She was a serious scholar, not a socialite. Wasn't exactly known for her charm and congeniality," he said ruefully. "She was a keen student of sciences and maths, and an utterly brilliant linguist. Spoke a half-dozen languages by the time she was twelve, a half-dozen more by her twenties. She fully intended to be the first woman to earn a full professorship at Oxford. Her job at the Foreign Office was to have been a step toward that dream."

"She sounds driven."

"She was. Intimidated the hell out of most men her age, as my grandfather tells it. She never married, never even dated, according to family lore."

"She still must have broken a few hearts if she was this beautiful," Lia murmured, eyeing the photos.

"She told more than a few people that she didn't see the value of courtship with men who didn't see the value of her studies."

Lia smiled. "I think I would have liked this great-aunt of yours very much. It's sad that she died before she could realize her dreams and ambitions."

"My grandfather thought the same. He looked for Sophie for a long time after the war. He refused to believe that she had abandoned her post, knowing just how important that job was to her. He wanted so badly to believe that she had somehow survived." He leaned his hip against the edge of the table. "He never found anything, of course, but my grandmother said his search saved him."

"What do you mean?"

"He was injured and struggled with depression when he came home from the war. My grandmother was a nurse, hired to help with his recovery, and she ended up helping him search for his sister. It gave him purpose again, she said."

"And they really found nothing?"

"Nothing. But hope is a powerful motivator, especially when it's mixed with stubbornness. I can't imagine how devastating it would be to return home to find that everyone you loved was gone. I can't imagine anything worse than losing your family without ever having a chance to say good-bye. If I had been in my grandfather's shoes, I would have done the same."

"It sounds like your family is close." Lia sounded almost wistful.

"We are. Probably too close for my sister's liking at about the time she started dating. The Spanish Inquisition had nothing on us."

"Your poor sister."

"I regretted nothing. At least until I brought a girl home for the first time."

Lia laughed.

"Are you close with your parents?" he asked.

"I suppose. They were busy with their jobs and travelled a lot when I was younger. And now I travel with my own work. We try to keep in touch as much as possible."

Gabriel only nodded, finding it hard to imagine not speaking to or seeing his family regularly. It was also none of his business, he reminded himself.

"Was there anything else in that envelope?" he asked, guiding the conversation away from the personal.

"Yes, two more photos." Lia handed him a smaller photo that lacked the professional, posed composition of the others. This was the spontaneous sort that one took on holiday, and it featured the same flaxen-haired woman sitting bareback on a horse, squinting into the sun and laughing. Gabriel turned it over. *Zawsze będę pamiętał* had been scrawled in faded ink across the back.

"*Zawsze będę pamiętał?*" Lia read over his shoulder. "Is that Polish?"

"Yes," Gabriel said, "though my Polish is appalling, I'm afraid." He pulled out his phone to translate. "It says 'I will always remember.'"

"I wonder who took it," Lia mused.

"Someone Polish, I presume." He looked up. "And the other photo?"

"This." Lia's voice sounded strange as she held it up.

It was a black-and-white photo of a large home that could have been a country house anywhere between Manchester and Munich. The background offered no specific details that would suggest location, and there was nothing written on the back of this photo. One of the edges had been damaged and creased, but the image was clear. And distinctly familiar.

"It's the house in the painting, isn't it?" Lia breathed. "Millbrook. Your family house."

"Yes," Gabriel said rather stupidly.

They stared at each other.

"Holy shit," Lia said presently.

"Yes," Gabriel agreed.

"Your aunt didn't die in Warsaw in 1939."

"No, it doesn't seem that she did."

"Those photos are really her."

"Yes, they are."

"And she was here. In this apartment. With my grand-mother."

"Yes." Gabriel was trying to sort the thoughts and questions that were exploding into his brain but it felt a little like an uncontrolled game of Whack-A-Mole.

They continued to stare at each other.

"Do you think your grandfather found evidence that she didn't die in Poland? Something specific that made him look for her?"

"I don't know."

"Do you think she had a connection to the art hidden here?"

"I don't know."

"Do you think that she was working with my grandmother? Hiding people during the war?"

"I don't know." It seemed that Gabriel had lost the ability to say anything else.

"Huh." Lia was looking at the three Degas dancers on the wall as if she was willing them to speak. To spill their secrets. "Well, whatever your aunt was doing here in Paris after 1939, I don't think it had anything to do with the Foreign Office or translation."

"No," Gabriel agreed faintly. "I don't think so either." He put the photo of Millbrook on top of the others with exaggerated care.

"I think she might have been a spy."

CHAPTER

10

Sophie

HAMPSHIRE, ENGLAND
4 MARCH 1943

S ophie was wakened by a blow to the head.

It wasn't hard, not enough to cause any real damage, but it left her momentarily stunned as she was dragged from her bed. She blinked against the harsh light that flooded the room, trying to get her bearings.

"Move!" The command was issued in German. She stumbled, the floor freezing beneath her bare feet.

Rough hands grasped her upper arms and propelled her forward with bruising force. Sophie twisted her head, trying to get a glimpse of the men who held her, and was rewarded by a backhand to the side of her head. "Eyes front," one of her captors barked.

Sophie was half carried, half dragged through the hallway outside the bedroom and then down a flight of stairs. She was manhandled into a darkened room, empty save for a single chair and a bare bulb that flickered feebly above. The men shoved her into the chair, yanked her arms behind her, and tied her wrists with rope. Then, without a word, they turned and left.

Sophie forced herself to take a deep, calming breath, trying to slow her pulse and her breathing. She had not heard the men come into her bedroom, and there was a distinct regret in that. But for right now, she needed to focus on what she could control. What she could see, hear, smell, touch. What she could use.

The room was freezing, and her thin nightdress offered little in the way of warmth. She could see nothing but blackness beyond the pitiful pool of light that surrounded her. The room smelled of damp and mildew, though cigarette smoke and the rank scent of an unwashed body nearby lingered underneath. Farther away in the darkness, someone coughed. There were at least two people down here with her, unseen and unknown.

Sophie casually shifted her weight, and the chair groaned and creaked, its legs wobbling beneath her. The thin spindles of the chairback pressed against her spine. Unsure who might be watching, she surreptitiously tested the bonds around her wrists next. Not as tight as they should have been. By curling her fingers, she could already feel the knot slip. Sloppy, sloppy.

"What is your name?" The sharp question came out of the darkness.

Sophie kept her eyes fixed straight ahead. "My name is Sophie Beaufort."

"What are you doing in Paris?"

"My husband, he has a cosmetics company. He sells cosmetics. I am helping him." The knot at her wrist slipped a little farther.

"Cosmetics?" Someone laughed. "In the middle of a fucking war? You're lying."

"I am telling the truth. You can look at my papers. You'll find them all in order."

Sophie gasped as something hit her in the face. It took her a moment to realize that someone had thrown a pail of icy water at her.

"You are a spy," the voice continued. "You are travelling across France and spying."

"I am n-not a spy. M-my family owns a s-small company in Marseille. My husband took over from my father when he died. We make lipsticks and powders." The shock of the water was starting to wear off, though Sophie was shivering. "We wish to sell them here, in Paris."

"And who the fuck buys lipstick and powder?"

"We sell to German officers' wives. Sometimes Frenchwomen." She slipped one hand free of the rope, catching it with her fingers. "It is simple economics, Monsieur. We have something to sell that is very much in demand. And in Paris, we can get a better price."

A man stepped into the pool of light, the runes on his collar displaying his SS rank of major. The hard soles of his boots struck the stone floor as he dragged a small table beside Sophie. He was heavy featured, his dark eyes flat and hard and his expression cruel above the lifeless grey of his uniform. Despite her best efforts, a shudder of revulsion rolled through her.

"Do you know what we do to spies, Madame Beaufort?" the major asked.

Sophie averted her eyes and forced herself to continue to stare straight ahead. "I'm not a spy. I work with my husband."

"I don't believe you. What could you possibly do to help him?"

"I take photos of our clients for our adverts and to promote our products. The photos are with my papers. You can see for yourself."

"Oh, I saw the photos. The Führer abhors cosmetics on his women, and I can see why. A passel of painted jezebels pretending to be someone they're not. And half those photos you speak of were of you."

"Sometimes I model our cosmetics too."

"You model cosmetics?" he sneered. He reached for a leather tool belt that was laid out on top of the small table and withdrew a pair of pliers. "Not for much longer, I'm afraid. I can't imagine there is much demand for a model with no teeth. You'll tell me who you're working for, what information you are passing on, and where I can find these people. Because after we finish with your pretty teeth, we still have your nails to attend to."

Sophie slipped the rope from her other wrist and wrapped the end around her palm so that the rope was caught between them, effectively creating a crude garrote. She turned her hands and gripped the outside spindles of the chairback with her fingers. "I have nothing to tell you, Monsieur. I am who I say I am. I have no reason to lie to you."

The man considered his pliers, turning them over so that they glinted dully in the meagre light. "You're still lying."

He lifted his eyes to Sophie, and this time she met his gaze.

"I am telling the truth." Fear rose, and she didn't fight it, only examined it the way one might examine an unwelcome insect that had crawled into the light.

It wasn't the threat of physical pain she feared, she discovered. No, what made her afraid was the possibility that the rage and hate triggered by the grey uniform and the arrogance of the bastard who wore it would distract her from what she needed to do. It was the possibility of failure that made her afraid.

She lifted her chin and ruthlessly quashed her emotions. There could be no distractions. Not here. Not now.

The Gestapo officer took a menacing step toward her, and then another. "This doesn't have to happen," he said. "You can avoid so much pain." He put his palm on her forehead and wrenched her head back, his other hand still gripping the pliers.

That was all Sophie needed. She lunged to her feet and swung around, the chair she still gripped behind her back colliding mercilessly with the ill-prepared major. The chair broke into a dozen pieces, the wood clattering loudly on the stone floor. The officer released her with a grunt of surprised pain and staggered back, but Sophie was already moving, cutting behind him. As he tried to straighten, she brought her hands down, slipping the rope over his head and across his throat.

The major gurgled, his hard-soled boots slipping on the wet floor, his fingers scrabbling at the rope that was choking him. He wasn't a tall man, and Sophie had the advantage of height and leverage. She tightened the garrote, the rope cutting into the edges of her palms.

"Jesus Christ, stop afore you kill him!" The room was suddenly flooded with light.

A man was standing behind a long table against one of the walls, three of Sophie's instructors sitting beside him.

Sophie relaxed her grip, and the man in the German uniform stumbled away, coughing and gagging.

"What the hell was that?" The man on his feet behind the table leaned toward Sophie, his face red.

Sophie unwrapped the rope from her hands and let it fall to the floor. "You would have preferred I use the chair?"

"I beg your pardon?"

She picked up a broken spindle and examined the ragged, pointed end. "You did not tie me securely and gave me three weapons," she said, frowning. "The rope, the chair, and whatever treasures lay on that table beside the pliers. I chose the rope. Most efficient and cleanest, I thought."

Sophie saw two of her instructors exchange glances.

"That wasn't the point of the exercise," the red-faced man sputtered. "The exercise was merely to measure your resistance to interrogation." He turned to the instructors sitting beside him and glared at them accusingly.

"We warned you," the instructor in the middle said with a shrug.

Sophie's interrogator in the Gestapo costume had straightened and was rubbing his throat and his shoulder, his breaths coming in hoarse, heaving gasps. "What the hell is wrong with you?" he rasped. "Bloody, unnatural bitch."

Sophie stared at the interrogator. For a moment, she was eight years old again, her stomach churning in a library.

You are an unnatural creature.

Maybe Mrs. Postlewaithe had had it right all along.

"Yes" was all Sophie said.

The interrogator coughed and gagged again.

"You may go, Celine," the instructor said, addressing her by her code name. "Return upstairs and change. This exercise concludes your training. We will compile our report and final evaluation shortly." He closed the folder in front of him. "It will be added to your file for consideration."

CHAPTER

11

Estelle

E stelle slipped the pink ribbon off the small wooden box. She had kept it hidden in the bottom drawer of her writing desk for the last year, unable even to look at it without feeling like her heart was being torn from her chest. With fingers that weren't quite steady, she opened the top of the box, the two pendants that still nestled against their bed of velvet gleaming in the low light.

She'd not been able to get to Serge and Rachel. They'd been imprisoned in the Vélodrome before they'd been shipped out of the city. None of the German officers she'd discreetly queried in the days that followed their arrest and deportation from Paris had been able to tell her exactly where they'd been taken. After all, they weren't the ones who had perpetrated the roundup—that operation had been conducted by French police. But—they had all agreed with a sickening degree of smug satisfaction—the Jews were not coming back. Ever.

A shadow fell in front of Estelle, and she looked up.

Aviva was standing before her in the circle of light, rubbing her eyes.

"I thought you were sleeping." Estelle stood and slipped the ribbon back on the box before sliding it into the pocket of her robe.

The little girl shook her head, her eyes overly large in her pale, drawn face.

"Would you like me to tuck you back in?" she asked.

Aviva shook her head again.

Estelle held out her hand, and the little girl took it without hesitating. She tried not to notice how fragile the child's bones felt beneath her touch. Or how silence and sadness had replaced the laughter and vitality as the months had crept by. Or how long it had been since Aviva had last asked about her family. Or spoken about anything at all.

"I have a surprise for you," she said, leading Aviva through the living room, past the rumpled blankets and storybooks on the sofa where the girl had been napping. Evenings and early mornings were the only time Aviva came out into the apartment. Estelle was too terrified to let her roam the apartment during the day in the event that she would be discovered.

The new tenants in Estelle's building who had appropriated the desirable apartments left empty by the Jewish roundup last year, including the Wylers', were predominantly German or the families of French industrialists, all becoming wealthy with their Nazi partnerships. She was now surrounded by sympathizers and collaborators, all of whom would be only too happy to denounce Estelle if they knew what secrets she hid in her apartment. Only her social reputation and continued visibility as one of them kept her safe. Kept Aviva safe.

Estelle no longer hid Allied airmen—the little girl hiding in her wall made that too dangerous—but she did continue to frequent the bars and restaurants at the Ritz, though not as often as she once had. She still listened to the men in grey who gorged themselves as Paris continued to starve and reported what she heard. She still had no idea if anything she had ever shared had made any difference. Even once. But she would not dwell on that.

Estelle brought the little girl into the bedroom and opened the wardrobe. The hidden door was already open. "Look," Estelle said, stepping inside. "Look what I found for you."

Aviva let go of Estelle's hand and crawled up onto the bed, staring up at the three paintings Estelle had hung on the wall of the hidden room. They were the Degas paintings, the ones that had once graced the Wylers' apartment. It had taken her an hour to extract them from behind her dressing room wall but, looking at Aviva's rapt expression now, it had been worth it.

"What do you think?" Estelle asked.

The child reached up to touch the corner of the closest one. Across the canvas, a collection of girls in a pastel palette of gauzy costumes rose up on their toes across a stage, all under the watchful eye of their teacher. Aviva smiled—the first time in months she'd seen Aviva smile. Estelle looked away, her eyes burning. Aviva deserved to be surrounded by family and friends and laughter, not silence and fear and darkness. Estelle wasn't sure how long the little girl would last living like this.

The bed creaked, and Estelle looked back to find that Aviva had lain down on the bed, curled into a ball, and was simply gazing up at the three paintings.

"There's something else," she said before she could reconsider.

Aviva sat up.

"I have another surprise for you." She sat down on the bed beside the little girl and withdrew the box from her pocket. "Open it," she said, handing it to Aviva.

The child took it, turning it over carefully in her tiny hands. She tugged on the pink bow, letting the satin fall to the side, and opened the box. Aviva touched one of the enameled pendants gently, a peculiar expression on her drawn face.

"I got these for you and your aunt for your birthdays," Estelle said, taking the box from Aviva's hands. "But I didn't get a chance to give them to you before your aunt Rachel had to go." Estelle steeled herself against the emotion that was making it hard to speak. "I'd like you to have it now." Estelle drew a pendant and chain from the velvet. "Would you like that?"

Aviva looked up at her and nodded.

Estelle bent and fastened the chain around the little girl's neck. Aviva wrapped her fingers around the pendant at her throat.

"And you can keep this one safe for your aunt for when she gets back." Estelle closed the box and held it out to Aviva.

Aviva shook her head and pushed herself up to her knees. She opened the box, pulled out the second chain, and held it out to Estelle.

"You want me to wear it?" Estelle asked.

Aviva nodded. Estelle took the chain from the child's hand and fastened it around her own neck with the realization that Aviva had given her the pendant because she already knew Rachel was never coming back. Estelle tried to stop her tears from escaping but failed.

The death of hope was a truly awful thing.

Aviva crawled into her lap and wrapped her arms around Estelle's waist. She stroked the little girl's hair until Aviva's breathing became steady and her body became heavy with the weight of sleep. With care, Estelle slipped out from beneath the slumbering child and tucked the blanket around her.

She returned to the living room and gathered the books, putting them back in their place in the hidden room. She closed the wardrobe and double-checked the apartment, but there was no evidence that a child had ever been here. She went into the kitchen and made sure that the dishes from dinner had also been put away. Though a visitor at this late hour was highly unlikely, one could not afford to be questioned about the need to wash two sets of dishes and cutlery after a meal when one presumably lived alone—

A familiar pattern of taps at the door of her apartment froze her in her tracks, a glass nearly slipping from her fingers. She set it aside and bolted to the front of her apartment, unlocking the door as quickly as she could.

Trepidation and relief coursed through her in equal measures as the man on the other side slipped in. She glanced across the dim landing and down the stairs, but everything remained silent and still. A dozen questions sprang to her mind but she uttered none of them, instead closing the door as silently as possible after him. It had been months since she'd seen Jerome. Months since she'd even heard from him, though rumours had been flying fast and furious of men and women arrested and carted off to prisons or worse for assisting the enemy.

She put up a hand to silence Jerome when it looked as though he was going to speak. Instead, she bade him follow her deeper into the apartment. She retraced her steps back into the living room and set a record on the gramophone. Only when the music started playing quietly did she speak. She couldn't be too careful.

"Why are you here?" Even hushed, the question came out more reproachful than she had intended.

Jerome pulled his cap off his head, his hair disheveled and badly in need of a cut. "I was in town. Thought I'd drop by for a drink. Maybe a game of cards. It's been awhile."

"That's not funny."

He dropped his eyes. "You're right. I'm sorry."

He looked utterly exhausted, Estelle thought, as she studied him. Dark circles under his eyes, a week's worth of stubble darkening his cheeks, and a stoop to his shoulders that betrayed his fatigue.

"No," she said. "I'm sorry. What do you need?"

He looked up at her. "A safe place to stay tonight."

"And you came here?"

"You have a very nice sofa. Two of them, in fact."

"Are you being serious?"

"I didn't know where else to go. We've lost three of our houses in the last week, and Diedre's brother was arrested. This was the safest place I could think of—" He stopped. "You've been crying."

"I have not." The denial was absurd because she'd never been a pretty crier. Just the threat of tears made her eyes puffy, her nose red, and her face splotchy.

"Is it Aviva? Where is she?" Concern shadowed his face.

"Safe. Sleeping."

Jerome ran a hand through his messy hair. "Then what is it?"

"It's just... it's been a year. Since they... took Rachel. Today would have been her birthday." She was aware she was speaking of Rachel in the past tense. "And every day since then, I've wondered what I could have done differently. What I could have done in those precious two minutes that might have saved Rachel and her family. Aviva would still have a family. And so would I."

"What happened wasn't your fault. You couldn't have known what was going to happen."

"I should have."

"Look, Allard, you—"

"I didn't do enough. I didn't act quickly enough." She didn't want to hear the excuses that he would make for her. God knew she didn't want to hear her own.

"You did everything you could."

"They came the next day, you know," she murmured. "Stripped the Wylers' apartment of everything valuable. The furniture, the rugs, Serge's books, Rachel's jewelry, the fine plate and silver that had belonged to her mother. I think, on that day, deep down, I knew they weren't coming back."

"You have to forgive yourself, Allard."

"I don't know if I can."

Jerome stepped closer to her. "How can I help?"

It was the gentle way he'd said it that broke her. She looked away, not even bothering to wipe away the new round of tears she could feel leaking down her cheeks.

Jerome reached out and gently wiped them away with the cuff of his sleeve, and somehow that made the tears come faster. This time, he simply put his arms around her and drew her into his embrace.

"I'm afraid," she said when she was able, her words somewhat muffled by the front of his shirt.

"Of what?"

"Not of. For. I'm afraid for Aviva." She sniffed gracelessly. "I'm afraid that that little girl is not going to survive this war. I'm afraid that I won't be able to keep the promise I made to Rachel to keep her safe. I'm afraid that this damn war has no end."

"I wish I could help. I wish I could take her out of France for you," he said. "But we can't take a child. She'd never survive the journey into Spain. The mountains or the rivers would—"

"I know," Estelle said, nodding miserably. "I know you can't. That's why I've not asked you. I don't even have papers for her."

Jerome winced. "God, I'm sorry, I can't even help you with that. I don't know who the forgers are in Belgium but I could try and find out—"

"No. Those sorts of questions draw attention and could expose you. You are too important to the men whose lives depend on you."

"What about Vivienne? She might know a local forger who could—"

"Who could betray both Vivienne and Aviva." Estelle had long ago considered and dismissed the notion of confiding in the petite woman. "I trust your cousin but I don't trust anyone else. I'm not willing to take that risk."

"I understand," he said. "For now, Aviva's safe here with you. Even if it's hard, she still has you. Just being there for her when she needs you is enough."

"I don't know if that's true anymore."

"It is."

"How do you know that?"

He was quiet for a moment, only Tino Rossi crooning

on the gramophone in the other room filling the silence. "Because it is for me."

Estelle drew back and looked up at him.

"I came here tonight because you are my safe harbour, Allard. When everything is going to hell, I know I can count on you. And so can Aviva. You will always do what's best for her, this I know. Rachel knew it too. That's why she left her with you."

"You sound so sure."

"I am."

Estelle blew out a shaky breath. "Thank you," she said. She put her hand on his shoulder and yanked it back as he hissed and flinched.

"You're hurt," she said.

"I'm fine."

"You're not."

"I'm a damned medic, Allard. If I say I'm fine, I'm fine."

"Take off your coat."

"That's rather forward of you, don't you think?"

Estelle glared at him and pushed the coat from his shoulders, lifting it carefully away from his skin. Beneath his coat, the shoulder of his shirt was stained a dark, rusty red. "Follow me."

"You're awfully demanding," he said but followed her anyway.

Estelle stalked into the kitchen and pulled out one of the two chairs that were pushed under the small table against the near wall. "Sit," she ordered the man who had followed her.

"Yes, Mademoiselle."

"Now your shirt." She busied herself fetching a clean cloth, soap, and a basin of water.

When she turned back, Jerome had his shirt off, the gash on his shoulder clearly visible.

Estelle bent and examined it critically. "Blade?" The wound wasn't deep, but long.

"Edge of a metal fence."

"I don't think it will need stitches. But you'll want to keep it clean and covered when you head back out."

"Did you miss the part where I reminded you that I am a medic? I know this."

"Then you should start taking your own advice." She dampened her cloth and gently wiped the dried blood from his skin. "It would be a shame to amputate your head because gangrene climbed up your neck."

"Very funny, Allard."

"Five inches to the right and your head just might have come off."

"Hardly. Besides, I'm like a cat."

"What?"

"I have nine lives. It's what my mother used to say. I wasn't an overly careful child, and probably took a few years off of hers."

"Well, a cat didn't do this." Estelle put the cloth back in the basin, watching as the water turned pink. "How did this happen?"

"Doesn't matter."

"Please don't do that."

"What?"

"Shut me out."

His forehead creased. "Not knowing should make you feel safer."

"It doesn't." She sat down on the chair next to Jerome. "It just makes me feel . . . alone."

"Alone? You've hardly been alone here, Allard. Your apartment has been the damn Ritz Hotel of our escape line."

"You're right, I suppose."

"I hear a *but* in that."

She sighed. "But did you know that, out of all the men who have stayed in this apartment, I've never known any of their true names? I've never sat down with them over a meal or a glass of wine to talk about anything personal because it's safer for everyone if no one knows anything about you.

"I arrive at those damn hotels and restaurants alone, pretending to be someone I'm not, feigning friendship, concealing the hate, and trusting no one. Safer that way, you see. Later, I pass on what information I collect to people whose real names I will also never know, people who will likewise never ask mine."

Jerome was quiet, his long fingers splayed over the knees of his patched trousers.

"Aviva depends on me to be smart and stay safe, so all this complaining I'm doing right now is stupid, I know. But there are just moments when the selfish part of me would like to feel...seen. By someone who knows me. Just once, I would like someone to call me by my real name and ask how my day was." She laughed weakly. "I'm sorry. Just ignore my ramblings. I'm not sure why I'm like this tonight—"

"Estelle."

She stilled. It was the first time Jerome had called her anything other than Allard, or driver, or mademoiselle.

Slowly, he stood up from the chair. "The Gestapo were all over Gare du Nord this morning. Checking papers, forcing people into trucks, taking them who knows where. I had an airman with me who spoke no French. We backtracked through the rail yards before they saw us and escaped under a fence." He touched his neck. "It was a tight fit."

"Ah. Is he safe? Your airman?"

"Yes. He is no longer in Paris, because this city is no longer safe. Not that it ever was," he rushed on, "but they are getting bolder in their cruelty."

"You don't need to tell me that."

"No, I don't suppose I do." He stopped in front of her and pushed a loose strand of hair behind her ear. "Instead, why don't you tell me about your day? It had to have been better than mine."

"I didn't save anyone."

"I disagree. You save a soul every day. And the proof of that is sleeping behind your wardrobe."

Estelle smiled sadly.

"What did you two do today?"

"We worked on reading and writing today. I read her half of *The Sword in the Stone.*"

"Is that a book?"

"Yes. And an Arthurian legend." She pursed her lips. "You haven't read it?"

"My fancy tutors must have skipped that one." He grinned. "Tell me about it. It sounds like a war story."

"Not quite. It is the story of the son of a king who is hidden to keep him safe from the jealous nobles who would kill him to claim the throne. He is called Wart, and he believes himself to be an orphan boy aspiring to become a squire to his friend Kay. One day in the forest, Wart meets Merlyn, a powerful wizard. The wizard becomes his tutor and, through-out the story, turns Wart into a succession of creatures so that he might learn wisdom."

"If the wizard was so powerful, couldn't he just have turned his enemies into slugs?" Jerome interrupted. "Seems more expedient."

Estelle huffed. "Do you want to hear the rest or not?"

"Yes."

"The boys become young men, and on the day that Kay is to be knighted, he forgets his sword at the inn and sends Wart back to fetch it. Only the inn is locked so Wart needs to improvise. In a churchyard, he sees a sword stuck into an anvil. He figures that it'll have to do so he pulls it free and races back to his friend with it. Except it is no ordinary sword. As it turns out, it is a magic sword, and only the person who will become the next king could pull it free. Merlyn tells Wart that his name is, in fact, Arthur, son of the late king. Arthur, of course, goes on to be a wise and fair king because of all he has learned, and everyone lives happily ever after."

"So you're like Merlyn."

"What?"

"Keeping those you love safely hidden from terrible people who would wish them harm simply for who they are. So that one day, they can emerge and raise their swords and continue to be good and wise. So that one day, everyone will live happily ever after."

Estelle stared up at him for a long moment. "I don't think I'm anything like Merlyn. Because I would use my power to turn every single Nazi into a slug and stomp on them all."

Jerome leaned his hip against the table. "I would help you with that."

"I know you would."

"And no matter what you think, I see you. I've always seen you." He reached for her hand and caught it with his own. "You're not alone, Estelle."

Estelle stood and pulled her hand from his and flattened her palms against the smooth ridges of his bare chest. She bent her head and pressed her lips to the heat of his skin, over the spot where his heart beat. "Nor are you."

"Estelle." It was a question and a plea all at once.

"Follow me," she said, and led him toward one of the very nice sofas Jerome had sought.

And for a while, neither of them was alone.

CHAPTER

12

Sophie

The flat in London's Orchard Court, just off Baker Street, had not changed in the months since Sophie had first been brought here. Miss Atkins, of the Inter-Services Research Bureau and of a rank that continued to elude Sophie, still sat on the other side of the desk. Her blue-grey eyes were still calm and assessing, her hair neatly styled, her civilian clothing tailored and tidy. At her elbow, the same ashtray still overflowed with spent cigarettes, and her hands were folded over another file she had yet to open.

"Welcome back to London, Celine. You made an impression on your instructors," Miss Atkins said.

"Madame?"

"Clever, resourceful, lethal with a variety of knives in close combat, a keen shot," Miss Atkins recited, though she never once looked down at the file in front of her that had *Celine—S. Kowalski* written at the top, MOST SECRET stamped across the front. "I am told that you took to your training in a way that, quite frankly, astounded men who I'm certain still believe women shouldn't be serving behind the lines at all."

"It was good to feel like I was doing something real," Sophie replied. Something more than translating messages of death and destruction. Her training had provided an outlet for her frustration and guilt, and it had been gratifying beyond words. "It's been hard waiting for an opportunity, though I've tried to be patient." Sophie tried not to sound too hopeful.

"Indeed," Miss Atkins said. "Your instructors mentioned that you possessed a rather unnatural patience. They also said you were cold, intense, and fearless."

"You disapprove."

"On the contrary. If you weren't a woman, they'd likely hang an award of some sort on your chest. However, it is the assessment of fearless that gives me pause." She tapped the file with the tip of her finger. "For fear is what keeps my agents alert and alive."

Sophie looked toward the window. The blackout coverings had been pulled to the side to allow the early morning sun to stream through. An empty cut-crystal tumbler had been left on the sill, and tiny rainbows were scattered across the polished floor. "I am not fearless," Sophie said slowly. "I feel fear like anyone else. But embracing that sort of emotion does nothing but cloud judgement and make otherwise intelligent people make stupid decisions." She lifted her chin and returned her gaze to the woman across the desk. "I set out to prove that I can be far more useful somewhere other than behind a desk at Bletchley Park. I hope I have done so."

"Ah, yes. Back to Bletchley." Miss Atkins reached for her cigarettes and took her time selecting one before looking back up at Sophie. "Exactly how much do you know about the coded messages that you translated there?"

Sophie smoothed her skirt over her legs. Miss Atkins did not ask aimless questions. She considered her answer carefully.

"There was very little information shared. No one talked much about what they did at Bletchley. My duty was to translate only. I don't know a lot."

"But you know some."

"I know that the Germans keep changing the cipher somehow. I know that whatever we were using earlier doesn't decode more recent messages or, at the very least, doesn't decode them fast enough. I know that since last year, Nazi U-boats and troops and tanks are once again invisible. Until they're not."

"Until they're not," Miss Atkins agreed flatly. "And you're right. They keep changing the rules just when we think we have the game figured." She rolled her cigarette between her fingers. "There is a new device that the Germans seem to favour. It's being referred to as Tunny by the minds at Bletchley. It is not dissimilar from the encryption device that the Nazis have been using since the start of this war, the one that we broke." Miss Atkins slid a photo from the folder beneath her hands. It was an image of what looked almost like a typewriter, a plug board of some sort fronting the device. The top surface was flat, with raised letter keys at the front and a second set of letters set flush to the surface behind. Three rotors were set into the board near the rear. The entire device was nestled neatly into a hinged wooden box. "This is the German military Enigma machine that Bletchley's been deciphering for some time now. They think that this new device is very similar, though they believe there to be far more than three or four rotors. They are guessing that the new device is significantly larger than this one and attached in line to a teleprinter. Guessing, because, unlike the Enigma, we have not yet been able to recover individual pieces, a whole working machine, nor the operator codebooks or instructions that accompany it." The photo disappeared back into the folder and two more appeared. "These are what the codebooks for the Enigma look like."

This was a photo of what looked almost like a school primer. The familiar eagle and swastika were stamped front and center, *Special Machines Key* written in fancy lettering above it. The second photo was of the charts inside, each containing dozens of lines of letters and numbers. Sophie turned the photos over. What looked like a file number had been written in black ink next to the words *Operation Overlord* on the bottom corner of each. Without comment, Sophie handed them back to Miss Atkins and they, too, vanished back into the folder.

"I've been briefed that Bletchley is working on a new solution for this Tunny device based solely on a feat of reverse engineering," Miss Atkins said. "That they are developing a new machine that can solve these encryptions in hours instead of weeks. But like anything new, it is taking time. And we do not have the luxury of time. Not weeks, not months, not when supplies and men are sinking to the bottom of the sea faster than they can be loaded." She smoothed her hands over the top of the folder. "And not when there are plans being made to take back Europe at this very moment."

Sophie leaned back in the hard chair. "What sort of plans?"

Miss Atkins gave her a long look.

Sophie felt her cheeks heat. A stupid, amateur question.

Miss Atkins reached for the lighter lying on the desk next

to the ashtray. "I can only tell you that it has been made abundantly clear to me that our ability to take back Europe hinges on knowing what the Germans are thinking. What they are planning. What they believe we will do and from where we will launch our attacks. We need to know where they will position their troops and tanks and planes and ships in anticipation of our operations." A flame jumped as she lit her cigarette. "We need to have the ability to listen, and we need to have it as soon as possible."

Sophie remained silent, waiting for Miss Atkins to continue.

"Hitler and his High Command have adopted this particular device to send communications to military headquarters throughout occupied Europe. Including those in France. Our listening stations have picked up renewed traffic."

"I'm being sent to France." It was a peculiar feeling saying those words out loud. A realization that everything up until now had led to this point. That this was exactly where she was supposed to be.

"Yes." The silver lighter was returned to the desk with care. "To Paris. You will, ideally, be in and out of France within four weeks."

"And there is one of these encryption machines there? In Paris?"

"The Ritz Hotel is headquarters of the Luftwaffe, and Reichsmarschall Hermann Göring, one of Hitler's closest confidants, occupies the Imperial Suite at the hotel. Intelligence that has, regrettably, only now come to our attention suggests that the existence of one of these machines in the hotel is a possibility. And crumbs of possibility, enough to leave a bread trail at this juncture of the war, are more than enough to make us take action."

"That sounds quite irregular. Having a machine like that in a hotel?"

"I can assure you, it's not. There have been other efforts to capture cipher machines in other hotel headquarters." Miss Atkins's gaze seemed to grow distant for a moment before she came back to herself. "Should something happen to Hitler, it is very possible that Göring would be the man to step in to the Führer's role, given his rank within the Reich. It is not unreasonable to believe that he might have communication equipment at his immediate disposal within Luftwaffe's headquarters."

"The machine would need to be protected. And there would be operators." Sophie's mind was already racing.

"A team of three, maybe four, operators, our intelligence suggests, but no more. The Tunny does not require translation into Morse code, making the sending and receiving of messages far less laborious."

"And the exact location of the machine?"

"The report claims that it is enclosed in a renovated space within close proximity to Göring's suite, which suggests that it might have been relayed by a hotel employee. Though to be honest, I'm not entirely sure how believable that is. It will be up to you to determine where it might be as, no matter the briefings or my opinions, it's possible that the cipher machine may have been moved since then. You will be provided with blueprints of the hotel with the area in question marked and a dossier on whatever details we have on the current residents, including Göring." Miss Atkins slid Sophie's file to the side, revealing a second folder beneath. "You will travel to Paris with your husband, to quietly offer quality cosmetics to the very wealthy French and German women who patronize the Ritz or call the hotel home."

"Madame and Monsieur Beaufort." Sophie's training suddenly made perfect sense.

"Yes. The cover that was given to you—that you've already established during your training—will be the cover you use in France. Shortly, you will meet the agent posing as your husband, who has established the same cover story. His code name is Tempo, and like you, he has been selected from amongst the recruits for his command of both French and German, the competency he has proven in his field training, and, most importantly, his familiarity with the Ritz Hotel. His mother was French and used to work as a chambermaid at the Ritz. He grew up in and around the hotel and is intimately familiar with it."

Sophie considered that. "Is it possible that he may be recognized?"

"A valid question. We feel comfortable with the time that has elapsed. He was last there as an adolescent, though we've taken no chances. You'll see for yourself shortly. The agent is currently with Colonel Buckmaster receiving his own instruction, and once they're finished, they will join us so you can both be briefed on your shared mission." She leaned forward, cigarette smoke curling around her head. "There are other matters to discuss before they arrive, however."

"Which are?"

"Communication to your family and the matter of your pay." Miss Atkins put up a hand before Sophie could speak. "I am aware of the circumstances surrounding your family. Normally, when I have an agent in the field, I send brief, periodic letters to that agent's parents or relation, assuring them that their daughter is doing well in her supposed FANY service. To keep morale up at home, you understand."

Sophie looked down and clasped her hands neatly in her lap. "Of course."

"Is there anyone else to whom you might wish me to send correspondence? Extended family perhaps? A friend?"

There was the staff at Millbrook, Sophie supposed, but they believed her to be dead, and in truth, she hadn't been back to Norfolk in almost a decade. There was a second—or was it third?—cousin somewhere in Hampshire and a childhood acquaintance Sophie hadn't seen or heard from since she left for Poland. But Sophie didn't even know if they were still alive, much less where they might be now. "No. There is no one who will be worried about me."

"That's not true. I will worry about you."

Sophie looked up and met Miss Atkins's gaze. She swallowed with some difficulty and nodded. She rather thought that the woman across the desk probably said the same thing to all of her agents, but still, the words made Sophie feel less alone somehow.

Miss Atkins abruptly crushed the cigarette that she had barely smoked into the ashtray. "And your pay? Where would you like that sent while you are in the field?"

"You can send it to Millbrook Manor. It's in Norfolk." Imogen, the housekeeper, could be counted on to keep any correspondence for Sophie, even if she was presumed dead. When this was all over, Sophie could return to Millbrook to fetch whatever was sent there. Maybe she would even stay.

Or maybe not.

"Very good. But I will need the address." She slid a blank slip of paper and a pencil toward Sophie and watched as Sophie scribbled down Millbrook's address. "I will also send whatever personal effects you have there."

Sophie glanced down at the wedding ring on her finger.

"You will have to leave that behind," Miss Atkins said quietly. "Even from where I sit, it looks like a family heirloom. Something that means a great deal, and given that you are still in possession of it after your escape from Poland, I think I am right. You will be given something less noticeable and more generic. Something that you will never hesitate to pawn or use as a bribe if you need to."

Sophie twisted Piotr's ring from her finger, the small ruby glowing with dark fire in the light. She held it in her palm, suddenly unwilling to let it go.

"I will send it safely to Millbrook also."

Sophie nodded and handed the ring across the desk, looking away as deft hands slipped the ring into a large envelope. She knew that Miss Atkins spoke only good sense. She had known that she could not take this part of Piotr with her.

Yet she couldn't bring herself to reach for the photos in her pocket.

Miss Atkins set the envelope on the desk and paused, as if choosing her next words carefully. "May I ask how he died?" she finally said.

"I beg your pardon?"

"Your husband. It says in your file only that he was a Polish cavalry officer killed in action."

Sophie looked away, though she could still feel the weight of the woman's sharp grey-blue eyes. "What does it matter?"

"It matters because I like to know the motivations of the women I send behind enemy lines. Some risk everything to fight for their country, some fight for their principles, others fight for those close to them. And there are always a few who simply fight because they are good at it." She paused. "There are no right and wrong reasons for fighting, Celine. It is my job not to judge, but to understand, and make sure that those reasons do not become a liability. And your motives are still a mystery."

Sophie gazed out the window. A sparrow had landed on the sill outside. "You think I am fighting for revenge?"

"Are you?"

"Maybe I am."

"How did he die, Celine?"

"German guns."

"How do you know?"

The old familiar feeling of loss and powerlessness made her muscles go rigid.

"I was there." The sparrow startled and flew away. "And I am alive because he isn't."

Miss Atkins remained silent.

"And after he died and before I could make it home, German bombs killed my parents and German planes shot down my brother." Sophie returned her gaze to the woman who remained motionless across from her. "All sacrifices that I will not let go unanswered. That will not be forgotten."

Miss Atkins picked up another cigarette but made no move to light it. "I am told you almost killed the interrogator dressed as a Gestapo officer during training."

"I thought it was part of the exercise. And he came nowhere close to dying. Trust me."

The spymaster sat back and rolled her cigarette between her fingers. "I do."

"So my answers do not change anything? My motives?"

"I think that they are what make you dangerous. And I think that they are what will make you successful. But remember this. From the moment you set foot in France, you are not fighting the Nazis. Your job is to find intelligence and information that will help all of us fight the Germans and bring it back. Do you understand the difference?"

Sophie blinked.

"You will need to befriend your enemy, earn their trust, learn their secrets. Only then will the sacrifices you speak of not be in vain. Understood?"

"Yes."

"Good." Miss Atkins returned the unlit cigarette to the desk. "Do you have a will?" she asked briskly, and the abrupt change in topic momentarily threw Sophie.

"No." She shook her head. "I own nothing of value other than that ring and whatever pay I earn."

"Very well."

"I have this though." Sophie withdrew a small, sealed letter from her handbag and placed it on the desk.

"What is that?"

"A letter to my brother," she said. "In case I don't come back and he does."

Miss Atkins only nodded, and for that, Sophie was grateful. She didn't insist that Sophie would be fine, because she couldn't know that. Nor did she try to gently temper Sophie's expectations that her brother would ever return or that he might yet be alive. The woman across from Sophie said nothing. She simply picked up the letter and added it to the envelope with Sophie's ring.

A sharp rap on the door made Sophie twist in her seat. Miss Atkins slid the envelope and the file with Sophie's name into a desk drawer.

"Come in," she called.

Colonel Buckmaster strode into the room, a man Sophie had never seen at his heels. The newcomer walked with a stoop and a pronounced limp and was perhaps fifty, his dark blond hair greying at the temples and heavily brilliantined away from his forehead. He had a fair complexion and brown eyes partially hidden behind a pair of gold-rimmed spectacles.

The colonel stopped and gestured toward his charge. "Sophie Beaufort, may I introduce Gerard Beaufort."

Sophie had known that there would be no real names used but to be introduced by a different name brought the enormity and gravity of what she was about to do sharply into focus. Miss Atkins had referred to him as Tempo. From this moment, Sophie would think of him only as Gerard, her husband. Till death do them part.

Slowly, Sophie stood.

"Good God, you're a bloody Amazon," Gerard muttered, looking Sophie up and down.

Behind him, Buckmaster winced.

Sophie merely extended her hand. "Sophie Beaufort," she said. "I am pleased to make your acquaintance."

Gerard only grunted. He straightened as he strode forward to shake her hand, his shoulders broadening and his limp disappearing. Sophie rapidly revised her estimation of his age. Closer to forty, she guessed. He might lack tact, but one could not fault his ability to appear as something he wasn't.

"Shall we get down to business?" Miss Atkins asked, her voice cutting through the space.

"Indeed," Gerard declared. He waited for Sophie to resume her seat before taking the empty chair next to her. Buckmaster took up a position behind Miss Atkins, leaning against the wall, his arms crossed.

"Since you are both familiar with your cover stories, let's not waste time," Miss Atkins started. "You will be inserted into France southeast of Rouen, at a farm near Gasny, as soon as conditions allow. You will be met by a reception committee of Resistance agents who are expecting you. From there, you will travel to Paris, where you will make contact with a woman who will be able to provide you both with the social introductions you will require at the hotel."

"She is part of the Resistance also?" Sophie asked curiously.

Buckmaster cleared his throat. "Yes. In a way."

Sophie didn't bother to ask Buckmaster for clarification.

"Your objective is to put yourselves into a position where you can confirm the existence of the cipher device at the Ritz Hotel," Buckmaster said. "Once that is confirmed, you are to study the machine, photograph it at best, sketch it at worst. But, most importantly, you are to copy whatever tables or codebooks accompany it that detail the settings of the device. If the device settings of the ciphered message are known, I am told we have a hope of decoding it quickly enough to make a difference."

"I'd prefer to steal the books," Gerard said. "It would be faster. Copying sounds time consuming. Risky."

"We do not want the Germans to know what we know," Sophie said quietly. "Or they will change the rules again."

"I beg your pardon?" Gerard was frowning at her. "What's that supposed to mean?"

"It means that Madame Beaufort is correct," Buckmaster said. "No matter what happens, your efforts cannot be discovered. You cannot be discovered. If it comes to it, destroy whatever evidence you've collected. We cannot afford to start over should the Germans fear we've penetrated their ciphers. Not now."

Gerard crossed his arms.

"You will be provided with everything you need at the time of the drop. Weapons conducive to concealment—blades and the like, whatever you favour—though you will not carry fire-arms when you travel," Miss Atkins continued. "The Nazis are very suspicious of anyone who is armed, and we do not want to give them a reason to look too closely. Tempo's purported injury and age should prevent him from being an obvious target of roundups for German factories. There is paperwork and a supporting address in place in Marseille should the credentials of Enchanté Cosmetics be scrutinized. Your French identification papers are in order, and you'll have train passes and ration books. You should get through inspections but, of course, we can offer no guarantees. I cannot stress enough that what you will be doing is extremely dangerous."

Gerard uncrossed his arms and glanced at Sophie, still frowning fiercely.

She gazed back, wondering if the man was as disgruntled as he appeared or if his expression was merely one of con-centration as he considered the details of the mission. It was difficult to tell.

"When do we leave?" Gerard demanded.

Buckmaster cleared his throat. "With luck, a fortnight. A bus will take you to Tempsford today. Major James Reed will be waiting for you there. We need a full moon and favourable weather conditions—let's hope we get them and hope that ground conditions remain the same. The countryside is too often crawling with Gestapo and police. You should also be aware that the pilot may be required to abort the drop if the re-ception committee fears they've been compromised in any way."

Miss Atkins slid the bottom drawer open and withdrew two

thin folders. She handed one to each of them. "What we have on the current residents of the Ritz. Study the information, commit it to memory, and then destroy it. Clothes, money, and the cosmetics that you will need for your cover will be given to you just prior to departure. I would also suggest that you use this time to become familiar with each other and practice your stories. Review the details of your pasts. How you met, where you married, favourite colors, the things that a husband and a wife would know. Keep it simple but keep it consistent." She glanced at Buckmaster. "Anything else?"

The colonel shook his head. "Not at this time. Major Reed will cover remaining details prior to deployment."

Sophie wasn't surprised. There would be no specific names, addresses, code phrases, or contact information given until their departure was imminent.

"Very good. Good luck to the both of you." Miss Atkins brought the meeting to a close.

Sophie and Gerard both stood and exited the room, heading down the hall.

Sophie tipped the folder in her hand. "If it's agreeable to you, I was thinking that perhaps we could photograph the pages of the code—"

"I do hope you understand your role in this mission," Gerard cut her off.

"My role?"

"Like Colonel Buckmaster said, these will be very dangerous circumstances. I understand that I've been assigned a woman out of necessity—to avoid the suspicion that would normally fall on a male travelling alone through France. However, once we reach Paris, I think it's best if you stay safely removed from any sort of danger."

Sophie stopped in the middle of the hall. "I beg your pardon?"

Gerard also stopped and turned back toward her. "In Paris, I will make contact and take any necessary steps for the success of this mission. I cannot be worried about you and trying to find this bloody machine and its codebooks at the same time."

"I see," Sophie replied evenly. "Did you mention your concerns to Colonel Buckmaster?"

"I did." Gerard removed his spectacles and scowled at her. "He has assured me that you are a capably trained agent and did not seem to share my concerns." He shook his head. "And while I won't deny that you look quite...capable, Madame Beaufort, war is a man's domain. Thousands of years of history have taught us that, regardless of what Colonel Buckmaster says. As a woman, you cannot possibly begin to understand what it will be like facing the enemy on the front lines. The very fact that you are here is unnatural."

Sophie stared at him, momentarily robbed of speech. That damn word again.

"Perhaps you believed that this might be more exciting than whatever mundane, domestic life you lived before but I must impress upon you the dangers of this undertaking. I've had extensive instruction in languages, weapons, and stealth and am fully prepared for the rigours of this mission. As such, I am confident that I will be able to use my considerable charm, ability, and intellect to put myself into a position that will guarantee success."

"How reassuring," Sophie remarked acidly despite her best intentions to remain unruffled.

"Indeed," Gerard confirmed, seemingly oblivious to her

sarcasm. "Now, there is a small chance that I may need you to act as a distraction at some point. Dressed in a pretty frock and red lipstick, you'll most certainly draw a German officer's eye away from my endeavors. But I doubt it will come to that."

Sophie took a deep breath and forced herself to consider the man called Gerard Beaufort much the same way she had considered the fear she had felt tied to a chair in a Hampshire cellar. She reminded herself that he was not her enemy, no matter how arrogant he might be. The truth of the matter was that he was now her partner. Months of training and preparation had already gone into their cover and their mission, and to complain or protest not only served no purpose, it would undermine everything she had already accomplished as a female agent.

Gerard's opinions were simply that. Opinions. No different from the matriarchs appalled at her extensive studies, the clerks resentful of her embassy position, the officers who didn't believe she had a place at Bletchley, or the espionage instructors who had waited for her to fail.

The opinions of others had never stopped her before. She would simply focus on what mattered. Indignant outrage in the face of unpalatable sentiments served no purpose.

Sophie gripped the folder she held tightly. "During the course of your . . . extensive instruction, did you train alongside any female agents?"

"One," he sneered. "And like most women, she was overly emotional and prone to hysterics. She lasted not even a week."

"Hmm. That is unfortunate. And how many men washed out of that same training?"

Gerard sputtered. "That is not the point. I know what

you're trying to do here. But you also know that I am only speaking good sense."

"Of course."

"Of course?" Gerard narrowed his eyes. "What, no distraught protests?"

"Monsieur, one thing that you will come to learn about me is that I pick my battles very carefully. You are but a single man, and your opinion of me is not a battle worth waging. An argument in this hallway over my capabilities will waste both my time and energy, and I have no inclination to waste either. You may evaluate my capabilities at a later date. I'd suggest somewhere in France. Before we enter Paris would be my recommendation."

Gerard looked at her, nonplussed.

"I think we can both agree that we have far greater enemies than each other, no?" Sophie gave him a pleasant smile that was not a smile at all. "Now, shall we decide where it was that we met?"

CHAPTER

13

Aurelia

LONDON, ENGLAND
6 JULY 2017

L ia considered her surroundings with interest.

In the time since Gabriel had amassed and secured the art from her grandmother's apartment and accompanied it all back to his studio in London, she had been looking forward to seeing exactly where he would be working on it.

She had never been to an art appraisal office before and hadn't been entirely sure what to expect, but whatever she had had fixed in her mind, this was not it. The front office of Gabriel Seymour's place of business looked nothing like the kitschy, cluttered workshop she had vaguely envisioned. The space was located in a converted warehouse in Shoreditch, and the units were sleek and modern with a nod to the building origins—new glass and steel set against old brick and wood.

"You look troubled," Gabriel said, glancing up from behind an antique ebony desk. He was sorting through a stack of papers, each with an eight-by-ten photo attached to the front, and comparing them to the laptop screen in front of him.

"Not troubled," Lia told him, eyeing the room in which she stood. A long mahogany table from a century past sat off to the right of the desk, surrounded by eight silk-upholstered chairs. Two large screens were mounted to the wall above it, a wide easel set in between. A Persian rug in shades of grey covered the wooden floor, complementing the dove-grey walls. To the left of the desk, a collection of four small Impressionist paintings had been hung, each illuminated by a light mounted above. The entire effect was one of refined gentility, tempered by modern convenience.

"Just...surprised," she finished awkwardly. "I didn't know what your office or studio would look like."

"You were expecting Geppetto's workshop?" he asked with a smile.

"Maybe." She smiled back.

He stood behind the desk. "Sorry to disappoint."

"Never."

"Did you get checked in all right?"

"Yes." Not far from Gabriel's studio, the little hotel where she was staying wouldn't be winning any hospitality awards anytime soon but it was perfectly adequate for her needs.

"I'm glad you could come to London so quickly." He shoved his dark hair away from his face. He was wearing faded jeans and a simple, long-sleeved black sweater and looked somehow professional and casual all at once. And effortlessly handsome.

"Of course. I was anxious to come. The apartment felt oddly empty without the paintings." *And without you,* she added silently. Whether she wanted to admit it or not, she had missed him. His steady presence as they had peeled back inexplicable layers of Grandmère's life, including the extra-ordinary evidence that linked their two families, had been a comfort she hadn't known she'd needed.

"I have all your grandmother's paintings catalogued and properly stored here on-site. We can go over the paperwork for each, and I'll walk you through exactly what I'll be looking for. I'll get started on any restoration work as soon as possible."

Lia nodded.

"But before we do anything with the paintings, I wanted you to see this." He came around the side of the desk and handed her a small frame that contained a black-and-white photo. "Recognize her?"

A blond supermodel in a long-sleeved blouse above a pleated skirt stared back at Lia. "Your great-aunt."

"Yes. This photo was at my parents' London home. I borrowed it to show you."

Lia wandered over to the table and put the framed photo on the surface. She set her backpack beside it, unzipped it, and withdrew a heavy file. The photos and identification papers they had found in Lia's grandmother's apartment had each been put into a protective sleeve and were carefully organized inside. She laid them out beside the framed photo. There was no doubt that the women in both were one and the same.

"Have you spoken to your grandfather about these?"

"Not yet." Gabriel pulled out a chair for Lia and then took his own once she had been seated. "It seemed like a conversation best had in person and not over the phone. Because I did speak to my father about it. And he is adamant that Sophie Seymour died in Warsaw in 1939."

"Hmm."

"I was going to head up to Millbrook this weekend to talk to my grandfather. About what made him look for his sister after the war and what he might have found. And what, if anything, he might know about your apartment and its contents."

"Then take these," Lia said, gesturing at the photos in the file. "Your grandfather should see them." She paused. "Will you tell me what you learn? What he says?"

Gabriel hesitated.

"You don't want to show him the photos?"

"I do." He toyed with the edge of the folder. "At the risk of sounding like a serial killer, I was wondering if you might want to accompany me."

"To your family home?"

"I understand that you might need to get back to Paris right away, but I thought—"

"No," Lia interrupted. "I mean, no, I don't need to get back to Paris. Not right away. And, yes, I'd very much like to come with you."

Gabriel smiled at her, his grey eyes crinkling in the corners. "Good. I'm glad."

Lia's stomach did a ridiculous somersault. "I would very much like to come with you because it would seem," she said, shoving the sensation aside, "that some of the answers I'm looking for about my grandmère might be found in the same place." Not because Gabriel Seymour was handsome and charming and kind.

"I hope so." He held her gaze for a second too long before he looked away and cleared his throat. "It would be even better if we could find some answers about your paintings as well."

"Have you been able to identify any?" she asked. "Find out who might have owned them?"

"Yes, to the first part of your question. Identifying the artists and their work is the easy part of this equation. Identifying the people who once might have owned those works is going to be far more difficult. And you should be prepared for the possibility that we might never be able to."

Lia nodded.

"I've reached out to a friend, Patrick Langford, whom I graduated art school with and is now at Sotheby's. His job is to verify the provenance of every painting and objet d'art that comes through Sotheby's doors and ensure that what the auction house takes on consignment is not stolen. Over the years, he's become a specialist when it comes to art looted by the Nazis during the Second World War. He spends a great deal of his own personal time researching and searching for lost treasures from those years."

"And he's agreed to help us?"

"God, yes. He nearly passed out when I showed him the photos and told him where the paintings were found." Gabriel grinned crookedly. "Patrick has contacts in museums and auction houses all over the world and works closely with organizations such as the Monuments Men Foundation. He's got multiple databases at his fingertips here in Europe and abroad. He also has access to the detailed records the Nazis themselves kept, and those records, ironically, have proven exceedingly valuable."

Lia nodded. "You told him that I'm not ready to sell these paintings even if I can? Not yet, anyway?"

"Don't worry. I made that clear." Gabriel tapped his fingers on the edge of the table. "Both he and I ran a search of the name Aviva. We both came up empty with anything that might give us a lead, though that isn't all that surprising given that, presumably, she was a child."

"That would have been too easy, I suppose."

"Yes." Gabriel paused. "Have you given more thought to what you'd like to do with the paintings? In the short term, at least?"

"I'd like to exhibit them."

"In Paris?"

"To start. They deserve to be shared, not hidden in a dark room. What do you think?"

"I think it's a good idea. And I think that, if we're serious about getting these paintings back to their rightful owners, having more eyes on them will increase the chance someone might recognize a painting that once belonged to their family. Patrick can help us with that too."

"How would I go about setting up an exhibit?" Lia asked.

"Leave that to me. There are a few galleries and museums in Paris I have in mind that I think would suit, both in size and security. Your paintings are not exactly the Gurlitt Hoard, but I suspect that this collection will draw quite a crowd."

His phone buzzed, and he stood to retrieve it from his desk. He glanced down at the screen. "I'm sorry, I have to take this," he said. "Please. Feel free to look around. My studio is just through there." Gabriel gestured toward a wide doorway and shot her an apologetic glance as he took the incoming call.

Lia waved off his apology and stood, wandering toward the studio. The brick walls and ancient wood floors continued in here as well. But that was where the similarities ended. His brightly lit studio looked a little like a well-organized cross between a hospital lab and a museum. A massive table dominated the center of the space, the Munch canvas laid at one end. Above the table, an array of instruments snaked down from the exposed rafters of the ceiling to hover over the table's surface: a sleek, suspended microscope that could be maneuvered from its arm, an array of what looked like vacuum hoses, two hooded lights, and a wide magnifying lens. Surrounding the table was a fleet of wheeled carts, each cart containing neat rows of brushes, jars, tools, and extensive collections of containers and bottles. On her left, long white cabinets, presumably containing more of the same, ran the length of the room. In the corner to her right, a set of desks and tables stood, each home to a piece of laboratory equipment that included a spectrophotometer, a portable X-ray machine, and two more microscopes. Cords and cables were coiled neatly beneath, screens and keyboards mounted above.

Lia wandered farther into his studio, her eye drawn past all of that to the paintings that were hanging on the far wall. It was an eclectic collection, some of the paintings obviously old, others much more recent. The subject matter and styles were just as varied, portraits executed with impeccable realism mixed with Impressionist landscapes and abstract still lifes. Each and every one glowed with color and life—evidently all beneficiaries of Gabriel's restoration talents.

In the corner, a narrow door stood ajar, more paintings visible beyond. Intrigued, Lia stepped through, turning in a slow circle, the cool, bright light from the large northwest windows illuminating a riot of color. Because in this room, there were dozens of paintings, some hung on the walls, others resting on the floor and propped against the wall. The distinctive scent of oil paint and turpentine laced the air in here, evidence of creation, not merely restoration. Two easels had been set up in the center of the space, a canvas on each. Lia approached the first, unable to tear her eyes away.

It was a painting of a ballerina, the dancer caught as she soared into the air, her ivory skirts swirling about her legs, her arms outstretched in graceful lines. Against a background of dark shadows, the brilliance was startling, as if the dancer were leaping right off the stage, up toward the viewer. Yet it was her expression, caught in strokes of color and light, that made Lia catch her breath. The ballerina was gazing beyond the viewer as she danced, and the joy that the artist had captured in her features was riveting. As if this woman lived and breathed her art and each movement was a celebration of that love.

"What are you doing in here?" Gabriel's voice came from behind her.

"The door was open. You told me to look around."

"I meant my studio. Not...this."

"You painted all of these, didn't you?" Lia asked.

"Yes." His answer was curt.

"You're an artist," she said, her eyes still on the ballet dancer.

"No. I'm an art appraiser and restorer," he replied. "Who paints to amuse himself."

She frowned. "These were not done by a man who seeks merely to amuse himself."

"While I appreciate your kind words, you are hardly an expert in the matter, Miss Engineer." He sounded almost defensive.

"No, I suppose I'm not." She stepped closer to the easel. "This woman you've painted—you know her well. She's a friend. Maybe a lover?"

"A friend," he replied with clear surprise.

"Ah."

"She was my neighbour when I was in art school. She and her husband are both dancers for the Royal Ballet. It's how they met." He paused. "How did you know she was a friend?"

"This is a painting of her personality, not just her image."

Gabriel moved to stand beside her but didn't speak.

"What it's called? This painting?"

"Um."

"Tell me it has a name."

"It does." He stopped. "It's called *First Love*."

"Ah." Lia smiled. "Yes. I can see it. Has she seen this painting? Your friend?"

"No."

"Why not?"

"Because, like I said, these paintings are merely a hobby."

"I disagree." Lia stepped away from him to approach the second canvas on the easel behind.

This was a painting of a couple dancing what was unmistakably a tango. The background was done in deep purples and blues, the illusion of a single spotlight illuminating the two figures. One of the woman's hands rested on her partner's shoulder, her other clasped in his. Her back was to the viewer, her gold dress and blond hair a brilliant contrast to his dark suit and his hand where he held her at the small of her back. The dancers' faces were hidden, their heads bent toward each other intimately. Their silhouettes were slightly smudged on the edges, as if their movement could not quite be contained.

Lia felt her throat close. She couldn't look away, the image stirring an intense longing in her that caught her unaware.

"Lia? Are you all right?"

She shook her head, trying to clear the emotion that was clogging her throat. "You're an idiot," she managed.

"I beg your pardon?"

"This painting. It's..." She fought for the right word. *Beautiful* wasn't adequate. *Stunning* wasn't even sufficient.

"A hobby," Gabriel intoned.

Lia ignored him. "When I look at this, I want to be this woman. I want to hear the music, feel the heat of another body pressed against mine. I want to live in this moment when no one else in the world exists except the man who is holding me as though I were the only woman on earth. I would like to dance, just like this."

Gabriel didn't answer. Lia turned to find him staring at her, his eyes searching hers, a peculiar expression on his face.

"What's this one called?" she managed.

Gabriel ducked his head, looking uncomfortable.

"What's it called?" Lia pressed.

"*Après.*"

"Who are they? The couple in this painting?"

"I don't know."

"You don't know?"

"I was in Gijón for work," Gabriel said. "I was walking back to my hotel, and it was late, after the bars and theaters and restaurants were closed. They were under a streetlight, on a walkway above the sea. No music, no audience. Just dancing after everyone else had gone." He paused. "Dancing for no one but themselves. I suppose it left an...impression."

Lia swallowed, emotion still making her throat tight. "What do you do with your paintings?" she blurted. "Do you sell them?"

"No." He jammed his hands into his jeans pockets. "When I run out of space here, I move them to Millbrook. If the walls of the manor were good enough for my forefathers' art, they are good enough for mine."

"But you've never exhibited your work?"

He looked back at the canvas. "I've considered it. My grandfather and father hound me all the time."

"But?"

"But it would only be a distraction from my real job. There is no need. Such a thing would be frivolous and a waste of time and money."

"Frivolous?" Lia crossed her arms. "Well then, I suppose that there is no need for me to exhibit the paintings I found in Grandmère's apartment either."

"I know what you're trying to do. And it won't work. The art that came out of that Paris apartment and what I create— it's not the same."

"Isn't that rather the point? That each piece is different? That each work instills and evokes different emotions depending on the individual who gazes upon it?"

"Now you're just being difficult."

"No. I'm being honest. To call what you've done here a hobby is doing yourself a great disservice."

"On the contrary, I do myself a very great service by recognizing my limitations. Which is far more than I can say for the generations who have come before me."

"What does that mean?"

"My great-grandfather, my grandfather, even my father, have all spent extraordinary amounts of time and money chasing the impossible dream of achieving fame and fortune from their art. And for their efforts, they were rewarded with nothing but disappointment and rejection. Had our family not been lucky enough to own vast tracts of productive land and a manor that could be turned into a business, and had our family not been fortunate to have practical, intelligent females who saw to business and ensured their menfolk did not bankrupt them in the pursuit of an impossible dream, things might be very different right now."

"I don't think that your forefathers had the talent you do," Lia murmured, thinking of the hopeful little landscape that had ultimately brought her here.

"You're not listening to me. Talent is only part of the equation, and even then, it is a fickle and capricious creature, subject to whims and luck. It cannot be relied on. So, yes, while I seem to have inherited a love of art, I have not inherited the mistaken notion that it is enough. I married that love to common sense and the knowledge that whatever skill I possess can be used for a far better purpose."

"That sounds very...practical." And not a word that had any place amongst the emotion and brilliance of the canvases that surrounded her.

"I'll take that as a compliment. The men in my family have long been considered hopeless romantics, indulged by their families. I have no interest in being indulged."

"And you think I'm expressing admiration to indulge you?"

"Look, I appreciate the vote of confidence, and my ego thanks you. But I have found my niche within my chosen field, and there I have realized immense satisfaction and happiness."

Lia turned back to the two dancers and ran her finger lightly along the bottom lip of the easel. "Sell me this painting."

"I beg your pardon?"

"I'm asking to buy this painting."

"I don't sell my paintings."

"Fine. Let's trade, then."

"I—what?"

"Pick a painting that you took off the living room wall in that Paris apartment. One of the landscapes that I'm fairly certain actually belonged to my grandmother. Whichever one catches your fancy."

"Don't be ridiculous," Gabriel scoffed. "Each of those paintings is worth a significant sum."

"And they mean nothing to me. I look at them, and I feel nothing."

"I will not let you do that."

"Then sell me this painting." She turned and looked him squarely in the eye. "All the practicality and common sense that you just boasted of—I can't think of a better way to demonstrate them. A sale will save you the hassle of transporting it to Norfolk to be hidden away. That manor must be running out of rooms three generations later, no?"

Gabriel scuffed the floor with his toe and looked distinctly awkward. "I . . ."

"Please."

"Fine."

"Fine?"

"If you insist, I will sell it to you. I do not wish to argue."

"Good." Lia felt absurdly pleased. "And I'll buy the ballet dancer too."

"You're shameless."

"No. Captivated. Moved." She set her hands on her hips. "We can talk price on the way to Norfolk."

CHAPTER

14

Sophie

Tempsford Hall sprawled elegantly, surrounded by lush greenery. Sophie immediately pictured dignified Victorian ladies and gentlemen in lavish dress and dashing hats speaking about nothing more important than the pheasant served at luncheon. In her vision, there were carefree children running and playing across the lawns, balls bouncing ahead of them, puppies barking at their heels.

Silly, Sophie knew, but just for a moment, she wanted to imagine Tempsford Hall in a happier, more tranquil time. Before it became the staging ground for agents flying out of the nearby airfield. Before the people who crossed its grounds wore uniforms and walked quickly with grim purpose while casting suspicious glances at newcomers. Before its guests and residents were continually deposited into enemy territory.

"How are you feeling?" Sophie asked the man walking

beside her as they entered the house. Gerard had said nothing on the journey from London.

In fact, in the time they'd spent together since they'd been given their orders, Gerard Beaufort had spoken only rarely to Sophie and only when absolutely required.

"Hungry," he snapped.

"No, that's not what I meant. I was wondering if you had given any more consideration to how we might best—"

"God's teeth, woman, I've made my expectations of our...partnership clear. I don't need you pecking away at me incessantly for the next two weeks until we depart." He jammed his hat farther onto his head and then cursed when it slid too far down his brow. "I don't need you at all, in fact," he mumbled, shoving the hat back up his forehead.

"I understand that you might be anxious—"

"I'm not anxious," he sneered. "Nor am I frightened or intimidated or worried or whatever else you're feeling and projecting onto me right now. I am a soldier, and soldiers do not fear anything."

Sophie sighed. "That's not at all—"

"Good afternoon." The greeting came from a harried-looking middle-aged woman. She had a tailor's tape around her neck, spectacles perched on top of her greying hair, and a pencil stub impaled in the bun at the back of her head.

"Good afternoon," Sophie replied.

"*Merde*," the woman said as she stared at Sophie, her fingers sliding on the tape as if itching to start taking measurements. "The best couture houses in Paris would have fought over dressing you."

Sophie bit her lip. "You are too kind."

"I'm not. Not at all. Kindness does not build a label. Only

appearance does that. Careful maintenance of a mirage that can convince people they can be something they're not if they possess the right things. All the best houses in Paris know this too."

"You've worked in these houses," Sophie said. When she had lived in Paris, she had often walked by the couture houses along the Place Vendôme. And she had seen the women who shopped there.

"In another life. It's what makes me good at this now, no? Dressing people who are something they're not." The woman gave a very Gallic shrug. "I am Marie. Major Reed, he says you need to be dressed, yes? Socks, coats, luggage, shoes?"

"Yes. Everything down to our knickers."

"*Bonne.* Follow me, *s'il vous plaît.*" Marie led them to what had probably been the study or the library before the war.

Now the space looked like a haphazard department store, full of coats and suits and dresses hanging on wheeled racks and draped over chairs and tables. Boxes of what Sophie could only imagine were shoes and accessories were stacked along one wall, and nearby, two women bent industriously over sewing machines.

"Is it really necessary I be here?" Gerard asked, looking around. "Surely my...associate can pick out something for me. She is supposed to be my wife, after all, and this is most certainly women's work."

Sophie kept her expression impassive.

Marie's lips thinned. "All agents must personally get fitted. No exceptions."

Gerard sighed loudly. "I'd rather just pick up my papers and go for a pint while we wait."

Wouldn't we all, Sophie wanted to say. She refrained.

"Clothes here first," Marie intoned, her annoyance clear.

"Papers, money, weapons at the airfield. You will be searched there too. No part of England can go to France, yes? That is how agents do not come back."

"Fine." Gerard sighed loudly again as if to underscore his displeasure at the inconvenience.

Marie turned her attention back to Sophie. "Tell me what you need. What mirage you wish to create." She yanked the pencil from the back of her head and snatched a tiny notebook from a cluttered tabletop.

"Clothes that might have been expensive at some time but have seen wear. Something that would belong to a wealthy business owner and his wife. But something forgettable."

"Hmmm." Marie made a notation and looked critically at both Sophie and Gerard. "Yes, yes. This is no problem."

"And I'll need a dress that would not be out of place in a more glamourous setting. Gloves. Accessories."

Marie brightened and rubbed her hands together. "Something not so forgettable, yes?"

"Yes. And anything that you might have with a laundry mark or label that might have been found in Marseille would be an advantage."

"We have labels and items from many French cities," Marie said, almost proudly. "Some come to us as . . . gifts, others we copy for ourselves. This also is no problem." She settled her spectacles on her nose and considered Sophie more carefully. "*Mais*, your height, Madame, may be more of a problem. I will need to see what I have."

Gerard scoffed under his breath.

Marie's eyes snapped to him. "You, on the other hand, are a nice, small man, yes? Finding you clothes will not be a problem. We can hem right here."

Gerard flushed, and Sophie suddenly found a loose thread on the cuff of her sweater fascinating.

"Come," Marie said, beckoning them deeper into the study. "I will make clothing for Madame and Monsieur that is both forgettable and unforgettable. I will make sure you are ready for your time in France."

★ ★ ★

Sophie lay on the cold metal floor of the Hudson bomber, feeling the vibrations from the engines right through her bones. At the front of the plane, the pilot and the navigator were absorbed in their duties. How these men could know where they were in the dead of night with only math and the moon and the occasional blackout-defying soul to guide them amazed Sophie. As did the gunners at the front and rear who scanned the ground and air with unwavering intensity. They had been told to expect flak from antiaircraft guns, explosions that could toss the plane even if they were too far out of range to cause real damage, but thus far, the flight had been blissfully uneventful.

Around her were over a dozen cylindrical containers as tall as she was, each attached to its own parachute. Their luggage and a suitcase full of silver powder compacts, tubes of bright lipstick, and an assortment of mascara and eye shadow pots were in one. The contents of the others were a mystery to her, though it didn't take much to guess that they contained weapons and supplies for the Resistance forces that would meet them.

Across from Sophie, Gerard also rested on the floor of the plane. The unrelenting din from the bomber's engines prevented any sort of casual conversation, not that her partner seemed any more interested in speaking to her than he had earlier. In fact, he hadn't said a word since they'd both stuffed themselves into their coveralls and helmets and securely strapped on their parachutes.

Sophie tried not to worry about his recalcitrance. She had to believe that, once they were on the ground, he would come to the realization that they were truly in this together. She didn't need him to like her, but she needed him to trust her.

She turned her head and watched as a squadron crew member moved through the plane, expertly double-checking the parachute harnesses attached to each cylinder, the beam of his small torch bobbing up and down. He stopped by Sophie and crouched down.

"First jump?" He shouted to be heard above the engines.

The glow from the little torch illuminated an airman who couldn't have been more than eighteen, with bright blue eyes that instantly reminded her of Piotr.

"Yes," Sophie replied. "But not your first time at this, I take it."

"This is my thirty-eighth visit to France. Over France, at least. You lot keep us busy." He rapped on the fuselage fondly. "Never been to Paris though. Always wanted to go. Me mum went once and thought it was the most beautiful city she ever saw. She said Sacré-Coeur was like standing on the top of the world."

"She was right," Sophie told him.

"Not so beautiful now, I imagine, with all those feckin' Nazi flags hanging everywhere."

"Working on it," Sophie said, smiling. It was impossible not to like him.

"Pilot reckons we're about five minutes out." He gestured to the cylinders. "Just remember, once the pilot verifies the ground signal and gives the all clear, we'll drop the cargo first so it doesn't land on top of you," he said with an easy grin. "'Cause that would put a damper on things."

His expression, coupled with the color of his eyes, so reminded her of Piotr that Sophie put a hand to her mouth and sucked in a harsh breath.

The airman's grin faded. "Oi, you'll be all right. Nothing to jumping."

"It's not that. You just...you just remind me of someone. My husband," Sophie finished awkwardly.

The airman glanced across the fuselage to where Gerard lay silent and motionless.

"He's not my husband. Just my...partner."

"Ah. That makes more sense." Another grin split his young face. "Lucky man, your husband. Maybe one day I'll be so lucky to find a wife willing to jump out of a plane with me."

Oh, Piotr, you would have liked this boy, Sophie thought, a shard of grief driving deep into her chest. Years gone and still those lingering fragments caught her at unexpected times, the pain as excruciating as it had ever been.

"Best of luck to you," the airman said. "Blow the feckin' Jerries right out of France." He stood and continued his inspection of the cargo.

Sophie crawled carefully around the opening that they would be jumping through shortly. "Five minutes," she shouted at Gerard.

He looked at her and then looked away just as quickly. Even in the dim light, she could see that his face was set in grim lines.

"They'll drop the cargo and then we go after," she continued. He didn't respond.

"Did you hear me?" she asked. "We wait for—"

"I heard you the first time," he snarled. "I know what I'm doing. I don't need you nagging me like a bloody fishwife."

Sophie raised her hands in a placating gesture and returned to the far side, ahead of the drop chute. The young crew member, with the help of a second, was working his way back now, this time hooking up the cylinder harnesses to the static line with practiced efficiency. She remained where she was, out of the way, as the sound of the engines changed and the plane banked. The pilot dropped the big bomber, flying low, presumably looking for something on the ground. The signal from the reception committee, Sophie surmised, though how a pilot of a bomber this size could spot the lights from a handful of torches on the ground was a mystery.

The engines rumbled and whined, and the plane rose again sharply.

"We're good to go!" the crewman shouted. "Holding for altitude."

The plane leveled off again after a moment, and Sophie watched as the two men manhandled and dropped each cylinder through the chimney-like opening with practiced movements. She closed her eyes and slowed her breathing, visualizing what she would need to do in the next few minutes once the plane banked and made its final pass. *Stand up*, she recited her training orders in her head. *Hook static lines. Wait. To the door. Jump—*

"Oi!" A panicked shout just to the rear made her eyes snap open.

"Jesus feckin' Christ!" the second airman was yelling at the same time, though his words were nearly drowned out by the roar of the rushing air and the growl of the engines.

The two airmen had finished dropping the cylinders and were resuming their positions near the front of the plane but both were now looking back in horror.

Sophie twisted and followed their gaze to see that Gerard had stood and hooked his harness to the static line. He was standing on the edge of the drop chute.

"Wait!" Sophie yelled, scrambling toward him.

Gerard barely glanced at her. "You won't have it in you. Better if I'm on my own." He straightened his arms by his sides and clutched his coveralls.

"You need to wait—"

Gerard jumped.

"Shit, shit, shit." The young airman had reached the drop chute and was looking down in disbelief.

The pilot and the navigator were both yelling questions at the two crew, though Sophie couldn't hear what they were asking.

"He was supposed to wait for the second pass," the airman blurted, looking up at Sophie, wide-eyed. "He'll be in the feckin' trees."

"What?"

"There's a forest on the eastern side of the potato fields. It's why we do two passes. First for cargo, second for jumpers. Shit." The plane was banking again.

"I'll look for him," Sophie yelled.

"You'll need to backtrack east. He'll have come down on top of the trees. No way he'll have made it through the canopy to the ground. If he's lucky he'll just be hung up." He didn't need to say what the consequences of unlucky were. "He'll be a sitting duck in the trees if he's discovered." The plane straightened. "Get ready!" he shouted and moved back toward the front of the plane to speak to the pilot.

Worry for Gerard and the damage he might have inflicted on their mission with his foolishness overrode any fear about the jump itself. Above her head, the red light blinked on. She stepped to the edge of the dark opening, the air howling and shrieking beneath her. The light went green, and Sophie jumped.

Falling unchecked through space was a peculiar sensation, terrifying and exhilarating all at once. Training on familiar ground was one thing but hurtling downward toward the unknown was something else entirely. It was also, Sophie reflected, oddly peaceful—the teeth-rattling vibrations abruptly ceased, and the thunder of the engines receded to a distant whine.

The air rushed by her, the small strings in the folds of her parachute snapping in quick order until the last one snapped off and the parachute opened. Sophie was jerked upward, her fall suddenly slowed. Above her, the moon shone brightly. Pale light glittered off a river that curled away to her right and created uneven shadows on the ground below her. To her left, beyond an inky black strip of what she assumed were trees, she caught a glimpse of what looked like a roof, the smooth surface a pale canvas against the dark.

Sophie concentrated on the ground, trying to anticipate the landing. As she drew near, she reached up as far as she was able, grasped the harness, and yanked it down. Her feet made contact with the ground, and she let herself fall to the side, landing hard on her hip. Her parachute billowed and yanked her forward a few feet before it collapsed like a spent balloon.

Sophie lay still for a moment, catching her breath. The

ground beneath her was damp with dew, the faint scent of decomposing vegetation mingling with the more earthy tones of rich soil. Sophie pushed herself to her knees and disengaged her harness. She pulled her helmet from her head and glanced around. She was on the edge of a long field, a dark wall of bushes or trees surrounding all four sides and swallowing any moonlight. There was no sign of any of the canisters that had been dropped prior to her jump. She had no idea where or when the reception committee that was supposed to meet her would materialize but for now she needed to take care of her parachute and get out of the open. Quickly, she gathered the lifeless silk in her arms and dragged it toward the nearest tree line, away from the exposed field.

In the shadows of the trees, the silence was unnerving, broken only by a tentative rattle of the leafy branches above her head as the breeze meandered through. Sophie strained her eyes but nothing moved. She whistled, two descending notes that should have identified her to the reception committee, but there was only more silence in answer. As the minutes ticked by, she wondered if she'd been dropped in the wrong spot. Or if she had somehow drifted far, far off course.

But staying here, crouched in the damp and the dark, was accomplishing nothing. She couldn't still be here when the sun came up in a few hours. She stuffed her parachute and helmet under a low bush and stripped the supporting bandages from her ankles, adding them to the concealed pile. Then, as silently as possible, she struck out toward the building she thought she'd seen on her descent.

An owl hooted in the distance, the eerie call echoing through the trees. Sophie focused on keeping her breathing quiet and even and her footsteps deliberate and careful. A thick layer of damp and rotting leaves muffled her footsteps as she moved forward until she arrived at the edge of what looked like an abandoned farmyard. Was this the right farm? Was she even near Gasny?

Closest to her, a small cottage squatted, its windows boarded up, the door drawn tightly closed. There was no telltale smoke curling from the chimney nor laundry hanging from the empty line to the side. Beyond the cottage, the larger outline of a barn loomed. Sophie crouched low and hesitated, unsure if she should approach—

She froze as a glimmer of light appeared beneath the cottage door. It was snuffed out almost as quickly as it had appeared but Sophie knew that she hadn't imagined it. She was not alone. Again, she hesitated.

It was possible that it was a trap. It was possible that there were ranks of Gestapo or gendarmerie hidden in that building like a ravenous spider waiting to devour prey that ventured too close. Waiting to ensnare the unwary into their web of torture and depravity.

She frowned. Given the number of canisters that had been dropped prior to her own jump, given the time her descent had taken and the time she had been exposed on that field, hiding in an abandoned cottage seemed an ineffective way to hunt. More likely the people whom she would find assistance from were hidden within.

Sophie moved out from the protection of the trees, hurrying across the open expanse of farmyard. She ascended the cottage steps, the tired wood creaking beneath her weight. Very slowly, she lifted the latch of the door and pushed it open. There were no shots, no shouts, and no one appeared to challenge her. Sophie stepped forward into the cottage, purposefully leaving the door open to facilitate a quick escape, and tried to see into the darkened space.

For she wasn't alone. The scent of unwashed bodies was detectable under the mustiness of a building closed for too long. Someone coughed in the darkness, the sound small and frail. Sophie fumbled in her coveralls pocket for her small torch. She flicked it on and nearly came out of her skin. At least two dozen pairs of eyes gazed back at her, set into gaunt, pale, terrified faces, and not one older than the age of ten.

"Are you here to take us to the funeral?" The question was thin and reedy and had been asked by a small girl who crept forward a step.

"The funeral?" Sophie repeated. What the hell had she stumbled into? "Are you here alone?" she asked the group, trying to understand what was happening and who these children were. "Where are your parents?"

The girl scuttled away back into the safety of her comrades, what looked like fear stamped across her features. One of the smaller children started to cry.

"Do you need help?" Sophie tried. "Can I—"

"Who are you?" The demand came from the open door, a figure in a bulky coat silhouetted against the pale light of the moon outside. He was holding a gun—Sophie could see the dull gleam of the barrel.

"You first." Sophie switched off her light and slid in front of the children. She adjusted her grip on the torch. Not much of a weapon but it was better than nothing. She'd worked with less.

"Get back against the wall." The gun barrel twitched toward the side of the room. "Now."

"I'm not moving—"

The girl who had asked the question suddenly detached from the cowering group of children and threw her arms around the man's waist with a torrent of barely comprehensible words.

The gun in the man's hand remained pointed steadily at Sophie. "How many of you are there?" he demanded.

"What?"

"I said, how many of—"

"Georges, put the damn gun down." A new voice interrupted him.

Another torch flickered on, aimed at Sophie, and she winced, holding her hand up against the disorienting glare.

"*Merde*," the newcomer muttered. The light was extinguished, and he whistled the two descending notes that Sophie had tried in the trees. "You were supposed to wait for us outside."

Sophie repeated the whistle and then said, "I did wait."

"You know this woman?" the man named Georges asked angrily, though he lowered the gun.

"No. Yes." The newcomer waved his hand. "She is on our side."

"Hmph." Georges grunted. "She shouldn't be in here."

"Yes, yes." The reply was weary. "I will remedy that immediately." He stepped to the side, his silhouette merging with the fluid blackness inside the doorframe. "After you, Madame."

Sophie glanced once more at the small girl still clinging to the man with the gun, her face a pale oval in the meagre light. "Apologies," she whispered and then retreated back outside the cottage.

The door shut behind her, her escort at her heels as if afraid she'd turn back.

"Who are these children and why are they here?" she demanded.

"That would be none of your business. Why were you even in that cottage?"

"Looking for you, obviously." She stopped, refusing to move until she got answers. "If you mean those children harm—"

"Harm?" The man sounded indignant. "I can assure you, Madame, we're not harming them."

"They're so thin. One of them sounded ill."

"That's what happens when you've survived this long hidden in attics and ghettos."

"They asked me if I was here to take them to the funeral," Sophie pressed. "I want to know what you are going to do with them."

The man cursed under his breath but answered her. "We're taking them out of France."

"How?"

"Not in a cattle car to be exterminated," he hissed in a low voice.

"How many children?"

"As many as we can."

"And the funeral they spoke of?"

"It's one of the ways Georges gets them across the Swiss border. Dress them up as mourners."

"Then what happens to them?" Sophie demanded.

"*Merde.*"

"What happens to them?" she repeated.

"They are placed with families who can look after them. Satisfied?"

"Yes."

"Good. Because I am not saying anything else on the matter, for my safety, your safety, and theirs. Understood?"

"Yes."

"Follow me." He stepped in front of her. "Our business is in the barn."

Sophie did as she was bade.

"I am Henri," he said as they skirted the cottage. "You are Celine?"

At the sound of her code name, a sudden, unexpected relief flooded through her, making her almost giddy. Relief that she had survived the jump, relief that she was where she needed to be, relief that she was not alone.

"Thought there was supposed to be two of you," Henri said.

"There was. Is. He jumped too soon."

"Did you see where?"

"To the east." Sophie repeated what the bomber's crewman had told her.

A low curse was uttered. "Your parachute?"

"In the trees under a bush along the field."

"I'll send someone to fetch it. Follow me."

Sophie followed Henri as they crossed the farmyard with its empty paddocks. The carcass of an ancient tractor had been abandoned in the center of the yard, and even in the dim light, its plundered innards were visible where they spilled out onto the ground. As they drew close to the barn, Sophie could now see the faintest line of light coming from beneath the wide door.

Her guide lifted the latch, pulled it open, and ushered Sophie inside. The door closed behind them silently on well-oiled hinges. Sophie blinked in the low lantern light and looked around. The barn was devoid of livestock, its windows boarded up, the floor littered with dusty straw. A sturdy ladder led up into the hayloft, where two men were winching a cylinder that had been in the plane with Sophie up into the darkness.

"You got them all?" Henri pushed past her to address the two workers.

In the light, Sophie could now see that Henri was no more than thirty, with curly brown hair escaping at the edges of a cloth cap pulled firmly down over his forehead. He had dark, intelligent eyes set into a broad face and was dressed in the rough clothes of a labourer or farmer, his coat patched at the elbows and collar. He moved with the ease and efficiency of an athlete, his questions clipped but not rude.

"Last one," the taller of the two men told him, glancing at Sophie. "Explosives are at the rear, away from the guns and ammunition."

"Good."

"Her things are down there." The man gestured to the side of the barn where the light didn't reach.

He did not introduce himself. Sophie likewise volunteered nothing.

Henri turned back to Sophie. "You can take your coveralls off here. We'll get rid of what you don't need."

Sophie nodded and extracted a packet of papers from the deep pocket of her coveralls, her identification and ration books all wrapped securely in oilskin. She set the papers aside and shrugged out of the heavy coveralls, balling them up into a tight bundle.

The men in the loft had finished their duties and climbed down the ladder. They had a brief discussion in low tones with Henri before departing. Once the door had closed behind them, Sophie reached under her sweater and pulled out the stacks of forged currency that had been strapped to her waist, dividing it according to the instructions she had been given before they had boarded the bomber.

"Georges is a good man." The comment came from behind Sophie, and she spun, finding a petite schoolgirl with twin braids and dressed in boy's clothes watching her. She was leaning against a rough post, a worn canvas satchel strapped across her chest and an unlit cigarette dangling from her lips.

No, Sophie realized. Not a schoolgirl at all. Cigarette aside, the steady brown eyes that looked back at her were much too old, cold cynicism where youthful innocence should have been. Sophie had no idea where she'd come from.

"I don't know who or what you're talking about," Sophie replied.

"Hmm." The girl considered her. "Good. I'm glad we understand each other."

Sophie set the stacks of currency on a rough table.

"Nothing wrong with your type being in places you aren't supposed to be so long as you don't get caught," the girl said. "If you want to live to see the end of this war, you should try to avoid discovery in the future."

"Noted."

"Good, you've met." Henri appeared behind the woman, heading toward the far side of the barn where the lantern sat. "Celine, Vivienne. Vivienne, Celine."

The tiny woman nodded, and Sophie nodded back.

"You can give Vivienne whatever money London has sent," Henri instructed in that brisk way of his. "She'll get it where it needs to go. She also gets information and messages where they need to go. She's in and out of the city twice a week for us." He continued toward the side of the barn.

Sophie handed three of the piles of forged notes to the courier, and they vanished into her satchel. "I am to meet a woman in Paris."

"I know," Vivienne replied. "La Chanteuse."

"Yes. Is she part of your network?"

"In a way," Vivienne said.

"Do you trust her?"

Vivienne gave her a hard look. "With my life. I've worked with her since this nightmare started."

"Mmm."

"I will tell you how to find her. And I will also give you instructions on how to find me should you require. I deliver vegetables on a schedule," she explained. "To the hotels and restaurants and cafés."

"I see."

"Will you require regular radio access to London while you are here?"

"No. Not right away, at least."

"Do you know how long you will be in Paris?"

"We are to be flown out. This same location, next full moon."

"I thought there were to be two of you. Where is your partner?"

"I'm not sure, exactly."

Vivienne's brows shot up her forehead. "You're not sure? What do you mean you're not—what are you doing with all that?"

Henri had returned just then with the lantern, a knife, and a long coil of rope that he had slung across his body. He exchanged a glance with Sophie. "We're going to go look for a spy."

CHAPTER

15

Estelle

E stelle stood beneath the trees, just to the west of the wide stone staircase, looking for a spy.

Behind her, Sacré-Coeur rose up against a cloudless curtain of blue, impervious to the mortals suffering and surviving beneath it. The pristine, bulging white spires that reached to the heavens were bejewelled in dazzling sunshine, a peculiar juxtaposition against the worn, gaunt, and drab mass of humanity over which they presided. Atop the corner closest to Estelle, over the triple-arched entry, Joan of Arc sat frozen in bronze, clutching the reins of her horse in one hand and wielding her sword impotently in the other. Idly, Estelle wondered what Joan would think of what had become of her country. Her life sacrificed to chase the English out of France only to have them replaced by the Germans five hundred years later.

The basilica was crowded today, devout Parisians making the laborious trek up the long stretches of stairs to the top

of their city to pray. Not that praying had seemed to have
done the city or its residents much good these past years. The
constant presence of the Geheime Staatspolizei that drifted
around the cathedral grounds like an omnipresent miasma was
testament to that.

Though today, there seemed to be more of them than
usual, and Estelle didn't like it at all. A week ago, Vivienne
had told her to expect two Allied agents to make contact with
her following the last full moon. That full moon had come
and gone, and the agents had failed to materialize. It was
likely that something had happened and their arrival had been
aborted or compromised. London would try again on the next
cycle, no doubt, and Estelle would wait here again, at the top
of Montmartre, bright red flowers still tucked into the brim
of her hat.

She'd stopped meeting couriers and agents anywhere near
the train stations long ago. Train schedules had become
increasingly erratic and unpredictable, and the stations themselves had become obvious targets of the Gestapo. She couldn't
risk being noticed and remembered. It was much easier, if it
came to it, to justify regular sojourns to a basilica than to a
train station.

Two Gestapo officers in their grey coats walked by, seemingly looking for something or someone. Estelle adjusted her
hat, grateful for the wide brim. Time for her to go—

"Excuse me. Can you tell me what time mass is held in the
afternoons?"

Estelle froze before she turned slowly. The question had been
asked by a woman, dressed plainly in a deep green dress that
might have been expensive at one time but was showing signs
of wear at the hem and cuffs. Similarly, her shoes were of fine

quality but worn noticeably at the heels, and the handbag she carried had a frayed strap. She was strikingly tall, with flaxen blond hair braided and secured on the top of her head in a very German style. Her complexion was flawless, her eyes a pale blue. She looked, Estelle thought, like a damn poster for the sturdy, wholesome maidens of the Bund Deutscher Mädel.

"Three o'clock, but only on Fridays," Estelle said slowly.

It was the correct response for the correct question, but it had been asked by a single agent. Not a pair.

Estelle glanced about but there was no one nearby on the lawn next to the basilica. "You are Celine."

"Yes. And you are La Chanteuse."

Estelle stared at the blond woman, wondering where she was from. She spoke like a Parisian native. "Are you alone?"

"Yes."

"Where is your partner?"

"Dead."

Estelle shifted the straps of her handbag uneasily. There were any number of reasons an agent might die, discovery and capture being the one that most concerned her. If the surviving agent hadn't been careful, she could be being watched right now—

"He died from the jump," Celine said, as if reading her mind. "Well, not the jump so much as the landing."

Estelle couldn't tell if the woman was in shock or if she was as unmoved at the disaster as she seemed to be. "The landing?"

"He missed his jump and landed in the trees. It took us hours to cut him down." Celine's explanation was made with no fanfare, merely a measure of regret.

Not in shock at all, Estelle decided. Simply methodical. A

veritable ice princess. Estelle wasn't sure if that reassured her or not. Involuntarily, her hand went to the pendant at her throat, the tiny, enameled locket lying warm against her skin.

"That's a pretty necklace," Celine said, making Estelle start.

Estelle released the pendant and pulled the collar of her coat up. The woman was watching her with those unflinching, icy eyes, and she didn't like it. It was as if she was peering directly into Estelle's thoughts. "What do you require from me?" she demanded with more sharpness than she had intended.

Celine did not seem to take offense. "Your help."

"The instructions I received were that I was to provide you with society introductions at the Ritz Hotel. I am assuming that that is still the case."

"Yes and no."

Estelle frowned. "I don't like riddles. Speak plainly."

"My partner, who was the other half of my cover story, is dead. I need a new one."

"A new partner or a new cover story?"

"Both."

"And what does that have to do with me?"

The tall blond woman reached into her handbag. She withdrew a small brass cylinder, a logo in crimson ink swirled across one side. "Here."

Estelle took it from the agent. "Lipstick?"

"Yes. And this." Celine delved into her handbag again and withdrew a beautifully engraved silver powder compact with the same logo across the top. She passed it to Estelle.

"What are these?"

"A sample of the small fortune in black market cosmetics I currently have in my hotel room. What I was supposed to help my husband sell."

"Sell to whom?"

"To the wives of the German officers and diplomats staying in the Ritz suites, the mistresses of collaborators and
industrialists enjoying their new position in high society in the
Ritz dining rooms, and the actresses and starlets that seem to
crawl out of the Ritz bedsheets at regular intervals."

Estelle stared at her. "You're well informed."

Celine shrugged.

"And is this still your intention? To sell to the . . . women at
the Ritz?"

"Perhaps. I still need entrance to the hotel."

Estelle opened the compact and examined the pressed
powder. "With an introduction from me," she said, snapping
the compact closed again, "these will sell quickly. These
women you speak of will be delighted. Though I warn you,
competition for the best of what you offer will inevitably
incite fierce grudges."

"Mmm."

"The couture houses that still remain open would likely
buy the whole lot from you without even blinking," Estelle
added, "if you needed to get rid of these and were considering
a different approach."

Celine seemed to ponder her answer. "How would you
have introduced us if I had arrived with my husband?"

Estelle handed the compact and lipstick back. "Something
very casual. A couple I met while shopping, perhaps. We fell
into conversation, you mentioned your reason for being in
Paris, and I would have suggested that you might get a better
price presenting your wares to the discriminating individuals
at the Ritz as opposed to wholesale liquidation to a couture
house."

"Clever."

"Not clever. Safe. You know nothing about me, and I know nothing about you other than what we've presented publicly. Keep distance maximized and lies minimized."

The agent gazed at Estelle, her expression impenetrable. Estelle hid a frown. She was generally very good at reading people but she couldn't read this woman.

"I need someone who knows the Ritz," Celine said after a long silence. "Its residents and, more importantly, its layout."

"And you think that I have this knowledge?"

"You spend a great deal of time at the Ritz. With your wealth, your beauty, your style, you are accepted as one of them."

Trepidation stirred within Estelle. "Who told you all that?"

"No one told me anything." Celine shrugged and slipped the cosmetics back into her handbag. "Most of that was conjecture. Based on your appearance, your speech, and your familiarity with the possible reaction of the Ritz residents to my presence, as well as the needs of couture houses."

"Conjecture?" Estelle repeated.

"Was I right?"

"Jesus." This ice princess was disturbing. Estelle started walking, heading back toward the front of the basilica.

Celine fell into step beside her. "I need to become one of them too. Blend in. Just long enough to get what I came for. And I need you to help me do that."

Estelle stopped. "You don't need me. All you need is an empty Luftwaffe bed that requires warming," she snapped. "You simply need to become a horizontal collaborator. That would seem like the obvious answer, no?"

Something flickered across Celine's face, an emotion so

fleeting that Estelle was unable to name it. "I've considered that. I'd prefer not to do so."

Estelle regretted her impulsive words almost immediately but there was something about this particular agent that had her on edge. A cold intensity that Estelle wasn't sure she could trust.

They had almost reached the top of the wide stone steps, still in the shadows of the low, overhanging branches. People were trudging up and down the expanse from the narrow street that snaked around the basilica, still more on the lower staircases below that fell away toward the city. Estelle scrutinized the crowds but saw nothing out of place. Still, she couldn't shake the sense of disquiet that gripped her.

Estelle lowered her voice. "Look, I can provide you with introductions to these wives and mistresses and likely whatever officers or artists or industrialists you require. But I can't get involved in whatever they've sent you here to do," she said, shaking her head. "I have my own obligations and duties. I have people who depend on me, and I cannot afford the additional risk."

Celine said nothing.

"I'm sorry. I truly am," Estelle said. "There is a café in which you can find me at a certain time during the week. Vivienne will be able to tell you the specifics if you still wish me to make introductions. But beyond that, I can't help you—" She stopped abruptly as her eye was caught by a man emerging from the center of the three massive archways.

Jerome was wearing his usual threadbare suit, a paper tucked underneath one arm, and he looked not unlike the other men milling at the entrance to the basilica. Except for the fact that he wasn't milling. He was walking with purpose in her direction, looking neither left nor right, the expression on his face ominously tight. After the night they'd spent together, he'd vanished completely again, as Estelle had known he would. What she hadn't expected was to see him here, now, at the basilica in broad daylight unless he was—

Estelle's eyes flew to the space behind Jerome, and sure enough, a second man walked, following in his footsteps. He was young with sandy brown hair, a square jaw, broad shoulders, and deep-set eyes shadowed with fear. One hand was in his pocket, toying with whatever coins or possessions were in it, a cigarette held between the first two fingers of his other hand. He kept glancing over his shoulder, his entire bearing that of a flighty horse about to bolt. He took a desperate drag on his cigarette.

"*Merde*," Estelle whispered. The airman hadn't been adequately briefed on habits and mannerisms or had forgotten everything.

"He smokes like an American," Celine commented casually. She had moved to stand beside Estelle and had followed her gaze. "A nervous one."

And it was going to get him noticed, arrested, or killed. Worse, it might very well get Jerome noticed, arrested, or killed. Though death would come after both men were carted off to avenue Foch and put into sealed rooms where no one, save the Gestapo, would hear their screams. Where no one, save the Gestapo, would hear whatever secrets were torn from their lips. Like the identities of those who helped the line. Now and in the past.

The two Gestapo men who had passed Estelle earlier were now farther down the promenade, heading past the basilica, their backs still to her. But another pair of uniformed men had emerged from the shadows of the arches, moving slowly, craning their necks as they wove their way through a group of women. Their attention fell on Jerome, and one of them shouted and pointed.

Jerome was almost even with Estelle now. She could see the fear that dotted his forehead with perspiration. He looked up, shock blooming across his face as he recognized her. In a smooth motion, he dropped his paper and bent to pick it up.

"They were waiting," he said before tucking the paper back under his arm. "They're looking for me. Get him to Troyes. You know the house. Please." His desperation was clear. He continued down the wide stone steps without a moment of hesitation.

"Your friend?" Celine asked, neither woman watching him go.

"Something like that." Estelle was trying to think fast but right now her thoughts were muddled, her ability to deliberate and calculate frozen by fear. Which was even more terrifying. She needed to get the airman away from here. But how to do that without implicating or compromising herself?

There was a tiny part of her that simply wanted to run. To turn and walk away and not look back. But that safety would only be temporary.

"You two meet these…individuals often?" Celine asked quietly.

"Something like that." Estelle would worry later about the consequences of the obvious conclusion the agent had made.

The two Gestapo men on the promenade were now storming back in pursuit of Jerome, people scattering in front of them as they gave chase down the staircase. Estelle shrank back, away from the top of the stairs and farther beneath the canopy of the tree, as if she could make herself invisible. Jerome had almost reached the narrow street at the bottom of the stairs below. If he could make it a little farther, he would be quickly swallowed by the twisting tangle of Montmartre streets that fell to the west—

Another pair of Gestapo soldiers appeared at the bottom of the stairs. Jerome came to a stumbling stop, frantically looking back and forth between the men who had him trapped and were closing in. He spun in indecision, his hesitation costing him everything. The men who had been chasing him from above reached him first and knocked him forward. He fell down a handful of steps, landing awkwardly on his side. The men from below closed the gap, and the smaller of the two delivered a vicious kick to his head.

Jerome went limp, and in the next second was hauled to his feet and dragged the rest of the way down the stairs. A black car had pulled up, and one of the four men pulled the back door open. An insensible Jerome was shoved into the back, two of his captors getting into the car with him. The vehicle rolled off quickly and quietly. People who had stopped or cowered from the scene resumed their travels, eyes fixed firmly on the pavement as if nothing had happened.

Estelle grasped the balustrade, trying not to give in to the helpless terror and panic that was crashing around in her chest. She heard a high-pitched, muffled whimper, and it took her a second before she understood that it was coming from her. She dropped her head and focused on her breathing. Focused on what had not happened instead of what had. Jerome had not been killed. He was not dead. Not yet.

And the airman he had been guiding had not been caught with him.

Estelle's head snapped up. The American airman. Where was he? She turned and scanned the promenade.

The American had stopped like a cornered hare at the top of the stairs in front of the basilica, looking wildly about. Even a child would have been able to identify him as someone other than a Parisian visiting the basilica, and the two remaining officers were starting back up the stairs, heading directly toward him. Estelle had no idea what she could do to stop whatever was about to happen. She did know that Celine could not be here. Estelle turned to tell her just that but the agent was gone. She couldn't see Celine anywhere. Just as well.

With shaking limbs, Estelle pushed herself away from the safety of the shadowed balustrade. She did not know what she was going to do but she had to do something. She hadn't gone more than three steps before she stopped abruptly, horror mingling with disbelief. Celine was bearing down on the airman like a woman greeting a long-lost relative. Or lover. It was difficult to tell which.

Celine reached the airman, put a hand on his arm, and yanked the cigarette from his mouth, tossing it to the side. "Do you speak French?" she demanded.

The man looked at her without comprehension.

Estelle cursed inwardly. Of course he didn't.

"Don't speak no matter what," Celine said in a low voice, switching to English. "And for fuck's sake, look stupid."

The American gaped at her, which, Estelle suspected, was exactly what she had intended with her language. She angled him casually away from the top of the wide stairway, where the Gestapo officers were almost upon them now, their boots thudding with an ominous rhythm. Estelle turned away slightly, still far enough away to avoid notice but still close enough to hear the conversation.

"Where have you been?" Celine's sudden exclamation was loud enough to startle Estelle and make the people nearest her turn and stare. "I've been looking everywhere for you. You know what I've told you about wandering away from me." The agent was checking the airman over with her hands the way a distraught mother might examine a toddler after he had a tumble on a playground.

No, not checking him over. Subtly searching his pockets. With her back to the approaching officers and the nimble fingers of an accomplished pickpocket, Celine lifted his papers from his coat pocket, glanced at them, and tucked them into her handbag. With the same easy movements, the agent adjusted her cuff and palmed a long, thin knife. The narrow blade flashed briefly before it vanished once again beneath the sleeve of her dress.

Estelle swallowed with difficulty. A small voice in the back of her mind wondered if this woman London had sent was not so much an agent as an assassin. And if she would spill blood on the pavement here long before she had a chance to reach her real target.

"You there!" thundered a voice. "Stop."

Estelle's heart hammered in her chest, fear crackling through like a lightning storm, and she edged a little farther away.

The officer who had spoken was broad and tall, silver hair visible beneath the brim of his hat. He wore a grey uniform with braid at his shoulder, the pair of jagged Ss on one side of his collar and the diamonds on the other. His partner was younger—much younger—with a narrow face, sharp nose, and equally sharp eyes. Estelle recognized him instantly. The

Gestapo officer who had once watched her sing at the Ritz and then questioned her with the intense suspicion of a raptor. She searched her memory for his name.

Sergeant Schwarz.

He lacked both braid and diamonds on his uniform, though the strip of black at his shoulders still marked him as a sergeant. Clearly, the ambition that Colonel Meyer had alluded to that night had not come to fruition. His expression was drawn and bitter, and that, more than anything, terrified Estelle. He said nothing, only studied Celine and the American with the same intensity he had once regarded Estelle in a Ritz salon.

Celine turned and looked at the Gestapo officers, and her face split into a blinding smile full of gratitude. "Oh, thank you all for finding him," she said. "I was so worried."

The officers' expressions momentarily matched that of the American—blank and confused.

"He keeps getting away on me," Celine continued, switching effortlessly to German with a fluency that put Estelle's to shame. "I can't leave him alone for a second. Yesterday, he followed a child holding a kitten. Today it was someone else."

The older officer—maybe a major, Estelle thought—stepped closer to Celine. "You sound German," he said.

Another brilliant smile was bestowed upon the officers. "Half," Celine said proudly. "My mother was from Berlin."

"What is your name?" he demanded.

"Sophie Beaufort," Celine replied earnestly, with just the right amount of respect.

"And this man? Who is he?"

"He is a family friend. Our mothers grew up together

in Berlin. We've known each other forever. In fact, I think our parents hoped we would marry one day," Celine babbled on.

"He should answer for himself," the major growled.

"He can't," Celine explained.

The airman, to his credit, was staring vacuously up at the gleaming cathedral spires and seemed oblivious to the entire conversation.

"What is wrong with him?" Schwarz finally spoke, his hand playing with the holster at his waist.

"He was in Blois when it was bombed by the Luftwaffe," Celine explained. "The doctors said it damaged his mind and his nerves."

"Ought to put him out of his misery, then," the sergeant suggested coldly.

Celine gasped. "What?"

The man shrugged. "You'd do the same for a dog. A kindness to just put him down."

Horror boiled up into the back of Estelle's throat. She'd seen men, women, and children shot in the streets for lesser reasons than being a simpleton.

"You can't," Celine said, her pale eyes widening and suddenly brimming with tears. "He helps keep me safe. A deterrent to those who would take advantage of an unaccompanied woman. He may not be the same man he once was, but he is still a good man."

The American was now watching a pair of doves quarrel in the branches of the trees, an empty smile on his face.

"No one is putting anyone down." The major frowned at his subordinate before turning back to Celine. "What are you doing here? In Paris?"

"Well, officially I am in Paris to sell beauty products. Cosmetics," Celine said. "But—"

"Cosmetics?" It was Schwarz who interrupted her, his question thick with suspicion.

"Why, yes." Celine slipped a hand into her bag and withdrew the lipstick and compact she had shown Estelle. She held them out to the older officer, who took them gingerly. "It's a family company," she went on. "You can keep those samples, of course," Celine told him with renewed enthusiasm. "Perhaps you have a wife or a special girl who might like them?"

The major looked pleased with her suggestion. "I do, yes." The makeup vanished into his pocket.

"I think she'll be very happy. The lip color is most popular—"

"You're not wearing cosmetics," the sergeant accused.

"Of course not," Celine said with a faint frown. "I'm not working today. I was praying."

"Praying?" His question was dripping with scorn.

"Yes. Before she died, my mother asked that I take Colin to Sacré-Coeur. She wasn't Catholic, of course, but she said that this was as close to heaven as one might get in Paris. She told me to pray for a miracle for him," Celine continued, with a slight wobble of her chin. "It sounds silly, I know, but I could not refuse her that request."

The sergeant was studying Celine with an expression of cold calculation. "You're lying."

Celine looked like he had struck her. "I'm not lying. I swear on the grave of my mother."

"Ah, yes, your mother. Your German mother. From Munich, you said."

"No, Berlin. She grew up not far from the zoo. She was enamoured with the aquarium."

"I don't think—"

"Let me see your papers." The older man interrupted the exchange while casting a look of annoyance at his subordinate.

Celine dug into her handbag again and produced her papers.

"And his? Where are they?"

She withdrew the American's papers next. "I keep them safe. God only knows where he might leave them."

Every muscle in Estelle's body tensed. If the American's papers were badly forged or missing crucial elements, she would be able to do nothing. Celine would be arrested no matter how well she spoke German and no matter how exquisitely she spun tales.

The major examined both sets and handed them back with a grunt. "You should have a care. There are dangerous men in this city. Spies and saboteurs and communists."

"I'll be careful," Celine promised. "This city needs more good men like you." Another one of her blinding smiles was directed back toward the German officers.

The major puffed out his chest and straightened his shoulders, blinking under the force of Celine's smile. "That's true. Good afternoon," he bade and moved off.

Schwarz didn't move right away. Instead, he gazed at Celine and then the American for a long moment before he finally followed.

Estelle leaned against the balustrade, pretending to rummage in her handbag for something. Her mouth was dry, and icy beads of perspiration were sliding down her spine. When she looked up again, Celine had linked her arm through the airman's and was leading him slowly and deliberately back toward the stairs.

She closed her bag and struck out toward them. "Stop at the bottom of the garden," Estelle said quietly as she brushed by them. "I'll find you." She immediately headed in the opposite direction, heading toward the basilica entrance.

Estelle stopped just outside the massive bronze doors of the sanctuary, pretending to be awed by the rendition of the Last Supper, the carved men still oblivious to the wolf in their midst. She would need to contact Vivienne. She would need to let someone in Jerome's network know what had happened.

She tried not to dwell on the image of him being shoved into that car, or the knowledge that he would be tortured and possibly killed. She tried not to think about any of that, not right now, because if she did she would fold into herself in a fog of fear and panic and that would help no one. Not Jerome, not Celine, and not the airman who had somehow remained unscathed.

If Estelle had been the praying sort, she would have prayed for the life of Jerome. She would have prayed for a way out of this wretched situation. She was not the praying sort, however, so all she did was lean against the cold stone while her pulse slowed and the terror drained slowly from her limbs.

She closed her eyes and forced herself to think.

Twenty minutes later, Estelle found Celine and the Allied airman at the base of the butte. Celine's arm was still linked securely through the American's, and if Estelle didn't know better, they might have been a handsome couple out for a stroll. Except upon closer examination, one might mark the pallor of Celine's complexion. Perhaps the agent wasn't as cold and remote as Estelle had thought after all.

"Follow me," she said as she walked by, the soles of her shoes tapping across rue Ronsard.

She didn't need to give Celine further instruction. The agent fell in a discreet distance behind her.

Estelle had made the difficult decision to take them back to her building. She'd considered using whatever hotel Celine was using but discarded that idea. The American, whoever or whatever he was, needed to be hidden somewhere safer than an unknown building with too many eyes. Estelle had no idea where he was coming from or where he was destined or who was supposed to have taken him farther, but she could sort those details out once the immediate risk was removed. She needed him off the streets and out of sight now.

She was less sure what to do with Celine.

In another forty minutes, they had reached her building, Estelle careful to take a circuitous route. She used shop windows and street corners to watch for any signs that they were being followed but she saw nothing and no one out of the ordinary.

Estelle entered her building and started up the stairs, stopping just high enough that she would be out of sight of anyone passing by on street level. Within three minutes, Celine and the airman also entered the building, Celine's arm still linked with the American's. She glanced up and nodded once at Estelle.

Estelle turned and made her way up to her apartment, unlocked her door, and let herself in. She left the door cracked open and swiftly checked the rooms to ensure that nothing had been left out that might betray Aviva's presence.

She was meticulous about that to the point of paranoia but Aviva's life might well depend on it.

She returned to the front entrance just as the pair let themselves in, closing the door quietly behind them. Without being asked, Celine guided the airman in, telling him in low tones to avoid the windows.

Estelle took off her coat and tossed it on the back of the sofa.

"Who are you?" the American asked, looking around.

"Doesn't matter," Estelle replied.

Celine said nothing.

"I'm supposed to be taken to a train this afternoon," he told them.

"That will have to wait," Estelle replied unapologetically. "Do you understand what just happened?"

The airman scuffed his toe on the edge of the rug and shrugged.

"Let me tell you, then," Estelle said, trying to keep her voice steady. "The man who was supposed to guide you through this city was taken by the Gestapo and is either dead or wishing he was." She stopped, her voice catching. She squeezed her eyes shut, willing herself not to think about what was happening to Jerome at this very second.

"What am I supposed to do now?"

Estelle opened her eyes. "You will say nothing and see nothing and hear nothing until I figure out a way to get you to the people who can take you where you need to go."

"How long will that take?"

Celine glanced sharply at the airman but remained silent.

"As long as it takes," Estelle replied, trying to answer him patiently. He would be anxious, no doubt. She tried not to blame him.

"I need my papers back." He was talking to Celine now.

The agent shrugged and retrieved them from her pocket, handing them to him wordlessly.

"And I would like to know what you—"

A harsh banging and muffled shouting interrupted whatever he had been going to say, freezing Estelle where she stood and sending her heart into her throat. An avalanche of memories blindsided her, recollections of another time when she had heard such banging. But, as last time, it was not her door that was being pounded upon. It sounded as though it was the apartment doors on the floors beneath her. Harsh, guttural demands to open up echoed up the stairway.

"What the hell is that?" the American croaked. "Is that them? The Nazis? Are they looking for me?"

"You were followed to the building." Estelle could barely get the words out around the renewed fear.

"No," Celine whispered. "I watched. I was careful."

"Not careful enough. We weren't careful enough." Not wary enough of the bitter sergeant whose eyes still burned with malice and ambition.

"What about the man who was arrested? Does he know about this apartment?"

Yes, Estelle thought but she was shaking her head. She would not accept what the agent was implying.

The unmistakable sounds of heavy boots on marble stairs added to the din. Someone pounded on the door opposite hers. A shout followed, another demand to open up.

"It doesn't matter. Your door is next." Celine had gone pale but when she spoke her voice was steady. "You should hide. They never saw you. Whoever is at that door will leave if I go with them. I'll say I lost him again." She gestured at the American.

"No." Estelle was shaking her head. An old, familiar anger reignited, reducing the fear to a brittle, blackened after-thought.

"Then tell them I broke in. Took you hostage, forced you

to let me inside." The wicked-looking knife appeared in the agent's hand again as if by magic. "I'll make it believable."

It might be tempting, if not for Aviva. But it would never work. Because once the Gestapo believed that they'd found a spy in this apartment, they would tear it apart looking for more. And inevitably Aviva would be found. The airman would be found. It was far better to do what Estelle had always done. Invite the enemy in.

"No. Follow me and hurry."

Estelle led them into her bedroom as silently as possible. With quick movements, she opened the wardrobe, swept the half-dozen hanging gowns to the side, and released the hidden door.

The little girl was sitting at the table, her pencils and paper in front of her. Estelle put her finger to her lips and offered Aviva a reassuring smile.

"Hello, darling," she whispered. "I need your help."

Aviva blinked at her.

"I have two friends I need you to help hide. Can you do that for me?"

Aviva nodded, her eyes wide.

"And I need you to be even quieter than a mouse." A ridiculous thing to say because Aviva still hadn't uttered a single word in almost a year. "Can you show them how?"

Aviva nodded again.

A fist crashed against her apartment door, making Estelle jump. She turned, pulled off her brightly adorned hat, and tossed it into the hidden room. "Get in," she ordered the agent and airman.

Both climbed in without a word, and Estelle latched the hidden door, replaced the garments, and closed the wardrobe.

The harsh male voice in the hallway had been joined by a shrill feminine one and the wail of a baby. Estelle hustled back out past the gleaming dining table just as a fist crashed against her door again.

She took a deep breath, smoothed her hair, arranged her features into one of perplexed confusion, and went to the door.

Scharführer Schwarz was standing in the doorframe, one hand again resting on the pistol at his waist, the other suspended in front of him. Beside him, Frau Hoffmann hovered, her small daughter on her hip. The German wife of a French industrialist to whom the war and all its financial opportunities had been inordinately kind, she had moved into the empty apartment less than a week after Rachel had been dragged from it. Estelle had exchanged less than a dozen words with the vitriolic frau, who seemed to resent everything French, including Estelle.

The door to the Wylers' old apartment was open, and Estelle could see into the space. Their once cherished bookcase was now filled with trinkets instead of tomes. The pretty carved rocking chair that Alain had made Hannah when Aviva was born was gone, replaced with a chunky cabinet filled with more baubles.

The rug that had lain at the entrance, once stained with Serge's blood, was also gone.

"Good afternoon, Frau Hoffmann," Estelle said, blinking rapidly. "Has something happened? Is something wrong? Is there an attack? I try to listen for the planes but I always worry that—"

"It's her," the woman said waspishly, speaking in German. She swatted her daughter's hand away from the string of pearls at her throat. "Arrest her. She'll be the one."

"What is happening?' Estelle asked again, feigning fearful confusion. "Who are you?"

"Scharführer Schwarz." He pinned Estelle with cold blue eyes. "It took you a long time to answer the door, Mademoiselle."

"You scared me. What is happening?"

The sergeant pushed his way into Estelle's apartment. "A woman and a man were seen entering this building. Traitors." He advanced farther. "We suspect they are hiding somewhere. We are checking all the apartments."

"You think they're still here?" Estelle wrapped her hands around her waist. "Are they very dangerous?"

"The enemy is always dangerous." He paused. "Do you live alone, mademoiselle?"

"Yes."

"I hear things coming from this apartment when she's not there, you know." Frau Hoffmann was standing just outside Estelle's door, nearly shouting to be heard. "There is someone living in there with her."

The hair rose at the back of her neck at the idea of the woman listening at her door. Listening for Aviva.

"I can assure you that I don't have anyone living with me. Perhaps it is the sounds from the street you hear. Or perhaps the apartment below."

"And I hear her come in late sometimes." Frau Hoffmann was not to be deterred. "When I'm up with the baby. Past curfew. Sometimes she's with someone. I can hear voices."

Schwarz went to the window and drew the curtains aside with the barrel of his pistol, peering down. "Is this true?" he asked.

"That I come in late? Of course it's true," Estelle said. "But I have a pass. And often an escort home."

"What?"

Estelle chose her words carefully. "I sing at the Ritz. Occasionally a cabaret if there is a special performance. I can show you my papers."

That stopped the sergeant. "I remember you."

"Oh?" Estelle blinked.

"I've seen you sing. And dally with the Luftwaffe officers at the Ritz."

"I merely try to offer a little entertainment. A distraction for those missing their families and their homes."

Schwarz sneered. "I'm sure you do."

"If you need proof of my passes, you may ask Colonel Meyer. He is the one who makes such arrangements for me."

"Colonel Meyer?"

"Yes," she chirped. "I had dinner with him just last week."

A momentary flash of uncertainty appeared across his face as he was no doubt trying to determine exactly what Estelle was to the colonel. The Boches, if nothing else, seemed to have an almost fanatical respect for the chain of command, and risking the displeasure of a higher-ranking individual seemed to be something that one could leverage. If one did so carefully.

Estelle wasn't sure what conclusion the sergeant might have come to but his smug arrogance was back. He released the curtains and circled the two sofas, stopping to pick up an issue of *Carrefour* Estelle had left out. He tossed it back on the table, where it slid to the floor. "I need to check the rest of the apartment."

Estelle widened her eyes fearfully. "Why? You think they got into my apartment somehow?"

"Did you know," Schwarz said, moving to the side table and picking up the photo of Estelle in the Mercedes her parents had gifted her, "that before I came here I was a police officer?

My father wanted me to be a doctor, but it wasn't the workings of men's bodies that fascinated me, it was the workings of men's minds. Criminal minds. The ability of an individual to lie so perfectly and so convincingly that they could, with the right representation, literally get away with murder."

Estelle wrung her hands, pretending to be completely oblivious to the clear threat that was embedded in his words. "I don't understand."

Faint annoyance washed over the sergeant's face. "We stopped a woman today, near Sacré-Coeur. She lied to us. My superior didn't think so, but I am sure of it. So I followed her and the simpleton she claimed to be with. And they entered this building. And now I have men checking every apartment. Yours included."

"Oh. Well, then I thank you," she breathed.

Schwarz frowned and muttered something under his breath. He set the photo down and stalked through the dining room and toward the kitchen. Finding it empty, he pivoted on his heel and marched down the hallway to her bedroom. Estelle followed him, leaning against the doorframe again and linking her hands in front of her. Like he did in the living room, the sergeant went to the window and peered out. Clearly finding nothing of note, he turned his attention to her dressing room, and wedged himself in. He poked his hand through the clothing, his gun still held in front of him. From there he crouched and looked under the bed, his weapon sweeping the space. When he stood, his face was flushed with frustration. He surveyed the room, and his eyes fell on the heavy wardrobe.

He lifted his gun and wrenched the door open.

Estelle's fingernails dug into her palms, and she forced herself to relax her hands.

"Look at this," the sergeant murmured.

Estelle's stomach plummeted. On unfeeling legs she stepped forward.

Schwarz was running his long fingers through the silk of a sapphire gown, embroidered and edged with tiny pearls at the bodice. "Fit for a princess, no?" He yanked the couture gown from the wardrobe.

"It's what I sing in," Estelle said, and the tremor in her voice wasn't altogether manufactured. She needed to get him away from the wardrobe before he completely emptied it. A cough, a sneeze, a pencil rolling to the floor, the creak of the cot—there were a hundred different things that might betray them all.

"Mmm." He tossed the gown on the bed and reached for another, the confection of lemon-bright crepe. "My wife would have liked to wear such things," he said. "I would like to have bought her such things. But I could never afford it, no matter how many hours I worked. Yet here, in Paris, a cabaret whore dresses like a queen. Lives like a queen." He was stroking the yellow-crepe gown with the muzzle of his gun. "Perhaps I might take her a gift. So many fine things in this apartment. So much to choose from." The yellow dress joined the sapphire one on the bed. He reached for another gown, this one the color of fresh cream and embroidered with yards of gold thread.

"Choose, then," Estelle said loudly as his hands closed over the cool silk. "Those dresses are all gifts from Reichsmarschall Göring. I'm sure he wouldn't mind."

The sergeant snatched his hand away as if he'd been burned and stared at Estelle.

She smiled prettily back. "The Reichsmarschall is very fond

of couture," she told him. "And he said he thought I looked like an angel in that dress. Perhaps your wife will too. Look like an angel, that is. I will tell him that."

He closed the wardrobe with jerky movements. Colonel Meyer's name had merely given him pause. The mention of Göring had had the intended effect.

Amid all the lies, sometimes the truth was the most useful.

The officer slid his pistol back into its holster. He retraced his steps through the apartment, Estelle trailing after him.

Frau Hoffmann was still skulking in her doorway, bouncing her fussing daughter. She glanced up, seemingly crestfallen when Schwarz returned empty-handed. "Did you find where she's hidden them?" she demanded. "The traitors? Because I know she has."

"There is nothing here." The sergeant stared hard at Estelle, as if trying to understand what she was. Socialite, singer, whore, mistress, German sympathizer, or all of the above. Or maybe something else entirely. "But I won't stop looking. Traitors will always be traitors. People don't change."

CHAPTER

16

Gabriel

NORFOLK, ENGLAND
8 JULY 2017

Millbrook House hadn't changed in two hundred years.
Well, that wasn't entirely accurate, Gabriel reflected, for the house had electricity and modern plumbing,
and a collection of ride-on lawn mowers and small tractors
now lived in the outbuildings where horses had once dwelled.
But every time he came here, he liked to envision the people
who had built this house.

There would have been a small army of skilled labourers
who had crafted the beautiful manor, and no expense had been
spared with an eye to design. The house was three stories,
rows of large, rectangular windows set uniformly into the rich
burnt-umber stone and topped by a smooth slate roof. The
center of the house was dominated by a wide expanse that extended forward from the wings, rising to a triangular roofline
with small crenellations on top, giving it a slightly medieval

flair. A massive arched doorway at the bottom welcomed guests in grand style.

But it was the location that awed their visitors. Set up on a gentle rise and surrounded by carefully maintained and manicured gardens that had once made the cover of the BBC *Gardeners' World* magazine, Millbrook had a breathtaking view of the sea. Stretching away until the water joined the horizon in a merging of cerulean and azure on bright days, lead and silver on broody days, the vista never grew tiresome.

"Oh," breathed Lia as they turned off the main road and started the easy climb up the long, tree-lined drive. "What a beautiful spot."

"It is," Gabriel agreed, glancing over at her in the passenger seat. She had her nose pressed against the glass with the excitement of a small child, and it made him smile.

The ride up from London had been passed in relaxed companionship, some of it in comfortable silence, other parts in easy conversation. She'd been waiting outside for him when he'd fetched her from her hotel in the morning, and it had been easy to pick her out of the crowd long before he pulled up in front of the aging building. She was wearing another one of the pretty sundresses she seemed to favour, this one a deep emerald shot through with a swirling lawn-green pattern. It made her eyes seem more green than brown today, her cheeks flushed with color above her familiar smile. She'd tossed a well-travelled pack in the backseat of his car and slid into the passenger seat, and he'd had the alarming sensation of butterflies waking beneath his ribs.

As they drove, Lia had told him about her work and the many places it had taken her. In turn, she'd asked Gabriel dozens of questions about restoration, his schooling, and his travels. All light and easy-to-answer queries, and he wondered if that was on purpose. She did not raise the question of his own art again, nor did she inquire any further about the two paintings she'd asked him to sell to her.

Gabriel's knuckles tightened on the steering wheel as he turned up the drive to Millbrook. The idea that she admired his work enough to buy it was oddly thrilling. He hadn't had any plans at all for those two pieces, so it wasn't as though he regretted parting with them. But he'd meant what he'd said when he had made it clear in no uncertain terms he would not fall into the trap his grandfather and father had. Yet somehow Lia had turned his own words back on themselves and presented an argument that seemed unbeatable.

"Do you have an event here this weekend?" Lia asked, twisting back in her seat and yanking him out of his ruminations.

"A wedding," he replied, glancing at the staff who were setting up a gauzy white arbour and rows of white folding chairs near the center of the gardens. "And a movie shoot this week."

She rubbed her hands over her bare knees. "You must be booked solid over the summer."

"Elaine tells me we are." He guided the car past a florist's lorry and toward a small lane guarded by a sign stating that only employees were allowed past this point. "Elaine is our events coordinator," he explained. "She lives on the property in a converted cottage, and she is very good at what she does. My mother hired her almost fifteen years ago when she expanded the business from a small bed-and-breakfast. We now have the capacity to host much larger occasions like weddings, and we've opened the house up to the film industry." He followed the narrow road around the back of the house, bringing the car to a stop in a small lot where four other cars sat gleaming in the sunshine. "Elaine has systems and org charts and processes that only her assistants dare mess with, and even then, I'm not so sure there aren't bodies of assistants who messed just a little too much buried somewhere in the gardens."

Lia laughed. "What does your grandfather think of all this?"

"My grandfather doesn't have anything to do with the business, of course, and he lives entirely in the suite of rooms on the west corner of the manor. But I think he likes having people around. I think he enjoys knowing that the house is loved and utilized. It was my grandmother who first opened the house to weekend guests. Both she and my mother were of the same mind that a house of this size needed to work for our family if it was ever going to be sustainable." He paused, pulling up on the parking brake with far more force than was necessary. "That, and the fact that their respective husbands were chasing an unsustainable, entirely futile career path."

"Ah." Lia didn't comment on his last words and instead simply got out of the car and shaded her eyes as she squinted up at the manor. "That's a lot of space to heat in the winter."

Gabriel unfolded himself from his own seat. "You sound exactly like my mother. She looks at this house and sees an accounting sheet full of neat numbers and sums."

"Then I'll take that as a compliment." She dropped her hand, her lips twisting into a wry smile. "I, too, am rather partial to neat numbers and sums."

Gabriel leaned on the door of the car and watched Lia as she spun in a slow circle, taking in her surroundings. He suddenly had the urge to paint her just like this—the green of her dress a jewel floating against a backdrop of fern and olive that comprised the lawns and vegetation behind the house. The curve of her soft rose-colored lips, the halo of amber and gold around her head where the sunshine illuminated the flyaway wisps that had come loose from her ponytail.

His fingers curled, as if he held a brush in his hand.

"Do you think I could look at the gardens and the view out front before we go in? Just for a moment? Before they finish setting up?"

Gabriel straightened and cleared his throat, pressing his fingers flat on the roof of the car. "Of course. Come, follow me."

He resisted the urge to reach for her hand and instead simply waited for her as she skirted the car. They walked back up the lane, their feet crunching on the gravel.

"Are you a lord of something?" she asked conversationally as they rounded the side of the manor. "I meant to ask that earlier."

Gabriel glanced at her. "A lord?"

"This house is rather lordlike. And it sounds like it's been in your family a long time. It seemed like a reasonable possibility."

"Alas, I am not a lord of anything," Gabriel told her. "Nor is anyone in my family. Though the house was intended for one."

"Really? Who?"

"As my grandfather tells it, a rather self-absorbed viscount who decided, on something of a whim, to build himself a fine manor in 1814. Unfortunately, also on a whim, his lordship decided that he would look quite majestic in a military uniform. Despite his family's horrified protestations, he purchased himself a commission, marched off to Belgium in 1815, and, regrettably, did not survive the French. The house was never completed, fell into disrepair, and the viscount's family eventually sold it to the first person with enough money and the ambition to take on an unfinished pile of brick and stone. It's been in my family ever since."

"So the house outranks you," she teased.

"Completely." He led her into the neat maze of low hedges and past the arbour that was now upright. Two young women were twining white roses into the pillars. "You have an interest in the British peerage?"

Lia shrugged. "A passing one, maybe. Leftover remnants of my boarding school days, perhaps, when such things seemed to matter."

Gabriel suddenly understood. "Ah. That explains it."

"Explains what?"

"Your English is remarkably English."

"Dr. Sullivan would be very pleased to hear you say that. She was the headmistress."

"But you were born in France?"

"Yes, in Marseille."

"Yet you attended English boarding school." He phrased it less as a question and more as a comment, leaving it up to her if she wished to answer.

"Because my parents were away so often, boarding school seemed like the best option. They told me that it was important that I have a fluency in multiple languages. That I would appreciate the opportunities it afforded later on in life. They weren't wrong."

They had reached the edge of the garden, ringed by deep green hydrangeas covered in a riot of snow-white blooms. Narrow openings were spaced between them, and Lia slipped through one, Gabriel following her. Here, just on the other side of the garden, the view of the sea was unimpeded. The breeze was picking up, perfuming the warm air with a bouquet of sweet floral fragrances, rich tones of recently turned earth, and a subdued salty tang from the sea. Behind them a bee droned as it worked, and, above, a seabird shrilled as it wheeled across the sky.

"When I was young, I spent an Easter with my roommate's family farther up the coast in Scarborough," Lia said, closing her eyes, tipping her face up to the sun, and inhaling deeply. "It smelled exactly like this."

"You didn't spend those holidays with your family?" Gabriel asked and then regretted it immediately. All he had done was to repeat what she had just told him in a slightly accusing manner. The dynamics of her family were none of his business.

"My parents have always spent March to May in Portugal." Lia opened her eyes, and if she was offended by his question, she didn't show it. "Though they head to their chalet in Switzerland for the summers before it can get too hot. That's when I would go back to Marseille to stay with Grandmère, because she never travelled."

"Never?" Gabriel tried again to reconcile the photos of a vibrant, daring Estelle Allard he had seen in that Paris apartment with the sedentary picture Lia was painting of her grandmother.

"Not while I knew her. Though my mother told me that, when she was a child, Grandmère would go to Switzerland all the time. At least three or four times a year. As she got older, it was only once or twice, and then, eventually, she stopped altogether."

"Why?"

"I don't know. I don't know why she went or why she stopped. She didn't take my mother with her when she went."

"And your parents never took you with them on any of their travels either—" Gabriel snapped his mouth shut. He sounded like a judgemental idiot. Again. Just because his family did everything together didn't mean everyone else's did.

Lia shrugged, ostensibly still not bothered by his lack of tact. "No."

"That sounds...lonely."

"Sometimes, maybe. But you get used to being alone, I suppose. And often I had friends to stay with. And it's hard to complain or be ungrateful when I know I was given the best education money could buy. It's taken me far. No pun intended, because I have literally worked all over the globe."

Gabriel plucked a leaf from the hydrangea bush, thinking that the woman beside him would find the silver lining in anything that was thrown her way. It was an exceedingly admirable trait. And exceedingly attractive.

He held the leaf between his fingers. "Your grandmother must have liked the company during those summers."

"She did. And the older I got, the more I understood that." She rubbed her bare arms with her hands. "There was a period in my life, mostly when I was an oblivious teenager, when I resented those summers. When I had to decline invitations from my schoolmates who were going vacationing in Monaco or sailing in Spain or touring in Italy. I think, at that time, I saw it as a prison. A cage from which I could not escape."

"And now?"

"Now I think differently. There were no hugs and kisses and excited exclamations when I arrived in Marseille. But

Grandmère was always there at the train station to meet me, waiting on the platform before my train even pulled in. At home, the sheets in my room had always been freshly laundered, there was always a vase of cut lilies next to the bed, and the ancient bicycle that she kept in her shed out back always had fresh oil on the chain and not a speck of dust on the frame. And there was always a stack of new books, a collection of truly diverse nonfiction titles, with a little note in her handwriting suggesting what I might find intriguing about each one." Lia smiled in remembrance.

"You are an avid reader?"

"I became a reader. The purpose of the books, she always said, was not to learn what other people thought but to learn to think for myself. And whether she knew it or not, over time, she created a place for me. And I know this sounds a little backwards, but knowing I had that place made it easier for me to leave. Gave me the confidence and the freedom to venture far."

"What about your grandfather? You've never mentioned him."

"Never knew him. He died long before I was born, when my mother was still young. He was a prisoner for a time during the war. His health suffered afterward."

"And your grandmother never remarried?"

"Nope." She put her hands on her hips. " 'You only meet the love of your life once,' she said to me on the rare occasions when I asked. 'And if you're fool enough not to recognize that sort of love and treasure it for what it will become, then you never deserved it in the first place.' "

"That sounds tragically romantic."

Lia inclined her head. "Dramatic, at any rate." She gestured out toward the sea. "This is breathtaking. If I had to get married, I'd get married here."

"If you had to? I didn't take you for another romantic, Mademoiselle Leclaire."

She arched a brow and glanced at him. "Is that sarcasm I detect?"

"You make the institution of marriage sound like an incarceration."

"Have you been?"

"Incarcerated or married?"

She laughed. "Either."

"No. And no."

"Engaged?"

"No."

"Ever been tempted?"

The leaf tore between his fingers.

"Sorry. That was a personal question and none of my business."

"No, it's all right," Gabriel replied. "The truth of the matter is that my work has always been a priority."

"Now *that* I can completely understand," she said, "and endorse. Though I suspect you get far fewer well-meaning admonishments about your ticking biological clock than I do."

"Jesus." He tossed the shredded leaf away. "I'm sorry. People can be utter prats."

She gave one of her very French shrugs. "I ignore them. Not worth my time or energy."

"Have you? Ever been tempted?" He had no idea why he was asking this, other than that she had asked him first.

"No. I've never stayed in one place long enough for a serious relationship."

"Would you?"

"Would I what?"

"Stay. Would you stay if you met the love of your life? If you recognized what it might become, like your grandmère said?" He was veering into dangerous territory here, places he had no business going with Lia—a client. Yet for some reason, he wanted to know what Lia the woman would say.

Her hands dropped from her hips. "I don't know. Maybe."

He met her eyes, his mouth suddenly dry. He stepped back. "Come," he said, hoping his voice sounded smoother than it felt. "Let's go inside, and I'll introduce you to my grandfather." He took another step back for good measure. "He may ask you a million questions about your job and where you've travelled but I can guarantee that he will not inquire about your biological clock."

Lia laughed, her eyes crinkling at the corners. "Lead the way."

They retraced their steps back to his car and entered Millbrook through a very ordinary-looking rear door. As they stepped into the cool interior, Gabriel let his eyes adjust to the light after the brightness of the morning. They were in the family rooms, as the maintenance and custodial staff liked to call them—the suite of a half-dozen modern rooms where his grandfather lived and any family that came to visit stayed. In the rest of the house, the hall and ballrooms, library and guest rooms, music room and morning rooms had been painstakingly restored to their former Regency-era glory, making it popular with filmmakers and those wishing for a fairly-tale setting for their nuptials. Part of the original kitchens had even been restored, while the other, separate half had been renovated to provide a state-of-the-art kitchen for event caterers.

The kitchen that Gabriel and Lia were now in was a small, simple one, featuring modern maple cabinetry, marble countertops, and stainless-steel appliances. He started for the narrow door on the far side only to be brought up short by a figure that sailed through with an exclamation of delight.

"Gabriel!" the woman greeted him with a broad smile. "I'm so happy you are here. It's been too long since you visited us."

"I know," Gabriel agreed, embracing the woman and inhaling the familiar scent of vanilla that he had always associated with her.

"And you brought a guest." She pulled back and turned her radiant smile on Lia.

"Abigail, this is Aurelia Leclaire. She is a client," he said, "who is...helping me with some research."

"Call me Lia, please." Lia stepped forward and extended her hand.

"And this is Abigail Denworth," Gabriel added. "The soul responsible for keeping Millbrook upright and all Seymours sane since 1972."

"I'm the housekeeper," Abigail laughed, ignoring Lia's extended hand and enveloping her in a welcoming hug.

"She's family," Gabriel corrected.

Abigail released Lia and patted her chestnut hair that was liberally threaded with grey. "If you're hoping to see your grandfather, he's in the reading room," she told him, her blue eyes twinkling. "He's already speculating what new book you've brought him this time."

Gabriel smiled. It was a long-standing tradition. "I've actually brought him something a little different. Some old photos."

"Oh? What sort of photos?"

"Some pictures of his sister from before the war." *And during*, he thought, though he didn't voice that.

"Oh, he'll like that, I think." Abigail clasped her hands together. "Such a bond, that William had with his sister. Like two peas in a pod, my mum often said. She spoke of Sophie often."

"Abigail's mum was the housekeeper at Millbrook before Abigail took over her duties," Gabriel explained to Lia.

"Could I see the photos?" Abigail asked. "I love looking at bits of history from this house."

"Of course." Lia pulled the familiar folder from her backpack and handed Abigail one of the photos in its protective sleeve.

Abigail pulled a pair of reading glasses from her sweater pocket and settled them on the bridge of her nose. "Oh yes, this is Sophie," she murmured. "Though she looks like a film star here. I've never seen photos of her like this before—the ones your grandfather keeps here at Millbrook are mostly childhood photos and those taken before she left for Poland. Wherever did you get this?"

Lia glanced at him, and Gabriel nodded.

"I don't suppose the name Estelle Allard means anything to you?" Lia asked.

"I don't think so," Abigail said. "Who is she?"

"She was my grandmother," Lia told her. "And I found that picture in her apartment after she passed. In Paris."

The housekeeper's forehead creased. "Good heavens. What a small world. They must have been friends, yes?" She tapped the edge of the photo. "I think Sophie studied in Paris."

"She did," Gabriel confirmed. "In 1933 and '34."

Abigail turned the photo over and squinted at the date

written in faded ink in the corner. "Wait. This photo says 1942. That can't be right. Sophie died before that. In the bombing of Warsaw."

Gabriel grimaced. "I'm not so sure anymore. That she died in Warsaw, that is."

"You think she's alive?" The housekeeper's head came up so quickly that her glasses slid down her nose.

"No. I don't think that, though I can't really prove anything one way or the other at the moment."

"Heavens. How...extraordinary." Abigail took off her glasses and handed the photo back to Lia. "And you've come to ask your grandfather about it?"

"Yes. There is an issue of...some artwork wrapped up in this anomaly. Property we're trying to return to rightful owners. My father doesn't know anything. About the art or the photos. I was hoping Grandfather might."

The housekeeper was shaking her head. "He doesn't speak of those years. Of the war, or anything that went on during it."

"I know. I'm hoping he might now."

"You be careful. I don't know what you're thinking or what those photos mean but William's heart is old and tired, and I'm not sure it could stand being broken all over again where his sister is concerned," Abigail warned. "My mum told me that the loss of his parents was one thing but it was the loss of his sister that almost accomplished what the prison camps had failed to do."

Gabriel shifted his bag on his shoulder. "I rather wish we could talk to your mum."

"Aye," Abigail agreed. "My knowledge of the war and all its tragedies and hardships is a secondhand account. Mum lived here through it all. Looked after a number of children that were sent here from London for safekeeping, as well as a few soldiers who came here to recover. She kept clippings and letters and leaflets and photos so that I might understand the uncertainty and the chaos of that time. If the war did anything, it turned Mum into a packrat, not willing to throw anything away. Though her efforts certainly kept me from ever being ungrateful for what I had growing up."

"Where?" Lia asked.

"I beg your pardon?" Abigail swung around to look at Lia.

"Where did your mum keep all of those things that she shared with you? Do you still have them?"

The housekeeper blinked. "I don't know. I haven't thought about all of that in years. I suppose anything that Mum might have saved would be up in the attic. We go up from time to time to look for pieces for the house, but I've never looked for anything Mum might have kept. Never had reason to."

"Could we take a look?" Gabriel asked.

Abigail shrugged. "No matter to me. It is your house, after all. But fair warning, stay out of the way of the wedding planners and guests or you'll have Elaine breathing fire down your neck."

Gabriel chuckled. "We've been warned."

"I don't know what she would have kept during the war that would tell you anything about your family that you probably don't already know," Abigail said dubiously.

"Worth a look, I think." Gabriel shrugged. "We'll pop in to see Grandfather and then take a look this afternoon when he's napping."

"Will you tell me if you find anything?" she asked.

"Of course."

"Well, good luck, then," Abigail said. "And remind your grandfather that lunch will be served at one."

★ ★ ★

Gabriel led Lia into the modest room they'd always called the reading room. The long, tall windows faced southwest, making the room almost perpetually bright, even on the days when the sun was hidden by banks of rolling cloud. Between each window, an equally tall bookcase stood, filled not with the leather-bound tomes that graced the study in the restored section of the house, but with well-worn, dog-eared novels that had been loved many times over.

Two comfortable couches sat kitty-corner to each other, an odd assortment of plaid throws draped over the dark grey cushions, and end tables covered in framed photographs flanked each. Mismatched wing-backed chairs were edged close to the windows, a collection of cross-stitched cushions depicting dogs and what Gabriel thought might be a chicken resting against the backs. A small television sat against one wall, though Gabriel couldn't remember ever watching much TV in this room, even growing up. It was a room for visiting or reading or deliberating over the wooden chessboard that had a place of honour on a table between the two couches.

William Seymour was sitting in a wheelchair by the farthest window, his eyes closed. Yet even at his advanced age, Gabriel could still see glimpses of the young man he had once been. His shoulders were still broad, his fingers long and graceful. The color in his complexion suggested he might have just come in from outside, and even the deep lines of his face did not detract from an aquiline nose and a square jaw.

He was wearing a pair of noise-cancelling headphones over his fringe of white hair.

"Is he asleep?" Lia whispered from behind Gabriel.

"No." Gabriel shook his head.

William suddenly barked out a laugh, a rough, harsh sound.

"He's listening to a book." Gabriel stepped into the room and knocked as loudly as he could on the door as he did so.

His grandfather's eyes popped open behind round spectacles, and his face immediately creased into a delighted smile. "Gabriel," he said, fumbling with the portable player that rested in his lap. He pulled the headphones from his head. "Abigail said you had arrived. I'm so glad you're here." His voice was gravelly, age roughening his words.

"Me too." Gabriel crossed the room and bent to embrace him. "I'm sorry I haven't been up to Millbrook more as of late."

"Bah," William said, waving his hand. "You're busy, and I'm glad for it. Young men should be busy. When you get to my age, there is plenty of time to sit in the sun and listen to others tell tales."

"What are you listening to?" Gabriel asked.

"Cornwell. I do so enjoy the adventures." His blue eyes shifted past Gabriel to Lia and a sly smile spread across his face and a bushy white eyebrow lifted. He put his headphones aside as Lia advanced into the room. "Abigail mentioned you had brought a guest. Do introduce us."

"Of course." Gabriel turned to Lia. "This is Miss Aurelia Leclaire, visiting from Paris."

"It is so wonderful to meet you, Mr. Seymour," Lia said, coming forward. She took his grandfather's outstretched hand and kissed both his cheeks.

"A pleasure to meet you as well," he rasped. "Forgive me for not rising." He stuck out his left leg, a pinned trouser folded over midcalf. "The old peg leg was achy so I didn't put my robot leg on today." He gestured to one of the wing-backed chairs beside him. "Please, won't you be seated?"

"Thank you." Lia smiled and settled herself in the chair, placing the folder in her lap.

"Would you like a refreshment?" his grandfather asked her, ever the gentleman. "I could see if Abigail might be kind enough to bring in some tea?"

"No thank you," Lia said easily. "I'm saving myself for lunch."

"At one o'clock," William said. "She asked you to remind me, didn't she?"

"Yes."

"I'm fairly certain lunch has been served at Millbrook at one o'clock since 1859," he grumbled. "When I forget that, then I give Gabriel permission to put me out to pasture."

Gabriel made a face and dragged a footstool from one of the couches over to the window. He sat down in the sunshine.

"Are you an artist by trade, Miss Leclaire?" William asked.

"No. An engineer. Chemical," she added when his brows rose again.

"Indeed? What a fascinating field of study." William sounded delighted with this revelation.

And judging by his expression, his grandfather was already imagining Lia's portrait in the hall with every other brilliant woman a Seymour male had managed to marry.

"I love my work," Lia told him.

"As you should." William looked back and forth between them. "Tell me how you two met."

"Lia is a client, Grandfather. I am doing some appraisal and restoration work for her."

"Oh?" William's attention transferred to Lia. "Then tell me about the art my grandson is working on for you."

"A fairly large collection of Impressionists," she said. "Degas, Pissarro, amongst others. Also some landscapes. A few Turners."

"Impressive, Miss Leclaire. How long have you been collecting?"

"I haven't. It was my grandmother's collection," she started. "We think."

"You think?"

"I found it hidden in an apartment in Paris. Until recently, I wasn't aware of the existence of either apartment or art collection."

"Hmph." William set his headphones aside on the small table next to his chair. "Sounds intriguing. I'd like to see the collection. Especially the Turners. I'm an artist myself, you know."

"Yes," Lia said. "I knew that."

Gabriel watched his grandfather's face for any sort of reaction to the revelation of a hidden art hoard in a Paris apartment where his sister may have been. But he saw nothing beyond expected interest.

"Gabriel is an artist too," William told Lia, sounding for all the world like he had just announced Gabriel's ascension to the throne of England. "He won't have shown you his art, but you should see it. This boy here has talent, and I think he should—"

"I've seen it."

"You have?" William narrowed his eyes at Gabriel. "He tends to hide that fact behind all of his fancy screens and chemicals and machines."

"I saw it by accident," Lia admitted. "But I've seen it all the same, and I agree wholeheartedly. He is extraordinarily talented."

"Are you listening, Gabriel?" his grandfather demanded.

Gabriel looked out the window, pretending to be absorbed by something beyond the glass, acutely uncomfortable with the turn this conversation had taken.

"When he was younger, he spoke of nothing but becoming an artist," William continued. "Exhibiting his work all over the world."

"Indeed?" Lia sounded contemplative. "So what happened?"

"I grew up," Gabriel growled. "And learned how to make a living. I believe we've been over this."

"He could sell his work," William insisted. "Should be selling his work."

"I bought two of his pieces," Lia offered. She still sounded thoughtful.

"You did?" William's voice rose in disbelief.

"I did," Lia confirmed.

"Well, it's about damn time," his grandfather said with clear delight. "I thought I would meet my maker before I saw that happen." He thumped the arm of his chair with his hand. "I thought he'd hide his talent forever."

"I'm not hiding." There was more defensiveness in his protest than he had intended. "I'm not hiding," Gabriel repeated.

"Then promise me you'll exhibit your work—just once— and I can die a happy man."

Gabriel stood and moved away from the window.

"Promise me, Gabriel," his grandfather nagged.

"Fine. I promise."

"Good."

"Miss Leclaire plans to exhibit her collection," Gabriel said, firmly changing the subject. "In Paris. We think some of the art may have been hidden prior to the war."

William sniffed, giving Gabriel a look that told him he had fooled no one. "Well, you can send me photos, I suppose."

"We actually have some photos that I'd like to show you now," Gabriel said. "We're hoping you may be able to tell us a little bit about them."

"Oh?" His grandfather leaned forward.

Gabriel walked over to where Lia sat and took the folder from her. He crouched at the side of William's chair and opened it. "We found these in Lia's grandmère's apartment, too, along with the art," he told him. "We think that these are photos of Sophie. Your sister."

This time, there was no missing William's reaction. His ruddy face paled, his body stilling.

Gabriel laid the first photo on his lap, one of the glossy, Hollywood-style shots.

William stared down at it without making any effort to pick it up.

"Is that her?" Gabriel asked. "Aunt Sophie?"

Finally William lifted the photo. His fingers traced the edge of her face. "It looks like her." His voice was barely audible. "But I don't understand why these would be in your grandmother's apartment. Were they friends?"

"I'm not sure," Lia said. "Did she ever mention a woman named Estelle Allard to you?"

William shook his head. "No."

"Ever mention anything about paintings that were hidden in Paris?"

"No." His answer was faint.

"There are more photos." Gently, Gabriel laid out the rest of the Hollywood collection.

"She looks different," William said, picking each one up in fingers that were trembling before putting them back down. "Different than I remember."

Gabriel nodded. "What about this one?" He put the small, battered photo of Sophie astride the leggy horse on top of the blanket.

William was shaking his head. "No, this isn't her. These all look like her but it's not her."

"How can you be sure?" Gabriel asked.

"Sophie didn't ride. Horses, that is. She never rode when we were kids. The neighbours—the Stantons—had horses, down the road. They'd let me ride their old mare whenever I asked, but Sophie never came. Didn't trust horses, she said."

"Do you think that maybe she could have learned later on? Maybe when she was working in Poland?"

William picked up the picture. "No. She would have told me. She sent me letters," he said. "Even when I enlisted and was moved around, her letters found me. Eventually. And that's something she would have told me if only because I was such a brat to her about it. That's not her."

Gabriel extracted the last photo in the folder. "I think it is. Because this one was with it." He put the picture of Millbrook on his grandfather's lap.

William seemed to hold his breath. Gabriel put a hand on his arm, more to reassure himself that his grandfather would start breathing again.

"Then this is her?" William's voice shook. His eyes were wet.

"Yes."

"Why didn't she tell me she had learned how to ride a

horse?" he whispered. He turned the photo over. "There's writing here. What does it say?"

"It's written in Polish," Gabriel told him. "And it says 'I will always remember.'"

His grandfather looked down at the collection of photos spread out on his lap. He suddenly looked every day of his ninety-eight years. "I've never seen any of these photos of her. I don't know who took them or where they were taken."

"I didn't mean to upset you," Gabriel said.

"Forgive an old man his sentiments. These photos are reminders of a time that I didn't have with her. Parts of her life I didn't get to share. Selfish of me, I know, but after all these years, I still miss her. She was my dearest friend." He removed his glasses and wiped at his eyes.

"Um." This was more difficult than Gabriel had thought it would be. He reached for the rest of the documents in the folder but Lia's hand suddenly appeared on his, stilling his actions. He hadn't heard her come up behind him.

"Gabriel told me that when you returned from the war, you looked for Sophie," she said to William. "That you thought that maybe she hadn't died in Poland working for the Foreign Office," she said. "Can you tell us a little more about why you thought that?"

Now it was William's turn to look out the window and evade their eyes.

"Grandfather?"

"It was foolish. And I can't...that is to say I don't..." He turned back, his lined face set in even harder lines. "I was off my head then, suffering delusions and imagining things that weren't there. Morphine, self-pity. Guilt that I survived when my family did not. I'm not proud of who I was when I got back. And I don't want to talk about it."

"I understand. But can you tell me what you imagined?" Lia pressed gently.

"What?"

"What was it you imagined that made you look for your sister even after you believed her to be dead?"

William set the photo of Sophie down on top of the one of Millbrook and stared at her.

"Please," Lia said.

"I imagined an angel."

Gabriel and Lia both remained silent.

"Like I said, off my head." William slid his glasses back on.

"Tell me about this angel," Lia replied.

"Now who's off her head?"

"Well then, we can be cracked together," Lia replied easily. "We'll make a good pair."

His grandfather didn't answer for a long time, and just when Gabriel was sure he wouldn't speak, he did.

"Very well." William's voice was rough. "The angel I imagined looked a lot like you, Miss Leclaire." He chuckled but it sounded forced. "I still have this very image in my head. She was standing before me, under a tree, wearing a white robe with a bright light shining from behind her. She told me that my sister had never believed I was dead. That Sophie had never given up on me. That she knew I would make it home." His gnarled fingers curled into the edges of the blanket on his lap. "Which is, of course, impossible. Because Sophie died long before I was ever captured."

"Where did you look?" Lia asked. "When you tried to find your sister?"

"The war offices, other government offices. Everything was so..." He seemed to be searching for a word. "Disordered. Confused. So many people missing, so much destroyed."

"Did you find anything?"

"Only her Foreign Office record. And they wouldn't let me take it, only look at it. There wasn't much in it. Personal information I already knew, an old letter of commendation for her work, and a letter of formal reprimand that she had deserted her post prior to the bombing. Which is utter rubbish." He sounded angry. "That job meant everything to her."

"What about the people she worked with?" Gabriel asked. "Surely, if—"

"I looked. But I couldn't find a single soul who had worked with her in Poland. Or anyone who knew her at all. Presumed Dead had been stamped across the front of her folder in red ink." He smoothed the blanket over his knees. "Smudged, like someone had been in a hurry. A hurried conclusion because any other explanation was too much of an inconvenience. I hated that red ink. I still hate red ink." He sighed, a wheezing, tremulous breath. "And I still hate that word. *Presumed*. Because presumed still allowed me to hope that she wasn't really dead, just gone. But over time, gone becomes far worse than dead."

Lia pushed the folder that was still in Gabriel's hands closed. "I'm sorry."

"Eventually, as the years passed, I was forced to accept the truth. If she had been alive, she would have found her way back." William slid his glasses off again. He dabbed at his eyes with the sleeve of his sweater. "I should not be maudlin so many decades later. If I were to be completely honest, my imaginary angel pulled me out of the doldrums. Gave me a purpose, even though it was futile."

Somewhere in the house a bell rang, pretty, chiming notes.

"Saved by the bell," William joked weakly.

Lia looked questioningly at Gabriel.

"The lunch bell," he said. "And I'm pretty sure that, too, has been here since 1859."

Lia's lips curled. She crouched down beside him.

"Thank you, Mr. Seymour," she said. "For sharing your memories." She gathered the photos that still lay on his lap.

William only nodded. He settled his glasses back on his nose, just as Abigail bustled into the room.

"Lunch," she announced, her keen eyes travelling amongst the three of them as if trying to discern what had been spoken of.

"Sounds wonderful," Gabriel said.

"Hmph." Abigail moved behind the wheelchair and deftly wheeled William toward the door. She glanced back. "Hurry up, you two."

Gabriel waited until Abigail and his grandfather were gone before he turned to Lia. "Why didn't you want me to show him the rest?"

"Because there was no point. Clearly, he knew nothing about the photos or how they might have ended up in Grand-mère's apartment. By his own admission, it took him years to accept her death. Why upset him all over again with more questions we don't yet have answers to?"

Lia was right. And kind and compassionate and far more intuitive than he. Gabriel had been ready to blunder ahead in his quest for answers.

"The angel he referred to. The one he said looked like you." Gabriel let those statements hang.

"You're thinking that Estelle Allard was here at Millbrook at some point after the war?"

"It's not any more unthinkable than anything else so far."

"I'm not disagreeing." Lia was toying with a seam in her emerald skirt. "There are probably more war records that have been archived and released to the public since your grandfather searched. Wouldn't it be better if we could give him real answers if they exist?"

"Well," Gabriel said, handing the folder back to Lia, "it's too late for us to get back to the city before the government offices close. We can tackle the archives of London tomorrow. But after lunch, let's start in the attics of Millbrook."

CHAPTER

17

Lia

L ia followed Gabriel through Millbrook House.

They were in the hall, a gleaming domain of light, polished marble floors, and richly papered amber walls. Elaborate plaster ornamentation adorned the soaring ceiling, and a chandelier showered sparkling ropes of crystal down from its center. Tall porcelain vases overflowing with white and yellow blooms framed the grand stairway. As the first space a guest saw when they entered Millbrook, it most definitely impressed.

And, as with her grandmother's apartment when she had first opened it, Lia had the distinct feeling of stepping back in time.

"This is lovely," she breathed, nearly crashing into Gabriel as he stopped in front of a narrow door.

"It is maintained very well," Gabriel agreed. He gestured to the stairs leading up to the first floor. "I'll show you the rest of the house once the wedding guests have left tomorrow, but for now, we'll skulk about on the servants' stairs. Far easier to avoid fire-breathing events coordinators this way." He grinned as he withdrew a key from his pocket and opened the door.

He led them up two flights of narrow stairs, their feet tapping on the wooden treads. Gabriel ducked through a second door, and Lia found herself at the end of a long hallway with bare floors, unadorned plaster walls, and plain wooden doors set in regular intervals on both sides.

"The old servants' quarters," he explained as they started down the hallway. He pointed to the neat labels that had been affixed to each door. "The rooms are used for event storage now," he said. "Holiday decorations, wedding decorations, lighting, table linens and settings, that sort of thing." He used his key again to unlock the door at the end of the hall. "Access to the attics." He held out his hand. "After you."

Lia slipped through the door and mounted the stairs. Here the air was stagnant, the scent of dust and age distinct. The stairway was lit only by the diffuse light coming from some-where above—daylight streaming through small windows, she guessed. At the top, she paused and Gabriel joined her, reaching just over her head to tug on a dangling string.

More light flooded the space from a series of exposed bulbs mounted above them, and Lia got her first look at the attic of the manor house. It was a little bit like a movie, she thought. In the center of the long, wide space was a collection of furniture from the previous two centuries. Chairs and headboards, small tables and desks, and even an old grandfather clock. On one side of the attic, large trunks of varying ages were stacked one on top of another, intermingled with a collection of cardboard boxes and plastic tubs. Along the other side, tall wooden braces had been built, hundreds of canvases and large frames stored upright in between.

Lia stepped closer to the wooden braces bolted to the floor. A small canvas leaned against the support nearest her, another hopeful little landscape of Millbrook. She would have bet her entire bank balance that if she picked it up, *William Seymour* would be scrawled on the bottom corner.

"Tell me that this is not where all your art goes," Lia said before she could stop herself.

Gabriel pushed by her into the space. "Some gets moved up here in preparation for the movie crews. Most is not period accurate or they have their own art props they wish to hang," he said, not answering her question at all.

Lia exhaled. Like in the reading room earlier, she could almost feel him withdrawing from her at the mention of his own work. A tall, narrow canvas jutted above the others, and from where she stood Lia could make out the torso of another ballet dancer, painted in swirling ivory and violet hues. Her fingers twitched with the desire to yank it from its banishment and bring it out into the light. She forced herself to look away.

"What are we looking for?" she asked, venturing farther into the attic.

Gabriel skirted the collection of furniture and set an ancient rocking chair aside to crouch in front of an old steamer trunk. "Probably a box or maybe a trunk like this." He put a hand on the top, wiping at the layer of dust. "Abigail's mum, Imogen, died in 1990. She lived at Millbrook all her life, so anything that wasn't discarded or donated after she passed would probably be up here somewhere." He peered at the latch. "Though I confess I'm doubtful that anything she kept might solve the mystery of how Sophie's photos ended up in Paris or what they might have to do with a cache of hidden art."

Lia knelt and slid her finger beneath the top of a cardboard box but then stopped. "I feel like I'm prying into the privacy of your family."

"Funny. I rather had the same feeling when we were rifling through your grandmère's apartment."

"Fair point," Lia conceded.

"I can, however, tell you with a fair degree of certainty that we will not find another Munch or a trio of Degas works up here," he said. "Honestly, I'm pretty sure that this is just a collection of rubbish that probably should have been given away or thrown out a long time ago. So don't trouble yourself and don't be shy," he said, releasing the latch on the trunk and pushing the lid open. "Just let me know if you find anything from the years just prior to or during the war."

Lia nodded and pulled the top off the first box.

They worked for a good hour, Lia sorting through boxes of old clothing, linens, toys, books, sporting equipment, kitchen detritus, and an assortment of instrument cases.

"Who played the violin?" she asked Gabriel, carefully lifting a violin case that had been stacked on top of a battered wooden trunk.

"Certainly not me," he replied, his voice echoing through the rafters. "I can't even play chopsticks on the piano." He sneezed. "Do you? Play the violin, that is?"

"Yes," she said. "Though I haven't for a long time."

"Are you any good?"

"I suppose. It was my grandmère who insisted I learn. She was quite accomplished herself, though she rarely played when

I was around." Lia fingered the clasps on the old case. "May I look at it?"

"Of course." Gabriel stood, wiped his palms on his hands, and glanced at his watch. "I'm not convinced we're ever going to find any answers up here in this mess. I think we'd be better off spending our time at the National Archives."

Lia nodded absently and released the clasps on the case and opened it with care. The violin nestled inside under a protective cloth was a varnished red-brown, the wood grain contrasting beautifully with the black chin rest, tailpiece, and neck. She lifted the instrument from the case, her fingers sliding over the strings.

"What a handsome piece," she said, turning the instrument toward the overhead lights.

"Don't suppose it's a Stradivarius worth millions," Gabriel said, coming to crouch beside her.

"I thought you said you didn't know much about violins."

"I don't. That about exhausts my expertise."

"Well," Lia replied, peering through the f-holes, "it's most certainly not a Stradivarius."

"Too bad." Idly, he brushed the dust off the top of the trunk the violin had been resting on.

"It is, however, a Collin-Mézin," she said a little breathlessly. She let her finger trail lovingly over the scroll. "My music teacher had one, though she never allowed her students to touch it."

"Then play it."

"What?"

"Play it. The violin."

"Now?"

"Why not?"

"Because the bow probably needs to be rehaired? Because it will sound terrible?"

"I won't know the difference. I'm happily tone deaf. And it would please me to hear you play it." He sat on the lid of the trunk and looked at her expectantly. "Go on."

"I can't."

"You won't, you mean."

"No, that's not—"

"I dare you."

"Are you twelve?"

Gabriel grinned at her. Lia's breath caught. No man deserved to look that good surrounded by dust and dares.

"Fine. But I make no promises that this will be anything less than awful."

Gabriel kept on grinning and leaned back on his hands.

Lia took a closer look at the violin. God, it was a beautiful piece. And her grandmère would have approved of how it had been stored. Someone had once treasured it.

Lia tested the strings and made careful adjustments. She examined the bow next and tightened the hair, all the while aware that Gabriel was watching her intently. She rosined the bow, grimacing. "This is old."

"Does it matter?"

"Yes, it matters. I'm not sure that it will sound—"

"I think you're stalling now."

"I'm not stalling."

"Then play."

Lia shook her head and then lifted the violin to her shoulder. She closed her eyes, thinking that she had been in Marseille the last time she had played. She had been sitting outside, the scent of lilies drifting on the summer air, Grandmère sitting across from her on the tiny porch in the fading light, watching her with a sad smile.

Lia drew the bow across the strings and played the piece she had played then. Or, rather, a part of the piece that had been Grandmère's favourite. She was rusty but the notes transported her to a summer's night in Marseille with a woman who had kept her secrets close to her heart.

She stopped after a few minutes, letting her bow come to a rest at her side.

Gabriel hadn't moved. "I would like to paint you playing."

Lia could feel herself blush. "That's not necessary."

"No, it really is. Necessary, that is." He paused, still staring at her intently. "Tell me what you just played."

"Beethoven. Sonata nine for the violin. Well, just a couple of minutes of it. A little dramatic, I know, but it was Grandmère's favourite."

"I thought you said you were all right. At the violin, that is."

Lia winced and lowered the instrument. "I know. It's been a while. And I really think the bow hair need replacing—"

"Jesus, Lia, I'm trying to compliment you." Gabriel stood and dusted off the seat of his jeans. "That was incredible."

"Oh. Thank you." Her face still felt overly warm. "I had a lot of hours on my own growing up. The violin was just something that I could do—"

He closed the distance between them. "Take it."

"What?"

"The violin. Take it. It's yours."

"No. I couldn't possibly—"

"Please. That instrument deserves to be played. Deserves to be heard. It does not deserve to be hidden up here. It deserves an audience."

Lia blinked at him. Gabriel was standing close enough that she could see the flecks of indigo in his irises and smell the faint scent of his soap that still clung to his skin. Her eyes searched his face, coming to rest on the curve of his lips.

"I'd like to kiss you," he whispered. "May I?"

Wordlessly, Lia nodded, certain that he could hear the pounding of her heart against her ribs.

Slowly, Gabriel lifted his hand and brushed away a lock of her hair that had fallen over her forehead while she played. His fingers drifted along the side of her face to settle gently around the nape of her neck. Electricity danced and crackled under his touch. His other hand slid over her bare shoulder, the warmth of his palm setting her skin on fire.

And then he bent his head and kissed her.

It was a soft kiss, his lips exploring hers unhurriedly and thoroughly, allowing her the space and time to pull away if that was what she wished. She had no such wish. Instead, she leaned into him and deepened the kiss. His hand slid around to her lower back, pulling her against him.

Lia lost track of time, lost track of where she was, lost track of everything save for the feel of this man against her. After minutes or maybe hours, he pulled back, his forehead resting against hers.

"You are extraordinary," he said.

Lia was trying to catch her breath. She lifted her head and gazed up at him. "That was..." She trailed off, words a herculean task that was seemingly beyond her at the moment.

"Yes," he agreed. He let his hand slip from her neck and stepped back.

Lia did the same, afraid that she'd give in to the urge to kiss him again if she remained where she was. Instead, she busied herself properly restoring the violin to its case.

"Just because I kissed you does not mean I'm taking your violin." She tried to make her voice light and breezy as if she could pretend her pulse wasn't still hammering out of control.

"Even though I insist?" He hooked his thumbs into his pockets, a smile playing over those very kissable lips.

"I'll think about it." She'd be thinking about a lot of things. Violins not being one of them.

"Good." He glanced down, and his movements stilled. "Huh. This might be something."

"What?"

He crouched down and rubbed at the top of the wooden trunk that the violin had been resting on. "Look."

Lia gently snapped the lid of the violin case closed. She set it aside and joined Gabriel, careful to keep a safe distance. He gestured to a yellowed label that had been glued to the top left corner of the trunk, its corners brittle and curling. RECORDS 1936–46 MILLBROOK was just legible in faded ink.

Gabriel was already working on the latches on either side. "What do you think?" he asked. "Something useful or a box full of receipts for coal and turnips?"

Lia bit her lip, welcoming the distraction. Her heart seemed to be slowing to a normal pace. "I'm having a faint sense of déjà vu," she said.

"You and me both." He shoved the lid up.

At first glance, the trunk looked as though a filing cabinet had been simply unloaded into its depths. Stacks of wide file folders were piled inside right up to the top, small scraps of paper peeking out from some like leaves lost in a windstorm.

Bundles of letters and what looked like bound ledgers were visible beneath. Gabriel lifted out the first of the thick folders and passed it to Lia, selecting another for himself.

She opened hers to find a collection of newspaper clippings. *The Times*, *The Daily Mirror*, and *The Sunday Express*, all dated, as far as she could tell, from 1944 to 1945. Each covered some part of the Allied invasion of France, their subsequent invasion of Europe, and, at the bottom of the pile, news of victory.

"This must be what Abigail was speaking of?" Lia guessed. "Some of what her mum clipped and kept?"

"I think so," Gabriel agreed, his head bent over the folder he held. "I have records here of children who were evacuated from London and who stayed at Millbrook. It looks like someone kept the tags that would have been pinned to their clothing, spent ration cards, and even a poster issued by the Ministry of Health urging parents to leave their children where they were safe." He sorted through the contents and set the folder aside. "Fascinating, and I should probably go through them and have these boxed up to be submitted and archived properly in London. I know people have tried for years to trace family members that were scattered during the war."

He reached back into the trunk and withdrew a stack of letters, bound by a single string. He thumbed carefully through the aged envelopes. "This is definitely Imogen's stuff," he said. "All these letters are addressed to her."

"Any from your grandfather or Sophie?" Lia asked.

"No. It looks like they're all from her own family." He placed them on the floor next to the folder. "Let's see what else she kept."

He and Lia emptied the trunk, examining the contents carefully. More newspapers, magazines, propaganda posters, bundles of receipts, several thick ledgers, and even some grammar and mathematics primers for children. But here was nothing that made any reference to Sophie, or even William.

Gabriel sighed as he pulled out the last of the contents, another bound stack of letters.

"More missives to Imogen?"

"No," Gabriel said slowly. "These are addressed to different people." He slipped the twine from the stack. "Soldiers, I think. Or maybe some of the children who stayed here. None of these names are familiar, though someone has made notes on the envelopes. Look." He passed one to Lia.

The sealed letter was addressed to a Private James Mac-Duggal, Millbrook's address listed below. On the side of the envelope, someone had written in a decidedly feminine hand, *Reenlisted RAF, September '43, Return to Sender.* Lia turned the envelope over. It was from a Cecily MacDuggal of Glasgow. "His wife?" Lia mused out loud. "Mother?"

"Maybe. There are three more for Private MacDuggal. One for a Corporal Frederick Smith, one for a Lieutenant E. Shields, and two here for a Nora Cooper." He passed them to Lia.

Return to Sender, Not at This Address had been scrawled next to Nora's name.

"Nothing to an Estelle Allard, is there? Something that might prove she was here? Or stayed here and made your grandfather think he imagined an angel?"

"Doesn't look like it."

Lia hadn't really expected a different answer. "I wonder why these were never put back in the post."

"Put aside and forgotten? Stuck in a to-do pile that never got done?" Gabriel murmured as he continued to examine the rest of the stack in his hand. "Who knows?"

Lia set the letters she held aside.

"Here's one to Sophie," Gabriel said. "The wrong Sophie, but a Sophie nonetheless." He held up a letter with a disappointed sigh.

It was larger than a regular airmail envelope, the stamps postmarked with smudged ink. SOPHIE KOWALSKI, followed by Millbrook's address, had been typed in neat rows across the front. *Return to Sender, Not at This Address* had been likewise written across the front in the now-familiar hand.

Lia reached for the envelope, and Gabriel handed it to her. It was thicker than the other letters and had a more official bearing. The left top corner was creased, something small yet bulky preventing it from lying flat. She turned it over. INTER-SERVICES RESEARCH BUREAU with a London address was stamped on the back of the envelope, the seal brittle with age and broken in some places. She stared at the top line before flipping it back to examine the postmark. The smudging made it hard to read the month and day but the year was clear. 1943.

"This might not be the wrong Sophie," Lia said slowly.

"What?" Gabriel had stood and had begun collecting the folders stacked around them.

"This letter is from the Inter-Services Research Bureau. Otherwise known as the Special Operations Executive."

"Special agents."

"Special agents, spies, saboteurs. Many who operated in France."

Gabriel dropped back to his knees beside Lia. "You think that this Sophie Kowalski was actually my aunt?"

"It's possible, I suppose." Lia held the envelope gently in her fingers. "The date on the postmark fits the photos we found.

And the first name fits, even if the last name doesn't. Maybe Kowalski was another code name. Like Beaufort."

"I don't know." Gabriel didn't sound convinced.

"Your grandfather would have searched for Sophie Seymour. Not Sophie Beaufort or Sophie Kowalski. Maybe that's why he never found anything. Maybe his answers are in here."

"Maybe."

"There is one way to find out," she said, holding out the envelope. "Open it."

"And if it's not the right Sophie?"

"Then we will do our best to get this to whatever family Sophie Kowalski might still have left with whatever information we find. Either way, we need to know what is in the letter."

"All right. But I'm not simply ripping it open here. I'll take this back to my studio where I can handle it properly. No matter who it belongs to, it is a piece of history and needs to be treated as such. This, and the rest of these documents, no matter who they belong to, should be properly archived."

Lia made a strangled noise and dropped her head to her chest. "The scientist in me recognizes the rationality of that and approves. The Agatha Christie reader in me wants to shriek and throw something in agonized impatience, and then tear this open with my teeth."

Gabriel chuckled and took the envelope from her. He bent to gather the rest of the letters. "If this letter indeed turns out to be tied to Sophie Seymour in any way, we will have a new starting point at the National Archives. Patrick, the friend I told you about earlier, is also well acquainted with the archives. He has an uncanny ability to know just where to look for information that would otherwise be missed. I suspect it's part of the reason he was hired to start with."

"This is wholly anticlimactic, you know."

"I'm sorry but not sorry."

"You can make it up to me."

"How?"

"Before we go, show me some more of your work. The pieces you have hidden up here in this attic."

He paused before resuming his task. "No."

"No?" Lia frowned. "Are you being serious?"

Gabriel didn't answer.

"You are serious," she breathed. "Why won't you show me?"

"Because it's personal. And my personal life is none of your business."

"Perhaps you should have thought of that before you kissed me."

"Then perhaps I shouldn't have. Perhaps that was a mistake."

Lia faltered. "It didn't feel like a mistake."

"Why do you care so much, anyway?" he demanded, straightening.

"Because your grandfather is right. You are extraordinarily talented. You shouldn't be hiding it."

"I'm not hiding."

"Is it true what he said? That you once wished to exhibit your work?"

"Those were the stupid ramblings of a child. That child grew up and watched his father and grandfather fail at that same dream over and over."

"So when you promised him this afternoon that you would exhibit your work, you were lying?"

"You don't understand."

"You're right. I don't. Is it failure that you're afraid of?"

"I'm not afraid of anything. Jesus, just because you convinced me to sell you two paintings doesn't mean you get any further say in my life or my career." He seemed angry.

"But I—"

"And may I remind you that while we are here on a mutual . . . quest for information that may have involved both our ancestors, you are simply my client."

"Right. A client." Her stomach dropped. "And one who has overstepped. It won't happen again."

Gabriel looked up at the ceiling and closed his eyes.

"Why did you ask me here?" Lia asked.

He opened his eyes but didn't look at her. "I wanted you to see my studio. All my clients are entitled to see where their pieces will be handled."

"No, I meant why did you ask me to Millbrook?"

He shook his head, at Lia or at himself, she couldn't tell. "As my client, I thought that you were also entitled to whatever answers we might find here. The art is still at the epicenter of this, as well as whatever history might be associated with your grandmother."

"Ah. An extra service, as it were, then."

"No. Yes. That's not— You're making it sound awkward."

He had no idea.

"Then what is your intention? To examine the letters we found here today and forward me any pertinent information that references my grandmother and her hidden collection that you may subsequently find?"

"Um. Yes. Though if we haven't found any traces of your grandmother here yet, I don't know that we will. I may be able to shed some light on what happened to my aunt but there doesn't yet appear to be a connection of any sort to the art."

"I see." Lia nodded. "Very well, then. We should probably

get going. If we leave now, I may be able to make a late flight back to Paris. I can be in Seville in two days. It will give me more time to prepare for the interviews."

"So that's it? You're just going to leave?"

"Is there a reason to stay?"

Gabriel ran a hand through his hair, the movement jerky. "What about the collection?"

"You are the professional when it comes to restoration and establishing provenance. Isn't that why I hired you? Why you agreed to take me on as a client?"

"Lia—"

"You will keep me informed throughout the process? If anything comes up?"

"Of course."

"For what it's worth, I apologize for whatever intrusion I subjected you to."

"This wasn't what I . . ." Gabriel stopped. "I still want you to have this." He bent and retrieved the violin case and held it out to her. "I meant what I said."

Lia shook her head. "I don't think that is a good idea, Gabriel."

"Why?"

"Because it belongs to you and your family. Not to me. And like the rest of whatever secrets live up here, it's where it belongs."

"Lia—"

"It seems like it's for the best." She turned and started down the stairs.

She did not look back at Gabriel or any of his paintings.

CHAPTER

18

Sophie

PARIS, FRANCE
20 AUGUST 1943

S ophie examined the painting hanging on the wall.

Rendered in a palette of wintery blues, frosty greys, and brilliant whites, each brushstroke brought an almost violent movement to the eye. A ship battled a turbulent sea, and Sophie could feel the bite of the wind that tore through the ship's sails and taste the sharp saltiness of the freezing spray that whipped over the bow.

When she and William had been twelve, their parents had taken them sailing off the Scottish coast. If she closed her eyes, she could still feel Will pressed beside her, laughing with abandon. Below their feet, the ship's deck had reared and bucked across the frothing waves, and above their heads, the sails snapped and cracked like rifle reports. Clouds had scudded across a cobalt sky, and the wind had torn Sophie's neat braid into a glorious mess and consigned Will's cap to a watery grave somewhere in the Irish Sea.

Will had painted nothing but seascapes for months after that.

"Is this a Turner?" Sophie asked casually without taking her eyes off the painting.

"I didn't take you for an artist." The woman Sophie still knew only as La Chanteuse sat on one of the ornate sofas in the low light, the silent, dark-haired, dark-eyed little girl tucked beside her, her small head in her lap, fast asleep.

"I'm not."

"A collector, then."

"Not really. My brother is the artist. I have merely been his unwitting student about the virtues of every artistic genius whom he studies." She paused, her eyes travelling over the collection of paintings that surrounded the seascape. "You have a fortune on your wall here."

"Yes." Her answer was flat. And uninterested.

"Turner's composition here is remarkable."

"It is." Another indifferent response.

"The American is from a fishing town in the northeast coast of his country," Sophie said, still considering the tempestuous waves. "His father was a fisherman, as was his grandfather. As he describes it, neither were happy when he chose the sky over the sea."

La Chanteuse didn't respond.

"His name is Frederick Rickman, though only his mother calls him Frederick," she continued. "His four sisters call him Freddie, or Flying Fred when they are feeling particularly playful."

La Chanteuse made a funny sound from behind her.

"What?" Sophie asked.

"It just seems rare. I know a person's real name anymore."

"Mmm." Sophie straightened the seascape, tipping the left

corner of its frame slightly upward. "He finished high school and signed up for the U.S. Air Force as quickly as he could run to the recruiting office. He said he was afraid that he would miss the action. He was flying in a B-17 as a tail gunner when they were shot down southwest of Brussels. It was his first sortie, and he was the only one who survived out of his crew. He likes American baseball, reading novels, and misses his family. He'll be nineteen in two weeks."

"And he talks far too much," La Chanteuse muttered.

"Beware the dog that does not bark and the man who does not speak."

"I beg your pardon?"

"Something the American said. I think he was referring to the child, who didn't say a single word the entire time we were in that room, no matter what story or joke we tried. Who hasn't yet spoken a word."

La Chanteuse scoffed.

"I don't even know her name. Real or otherwise."

The carved clock on the mantel ticked loudly into the silence. Just when Sophie didn't think the woman was going to answer, she spoke. "Aviva. Her name is Aviva."

Hebrew for springtime. A beautiful name for a beautiful little girl. A little girl who had remained as still as death throughout the invasion of the apartment.

When the immediate threat had faded, the child had resumed her drawing and had not objected when Sophie picked up one of her pencils. Together, they'd passed the hours drawing, Aviva rendering sketches of dogs and Sophie doing her best to portray a mare and foal galloping across a pasture. Aviva hadn't objected, either, to Sophie's lack of talent and simply bent her head, wrinkled her fine features, and added color to Sophie's efforts.

As the hours had dragged on, Aviva had left the pencils and papers where they lay and curled up in a listless ball on the cot, staring at three small paintings of ballerinas that had been hung high on the wall opposite. The airman had whispered stories about his childhood and Sophie and Aviva had listened. Eventually, he'd fallen asleep stretched out on the floor next to the cot, succumbing to the anxiety and exhaustion of his journey. He didn't wake when the hidden door had finally opened and Sophie and Aviva had emerged into an apartment with curtains pulled tight against the darkness outside.

La Chanteuse had served them a simple but surprisingly decent meal of bread, soup, and hard cheese. She had remained tight-lipped and said almost nothing, other than to explain that the airman would remain hidden in the wardrobe room until she could make further arrangements and that Sophie would not be returning to her hotel room tonight. That no one would be leaving the apartment tonight. Curfew had come and the city had once again gone dark.

Wordlessly, Sophie had helped tidy up the few dishes and had gazed around the apartment, thinking that it, along with the woman who lived in it, was a study in contradictions. The highly visible pro-Nazi literature that lay scattered about the apartment. The concealed room in which a small girl was hidden, presumably Jewish. The food in the cupboards and the stack of unused ration books and coupons. The array of fine classical art that hung on the silk-covered walls of the apartment and the three Impressionist Degas paintings that hung in that hidden room. A woman who had accepted a gift from Göring and used that circumstance to protect an Allied airman.

"Are the dresses in that wardrobe really gifts from Göring?" Sophie asked into the new silence.

"You heard that conversation." Not really a question, just a dull confirmation.

"When the wardrobe was open, every word. Did he tell you that you looked like an angel?" With La Chanteuse's rich, honey-colored hair, hazel eyes, and her graceful carriage, Sophie wasn't surprised.

"Yes. That was the truth." Her answer was flat. "I wear them to sing in."

"They're beautiful."

"They make my skin crawl. But all the best disguises do, I suppose."

"You sing often at the hotels."

"Just at the Ritz. But not as much since . . . since Aviva, but enough to remain routine. Welcomed. Included in conversations or, even better, dismissed as mere décor during others."

"I wondered."

"About?"

"Where *La Chanteuse* had come from."

"We can't stay here much longer." The statement was abrupt.

"I beg your pardon?"

"The . . . man who was arrested. He knows about me, about this apartment, and about Aviva. I would like to think that he would never betray us, but I . . ." Her face crumpled before she seemed to catch herself. With a visible effort she reasserted her outward calm. "I do not know how long he might hold out under their torture," she whispered. "I might have days or weeks or—" Her voice broke, and she stopped.

"Or maybe the man that they arrested today might only be imprisoned. Or he might already be—" Sophie stopped, unwilling to say it.

"Dead," the woman finished bleakly.

"Or he might be dead," Sophie agreed, trying to gentle words that weren't gentle at all. "You might be safe."

La Chanteuse looked at her, despair shadowing her features. "Or I might not. We might not."

"I just—"

"Enough." The woman cut her off, speculation about the fate of the man on the basilica steps at an abrupt end. "What do you want?"

The harsh, cynical question caught Sophie off guard. "I beg your pardon?"

"You did what you did at that basilica this afternoon for a reason. And for the life of me, I can't figure out what that reason is. But no one does anything without an agenda. Did you think that what you did would cast me in your debt?"

"What? No." Sophie turned, scowling.

"I don't believe you."

"If we are measuring debt, then whatever assistance I may have provided this afternoon has been subsequently repaid in kind. Had I taken the American back to my hotel, we would likely have been found, arrested, and I'd be having a far different conversation than the one I'm having now. If we're keeping score, we owe each other nothing, and in the morning, I will leave, and you will never see me again. I don't even know your name, which will make it easy for me to forget I was ever here."

La Chanteuse seemed to weigh Sophie's answer and came up wanting. "Why did you do it, then?"

Sophie didn't pretend to misunderstand. "Because I could." It was an honest, if incomplete, answer.

"I don't know what you've been sent here to do but the

fact that London sent two agents tells me that it is important or urgent or both. What you did was foolish and reckless and put you and your mission, whatever it is, at an extraordinary risk."

Sophie couldn't disagree.

"Do they teach you in spy school what the Gestapo does to your kind? Or mine? They don't just shoot us anymore. Instead, they like to see what they can get to fall out of our heads first before they kill us. The funnel, the press, extraction of fingernails and toenails, though that is usually done after they've driven needles and wooden wedges underneath them to pry them loose. They'll burn you, electrocute you, file your teeth, and slit the bottoms of your feet. They might not let you sleep for days, keep you in the dark for weeks, all the while beating you regularly—" She broke off, her expression again one of despair.

"I understand," Sophie answered.

"Then what were you thinking?"

"I was thinking," Sophie said slowly, "that I know another pilot. I was thinking that it's been three years since he was shot down and vanished. But that maybe, just maybe, he might escape from wherever he is and that people like you would help him get home. I was thinking that if the man in that room wasn't an American but an Englishman who loves cars and art and his bacon blackened around the edges, who found himself cornered in front of a French basilica, that someone might do for him what I did." She paused. "I was thinking that, one day, that man, or men just like him, will be better served by your continued innocence and anonymity."

La Chanteuse looked away. "I'm sorry about whomever it is you've lost but I don't know what you're talking about."

"Of course you do. You help get Allied airmen out of France," Sophie said. "You're part of a smuggling line."

"That's quite an assumption."

"It was at the time. It's no longer an assumption."

"Based on more of your conjecture?"

"Based on the fact that the man who was being hunted trusted you implicitly with the life of the American. He knew that you understood what needed to be done. I guessed then that it wasn't your first time."

"And now?" The question was biting.

"I don't need to guess. In that hidden room, there is a trunk that contains books in English and Polish. Men's clothes and identity papers and money. And train schedules, though they are over a year old and probably quite useless now."

La Chanteuse paled. With stiff movements, she slid out from under the sleeping girl, careful not to wake her. In a half-dozen steps she had crossed the room, facing Sophie. "You went through the trunk?" she whispered furiously.

"Wouldn't you in my position?"

"Your position?"

"Hidden behind a wardrobe wall with no weapon other than my knife to defend all of us should the Gestapo officer have been lucky in his search." She made a face. "The rifle would have been more helpful had it been accompanied by ammunition."

"I don't keep ammunition in there."

"So I discovered. And the rifle needs cleaning."

"That trunk was locked. For a reason."

Sophie shrugged. "It was. And then it wasn't. Something else they teach us at spy school."

"*Merde.*" La Chanteuse pressed her fingers to the temples of her forehead. In the background, Edith Piaf continued to sing softly on the gramophone.

"I know you didn't ask for any of this," Sophie said.

The woman sighed. "And neither did you."

"And yet here we are."

"Here we are," she agreed. She dropped her hands and looked up at Sophie. "Estelle," she said after a long pause.

"I beg your pardon?"

"My name. It's Estelle."

"Estelle," Sophie repeated. "Thank you."

"For what?"

"For what you've done. The men you've helped get home. You're very brave."

"Save your thanks. I'm not brave."

"Yes, you are—"

"No, I'm not," Estelle snapped. The child on the sofa stirred, and she lowered her voice. "I haven't been part of that network in over a year. Because I'm not brave. I'm terrified. Terrified that Aviva will be discovered. Terrified that, even if she isn't, she won't last this war. Terrified that the promise I made to keep her safe will mean nothing because every day I watch her fade a little more." She leaned back against the wall, gazing at the slumbering child. "I'm afraid to take her outside. I'm afraid to leave her in the apartment without being hidden. There are ears and eyes everywhere these days. Half my neighbours hate me because they see the black cars that have brought me home from time to time and think I'm one of *them*. The other half, those who have sold their souls to the Vichy cowards and Nazi pigs, are ravenous for the chance to denounce a neighbour. To prove that I am not who I pretend to be. I'm so afraid I'm going to fail her. I'm so afraid I'm going to make a mistake that will cost her her life." The words had poured out in a torrent, like the breaking of a dam, and Estelle's jaded defiance that she had worn like armour was replaced with desolate sorrow. "My world has shrunk to this apartment and the space between here and the hotels, but hers has shrunk to that room. And now even that isn't safe anymore."

Sophie didn't know what to say.

"She wants to be a doctor when she grows up," Estelle said. "Or maybe a ballerina. I told her she could be both." She made a harsh sound. "Right now, I'm not sure she'll even have the chance to grow up."

"You're doing your best," Sophie said gently.

"My best," Estelle sneered. "My best has yet to be enough. My best has failed at every turn."

"That's not—"

"Did you know that the paintings in that room used to belong to her family? The ballerinas? I put them in there thinking that they might make her feel less alone. That a part of her family was still with her." She was twisting a loose thread on the hem of her skirt around the top of her index finger, turning the tip of her finger white.

"What happened to them? Her family?"

"More of my best." The thread snapped. "Her father died on the front before he could be taken back to a field hospital in my ambulance. What was left of her family was arrested and shipped east in a liquidation I should have seen coming."

"That you should have seen coming?" Sophie repeated with raised brows. "You have a crystal ball?"

"Don't patronize me."

"I'm not patronizing you. Evil is unpredictable, cruel, and without mercy. I did not foresee the bombs or the guns that killed my husband. Nor, I would imagine, did my parents go to bed one night knowing that it was the last time they would do so."

Estelle traced a pattern with her toe on the rug. "I'm sorry," she said after a moment.

Sophie said nothing. She was sorry too.

"I shouldn't have said anything. You have your own heart-ache and trials, and neither Aviva nor I are your concern." Estelle blew out a shaky breath.

"Leave France."

"You think I haven't considered that?" Estelle hissed. "You think I don't want to? But just how far do you think I might get with a child who looks nothing like me and has no papers?" She held up her hand. "Let me answer that for you—not far enough to make me think I could pull it off. Though it seems that now I have no choice but to try. For Aviva's sake."

"I could get her out of France." The words were out before Sophie had stopped to consider them. Before she stopped to consider if that was something that she might actually be able to do.

Estelle stared at her. "What?"

"There are...people who smuggle children over the Swiss border. And there are families who provide a home for them after that."

"How do you know this?"

"I just...do."

"That is not very reassuring."

"You'd have to trust me."

"I don't know you enough to trust you."

"No. I don't suppose you do."

"Why would you do this?"

Sophie frowned. "What do you mean, why?"

"What do you want from me in exchange?" The jaded defiance was back.

"Jesus. We're back to this?" Sophie turned away to the wall of landscapes. Her gaze fell on a richly rendered image of a poppy field beneath an azure sky. The crimson flowers were scattered like drops of blood across the swath of earth, beautiful and oddly macabre all at the same time. "Again, I don't want anything from you in exchange."

"In this war, everyone wants something. But I'm having difficulty determining what it is you really want."

Sophie tried to temper the unexpected emotions that were bubbling up uncontrolled and flooding her chest, making it hard to breathe. "I'll tell you what I wanted this afternoon. For one beautifully horrifying second this afternoon in front of the basilica, I thought that I would simply draw my knife and bury it in the major's neck. I wanted to kill him. Later, I almost wanted the fucking sergeant to open that wardrobe door so that I'd have an excuse." She took a shaky breath, her hands closing into fists. "I hate them. The Nazis. So much so that sometimes it makes me afraid that I will not be able to think through it." She forced her hands to relax and turned away from the bloody poppies to face Estelle.

The woman was merely gazing at her, and if she was at all disturbed by what Sophie had just said, she didn't show it.

"I sound like a lunatic," Sophie mumbled. "Perhaps there really is something wrong with me."

"What?"

"It's been suggested a number of times that there is some-thing unnatural about me."

"Is there?"

"You tell me."

Estelle studied her for a long time. Sophie resisted the urge to squirm.

"If the Nazis have done anything well," Estelle said, "it's to make us capable of hate beyond logic."

"Yes," Sophie agreed faintly.

"That is not unnatural." Estelle continued to watch her. "I think I find it reassuring."

Sophie straightened her sleeve. "Tomorrow morning I will leave this apartment, and you will never see me again if that is your wish. And while I have asked for your help, know that with or without it, I will accomplish what I came here to do."

The woman who faced her toyed with the small pendant at her throat. "Have you come here as an assassin, Sophie Beaufort?" She used the name Sophie had given the Gestapo. "To kill?"

"No. I've come to use them." She chose her words with care, knowing she couldn't reveal too much. Not yet. "I've come to make their own Nazi arrogance their downfall."

The questions she had expected were remarkably absent. Estelle merely pursed her lips. A few times she looked as though she might speak before seeming to change her mind. The silence stretched.

Then Estelle's fingers abruptly fell away from the pendant. She paced to the sofa, crouching to gently sweep the hair from the little girl's pale face. "Help me get Aviva out of Paris—out of France—and I will become your new partner. I will help you do whatever you need to complete your mission."

"No." Sophie shook her head. "I am not leveraging the life of a child. Whether you help me or not has no bearing on this. That's not at all why I offered to—"

"When Aviva is gone," Estelle continued as if Sophie hadn't spoken, "I will take you to the Ritz and help you do whatever it is that you came here to do. But I can only do that if I know that Aviva is already safely away."

Sophie shook her head again. "I can't promise that. That she will be safe. I can't even promise that I can make this happen."

"But if you could make it happen?"

"Then all I can promise is that she will have a chance. A chance to survive. To live life again."

Estelle stared at her.

"I understand that that is a very frail promise. That it is probably not enough."

"It's enough."

CHAPTER

19

Estelle

I n the back of a café with cracked windows that overlooked rue Saint-Vincent, Estelle sipped her cup of whatever horrid, murky chicory mixture they were passing off as coffee and wondered if she'd been an utter fool to believe that the ice princess could promise anything. The café had been Estelle's choice. She had chosen it because it was always crowded, and the lack of anything that resembled real coffee, advertised loudly and unapologetically by the proprietors, generally kept away anything resembling a German. A good place in which information could be exchanged quickly and casually without notice at a set time.

Yet three days had passed, and Sophie Beaufort had not reappeared, and with each passing day, Estelle's trepidation grew. True to her word, the British spy had vanished into the streets of Paris the morning following her chaotic arrival and breathtaking promises. It was possible the agent had simply been unable to realize the hope that she'd offered. It was also possible her absence had far more sinister implications.

At least the American was gone. He'd left the same day as Sophie, trailing a discreet distance behind Estelle. He'd been dressed in a new set of clothes, his throat bandaged so that injury could be provided as a reason he couldn't speak, and a set of forged doctor's papers in his pocket declaring this so. Estelle had made the short journey with him to Troyes, every second on that train an exercise in dread, but the Germans who had asked to see their papers had looked harder at the copy of *Signal* they were both pretending to read than they did at their documents. Estelle had left the young gunner in a house she'd been to only once before, and if the elderly woman who had opened the door had been surprised to see Estelle and not Jerome, she didn't indicate it.

Estelle wrapped icy hands around what little warmth remained in her mug and finished her drink, examining her surroundings for anything out of place. She saw nothing. It didn't make her feel any better. She surreptitiously checked her watch. She couldn't linger much longer. She would have to try again tomorrow, but in the meantime, she needed to figure out an alternative plan to get Aviva out of that apartment and out of the city.

Estelle set her empty mug down on the surface of the table and dug into her pockets for payment.

Something thumped down on the table beside her, and Estelle started. She looked up to discover that someone had put a book down and taken a seat beside her. She glanced at the tome and, with a jolt, realized that the title was in German. *A Fatalist at War*, she translated silently. How poignant.

The newcomer pulled the scarf from her head, setting

it neatly on top of the book. Two schoolgirl plaits escaped over her shoulders. Estelle remained motionless as Vivienne ordered a cup of the same awful brew.

Beneath the table, Estelle clasped her hands together so hard that her knuckles went white. She hadn't yet told Vivienne about Jerome. Hadn't been able to find her, though Estelle had tried. But now that she was inexplicably here, sitting beside Estelle, the words wouldn't come.

Vivienne's drink arrived, and she blew gently on the steaming surface.

Estelle took a deep breath and forced herself to speak. "There is something you need to know—"

"I do." Vivienne cut her off.

"What?"

"I know what happened at Sacré-Coeur."

"Oh." There must have been others watching that day. Others who had seen what had happened. Hope flared. Maybe Vivienne had been missing these last days because they had found—

"We haven't found him. Not yet." The petite woman snuffed out her hope.

"Oh." Estelle managed again, looking down at her hands.

"What about young Frederick?"

"What?" The use of the American's name nearly jolted Estelle from her seat.

"Is he safe?"

"Yes." Estelle was trying not to stare at Vivienne. Nobody knew the airman's first name save for Estelle.

And Sophie.

Suspicion colored her next question. "What are you really doing here?"

"Celine didn't think you would trust her. Not with something this important." Vivienne paused. "Not with the life of a child."

Estelle froze.

"Was she right?"

Yes. Except Estelle didn't reply because she'd come to the sudden realization that the ice princess might know her better than she seemed to know herself.

"Do you trust me to help you with this?"

"Yes."

"I wish you had told me about the child before now," Vivienne murmured.

"I couldn't," Estelle managed. "I was trying to be careful."

"I understand." Vivienne set down her cup and ran a spindly finger around the rim. "But I know now. And everything is in place."

Estelle's fingers tightened so hard around the handle of her mug that she was afraid it would crack. She loosened her grip. The possibility of Aviva escaping—of her having a real chance to get out from under the constant threat of discovery, deportation, and death—had seemed distant. Now it was a real entity, a double-edged sword, capable of salvation as easily as it was capable of tragedy.

"Um" was all that came out of Estelle's mouth.

"Can you go through with this?" There was a sharpness to the question, as if she had been reading Estelle's mind.

Could she? What if she was doing the wrong thing? What if— She stopped. She couldn't go down this road. At some point in this godforsaken war, she had to trust someone. And at the moment, that someone was both Sophie and Vivienne.

"Yes," she whispered.

"She'll be in good hands." Those words were softer. "I promise."

"Yes," Estelle whispered again, because she didn't know what else to say.

"*Cimetière de Montmartre.* Jacques Offenbach."

Estelle swallowed. "I understand." Estelle had seen Offenbach's grave before. Knew exactly where it was.

"Three." Vivienne paused. "He won't wait."

"I understand," Estelle repeated. Three o'clock. Estelle would say good-bye to Aviva today.

"Make sure she's ready to leave you."

The words were soft but Estelle recoiled anyway.

Vivienne finished her drink and paid. She stood, picked up her scarf, and wrapped it tightly over her head.

And then, without another word, she left.

The book still lay on the table. Estelle shifted slightly and looked around the café but no one paid her any attention, preoccupied with their own thoughts, silent sufferings, or conversations. Outside the café on the street, pedestrians hastened past the cracked panes, their heads down.

Unhurriedly, Estelle set her own cup aside and picked up the book, putting it out of view on her lap beneath the table. She ordered another cup, drinking it slowly but deliberately, leaving a safe interval between their departures. Eventually she stood, paid the waiter, tucked her chair neatly back beneath the table, and exited the café in careful, measured steps. No one stopped her. On the pavement outside, Vivienne was gone.

Estelle walked back to her apartment, when all she wanted to do was run.

Once she got into her building, she took the stairs two at a time.

"In a rush to get somewhere, Mademoiselle Allard?"

Estelle stumbled to a stop on her landing, coming face-to-face with Frau Hoffmann. The woman was wearing another flowered dress, this one the color of her scarlet lipstick.

"You left early this morning." The frau put her hands on her hips.

Estelle shrugged and stepped around the woman. She wasn't going to answer.

"Another man?"

Estelle froze, unease pricking. "Pardon me?"

"I saw you the other day out my window. Leaving with a man. I was going to report you. I might still."

"Report me? Or the man I was with?" She tried to put scorn into her voice in an attempt to cover the unease. "Because I'm not so sure you want to do that."

Estelle was rewarded with a flicker of uncertainty. "But—"

"I do not question you about what goes on in your bedroom, Frau Hoffmann. Please extend the same courtesy to me."

"He could be a spy," Hoffmann spluttered, flushing.

"Did you get a good look at him?" Estelle went on the offensive and took a step closer to the woman.

"No, but that is not—"

"Discretion is a virtue valued not only by myself but by officers of the Wehrmacht. I'd hate for your husband's business connections to be...blemished because his wife made assumptions about important people. Put certain individuals into awkward situations." Estelle was making this up as she went but it seemed to have the desired effect. The flush of the woman's cheeks drained, leaving behind a crimson slash in an otherwise pale face.

"I think we can both agree that we can leave the matter there, yes?" Estelle prompted.

Frau Hoffmann stared at her.

"I'm glad we understand each other, then." Estelle put her key in the lock and opened her apartment door.

"You might fool them, but you don't fool me," the woman shouted as the door closed. "I know what you are!"

Estelle leaned against the back of the door, her heart beating loudly in her ears. Frau Hoffmann, for all her unhappy vitriol, was a real threat. Her husband did indeed dwell in high circles within the Reich, high enough that a complaint from him, if only to placate his wife, would have dangerous consequences. The noose around this apartment, and everyone in it, was tightening.

Estelle pushed herself away from the door, made her way to the dining room, and set the book on the table. With its faded cover and rusty water stain in the lower right corner, the volume looked sorely out of place against the gleaming rosewood. With exaggerated care, Estelle opened it. At first glance, the book was unremarkable. She flipped through pages yellowed at the edges, but there was nothing tucked inside. No notes, no papers, no instructions, no cleverly hollowed-out chapters. For a moment, Estelle wondered if she had lost her mind. If she had imagined everything.

She reached the end of the book. The inside of the back cover was also water-stained and torn along the bottom. Someone had tried to repair it at some point—

Estelle lifted the water-stained edge with her thumbnail. Someone had done more than repair it. A document had been tucked between the lining and the back cover, its edges just visible. Carefully, Estelle extracted it from its hiding place.

It was a birth certificate. For a Marthe Marie Varennes, born in Marseille, France, on 4 May 1939, daughter of Jules

Varennes and Edith Marie Bouchet. It had all the official stamps required, and all the creases and folds one might expect from a travelling document.

Estelle stepped away from the table and the document that lay on its surface. The clock on the mantel chimed noon. She had three hours left before she would say good-bye to Aviva Wyler.

★ ★ ★

The cemetery had been well chosen. It sprawled with organized abandon in all directions, avenues that cut through in an eclectic collection of angles, straightaways, and curves. With its collection of jutting monuments, squat mausoleums, and elevated sculpture, the sight lines were nonexistent. It would be an easy place in which to get turned around and lose one's bearings. It would be easy for a body to slip away into a myriad of hiding places. Which, Estelle assumed, was the entire point.

They entered on rue Rachel, Aviva's hand clutched tightly in hers. The breathtaking irony of the street name was not lost on Estelle. It was as if all the fates were conspiring to make her doubt what she was doing. To make her remember the promise she had made to this little girl's aunt to keep her safe.

Yet on their journey to the cemetery, the little girl had shrunk from other pedestrians, the occasional passing vehicle, and even a pigeon that had fluttered over their heads to land on the pavement just ahead of them. Inside the lining of Aviva's coat, Estelle had sewn the only picture she had of Aviva's family, the one she'd taken from the Wylers' apartment that horrible night. She'd written nothing but the date on the back of it. No names, no places, nothing that could betray Aviva's real identity if it ever fell into the wrong hands. But the idea of Aviva disappearing without at least a tiny piece of the family who had loved her was intolerable to Estelle.

The grave where they were to meet the people who would take Aviva to safety was up ahead. Estelle stopped, and in the lacklustre light beneath a bruised sky, she crouched in front of the small child, double-checking the buttons of her coat, as if she could stall the inevitable. As if such action could stay the tremble of her fingers and smother the sense of loss that was already rising to choke her. Another soul slipping away from her as silently and surely as smoke through her fingers.

"Are you ready to go on your adventure?" Estelle asked, knowing her smile was entirely too bright. She would not cry.

Aviva nodded, her dark eyes filled with nothing but the sadness that had haunted them for far too long.

"They are going to take you out of Paris," Estelle continued. "Somewhere you can play outside with friends your own age. Somewhere that you might even be able to have a dog."

Aviva stood up straighter at the mention of a dog. She reached for Estelle's hand.

Estelle took a deep breath. "Aviva, I can't come with you. We talked about this."

The little girl shook her head frantically, her forehead creasing.

"But I promise I will come and find you," she rushed on. "As soon as I am able. I'm going to look for your mama and aunt, too, and we'll all come to find you." Estelle refused to acknowledge that what she was saying was likely impossible. "Do you remember what I told you? That you can't tell anyone your real name. Or where you used to live. There are people who will take good care of you until I come to get you. All right? Can you do that?"

Aviva nodded uncertainly.

"You are the bravest person I know," Estelle said and hugged the fragile body close to her.

And then, with an almost physical pain, she forced herself back to her feet and tugged Aviva forward.

Three people waited in front of Offenbach's memorial, where a sculpted bust of his likeness stared sightlessly out over his final resting place. A round-faced man in an ill-fitting suit accompanied a dark-haired woman holding a folded umbrella in anticipation of the threatening rain. Beside them, dressed in a drab grey coat and her pale hair covered by a scarf, was Sophie Beaufort. The little knot of people stood at ease in front of the memorial, looking to all appearances as though they were simply sightseeing. Vivienne was nowhere in sight.

Sophie turned as Estelle approached and lifted a hand in greeting.

"Good afternoon," she said easily. "And good afternoon, Mademoiselle Varennes," she said to Aviva.

Aviva shrank away from her and pressed herself against Estelle.

Estelle extracted her hand and crouched down in front of Aviva. "These are my friends," she said. "They are going to take you somewhere safe. I need you to go with them."

Aviva stared at her, wide-eyed.

"Do you remember everything I said?" Estelle asked. "What I need you to do for me? And your mama and aunt?"

Aviva nodded.

"Good."

"My name is Edith." The dark-haired woman was smiling

kindly down at Aviva, but there was worry and wariness in her eyes. "But we have to go quickly." She held out her hand to the child.

Aviva looked up at Estelle.

Estelle nodded and forced her face into what she hoped was a reassuring smile. "It's all right. Go with her. Listen very carefully to what she says."

"Does she not speak?" The man had moved beside Estelle.

"Not for a year," she managed, watching the woman lead Aviva away.

"Probably for the best," he grunted and then set out after the pair.

In less than ten seconds, all three were gone.

"Walk." The ice princess's command was cold. She threaded her arm through Estelle's and forced her around. She started walking, half dragging, half propelling Estelle with her. She paused long enough to retrieve a small suitcase that had been left near the memorial, half hidden behind a clump of overgrown grasses.

"Who was that man? The one who took her?"

"His name is Georges," Sophie replied. "And that's all I can tell you because that's all I know."

"But where are they—"

"Somewhere safe."

"But—"

"Don't think about it anymore," Sophie said, dragging Estelle forward again. "You did the right thing."

"I can't not think about it." Estelle could barely get the words out. Tears were blurring her vision, and she thought she might be sick. "What if I just did the wrong thing?"

"You saved her life." Sophie was now propelling them back

toward the rue Rachel entrance. "And one day, when she is a very successful doctor and dancer, she will thank you."

Estelle squeezed her eyes shut and stumbled along with Sophie, leaning on the other woman as if she were a hundred years old. "I didn't think it would be so hard." Which was a stupid thing to say. She had known it would be awful. She just hadn't allowed herself to dwell on it while she was still with Aviva. Hadn't dwelled on the very real possibility that she would never see Aviva again.

She stopped and wrenched herself away from Sophie and retched into a pot of withered flowers. When she was done, she put her hands on her knees and tried to catch her breath.

"Here." A handkerchief appeared in front of her.

Estelle wiped at the tears that had leaked from her eyes and then swiped at her mouth. "I'm fine."

"I can see that. Just be a little more fine before we leave here," Sophie said. "We don't need a reason to draw any more attention than necessary." She slipped her arm back into Estelle's.

Estelle tried to return her handkerchief.

"Keep it," Sophie said.

"Where are we going?" Estelle croaked.

"Back to your place."

"Right." Estelle tried to get her thoughts in order but her mind couldn't seem to focus on anything. "You need me to start—"

"I don't need you to do anything now, except come back with me to your apartment, where you will grieve properly."

"I don't need to grieve. She's not dead."

"No, and nor will she be. But gone hurts just as much as dead. This I know."

Estelle sniffed, feeling slightly ashamed. This woman knew

better than most what grief was. And yet still, she was the one who was comforting Estelle.

"And when you are ready, we will discuss what happens next. What we will do to help end this all."

★ ★ ★

When Estelle woke, she was alone in her bedroom. She hadn't meant to fall asleep when they had returned, just rest for a moment to collect herself and her thoughts. But she had found herself weeping for Aviva, weeping for Jerome, and, somehow, she had fallen asleep despite her best intentions. Light now streamed through the breaks in the curtains, telling her that a night had passed and morning had arrived, and Estelle had slept through all of it.

She crawled out of bed, pulled on a sweater against the cool air, and deliberately did not look at the wardrobe. She wandered out of her bedroom and came up short in the dining room.

The ice princess was sitting at her dining room table, once again wearing the green dress Estelle had first seen her in. Laid out before her was the old rifle that had once resided in the trunk in the hidden room. She had placed a blanket on the table to protect the surface and was working a rag over the barrel of the gun. A sharp, oily scent hung in the air.

"How are you feeling?" the agent asked without taking her eyes off her task.

Estelle ignored the question. Mostly because she didn't know how she was feeling and partly because she didn't want to try to answer.

"Are you planning on using that at the Ritz?" she demanded instead.

Sophie shook her head. "No. I don't need a rifle. Not for what I need to do."

"Then why do you have it out?" Estelle had, apparently, also slept through Sophie entering her bedroom and accessing the room through the wardrobe. The thought of that was faintly unsettling.

"I'm cleaning it for you."

"You don't need to. It's not mine. I don't like guns."

"Then why do you have it?"

"A . . . guest left it here."

"I wondered. It's French." Sophie slid the bolt handle back with a smooth, practiced action. "Military issue, I think."

"I suppose you do? Like guns?"

The agent shrugged. "They are another type of language to be studied and mastered. A combination of mechanics and intangibles."

"Something else they teach you in spy school, I imagine."

"No. Well, yes, they do teach you about guns, but I was already familiar." The spy picked up the weapon, peered down the sight, and then put it back down. "I got my first gun for my eleventh birthday. It was also a bolt action. A twenty-two."

"You got a gun for your birthday?"

"Actually, it was my brother who got the gun. I got a water-color set. We traded because Will didn't want the gun and I didn't want the paints. They were gifts from an old family friend who still believed himself safe in his understanding of a world where boys shot guns and revelled in fisticuffs and girls painted landscapes and arranged flowers."

"What?"

"My brother and I spent summers on the coast, and he and I used to pass countless days up in the fields and forests overlooking the sea. He would paint, and I would study or shoot. There is nothing more satisfying than pulling the trigger and watching a tin can jump off a distant stump in a cross-breeze."

Estelle stared at the blond woman sitting at her table, wondering why she was telling her all of this. Or if anything she was saying was actually true.

"I eventually taught my brother how to shoot, though I think he learned to make me happy more than he did it for himself," Sophie continued, seemingly oblivious to Estelle's confusion. "Just like he learned to fly to make my mother happy. A useful skill set, my mother called it. She was, above all, a very practical woman."

The pilot Sophie had spoken of earlier. The one who had been missing for three years.

"My brother spent an exorbitant amount of time after each flying lesson painting inspired, sky-filled vistas," Sophie continued. "In the end, I confess, he became a far better pilot than a painter, though I will gouge out my eyeballs with a dessert fork before I ever tell him that." She resumed rubbing her rag over the barrel of the gun.

Estelle slid into the chair across from Sophie. "Do you really think he's still alive? Your brother?"

The rag stopped midbarrel. "Ah."

"I listen."

"I know."

With slow movements, Sophie set the rag down and silently slid an envelope out from under the corner of the blanket beneath the gun. She extracted a packet that contained ration cards for food, clothing, and tobacco; a birth certificate; an identity card; and a rail card. Things Estelle would expect from an agent. With those documents, however, was a collection of photos, all glossy, professional-looking pictures of Sophie. In each, her hair had been expertly styled, her makeup skillfully applied.

Sophie pushed the papers and photos aside. From the envelope, she pulled out two more small, square photos, both of them ragged around the edges, both creased and worn.

The first was an image taken in bright sunshine, the blond ice princess sitting bareback on a horse with her knees and elbows a muddy mess, laughing into the camera. The second was of a grand-looking house, settled amongst a diorama of shrubs and trees.

"One of the very first things they teach in spy school, besides guns, is not to talk about yourself unless one is alone with a fellow staff member who acknowledges that you are speaking under certain conditions. There was even a code name for those certain conditions."

"And what constituted certain conditions?"

Sophie smiled, though it didn't reach her eyes. "Funny you should ask, because I never really got a straight answer to that question. My interpretation was that it was an interval of official debriefing between staff or colleagues."

Estelle shook her head. "Is that what we're doing here? Debriefing? Because I'm pretty sure that we're long past debriefing. That the last five days has been a disembowelment of my entire life and every secret that I possess. While all I really know about you is that you grew up somewhere near the sea, you enjoy target practice, you have a brother who became a pilot, and that your parents and husband died. All of which could be completely made up."

"Mmm."

Estelle wasn't sure if that was a confirmation that Sophie had spoken the truth. Or a confirmation that she had not.

"Here." Sophie set the two photos in front of Estelle. "This is my acknowledgement that we are speaking under those certain conditions. Because I think you're right. We're long past the point of secrets." She paused. "My husband used to say that trust is everything."

"What?"

"You have trusted me. Maybe not on purpose at first. But in the end, you trusted me with your dearest secrets. Now I am trusting you with two of mine." She brushed her hair away from her face with the back of her hand. "Trust cannot be a single-sided affair, not when you may one day ask the impossible of each other. If we are going to be ... partners moving forward, I think that this is something that I need to do."

Estelle stared down at the photos. "Are these really personal photos?"

"Yes."

She looked up at Sophie accusingly. *You can't have these* was on the tip of her tongue but then she thought back to the photo she had sewn into Aviva's coat and the denunciation died unspoken. And, in truth, the battered photos revealed nothing. They could have been taken anywhere between here and Berlin.

Sophie tapped the photo of the house with her finger. "You want to know how I know that my brother is still alive? This is how."

Estelle frowned. "I don't understand."

"The house is called Millbrook. Every Saturday morning, for as long as I can remember, Millbrook hosted a market on the lawns. People from the nearby towns would come to buy or sell their wares. My brother, from the time he was eight or nine, until he enlisted, had a booth there from which he sold his paintings." She shook her head. "And he never sold one. Not once. The ones my mother bought don't count."

Estelle waited, baffled.

"It didn't matter though. He set up every weekend, rain or shine, smiled and laughed and made the best of it all. He saw his lack of sales as a challenge, not a failure. I mean, really, after a year, even the most optimistic of souls would have accepted their limitations and quietly withdrawn. But Will refused to accept defeat, and wherever he is now, he'll be doing the same. I have to believe that." She looked up at Estelle. "And so do you."

Estelle finally understood. The ice princess wasn't talking about her brother anymore.

"After this war is over, I will find those lost to me, and you will find those lost to you. I will help you do it." Sophie looked up from the rifle, her eyes steady. "And in the meantime, we will help each other."

Estelle nodded, her throat thick with emotion. "What's this one?" she asked, reaching for the second photo, needing the distraction.

"That's a picture of me the first time my husband took me riding," Sophie said quietly. "He wasn't my husband at the time. Not yet. But it was the day that he kissed me for the first time."

Estelle closed her eyes, wishing for her question back. "I'm sorry. I didn't mean to—"

"I lost count of how many times I fell off that damn horse." Sophie laughed but it was a sad sound. "As it turns out, horses are not a combination of mechanics and intangibles. They are the very definition of intangibles."

"That is a good description," Estelle agreed with a crooked smile.

"I miss him," Sophie said, her voice breaking. "So very desperately."

Estelle set the photo aside and put her hands over Sophie's. There was nothing she could say that could fix the bleak desolation on Sophie's face. And it was a reminder that Estelle was not the only one who had lost.

The agent took a shuddering breath. "It's fading faster than I thought it would. His face. And I'm afraid I will forget," she said. "I'm afraid I will forget what he looked like. I'm afraid I'll forget his smile, his laugh, his voice."

"You won't."

"But what if I do?"

Estelle let go of Sophie's hands and stood, making her way to the small writing desk. She returned with a fountain pen. "Write it down."

"What?"

"Write what you want to say to him on the back of this photo."

Slowly, Sophie took the pen from Estelle and then pushed the blanket and the rifle to the side. She reached for the photo and centered it in front of her. "I don't know what to say."

"That would be a first."

Sophie choked on another half laugh. She pulled the cap off the pen and pressed the tip of the nib to her fingertip. A smudge of ink appeared. She turned the photo over, her pen hovering over the blank square. And then she bent her head, the nib scratching quickly over the surface. She stopped and recapped the pen with deliberate motions and set it beside the photo.

Estelle gathered the photos and papers that were spread out on the rosewood surface and tucked them all back into the envelope. She kept out only the agent's birth certificate and carte d'identité.

"Put that picture in here with the rest of them," Estelle said quietly, holding out the envelope. "We'll lock them all up in the trunk where the rest of our secrets live. And when this is over, you can come and fetch it back."

Sophie pressed the photo to her chest, her eyes closed. After a minute, she tucked the photo into the envelope. "You didn't ask what I wrote."

"I don't need to know. What you wrote is for your husband and for your husband only."

Estelle put the envelope on the table and smoothed her palm over the flap. The clock on the mantel ticked into the silence, and, somewhere below, a door slammed.

"Does dead become easier than gone?" Estelle asked hoarsely.

Sophie didn't answer, only sat back in her chair and looked up at the decorative plaster whorls in the ceiling.

Estelle rubbed her face, hating how weak she sounded. "Everyone I have ever cared for in this life is just... gone. The friend I loved as a sister. The man I loved as a father. The man I wish I had a chance to love properly. And now Aviva. And every morning, I open my eyes, and there is this moment when I can convince myself that they are simply somewhere else and that they will find their way home. And then, a second later, I fall off that cliff of hope, and at the bottom, I crash into the certainty that they are never coming back. That they no longer live."

"Gone is always chained to hope. And hope can be as comforting as it is cruel." Sophie closed her eyes. "I know you want a different answer, but dead and gone both break my heart every single day. Neither gets any easier."

Sophie was right. Estelle wanted a different answer.

"But we are still here," the agent whispered, opening her eyes. "And we have to make it all count for something. It's all any of us have left."

Estelle cleared her throat and stood abruptly. Sophie was again right. If she never saw Rachel or Serge or Aviva or Jerome again, she had to make it count for something.

She picked up the envelope and then reached for the rifle. Wordlessly, Sophie handed it to her. Estelle took both and secured them back in the trunk and closed the wardrobe tightly behind her. She returned to find Sophie standing in front of the painting that dominated the space over the fireplace.

"For all its brilliance, I hate that painting," Estelle said without preamble.

"I hate the entire story," Sophie replied. "How Polyxena ends up as a sacrifice. It has never made any sort of sense to me."

"Achilles got what was coming to him yet she became the pawn."

"I think it's the idea that she's simply accepted her fate that I hate the most. Just look at her expression in that painting. She's accepted that the actions of others have put her in an untenable position. I want to scream at her to fight. To take something back. To balance the scales of justice. To choose her own bloody fate."

"To make it count."

"To make it count," Sophie agreed.

"That painting was my mother's original décor choice," Estelle told her. "But I had a different painting hanging there until the war started. The first piece of art I ever bought for myself, in fact. Done by a Norwegian who knows how to paint emotion, not pictures."

"Why did you take it down?"

"Because it was a painting of a woman who would rather die than accept her fate. It was a painting of fearless defiance and unassailable courage." She paused. "That, and it would be considered degenerate by the Nazis. I did not want to take the chance of losing it."

"So you still have it?"

"Yes."

"Would you show it to me? I think I would like to see what fearless defiance and unapologetic boldness looks like in paint."

"Perhaps." Estelle left the hearth to stand near the window, peering down at the street below. The earlier sun had been swallowed by another heavy bank of clouds, and Estelle shivered. It was still summer, but the sky reminded Estelle that fall and winter would be here far too soon, and with them, more death—if not at the hands of the Nazis, then certainly at the hands of cold and starvation.

"Tell me what you need from the Ritz." She turned from the window to face the British agent.

Sophie ran her fingers along the edge of the marble mantelpiece. She opened the glass face of the clock that sat in the center. "Are there many spies working at the hotel?"

Estelle felt her brows shoot up. "The Ritz is a hornets' nest of employed spies. In the kitchens and behind the bars, in the maids' rooms and management offices. The trick," Estelle said without humour, "is knowing what side they are on."

Sophie closed the glass face with a snap. "And is this something you know? Which side they are on?"

"More than most," Estelle allowed. "Why?"

"There is a machine somewhere in that hotel. A ciphered communication device that is used to send messages to and from some of the most important members of the Reich. I've been sent to confirm its existence and copy whatever codebooks accompany it so that we might have a chance of understanding intercepted messages."

Estelle opened her mouth and then closed it, a peculiar feeling crawling through her.

"The intelligence that such a machine existed was old, something that only recently came to light, so it's possible that the device has since been moved. We were not even able to verify the network that sent the original radio message or the source who provided the information in the first place, but it was likely someone who once worked or still works at the Ritz." Sophie winced. "Crumbs, is what my superior called them. Crumbs of possibility that nonetheless left a bread trail convincing enough to warrant my dispatch. You should probably know that before you agree to anything further. But finding this device is critical."

A mix of disbelief and euphoria was now dancing across Estelle's skin, making the hairs on her arms rise. "Crumbs?"

You never know what crumb might turn a tide. It was what Jerome once said.

"Have you heard anything of the like?" Sophie asked her. "Perhaps something a maid or servant might have mentioned? One of the serving staff? It's possible that someone like—"

"Me," Estelle interrupted.

"I beg your pardon?"

"It was me who sent that information. Well, that's not true. It was someone in Vivienne's network whom I told that to, and I can only assume that they included it in a radio transmission. But you're right, it was a long time ago."

Sophie had gone quite still. "What?"

"I've been in that room. With the radios. Or machines. Or whatever they're called."

Sophie had turned fully. "And it's still there?"

"As far as I know." Estelle stepped away from the windows. "I think it was installed exclusively for Göring's personal use. The room is accessible through the Imperial Suite, where Göring stays while he is in Paris. It's down in the cellars, to protect the devices from the threat of bombing, I assume. But Göring isn't in Paris right now. I overheard a colonel say that he was on the eastern front somewhere. Poland, maybe?"

"Yes, that was what we had heard as well right before we left." Sophie drummed her fingers on the edge of the mantel. "How often have you been inside this room where the device is located?"

"Only once."

"Did you see anything that looked like a codebook?"

Estelle shook her head. "No. But there are locked cabinets inside the room."

"Cabinets? Not a safe?"

"Cabinets," Estelle confirmed. "That open with a key. A small one."

"And what sort of lock is on the door to the room?"

"None."

"None?" Sophie's brows shot up.

"Access is through a closet with a false back."

"It's not guarded?"

"No. I've been in that suite a total of three times, and I've never seen anyone standing by the door. It's supposed to be a closet, after all. I don't even think it's used when Göring is not in residence. I've only ever seen men with dispatches coming and going from the suite when he is present."

"What arrogant fools," Sophie marveled.

"The floor that the Imperial Suite is on is restricted access," Estelle warned. "Not just anyone can wander about without being challenged. Hotel staff come and go to clean and maintain the room, of course, but they are known. You or I could not simply waltz into the suite unless we had a good reason to be there. And permission."

Sophie absorbed that. "How will the officers inside the hotel be armed?"

"They're not."

Sophie's head jerked around in surprise. "What do you mean, they're not?"

"Officers are required to surrender their sidearms at the door. Can't have such vulgarity in the hotel," she mocked.

"Why were you in his suite?" Sophie asked. There was no judgement in the question, merely curiosity.

"I've . . . offered him fine jewels on occasion. An occasional piece of art. It's kept me welcome amongst higher-ranking officers at the Ritz. And just as importantly, kept me welcome in the kitchens at the Ritz."

"Ah."

"What do you need in that radio room?"

Sophie was drumming her fingers on the mantel. "It's the codebooks I'm after, though I can't steal them, not even just to copy them. I can't take the chance that they will be discovered missing, and then returning them adds additional risk. Under no circumstances can the Germans think that their codes or encryption device have been compromised."

"I understand."

"I had always thought that the best approach would be to take photos of the device and then the pages because to copy codebooks by hand would take hours. I have a camera—a Riga. It's small, easily concealed." Sophie hesitated. "I practiced before I left for France. With the camera, that is."

"How long?" Estelle pressed, her mind racing.

"Assuming I can get through the locks with efficiency, maybe twenty minutes. Maybe less. Get in and get out and leave no trace."

"And what happens when you've done that?"

"I'm to smuggle whatever information I'm able back to London."

Estelle let out a bark of laughter. "You make it sound like you'll simply board the next ferry heading back to Southampton."

"I'm to make my way back to my original drop site on the next full moon. Where I met Vivienne and her network."

"That's still weeks away," Estelle protested.

"Yes. Until then, I'll need to disappear. Evade capture."

"You don't say," Estelle muttered.

"At that point in time, they'll send a Lizzie to fetch me. If not, I'll figure something else out."

"Who's Lizzie?"

"Not who, what. A tiny plane they use to recover agents." Sophie grimaced. "Though they are rather hit and miss, I've been warned. It's harder than you might think to land a plane in a field in the dark in the middle of a country crawling with Nazis."

Estelle looked back out the window.

"But that part is secondary at the moment. Of greater

concern is how I will get into the Ritz undetected, get into the Imperial Suite undetected, stay there for twenty minutes undetected, and get back out. Undetected. We need a plan."

Outside, on the pavement below Estelle's window, a woman had appeared, wrapped in a tattered coat that might once have been a vibrant shade of blue. She was moving slowly and unevenly, her shoulders hunched, her head covered by a dark scarf. As she reached the corner of the street, she simply sagged to the ground on her hands and knees, whether from exhaustion, hunger, or illness, it was impossible to say. Approaching from the other direction were two Wehrmacht soldiers in pressed uniforms, leather gloves, and polished boots. One of the men had a brochure or possibly a map in his hand, and they appeared to be in deep discussion. They stopped, inches from where the woman huddled, the taller one pointing up the street to the west. The Germans seemed to come to some sort of decision, and they moved off in that direction. Neither spared the woman a glance. It was as if she didn't exist.

Estelle left the window. "You won't be undetected."

"I beg your pardon?"

"Have you ever been to the Ritz?" she asked Sophie, coming to join her near the empty hearth.

"Once. Many years ago," the agent replied slowly. "But just to the dining room and the shops. I've since studied the blueprint though. Why?"

"Plain sight."

"What?"

"We'll do this in plain sight. Detected by many."

"And what, exactly, is it that we are doing and how are we doing it?"

Estelle looked up at the painting and the fatalistic maiden with her arms outstretched above her tunic that was still a vibrant shade of blue. Waiting for the dagger that would end her life. "If Polyxena is so intent on being a willing sacrifice, I have a far better cause for her to sacrifice herself for."

CHAPTER

20

Sophie

The lorry that stopped in front of the doors on Place Vendôme was expertly handled by a driver in the Ritz's dark uniform, gloved and groomed to the hotel's uncompromising standards. His assistant, a youth likewise outfitted smartly, hopped from the passenger-side door and hurried to the rear of the vehicle. He was joined by the driver, and both set to work immediately maneuvering a large, flat object out of the lorry. The object was the height of a man and perhaps half as wide, and it was wrapped in stiff canvas, bound neatly with rope.

The car that Estelle and Sophie were riding in glided to a rolling stop behind the lorry and beside the lines of black vehicles, many adorned with miniature versions of the swastika banners covering the façade of the hotel. Sophie swallowed hard and reminded herself that she was not here to fight these

Nazis. Not tonight. Tonight, she was here to be their friend. To help others one day obliterate them all.

She glanced up through the open window, following the lines of the Vendôme column up toward the unsettled sky. It was early evening but it seemed later, and the heavy clouds that had loomed earlier now sat squarely over the city, rumbling ominously and threatening rain.

A soldier hurried forward. He was painfully young, and his fair, flushed cheeks had probably never seen a razor. "Stop!" he said as the driver turned off the car. "You can't be here."

Sophie wasn't sure if he was speaking to the driver or themselves, sitting silently in the back.

The driver merely glanced at the young soldier as if he were a fly buzzing at the periphery of the vehicle. He exited the vehicle and then opened Estelle's door for her. Estelle gracefully slid from the vehicle. She was wearing the stunning yellow-crepe gown that had hung in her wardrobe. It clung to her in effortless style, and with her hair gathered in glossy waves and secured at her nape and her makeup applied with a skill that had startled Sophie, Estelle Allard had transformed herself from a heartsick woman to a femme fatale. Vera Atkins would have approved.

"Mademoiselle Allard," the soldier said, taking a step back, confusion crossing his face as Estelle advanced toward him. "It is a pleasure to see you again, but you can't be here. I must remind you that this entrance is reserved for officers only."

Estelle snorted inelegantly and let the strap of her gown slip from her shoulder. "Hauptgefreiter Müller, a pleasure to see you too. Tell me, how is the lovely Madeleine?"

The young soldier blushed. "She is well, thank you." He cleared his throat. "But you can't be here, truly. This is the officers' entrance."

"I know this," she said with a pretty laugh. "I also know that if you care to check in with Colonel Meyer, you will discover that he is expecting me. He did, after all, send a car for me. And transport." She gestured at the lorry. "I have a gift for the Reichsmarschall."

The young soldier blinked under the barrage of name dropping and effortless charm. From where Sophie sat, it was difficult to tell which had more impact.

"What sort of gift?" Müller asked.

"You are now the Reichsmarschall's curator?" Estelle asked as the two men from the lorry started toward the entrance with the package.

"What? No." His eyes darted toward the two men, who were getting closer to the entrance, clearly torn between stopping the errant entries and speaking with Estelle.

"Then be a dear and go tell the colonel that Mademoiselle Allard has arrived with the Reichsmarschall's art."

The driver had come around the other side of their car and opened the door for Sophie. She tried to exit with the same grace Estelle had. She wasn't entirely sure she managed it.

Müller's attention snapped to Sophie, and his eyes widened in a manner that suggested Sophie's efforts at glamour hadn't been wasted either. She, too, wore a dress fit for a starlet, courtesy of a French Tempsford seamstress. It was pale blue with a beaded bodice, the long sleeves she had requested gathered at her wrist with silk ribbon. Her hair fell in soft waves over her shoulders, and when she had emerged from Estelle's bedroom, the woman had, with a wry smile, called her an ice princess.

"Who are you?" the soldier asked warily.

Sophie only smiled in reply because, at the door, there

was a predictable fracas as the men carrying the package were stopped.

"Must I do everything?" Estelle huffed and stalked toward the door, her heels striking the pavement in a sharp staccato.

Müller followed her hastily, protesting as he went. Sophie simply slipped in behind the two at a discreet distance.

Another soldier, alerted by the fuss, had come forward, blocking their path. The two men from the lorry set their burden down on the pavement outside the hotel.

"If someone would be so kind as to let Colonel Meyer know that Mademoiselle Allard has arrived with a gift for the Reichsmarschall, we would not all be standing out here," she said before the second soldier could open his mouth.

"The colonel is not here. He is at dinner," the soldier told her. "He has a standing order not to be disturbed."

Sophie already knew this. Estelle had told her that Meyer rarely deviated from a two-hour routine that usually included red wine, braised lamb, buttered potatoes, and roasted vegetables, all served at Maxim's. And a pretty redhead named Collette for dessert, served somewhere else entirely.

Estelle put her hands on her hips and scowled. "Well then, after he has finished his dinner, you may be the one to tell him that the Le Brun that I had promised the Reichsmarschall was destroyed in the rain outside this hotel because you would not admit us entry."

The two young soldiers looked at each other with indecision.

The Ritz employees merely waited, their eyes averted. Sophie wondered where their allegiances lay. Given the muscle jumping in one of the lorry drivers' jaw every time the soldiers spoke, Sophie was reasonably certain that his loyalty, at least, did not belong to the Reich.

Thunder growled low, and a gust of wind raced across the

square, chasing a chill around Sophie's bare legs. The timing could not have been better.

"At the very least, allow me to have the painting brought in," Estelle snapped imperiously. "Before you are required to assume the cost and consequences of your inaction. Because I can assure you that you cannot afford it."

"Fine." It was Müller who finally spoke. "Bring it in."

At a wave of Estelle's hand, the two men lifted the awkward canvas-wrapped painting and maneuvered it carefully through the door.

"Where do you want it put?" the shorter lorry driver asked.

"We'll take it directly to the Imperial Suite. It's to be hung before the Reichsmarschall returns."

"W-we can't allow that," the young soldier stuttered.

"You most certainly can. Do you know how many pieces I have brought to the Reichsmarschall?" Estelle demanded.

"But—"

"Look," Estelle said, gentling her voice, "I understand that you are only doing your job here. But this is a very valuable painting, and the longer it sits unprotected the greater risk of damage. The safest place for it is in his rooms."

"Then we will have it taken there."

"Not without us, you will not," Estelle said primly. "I will not rest until I see it right to the end of its journey."

"Us?"

Estelle gestured at Sophie. "This is Madame Beaufort, recently of Marseille. At my request, she has come to Paris to deliver this painting. I promised the Reichsmarschall a Le Brun and he shall have it. I always keep my promises."

Sophie kept her gaze steady as she met the abrupt scrutiny of the soldiers.

"This is true?" the second one asked.

"It is," Sophie answered easily in German. "It is an honour to offer such a piece to the glory of the Reich." The soldiers straightened. The older lorry driver closest to Estelle gave her a speculative look.

"You're German." The soldier's tone had warmed considerably.

"Half," Sophie said, telling them the same thing she had told the Gestapo outside Sacré-Coeur. "My mother was from Berlin."

"Mine too," said Müller eagerly.

"That almost makes us neighbours, then," Sophie said, smiling at him, trying her best to focus on the fact that the boy in front of her was just that. A boy. It was easier to smile that way.

He blushed to the roots of his fair hair and smiled back.

Sophie looked away.

"It was the colonel who suggested that I find a suitable place in the Reichsmarschall's suite to best display the work," Estelle said, sounding bored.

And with that lie, the clock had started ticking.

"In the interest of the efficiency that he so values," Estelle continued, "as well as my own peace of mind, this work could be hung long before he finishes his evening. He can inspect it then, should he so desire. Or, alternatively, if you feel you must interrupt his evening to confirm his instructions to myself and Madame Beaufort, then please, go ahead. We'll wait—"

"Wait?" Sophie cut Estelle off, her words brittle and just loud enough for the soldiers to hear. "What is going on here, Mademoiselle Allard? You indicated that this painting was very valuable to the Reichsmarschall but it seems that perhaps you have oversold its importance? Reichsführer Himmler has also expressed interest in this work, and I'm wondering if perhaps I should offer it to him instead—"

"No." It was the young officer who interrupted her.

And Sophie knew they had won this first part.

"That will not be necessary," he continued hastily, no doubt imagining a conversation in which he was required to explain why a painting the Reichsmarschall supposedly coveted had been taken elsewhere. "Do as you wish, Mademoiselle Allard." He gestured toward the interior of the hotel. "I will accompany you."

"Thank you," Estelle said graciously and swept into the hotel, Sophie and the wrapped image of Polyxena with a knife to her breast following in her wake.

The procession made its way through the hotel, heading toward the staircase that would take them up to the Imperial Suite.

"Tell me, who is Madeleine?" Sophie asked the young soldier who was dogging their heels like a puppy. She spoke deliberately in German.

"My girl," he told her earnestly, blushing again. "She lives over near Notre Dame. She is something, truly. I never thought I would get so lucky."

"How long have you been in Paris?"

"Three months," he replied. "In truth, I didn't think I would see any action in this war but here I am. Not that this post is as important as what my countrymen are doing on the front lines," he said. "My mother cried when I told her that I was leaving."

"How old are you?"

"Seventeen," he mumbled.

"Your parents must be very proud of you," Sophie told him, the words coming out far more easily than she had anticipated. "Proud of your service."

His cheeks were scarlet. "Thank you."

"You should be grateful that—" Sophie stopped abruptly, taking two quick steps forward so that the painting was between her and the salon they were passing. Without turning her head, she glanced up at the tall mirror mounted on the wall closest to her, reflecting the occupants of that salon.

Scharführer Schwarz was reclining in a brocaded chair, a cigarette dangling from his fingers, frowning fiercely. He was sitting off to the side, not a part of the conversation that was taking place amongst a group of Luftwaffe officers. Instead, his eyes followed the employees carrying the painting and the woman in the yellow dress leading them.

Sophie lowered her gaze and bent her head, cursing inwardly. Had he seen her? And if he did, would he recognize her? She looked much different than she had in front of Sacré-Coeur but that didn't mean much.

"Madame Beaufort?" The question came from the young soldier. "Is something the matter?"

"Not at all," Sophie replied. "I'm embarrassed to say I simply tripped."

"Oh," he said, looking relieved.

They were almost past the salon. Sophie had no idea if Estelle had seen the sergeant or not.

As the group reached the stairs and no one shouted from behind to stop them, Sophie relaxed fractionally. She maneuvered herself so that she remained with the painting on one side, the wall on the other, and just ahead of the young officer.

If the sergeant was still watching, the officer would provide a modicum of cover.

They climbed the stairs and made their way to the Imperial Suite. Along the way, they passed other uniformed men, many greeting Estelle by name and asking after her health, and two asking if the wrapped painting the Ritz employees still carried was another treasure for Göring. Whatever Estelle had been doing to integrate herself with the occupants of the Ritz, she had done it well. Sophie remained where she was, generally hidden by the bulky canvas.

A man in another grey field uniform met them at the door of the suite. He lacked any decoration or indication of rank on his uniform, and Sophie took him to be an aide of some sort. He had a narrow, pinched face that nevertheless managed to convey a smug, haughty expression. A magpie. That's what Piotr used to call men like that. Loud, mean, attention-seeking birds that lorded over the scraps left by others but fled at the first sign of a challenge.

"Mademoiselle Allard. This is an unexpected surprise. I do hope you're aware the Reichsmarschall is not in residence at the moment." His greeting was rife with condescension.

"I'm not here to see the Reichsmarschall, Hesse. I'm here to see a painting hung in his suite in preparation for his return."

"He told me nothing about this before he departed."

"I cannot help that oversight," Estelle said, sounding impatient. "Please let us in."

"I don't think I will," the aide called Hesse said, crossing his arms and leaning up against the wall.

"Colonel Meyer wishes—"

"I do not care what the colonel wishes, for the colonel is not here. Therefore, I will do as I wish. And I certainly do not obey the whims of a whore." His last sentence he uttered in German.

Müller sucked in an audible breath.

Estelle's face remained utterly blank, looking back and forth between Müller and the aide.

"It is troubling," Sophie said, stepping forward and addressing him in German, "the disrespectful manner in which you speak to a loyal servant of the Reich."

"Who are you?" Hesse demanded.

Sophie ignored his question. "You took the *Führereid*, did you not? Pledged personal loyalty to the Führer?"

"Of course I did," he sputtered.

"Then that is troubling also. Tell me, Herr Hesse, is it self-interest or just disregard for the Reichsmarschall, and thus the Führer himself, that arouses such disrespect?"

The aide pushed himself off the wall. "How dare you—"

"'Posterity will not remember those who pursued only their own individual interests, but it will praise those heroes who renounced their own happiness.' You should keep that in mind."

The aide scoffed. "Of course a woman would say something so pitifully inane."

"Oh, those aren't my words, Herr Hesse. Those are the words of the Führer."

The color drained from Hesse's complexion.

"You may not like Mademoiselle Allard," Sophie said, taking another step closer to the aide so that she was towering over him, "but she has, in her own way, proven her dedication and loyalty to the Reich. I would hope you would demonstrate your own loyalty by putting your self-interest and personal feelings aside."

The aide's superciliousness had been wiped from his face, and he seemed unable to formulate a response. "You will open this door, and we will see this art placed in a location of honour deserving of both the artist and Reichsmarschall Göring," Sophie intoned coldly. "After that, we will return below, where I will order a Bee's Knees from the bar and forget all about your... unfortunate lapse. Are we agreed?"

Müller was watching her with something akin to awe on his round face. The two Ritz employees looked like they were trying to follow the rapid German without much success.

The aide's jaw had tightened. "I—"

"Colonel Meyer arranged for the assistance from the two Ritz employees you see here." Sophie didn't allow him to speak. "Hauptgefreiter Müller has agreed to supervise. Once you've opened the suite for us, you may go."

Hesse stared at her and then seemed to recover. He threw up his hands with a sneer. "This is your problem then, Müller," he barked. He yanked a set of keys from his uniform pocket and unlocked the door to the suite.

"Thank you," Estelle babbled. "Oh, I'm so happy you changed your mind. The Reichsmarschall will be so pleased, I know it."

The aide pushed the door open and stalked away, refusing to look at Sophie and muttering under his breath.

Müller entered the suite first, and Estelle indicated that the men carrying the painting should follow. When they were out of earshot, Estelle glanced at Sophie, her eyes wide. "That was... convincing," she whispered.

"You may thank my German tutor for the inspiration," Sophie whispered back. "She made me read *Mein Kampf.*"

Sophie entered the suite, and though Estelle had described

the space in great detail, the luxury was overwhelming even in the failing light. It took every bit of her concentration not to gape like an awed tourist, and instead she swept through the gilded space as though such surroundings were the expected and not the exception.

She stopped in the center of the grand salon and turned in a slow circle, ostensibly deciding where the painting would best be hung. "Turn on the lights, please," she said to Müller.

The soldier obeyed immediately. Sophie allowed herself a small sigh of relief. She had not been at all confident that she would be able to manipulate the arrogant aide who had barred their way into the suite but the young soldier was proving more than malleable.

"You may take the bindings off the painting, but leave it covered for right now," she said to the two men who had set their burden down just to Sophie's left. Without a word, they, too, obeyed Sophie's request and bent to their task.

She put her hands on her hips and let her eyes linger on the doors that led to the dining room. Beside them, close to the corner, were the subtle lines of the hidden door, exactly where Estelle had said it would be. Had Sophie not been aware of its existence, she might not have noticed it at all.

"What do you think, Madame Beaufort?" Estelle came to join Sophie in the center of the large salon.

"I think the painting should be hung out here. It will set a tone, if you will, for the Reichsmarschall's impeccable taste in fine art and to impress his visitors." She paused. "What do you think, Hauptgefreiter Müller?"

The young soldier was still standing near the wall, openly gawking at his surroundings, now brightly lit. He jerked at the sound of his name. "Pardon me?"

"I was asking your opinion on the best location for this painting." She turned a brilliant smile on him.

"Um." He advanced slowly into the room. "I'm sure I don't know."

"Well, take a peek at the work and tell me where in this room it would be most dramatic. Most impactful. Where the Reichs-marschall will smile with pleasure every time he looks at it."

"Er." He approached the men still holding the painting and lifted the edge of the cover, his forehead creasing. "It's very, ah...colorful." He let the canvas cover drop back into place and wrung his hands, as though this single decision might determine his future in the Luftwaffe.

"What about near the entrance to the dining room?" Estelle suggested. "Visible from here, sure to be commented on by any guest invited to dine. There is the perfect space just above that sofa."

"Yes." Müller nodded. "A good idea." He sounded relieved that the decision had been taken from him.

"I agree." Sophie turned to the two Ritz employees. "You may lean the painting against that wall for now," she said, gesturing across the space. "Perhaps one of you might move the sofa and tables?" She tipped her head as if deep in thought. "We will need a ladder and tools. Hauptgefreiter Müller, would it be possible for you to accompany one of these men to fetch those things?" She framed it as a question. "I would be indebted to you."

"Of course." The soldier nodded eagerly as the men set the painting against the wall.

"I will take care of the furniture." The older of the two men spoke loudly to his partner. "Joseph, you have heard what the madame has requested. A ladder, a tool kit, proper anchors.

The ladder you will find in the north cellars, the tools that you will need are in the workshop closest to the garden terrace on the Cambon side. Anchors should be there somewhere too. And please try to keep your return as discreet as possible. I don't need resident or guest complaints."

The man called Joseph had a thoroughly puzzled expression.

"You heard my instructions. Please heed them carefully."

Joseph's face cleared. "Of course."

"Thank you," Sophie told them easily, not looking at the man who had spoken. "We will wait here with the painting."

Müller and the younger employee vanished, leaving Sophie, Estelle, and the older man in the center of the salon.

"I'm not sure what you are doing, Mademoiselle Allard, but you need to do it quickly," the man said. "I sent Joseph and his Boche on a scavenger hunt, but they will be back soon. Fifteen minutes, maybe?"

"That's all I need. And it would be best if you left right now," Estelle told him. "For your own protection."

"But—"

"Please. If anyone asks, you can tell them I ordered you to bring us drinks from the bar. In fact, why don't you do that."

"You want me to bring you a drink here?"

"Why not? All this waiting is so wearing on a soul."

"Are you sure?"

"Yes. And please take your time. For your own sake."

"Very well," he said before he retreated and then vanished.

Estelle was already hurrying to the hidden closet, gesturing at Sophie to follow her. With quick, sure hands, she released the closet door. "Hurry."

Sophie ducked in behind her, finding herself in a small, cramped space. "Did you see Schwarz?"

"Yes. And I'm not sure if we'll have fifteen minutes." Estelle was feeling along the edge of the rear wall, and the click as the hidden door at the rear swung open sounded overly loud. "Just get what you came for and get out. There is a light at the bottom of the stairs same as this one. I'll wait up here and deal with Schwarz or anyone else."

Sophie pulled the tiny Riga Minox camera, smaller than the length of her hand, from her beaded handbag and started her descent into the darkness. The air down here was stagnant, a metallic scent hanging heavily around her. She reached the bottom as quickly as she dared in the darkness and found the light at the bottom of the stairs where Estelle had said it would be.

The Tunny machine sat directly in front of Sophie on a long counter. It was squat and square in shape, perhaps a bit bigger than a wooden milk crate. Or at least she was assuming that it was a Tunny machine, never having seen one before. However, Sophie had seen many teleprinters at Bletchley, all similar to the teleprinter that was attached to this machine. Rolls of paper ribbon were stacked up next to it on the counter, used, perforated fragments curling out of a metal bin underneath.

Sophie went directly to the boxy machine and discovered that the box itself was simply that—a metal cover placed over the machine that sat beneath, presumably to protect it from dust and debris. She lifted it carefully and was rewarded by a maze of small electronic parts and pieces, all sitting above a neat row of twelve rotors that looked like sprockets from a bicycle. Sophie took a half step back and raised the little camera. With some shock, she realized that her hands were shaking. After everything that had happened, after everything that had brought her here, this close to achieving her mission, her nerves chose this moment to make themselves known?

A bubble of hysterical laughter rose in the back of her throat, and she swallowed it lest she make a sound. This was absurd, she reflected, but reassured herself that it was only a natural reaction. And on the heels of that thought, another gurgle of manic laughter threatened, because if ever there was a time for Sophie to embrace the unnatural accusations hurled at her since she was eight, now would be it. She took three deep breaths through her nose and out her mouth, focused on the mountain of sprockets and wires and gauges responsible for messages that wreaked death across a continent, and began taking photos.

The steady clicking as she opened and closed the camera to advance the film was the only sound in the tomblike space. She took photos as quickly as she could from as many angles as she could without risking blurring the image. When she was satisfied that she had captured as much as possible, she replaced the machine's cover and turned her attention to the cabinets that sat exactly as Estelle had described.

She set the little camera down and pulled out her set of lock picks. It took her less than a minute to open the cabinet, the simple lock giving way easily. She pulled the upper of the two drawers open, and her stomach sank. It was empty. She crouched in front of the lower drawer and opened it. This one was not empty, and instead, contained a neatly organized stack of what looked like about a half-dozen thin manuals.

Estelle pulled the first one out, the familiar eagle above the swastika stamped on the red cover. SONDERMASCHINEN SCHLÜS-SEL was written above. *Special machines key*, Sophie translated, and it was almost identical to the picture Miss Atkins had once shown her in a Baker Street flat. This was what she had come for.

She laid the manual out and began taking photos. Four times she changed the tiny film canisters, sliding each completed one into an empty Gauloises packet from her handbag. When she had finished the last book, she restacked them and placed them back as they'd been found. She closed the drawer, relocked the cabinet, and switched off the light. She estimated that the entire process had taken less than fifteen minutes but still Sophie hurried back up the stairs as soundlessly as possible. She reached the closet and pushed the hidden door closed, making sure it latched behind her.

She smoothed her hair, took a deep breath, and edged her way to the suite door, listening hard. She put a hand up to push the door open but just as her palm made contact she stilled.

They were no longer alone.

CHAPTER
21

Estelle

Mademoiselle Allard. What are you doing up here all alone? I did not expect to see you again so soon. What a...happy surprise."

Estelle froze where she had been pacing and tried desperately to smother the horror that bloomed through her chest. She lifted her chin and faced Scharführer Schwarz. He was standing in the door of the Imperial Suite, the weasel-faced aide, Hesse, hovering behind him.

"Scharführer," she greeted loudly, not allowing herself to look anywhere near the dining room. "It is a happy surprise. Whatever are you doing here?"

"The same thing I was doing last time we met," he said. "Looking for a traitor."

"What?" Estelle let her voice rise, which wasn't very difficult. "What are you talking about?"

"Madame Beaufort. Where is she?"

"What?" Estelle stalled, feigning utter bewilderment.

"The woman you entered this hotel with. Where is she?"

"You think Madame Beaufort is a traitor?" Estelle said, making an epic effort to sound merely appalled and not terrified.

"Where is she?" Schwarz demanded again, ignoring her question.

"I don't know where Madame Beaufort is at the moment," Estelle said. "She left. We have been waiting and waiting for Hauptgefreiter Müller to find a ladder and whatever things he needed to get a painting hung up properly on the wall. But it's been an age, and she got bored of waiting. She probably went to get a drink. Did you check the bars?"

"She's not in the bars," the aide muttered in German. "I told you something wasn't right. And I told you this whore here can't be trusted."

"Mmm." The sergeant addressed Estelle in French. "I'll ask you again, Mademoiselle, and I'd like you to consider your answer carefully. Where is Madame Beaufort?"

"You think I'm hiding her?" Estelle exclaimed. "Look around. As you can see, she's not here." She turned on her heel and flounced into one of the bedrooms. Away from the dining room. Away from the agent. "And she's certainly not here either," she announced. "Look for yourselves."

The sergeant and aide followed her into the room. Estelle almost wept with relief. Sophie had minutes now in which she could slip from that damn closet and escape the suite and no one would see her go. Not from here, anyway.

"Tell me, how is it that you are acquainted with Madame Beaufort?" Schwarz asked.

"I met her while I was shopping the other day," Estelle

told him readily. "Her family owns a cosmetics company, you know. A stroke of luck indeed because to find a good lipstick these days is almost impossible. Such an inconvenience."

The aide was sneering at her again, and Estelle kept right on going, hoping with all her might that Sophie had found everything she needed and was on her way out of this suite and out of this damn hotel.

"Anyway, she had a painting that she wanted to gift to the Reichsmarschall while she was in Paris, and I was only too happy to offer my help. Her father is from Berlin, you know. Or maybe it's her mother. I can't remember. She seems very German, and I thought she might appreciate the hotel. You know, being amongst her people here."

"Her people?" The sergeant had a look of disgust across his face. "I am quite sure that we are not her people."

"What does that mean?"

"I think, Mademoiselle, that you are not telling me everything." Schwarz's eyes had narrowed. "I think you know more about this woman than you are telling me."

The aide beside him suddenly laughed. "You can't be serious," he said to the sergeant. "This...this woman here has the intelligence of a post. I've known her for years. She brings baubles to the Reichsmarschall like a pretty little lapdog hoping for a pat on her head. Though I suspect she gets that from him too."

"Even lapdogs bite," Schwarz said. "Perhaps I should have her arrested to be sure."

The ground tilted beneath Estelle's feet, and the edges of her vision dimmed.

"Mademoiselle Allard!" The feminine voice came from the salon. "Where have you gone? I've found a toolbox."

Estelle tried to get her lungs working again to clear the spots from around the edge of her vision.

Run, she wanted to scream. *Run as far and as fast as you can.*

Schwarz spun. The aide's mouth snapped shut.

"Mademoiselle?" Sophie's voice floated from beyond. "Are you still here?"

The two men crowded out of the bedroom, leaving Estelle behind. She forced her feet to move and followed them.

Sophie was crouched near the painting, the dusty little toolbox that had sat in the corner of the closet in one hand. She set the toolbox down against the wall beside the painting and straightened as the men approached, a blinding smile on her face. "Oh, it's you again," she exclaimed happily. "What a coincidence."

The sergeant stopped, Hesse nearly crashing into him. Estelle edged toward the door.

"Tell me why you are here, Madame Beaufort," Schwarz said coldly. "What have you been sent to do?"

"At the moment, we are trying to hang a painting," she replied without missing a beat. "I don't suppose you've run into Hauptgefreiter Müller? He's gone to fetch a ladder. Perhaps you would be so kind as to assist when he returns."

"How is your friend?" Schwarz asked, ignoring her query and advancing toward the agent.

"My friend?"

"The half-wit I met at the basilica."

Sophie's smile slipped. "He is not a half-wit—"

"No, I didn't think he was. Finally, we get to a truth from you. Where is he now, Madame Beaufort? And what is your mission here?"

"—and he is much better, thank you," Sophie continued

on, ignoring his interruption. "I took him to the Tuileries Gardens. He enjoyed the peace." She nudged the toolbox by her foot a little farther behind the painting before stepping away and wandering unhurriedly toward the door. Toward Estelle.

Estelle tried to catch her eye, to understand what was happening. To understand what the agent thought she was doing. But Sophie ignored her.

"Stop," Schwarz commanded.

Sophie ignored him, too, and continued walking.

"You were told to stop," Hesse barked.

"I don't know who you are working for but you'll not get far, Madame Beaufort," the sergeant shouted. "I have more men on their way up here now."

"I'll stop her," the aide said and pushed by the sergeant, launching himself at Sophie.

The agent unaccountably paused and allowed him to close his hands around her neck. He snarled in triumph, an expression of savage glee suffusing his narrow features.

Estelle never saw where the knife that punctured his neck came from, though the long, flowing sleeves of Madame Beaufort's dress had likely not been an accident. The aide dropped bonelessly to the rug, his mouth opening and closing like a fish, his eyes rolling back in his head.

In another movement so swift that Estelle barely had time to register it, Sophie turned on her, wrapping an arm around her neck and yanking her hard backward. With Sophie's height and startling strength, Estelle found herself held immobile, her fingers clawing at Sophie's forearm. A prick of warm steel against her neck stilled those struggles.

"No," Estelle gasped, none of the terror in her voice feigned.

Because she understood now exactly what Sophie was doing. "Don't do this."

"I must," Sophie said. She started pulling Estelle back toward the door of the suite.

Schwarz nudged the leg of the lifeless aide with his boot. "Fool," he breathed. "But useful in the end, I suppose. For he has shown me exactly what you are, Madame."

Estelle's gaze darted frantically around the room, past the Gestapo officer who was now circling them with a feral intensity. "No," she wheezed. "No, no, no."

"You will not come any closer," the agent said to Schwarz. "If you do, I'll kill this one too."

"Kill her, then," he said. "She is of no consequence to me."

"But she is of consequence to the Reichsmarschall. And you and I both know it, no matter how stupid she might be."

The sergeant hesitated.

"For what it's worth, the dead man was right," Sophie told him with scorn. "She really does have the intelligence of a post."

From outside the suite, the sound of boots on stairs rumbled.

Sophie jerked Estelle closer to her, turning away from Schwarz as if trying to listen to the sound coming from the suite's entrance. "You know what you must do," she whispered harshly in her ear.

Estelle squeezed her eyes shut, tears leaking from the corners. She nodded imperceptibly.

"Now scream," Sophie hissed.

Estelle took a deep breath and did as the British agent instructed, a hysterical, frantic sound that went on and on. Sophie shoved her toward the sergeant and bolted through the door. Estelle fell to her hands and knees, her teeth clacking hard, her breath coming in gasps.

Schwarz bellowed and pursued the agent out of the suite, joining the chase.

Alone, Estelle half stumbled, half crawled across the empty salon toward the painting. She tugged frantically at the tool-box, pulling it out from behind the frame. Sophie's pretty, beaded handbag rested exactly where Estelle had known it would be. She snatched it from behind the painting and tucked it under her arm.

As she did, the cover slid from the painting. Unsteadily, Estelle stood, her eyes fixed on Polyxena, still in her flowing cobalt tunic, her mother still desperately trying to reach her around the soldiers who held her firm. Except now, some-thing had changed. Perhaps it was a trick of light or perhaps it was something else entirely, but Polyxena no longer looked resigned. Instead she looked resolute.

Estelle turned away from the painting and made her way back toward the suite's door. She exited, pulling the door closed firmly behind her. There was no one about. Wher-ever Sophie had led her pursuers, they were gone. She wiped her face, straightened her shoulders, and, with Sophie's handbag securely clutched in her hand, made her way back downstairs.

"Mademoiselle Allard." A horrified-looking Müller met her at the bottom of the stairs. "There is a rumour that something has happened. Are you all right?"

"She tried to kill me," Estelle whispered, letting a few more tears slide down her face.

"What?" Müller's face went white. "Who?"

"Madame Beaufort," Estelle sniveled. "The sergeant is pursuing her. I think . . . I think she came here to kill the Reichs-marschall. I . . . I think she used me. She called me stupid."

Estelle swayed on her feet, and Müller leapt forward to steady her. "Are you all right?" he asked.

"I don't know." Estelle sniffed. "It all happened so fast. I'm not feeling well at all. I . . . I'd like to go home," she said, turning her tearful gaze on the youth.

"Yes, yes, of course," he said. "I will arrange it."

"Thank you," Estelle told him. "I don't know what I would do without you."

She allowed Müller to walk her through the hotel to the Cambon exit. They passed the bars and dining rooms and salons, the patrons focused on their meals and drinks and cigarettes and all oblivious to everything that was unfolding somewhere above their heads.

The young officer put her in a car and gave the driver instructions.

★ ★ ★

Estelle climbed the stairs to her apartment for the last time.

She opened the door and stalked through the empty flat, the bare space above the hearth a glaring reminder that she would not be coming back. She strode into her bedroom and set the little handbag on the coverlet. From beneath the bed, she pulled out a small travelling case, already packed. With care, she transferred the contents of Sophie's handbag into the interior lining of the case, beneath the samples of lipstick and powder. She pulled off the lemon-yellow dress, tossing it on the end of the bed, and changed into clothes more suited for a travelling saleswoman.

She picked up the case, left the bedroom, and deposited it on the dining room table. She opened the tall cabinet and chose a pretty crystal tumbler, carrying it with her into the kitchen. There, she poured herself a healthy measure of brandy from the bottle she'd kept hidden under the sink. She raised her glass in a silent toast to the woman who had risked everything and made a silent promise to her that her risk would not be for nothing. She tipped the brandy down her throat, embracing the burn.

Estelle left the crystal tumbler in the kitchen by the sink, fetched the case from the table, and made her way to the door. She put her hand on the knob and turned to look behind her one last time. Her gaze collided with that of the nude woman who glared silently back.

In the end, once the Le Brun canvas had been removed and wrapped, Estelle had retrieved this painting from behind her dressing room wall to show to Sophie. The agent had said nothing as Estelle had propped it up against her writing desk, only stared at it with an impenetrable expression.

"What do you think?" Estelle had asked finally.

Sophie transferred her pale gaze to Estelle, and Estelle once again had the unnerving sensation that this woman was peering directly into her soul.

"It's a painting of you," Sophie said simply.

"It looks nothing like me."

"Fearless defiance and unassailable courage. That is who you are." Sophie put her hand lightly on Estelle's arm. "And I am honoured to be fighting beside you."

Estelle had covered the agent's hand with her own, her throat tight. "And I you."

Estelle should have restored the painting to its rightful place above the hearth but there had been no time. And it was too late now. The nude woman, with her midnight hair and outstretched hands, would stay as she was, greeting whoever might enter this apartment next with her unapologetic boldness. She would remain a keeper of the secrets and stories hidden within these walls for as long as necessary.

And she would remain a reminder to Estelle of the faith and trust that Sophie had placed in her.

Estelle turned from the painting and exited quickly, locking the door behind her. From across the hall, she heard the muffled wail of a baby followed by a raised voice and a clatter. Steps approached from within, but by the time Frau Hoffmann opened her apartment door, Estelle was already down the stairs.

She had a plane to catch, somewhere near Gasny.

CHAPTER
22

Sophie

Sophie woke to blackness.

She thought her eyes were open but she could see nothing. Maybe she'd been blinded, she thought rather distantly. She tried to raise her hands to touch her face, but pain ripped through her and made her gasp. Her arms were broken, she was reasonably sure. As were both her legs. Her mind examined the pain there, as if she were poking herself from a distance, and decided that as long as she didn't move, the dull throbbing in her lower legs was merely a steady count of her heartbeats.

A peculiar thought.

She licked her cracked, dry lips, thinking how lovely a sip of water might be. No, she amended, a glass of lemonade the way Piotr used to make it. Not enough sugar and too much lemon but delicious for its startling tartness all the same. She smiled at the memory before sharp bee stings stabbed at her lips where they were split.

She'd seen Piotr yesterday. Or maybe it was the day before. It was difficult to keep track of time now. He'd been standing by her feet, in his uniform, looking rather dismayed at whatever it was that the Gestapo were doing to her. Sophie had focused on him to distract herself from the pain that had become her constant companion. She'd tried to keep him in focus long enough to see his face but he'd wavered, and Sophie had closed her eyes. When she'd awoken again, the Gestapo were gone and so was Piotr.

She hoped he was telling her instructors that they ought to be impressed, she thought disjointedly. They would, undoubtably, call her unnatural again but this time it would be with approval. She hadn't told the Nazi roaches anything other than what they thought they already knew. Lipsticks and powder and a chance to kill Göring when he returned. Miss Atkins would most definitely approve.

Sophie sighed. She would be sad, Miss Atkins would, when Sophie didn't come back. And so would Will, though he would read her letter and understand. And Estelle would complete what Sophie couldn't. Because, like Will, Estelle was a survivor.

A deafening bang reverberated, and an agonizing light flooded the room. Sophie groaned and squeezed her eyes shut but it didn't seem to help the new pain that sparked deep in her head.

"Sophie." Her name, called as if someone was yelling through a window.

"Sophie." Again her name, and this time it was accompanied by a blow to the head. A faint buzzing started in her ears.

Sophie opened her eyes. They were back, the roaches in grey and black, hovering above her. Back with their instruments and hammers and tools and electrical devices that hummed, determined to extract the secrets caught inside her head.

They would never have them. They had to know this by now. This made her happy.

"Sophie." A new voice from the corner of the room caught her attention. This was a voice she recognized.

"Piotr," she murmured, relief washing through her like a warm bath. She wasn't alone here anymore. This time he wasn't in his uniform. He was wearing the heavy sweater he'd been wearing that last morning. She could see his face clearly, and this time, he didn't look troubled. He looked the way he had when he had helped her to her feet the morning she'd crashed her bicycle.

"Did you make it count?" Piotr asked her.

"Yes," Sophie whispered.

"What did she say?" someone barked loudly in German. She ignored them.

"I knew you would." Her husband smiled at her. "Don't be afraid. You're almost home."

Sophie tried to nod but the buzzing inside her head had turned into a sound similar to a stream dancing over a bed of stone. And like the stream, whatever pain she had felt seemed to be draining away just as quickly.

"Chain her back up." Another loud, guttural command.

Sophie didn't take her eyes off Piotr. He glanced beside him and smiled, and Sophie could now see that he wasn't alone. A colt, the color of a new copper penny, was standing at his side. The foal shook its head and pranced, skittering away before coming to stand beside Piotr once again.

The sight filled Sophie's heart with joy. Her husband put one hand on the colt's withers and looked back at Sophie.

"Come home, Sophie," he said and held out his hand.

And Sophie reached for it, grasping it tight.

CHAPTER
23

Estelle

The English, like the French, often had the most literal names for their villages, Estelle reflected as she gazed north. Wells-next-the-Sea was exactly as advertised, perched stubbornly at the edge of a tidal flat that was even now giving way to the steady, creeping onslaught of the North Sea. The midmorning sun was warm on her skin, the breeze barely stirring. Here, the salty air was humid, thick with an underlying scent of earthy vegetation. Above her head, a bird shrieked and wheeled away toward the sea.

Perhaps it was the sight of the unending horizon, where the darker blue hues of the sea met the brighter, paler smudge of sky, that made her realize why she had come here. A thousand generations before her and a thousand generations after she was gone would stand in this same spot and look out at the same horizon. The line that stitched water to air would be found in the same place. It would never move. It would never leave or disappear. Not like the people who had once anchored Estelle's life. Gone, all of them, vanished without a trace like smoke in a gale.

Including Sophie Beaufort.

But the place that Sophie had loved was not gone. It had survived against the cruelty of time and man and beckoned to Estelle for reasons she hadn't been able to explain until she had stood looking at the horizon where sky met sea. She could find Millbrook. She could visit the place where Sophie had spent hours exploring the hills with her brother, shooting tin cans. Even if Sophie was gone forever, the home she had adored was not.

Estelle clutched her travel bag and turned away from the water, heading west. Millbrook was about two miles outside of town, a helpful gentleman at the train station had told her. All she had to do was follow the old mill road out of town, and it would take her directly to the estate. Just follow the people, he'd said, tipping the brim of his hat. For today was market day at Millbrook.

Estelle did as the kind stranger had suggested, joining clumps of people who were winding their way along the rutted track. Baskets were hung over arms or fastened to the rear of bicycles, and children darted from place to place, inevitably spilling into the tall grasses along the side of the road. An intrepid youth had set up a small table at about the halfway point between the town and the manor, selling ale by the cup.

If one did not wonder why there was no petrol for cars or why there seemed to be a disproportionate number of women and elderly folk in the migration of market-goers, one might convince oneself that the war had never existed. Here, the jagged holes torn into the fabric of everyday life were less noticeable than they were in the pockmarked, ragged cities like London. Yet in both places, time marched on, uncaring.

Estelle saw the house before she saw the market. Millbrook sat up on a gentle rise, as if surveying its domain, and Estelle recognized it instantly from the photo she had once examined on a gleaming rosewood tabletop. The tall shrubs that flanked the house were the same, though the sprawling lawns that rolled away from the manor had been torn up and turned into vegetable gardens. Stakes and the occasional scarecrow dotted an expanse that had, at one time, been a manicured carpet of grass.

The black-and-white photo had also been unable to capture the color that blazed from the house itself. Windows reflected the sun in a glittering array, and the stone façade glowed a rich umber. The building was architecturally impressive, a proud ambassador to a time long past. But if Estelle had been asked to describe it, she would have said none of those things. She would have said it looked like a home.

Perhaps it was the crowds of people who swirled at the base of the long drive that made it appear so. It was here that the market was set up under a canopy of ancient trees, and it was a jaunty, bustling affair, as if it were deliberately defying the years of want. A large collection of booths and tables had been set up in two rows, and someone, somewhere, was playing a fiddle. Brightly colored ribbons had been tied to the top of each booth, adding another element of festivity.

In the distant past, Estelle imagined that the tables and booths would have groaned under the weight of their wares. Today, the offerings were sparse, but still a rainbow of vegetables stuck triumphantly out of crates, barrels of apples and pears were set in rows, and there were ropes of skinned rabbits for the stewpot. Estelle wandered down the first row, sidestepping those haggling and debating the best value. Toward the center, honey was being sold in a haphazard collection of jars and bottles, and, farther down, a young woman was selling scented soap and knitted socks.

And beyond that, there was a collection of paintings.

Estelle walked toward the last booth at the end, coming to a stop in front of the small wooden structure. There were no crowds here, though occasionally a child stopped to inspect a particular canvas before skipping away. Estelle stepped closer and examined the collection.

It was certainly a bright effort, the colors of each composition vivid, if a little one-dimensional. There were renditions of the sea, of grass-tufted dunes, and of copses of trees under heavy, leaden skies. More still were dedicated to the sailboats and fishing boats that plied the waters, and a few depicted fluffy white sheep grazing bottle-green pastures. At the bottom of each, *William Seymour* had been signed with a proud flourish.

These would be paintings done by William, the artist who liked cars and art and his bacon blackened at the edges. William, who had traded a rifle for a watercolor set on his eleventh birthday. William, who learned to shoot to please his sister and had learned to fly to please his mum. William, who had never lived long enough to sell a painting.

Estelle's eyes burned. How was it possible that she still had tears left to cry? Maybe this hadn't been a good idea after all.

"Good morning." A cheery voice cut through Estelle's thoughts.

She blinked rapidly and straightened. "Good morning."

A buxom woman with kind eyes, a flushed face, and dark

hair just starting to silver was watching her. She wore practical shoes, a simple dress the color of autumn wheat, and an apron tied about her waist.

"Can I help you find something, lass?" the woman inquired.

"I wish you could," Estelle mumbled.

"You're looking for art?"

"Um. No."

The woman stared quizzically at her. "Then you were looking for William? I have to tell you, I'm not sure this is a good time."

Estelle put a hand out to steady herself against the booth. "He came back? He's here?" she blurted.

"Yes," the woman replied slowly, still staring at her.

Something deep inside her chest constricted painfully, joy and grief flooding through her all at the same time. William Seymour had survived. He'd survived impossible odds. His sister had been right all along.

The woman brushed her hands on her apron and came out from behind the booth. "May I ask who you are?"

"A friend," Estelle said. "Of his sister," she amended, realizing that she had no idea what Sophie's real name might have been. "I was a friend of his sister."

"Ah." The woman's expression instantly crumpled. "I'm sorry," she said, wiping at eyes that had gone misty. "You think you've overcome it, but it catches you at strange moments, the sadness."

"I understand."

"I'm Imogen," the woman said. "The housekeeper at Millbrook. I've known Will and Sophie their entire lives."

Estelle twisted the handle of her bag around her fingers, the strap biting into her skin. Sophie Seymour, she repeated silently in her head, letting the name sink in. Sophie really had been her first name.

"You're French, are you, lass?"

"Yes."

"You must have known our Sophie while she was studying in Paris, then?"

"Yes," Estelle said faintly. "In Paris."

"She is missed terribly. By none more so than Will." Imogen turned slightly and tipped her head toward the base of a twisted oak.

A hunched figure sat in a wheeled chair, his lower half covered with a blanket even in the warm air, his head bent in what looked like defeat. From this distance, it was impossible to make out his features, but the hair that fell over his forehead and shadowed his face was a familiar shade of pale blond.

"He's not himself yet," Imogen said. "He was barely recognizable when he came home." She sounded as if she was going to cry again. "They kept him in a...camp. He won't tell anyone what they did to him. But they took his leg."

"I'm sorry," Estelle whispered.

"As am I." Imogen wiped her eyes again with the edge of her apron. "Perhaps it was for the best that Sophie died long before the war ever became what it did."

"What?" Estelle asked in confusion.

"Oh, lass. I'm sorry to be the one to tell you this. Sophie was working in Warsaw when they bombed the city the first time." Imogen sniffed, patting Estelle gently on the arm. "She died in that bombing. And it's the only thing that offers any of us any consolation. Will especially. That she didn't have to see or suffer what he did. That she didn't have to grieve their parents." She wiped her eyes again and let her apron fall. "Small mercies, I know. But now they are all we have."

Estelle couldn't speak. Didn't really understand what had happened. What she did understand was that the British agent code-named Celine had kept many secrets, and not just from Estelle.

"I'm sorry, lass, for being so maudlin on such a beautiful day." The housekeeper shook her head as if she might shed her sadness the way a dog shook to shed water. "I thought, in truth, that maybe bringing William out here in the sunshine, where he could see the market and see his paintings, would make him remember the better times." She glanced at the hunched figure under the tree. "Would you speak to him? Will?"

Estelle shrank away. "I don't know him."

"But you knew his Sophie. Maybe you could share something with him about her? A happy memory, perhaps?"

"I don't want to upset him."

"I don't think that there is anything that you could say that would make his suffering worse."

Estelle bit her lip so hard that she tasted blood. Imogen was wrong. There was a great deal that she could say to the desolate man in the wheeled chair that would make this all worse. Estelle could tell him that she had not been able to save his Sophie. That his beloved sister and best friend had very likely died a slow, horrible death at the hands of the same monsters that had kept William Seymour captive for years. That Sophie had witnessed more hate and more evil than even an RAF pilot shot down in the opening salvos of the war.

"Please," Imogen said. "Please just talk to him. The doctor gives him medicine but I don't know that it helps any. It only seems to make him confused and nauseated. He's but a shadow of himself, and I am powerless to do anything except watch him fade away. You can't imagine what that's like."

"I can," Estelle whispered. She knew this woman's fear intimately and the feeling of helplessness that came along with it.

"Then you'll speak with him?"

Estelle could almost feel the hope in that question right down through her bones.

"Of course." She couldn't answer otherwise.

"Bless you, lass." Imogen was sniffling again.

Slowly, Estelle left the booth and walked toward the man in the chair. The ground was dappled here, the sun finding holes through the tree's canopy to splash a pattern of yellow-gold and grey-blue across the overgrown grass. Here, only the cowslips on the ground and the sparrows in the branches above would overhear their words.

She stopped in front of William but the man seemed oblivious to her presence.

"Mr. Seymour?" Estelle tried.

No response.

Estelle set her bag down in the grass and crouched in front of Sophie's brother. She looked up at him and sucked in a sharp breath. He was painfully thin, his face gaunt, with dark shadows beneath his eyes that could not hide the same magnificent bone structure that had made his sister a Nordic princess and, in a different time, would have made this man a Nordic prince. He had the same arresting, pale eyes as Sophie but, unlike his sister, Will's were empty and flat, his pupils mere pinpoints.

Morphine, no doubt. Estelle had seen it a million times in the field, along with the muddled confusion and disorientation that came with it. In truth, it probably didn't matter what she said to William Seymour in this moment because he probably wouldn't even remember any of it.

His hands lay listlessly atop the blanket that covered his lap. His bony knees jutted out beneath the blanket, and on the right, a booted foot rested on the ground below. On the left, there was nothing but an empty space.

"Hello, William," Estelle said quietly. She reached out and gathered his hands in hers. His skin was cold and clammy to the touch, and if he objected to her gesture, he didn't show it. Estelle was quite certain he wasn't even aware she was there.

"I was a friend of your sister," she started. "She talked about you a great deal, and I could tell how much she loved you." Her fingers tightened on his, as if she could make him acknowledge her by touch. "I didn't know Sophie long but I wanted to tell you how brave she was. How smart and selfless and brilliant she was. I admired her, William, so much. I didn't get the chance to tell her this so I'm telling you."

Estelle stopped talking, her throat closing on her again. William didn't stir.

"She saved my life," Estelle whispered. "She saved so many lives. Almost no one will ever know what she did. What she accomplished."

Because it had been Estelle who had watched the promised Lizzie drop from the sky at an alarming angle to land in a moonlit field. The little plane had been guided in by Vivienne's resistance fighters, and after touching down, the pilot did not shut off the engine. Estelle had been waved aboard, along with a man who identified himself only as Henri.

Less than two minutes after the Lizzie had landed, it was climbing back into the sky and banking sharply for the shores of England, Estelle hunched inside, braced for the thunder of guns that never came. She had wept silently as land had given way to the silver expanse that was the Channel. She had wept again after she had handed the little box of film to the woman named Miss Atkins in a Baker Street flat cloudy with cigarette smoke and explained why the agent named Celine was unable to do so. What she had sacrificed.

In front of her, William Seymour's eyes remained unfocused, his breathing shallow but steady, his hands limp in hers.

"So you don't get to give up now," Estelle said. "Because Sophie never gave up on you. Do you hear me?" She leaned closer to William. "When people told her that, even if you had survived the downing of your plane, you would not have survived being taken. And even if you survived being taken, you would not have survived the days and weeks and months that followed in whatever nightmare you were cast into. They told her that you were dead, and she refused to believe them. Do you understand?"

William's fingers twitched beneath her own before stilling again. His slack expression remained unchanged.

"You don't get to give up," Estelle repeated. She pulled her hands from his and stood, brushing at the bits of grass and earth that clung to the hem of her cream-colored skirt. She snatched her bag from the ground. A thready anger had gripped her, and it was better than the omnipresent sorrow. "I failed your sister, and I will never forgive myself for that. So don't do what I did. Don't fail her, not when you have been given this second chance at life. A chance she never got. Find a way to live again, William Seymour."

Estelle turned and walked away from him because she was afraid that anything else she said would be a continued, unjustified assault of harsh words borne from her own guilt and weakness and regrets. She stopped in front of the booth again, staring at the collection of landscapes and seascapes.

The housekeeper emerged from behind the booth to meet her, wringing her hands, her face a mask of worry. "Did he say anything to—"

"I'd like to buy a painting," Estelle said.

Imogen's jaw slackened before it snapped closed again. "I beg your pardon?"

"One of Mr. Seymour's paintings. I'd like to buy one."

The housekeeper was staring at her like she'd lost her mind. "Don't feel like you have to—"

"This one." Estelle stepped closer to the booth and lifted a small rectangular canvas that had been mounted in a simple wood frame. It was an image of Millbrook, the sky a bright blue over the distinctive house. The shrubs and greenery that had been dabbed around the base of the manor gave way to rolling lawns painted in sweeping brushstrokes.

She glanced back at William Seymour. He'd lifted his head and was staring out at something that only he could see.

"Why are you doing this?" Imogen asked as Estelle handed over her money. "This is too much."

"I am making an investment," Estelle replied. "One day, when he is a famous artist, this painting will be worth a hundred times what I paid today. You can tell him that I will accept nothing less."

She left the housekeeper staring after her and retraced her steps along the old mill road, back to the center of town. She stopped at the edge of the sea, where she had stood when she first disembarked. The horizon was still where it had been, the sky and the sea meeting in a breathtaking blue vista. She set her bag down on the ground and opened it, sliding the little painting inside, next to the sheet of paper that Miss Atkins had given her the day before Estelle had left for Norfolk.

Because Estelle had never returned to France. Instead, she had remained in England, working for the Inter-Services Research Bureau, teaching other agents, agents like Sophie, how to act, how to speak, how to eat, how to smoke, what to order in a café. Tiny details that might one day save their lives. She had been invaluable, Miss Atkins had told her on the day when people had finally danced in London's streets.

Estelle hadn't danced. Instead she had asked the woman for a favour.

That favour now rested beside the hopeful painting of Millbrook, and Estelle withdrew the long sheet, looking at it again, though she knew it by heart by now. There were three columns of names, prisoners who had been incarcerated by the Nazis at Amiens Prison before it had been bombed. The first column was a list of all prisoners. The second column was a list of those who had escaped when the walls of the prison crumbled beneath the explosives dropped from the sky in 1944. The third was a list of prisoners who had been recaptured.

Jerome de Colbert's name existed only in the first two columns.

It was time to return to France.

She would not return to the Paris apartment where her failures would forever haunt her. But the painting, along with the prison list, were reminders that second chances could exist.

That something lost could be found again.

CHAPTER

24

Gabriel

10 July 1943

Dearest Will,

If you are reading this letter, then you did what I could not and found your way home. As I write this I do not know where you are or what you may be enduring, but I know with all my heart that you will survive whatever comes your way. You've always lived without fear of failure.

I didn't live like that, not often enough and not soon enough. It may seem like I was daring and dauntless but I wasn't, not really, not like you. I kept myself safely insulated by my strengths, hidden behind my books and lessons because those were easy. It took falling in love to make me understand that the things worth most in life are hard. I was married, Will, to a man you won't ever get to meet, but whom you would have loved because Piotr was smart and funny and kind and he lived with the same courage you did.

I've tried to keep living like that. For you. And for him. To never give up, to keep fighting, to do hard things, and to refuse to fear failure. I hope, by the time you read this, I've made you both proud.

Good-bye, Will. Make every day count.

Your loving sister,
Sophie

Gabriel folded the copy of the letter and slid it back into the pocket of his jacket. He'd taken the letter out more from habit than anything else. From the number of times he had read it, Gabriel had it memorized. It was a strange feeling, knowing that the letter had been written to his grandfather yet feeling as though each word spoke directly to him.

His grandfather, surrounded by the rest of their family, had wept openly when Gabriel had read it to him. He'd had questions after that, most of which Gabriel had had answers for, because while Sophie Seymour had seemingly vanished into history, Sophie Kowalski, code name Celine, had not.

Her work at Bletchley had been carefully documented, commendations and notes on her extraordinary linguistic talents recorded by her superiors. Her training and service with the Inter-Services Research Bureau had been likewise documented, her mission linked to Operation Overlord. The revelation that William's sister had not perished in Warsaw but had, instead, become an agent revered for her cleverness and courage had been bittersweet.

It had taken time, but with help, Gabriel had managed to piece together the objective of the mission that had taken Sophie into France. Her fate had been dictated on a single sheet of typed paper, an illegible signature on the bottom of the page. Arrested, Paris, August 27, 1943. Gabriel could find no further records beyond that.

He had also been unable to find any reference to Estelle Allard. There had been, at the back of the bureau's file, a neatly typed report that made mention of a Frenchwoman, part of the Resistance operating out of Paris, who was referred to only as La Chanteuse. According to the report, the Frenchwoman had provided invaluable assistance to the SOE and had been smuggled out of France three weeks after Sophie's arrest. The report indicated that La Chanteuse had delivered an intelligence package on behalf of the British agent Celine to a Miss V. Atkins in London via Colonel James Reed at Tempsford. It did not say what was in the package, and what had happened to the Frenchwoman after that was lost to time.

Gabriel had decided that it was possible—likely, even—that the woman referred to as La Chanteuse had been Lia's grandmother. It seemed obvious that the Frenchwoman had been instrumental in helping the English agent named Celine complete her mission in 1943. And to Gabriel, it seemed just as likely that La Chanteuse had been the angel who had whispered hope into the ear of a suffering pilot on a sunny Norfolk morning.

Gabriel set the letter aside and sat back in his studio chair, gazing at the three Degas dancers caught forever in motion. They were the last of the collection he had worked on, most of the paintings needing very little in the way of restoration. He would crate and pack them properly after lunch and add them to the shipment that was set to be returned to Paris. The gallery for Aurelia Leclaire's collection had been selected, and the exhibition date three weeks from now decided upon. Advertisement for the exhibit had already garnered a great deal of interest.

The images of each painting had been showcased in art publications across the globe. International columnists from major newspapers had featured the collection in their respective arts and leisure sections, and art history professors from a storied collection of schools had incorporated the collection into lecture material. Each work had been uploaded into a variety of lost-art databases in the hopes that a rightful owner might be identified.

Thus far, Gabriel's office had received inquiries from museums and galleries and private collectors, all anxious to acquire various pieces. The museums and galleries had been engaged in conversation regarding loan or exhibition of pieces in the collection, and the private collectors had been turned away. But no one had come forward to indicate that any of the art might once have belonged to them or their family.

All of this, from the information he had uncovered about Sophie's past, the link to a French Resistance fighter called La Chanteuse, Gabriel's progress on each piece of art, and a warning that they might never be able to determine who may have owned Lia's collection, had been communicated to Lia in polite, professional emails and phone calls. She'd been gracious and pleasant, and yet every time Gabriel spoke to her, the hollow, awful feeling that had started that afternoon in the Millbrook attics had become a little more hollow and a little more awful.

You only meet the love of your life once, Lia's grandmother had once told her. *And if you're fool enough not to recognize that sort of love and treasure it for what it will become, then you never deserved it in the first place.*

Gabriel feared he'd let his greatest discovery slip through his fingers.

★ ★ ★

The night the exhibit opened in a Paris gallery in the Marais district, everything had been implemented exactly as Gabriel Seymour had instructed. Pale walls with polished floors that lent a minimalist, professional atmosphere. Subdued lighting except where the masterpieces hung. Comprehensive cards mounted beside each painting detailing the artist and the work itself as determined by Gabriel and his committee of experts. And all of it tended by a small army of people providing additional expertise or security or both.

An electrified hum of conversation swirled around each frame as scholars and artists and collectors and journalists clumped and drifted like flotsam through the space. The entire collection that had been in Estelle Allard's apartment was here. The Munch had a place of honour, as did the three Degas dancers. The rest of the paintings, including those that had been hanging in the living space and dining room of that Paris apartment, hung in tasteful arrangements.

But Gabriel wasn't at the exhibit to see the art. He'd come to see Lia.

He walked farther into the gallery, ignoring the stunning display of art on the walls. He stopped abruptly when he saw her, standing in front of a turbulent Turner seascape. She was wearing a dress the color of a crimson rose at dusk, her hair a curtain of rich chestnut shot through with gold. Her skin was sun-kissed, her extraordinary eyes almost a moss green in the low light. She had a small beaded clutch tucked under one arm and an empty champagne glass in her hand, her fingers toying absently with the ever-present pendant at her throat, as though deep in thought.

He swallowed, his mouth suddenly dry, and joined her in front of the seascape.

"I'm sorry," he said without preamble.

Lia turned slowly and looked up at him, her expression utterly inscrutable. "Good evening. It's nice to see you, too, Gabriel. I need to tell you that this exhibit is incredible. The gallery staff have been accommodating and extraordinary."

"I don't think you heard me."

"I heard you. I'm just not sure what it is you have to be sorry for, because all of this"—she waved her hand around her—"has exceeded my wildest expectations. And if you think I fault you in any way for being unable to uncover the history behind this collection or my grandmother's connection to it, please know I do not. The work you've done on my behalf has been worth every penny—"

"I need to apologize for lying to you."

Her fingers dropped from her pendant. "Lying to me? About what?"

"About kissing you. I've made a great many mistakes in my life, and kissing you was not one of them. The mistake I made was lying about it."

"Mmm."

He still couldn't tell what she was thinking.

"You were right that day. I was—am—hiding. From the

possibility of failure." He reached into his pocket and withdrew a folded paper, the edges worn. "I want to read you something."

"What is that?"

"It's a letter Sophie wrote to my grandfather. It was in the envelope you found in the attic at Millbrook."

Her lips parted, and he heard her inhale. "You don't have to do that. That is a private family matter—"

"No. You deserve to hear it." Gabriel took a deep breath and began.

When he was finished, he folded the letter back into its square. "My grandfather got his sister back, if only for a moment." He held the letter out to Lia. "And he was proven right. She never stopped fighting."

Wordlessly, Lia took the letter from his outstretched fingers.

"Sophie may have been writing that letter to William but the words she wrote spoke to my heart. I, too, have safely insulated myself because it was easy. I haven't had the courage to live as she did. I haven't really made each day count."

"Gabriel—"

"Hear me out. I am going to try to change that. Put myself in a position where I might fail. And maybe the paintings that you bought will be the only two pieces I ever sell in my life, but I won't know for sure unless I try, right? I won't know if I—" He stopped abruptly as Lia went up on her toes and kissed him.

Her lips brushed his with a butterfly-light touch, and she tasted of champagne.

"For the record, that was not a mistake either," she said.

"No," he whispered.

"Do you trust me?" she asked.

"I beg your pardon?"

"Do you trust me?"

"Yes."

"Good. Then come with me." She put her empty champagne glass on the tray of a passing waiter and caught his hand in hers, twining her fingers through his as if it were the most natural thing in the world.

She led him past the landscapes and Impressionists and into the short gallery, partially separated from the rest of the exhibit by a wall of frosted glass. There were people here, too, in small groups, speaking in hushed voices, or alone, simply standing in front of the images. The white, square wall that faced them was adorned with canvases blazing with saturated color beneath the lights.

Gabriel stopped, feeling fevered and freezing all at once. His skin prickled with a sensation he couldn't name, each breath an extraordinary effort. He pulled his fingers from hers.

"What have you done?" His voice was hoarse.

Lia didn't turn and kept her eyes on the canvas where two figures tangoed under a streetlight, alone against a backdrop of darkness. Beside them, a ballet dancer lifted her head toward her audience, the love of her craft caught in her eyes.

"These..." Gabriel stopped and tried again. "These paintings are..."

"Part of this story. They deserve a space on these walls just as much as any of the others."

"No. These paintings aren't part of this collection."

"Of course they are. Ironically enough, they may be the only part of this collection that truly belongs to me. These paintings are mine. To hang where I please. To share with whom I please."

Gabriel didn't answer but stepped forward and bent to examine the small card that had been mounted in the bracket next to the first canvas.

Après, the card read in bold letters. 2017. Artist Unknown. From The Private Collection Of Aurelia Leclaire.

"Artist unknown?" Gabriel straightened and turned to stare directly at her.

"I would never have forced you somewhere you didn't want to go. You are yet an unknown artist, just as the card says. The choice to claim your work as your own must be yours. Not mine." She opened her clutch and drew out a small white card.

She handed it to him. It was identical to the one already on the wall, except it read Après, 2017, Gabriel Seymour. From The Private Collection Of Aurelia Leclaire. "Replace the current card with this one. Or don't. It will have cost you nothing. You will have risked nothing. *Après* will stay here until the end of the exhibit a month from now, and after it is over, I'll take my painting home, and you can go back to hiding your work in the attics of Millbrook."

"You don't understand. It is one thing to exhibit my work. It is another to have it hanging here, an imposter amongst a gallery full of goddamn artistic geniuses."

"And who gets to decide who is a goddamn artistic genius?" Lia asked pleasantly. "You do yourself a disservice."

"We've had this conversation," he said through gritted teeth.

"And you were wrong then too."

"No, I wasn't."

"Yes, you were." This time it wasn't Lia who spoke but a familiar voice that came from behind him.

Gabriel spun in surprise. The woman standing before him

was lithe and graceful, with a round face framed by auburn hair twisted up into a crown on top of her head. A simple ivory dress floated around her body.

"Olivia," he said and bent to envelop the woman in a warm embrace. "It's so good to see you. It's been much too long." He pulled back in confusion. "What on earth are you doing here—" He stopped abruptly as he realized exactly why she was here. "Oh, Jesus."

"No, it wasn't Jesus who invited me," Olivia said, patting him on the arm. She slipped by Gabriel and Lia and stood in front of the second canvas as a knot of people drifted away. "It was Lia who insisted I come. And I'm glad she did. You titled this correctly, by the way. Dancing was always my first love."

Gabriel pinched the bridge of his nose with his fingers. "How did she find you?"

"As it turns out, there are not that many married couples who dance for the Royal Ballet," Lia told him, coming to stand next to Olivia as the woman gazed at her likeness on the wall. "It wasn't hard."

"All the years I have known you, Gabriel Seymour, and I never knew you could do this," Olivia said. "I never knew you had such extraordinary talent."

"It's not—"

"Do shut up," Olivia interrupted him. "Before you say something I won't be able to forgive you for."

Lia turned her head away but not before he saw her smile.

"My husband cried when he saw this, you know," Olivia continued. "And he's not much of a crier. In truth, we both cried. So when Lia tells you that you are a goddamn artistic genius, the smart thing for you to do is to nod your head and say thank you."

Gabriel closed his eyes briefly. "Um."

"Try again."

"Thank you."

"That's better. Here." Olivia turned away from the painting and extracted another small white card from her purse. "You need to put this up. It came with my invitation."

Gabriel took it from her. First Love, Gabriel Seymour, 2016. From The Private Collection Of Olivia Allen.

Gabriel's eyes snapped to Lia.

"I gifted it," Lia said. "To the person to whom it rightfully belongs."

"Oh." Gabriel stared at the card in her hand but made no move to take it.

"It's terrifying, isn't it?" Olivia mused.

"I beg your pardon?"

"Seeing a part of yourself exposed for the world to judge." The dancer's voice softened. "I get it. Because it's no different than what I do each night I step out on that stage and perform for an audience. No different than an author who tells a story, a composer who writes a concerto, an actor who portrays a character. All of us not knowing how we might be received."

Lia stayed silent, and he was aware she was watching him.

"What you have done here deserves to be recognized." Olivia went up on her tiptoes, kissing both of his cheeks. "Be brave, Gabriel Seymour," she said before vanishing into the crowd.

He watched her go before turning back to Lia. "What you've done is positively diabolical." It was hard to put heat into words he had already spoken in a Paris apartment.

"I've been accused of worse." She was smiling as she said it. "Did it work?"

"Maybe."

"Good."

"How did you convince the gallery to exhibit my work?"

Lia shot him a long look. "An entire collection of artistic geniuses gave me some leverage, Gabriel. You may have looked after the arrangements, but I am the de facto owner. The gallery director was not about to quibble over two additional paintings that I wished to have displayed as part of the exhibit."

"They never mentioned it to me."

"Because I asked them not to." She paused. "I think you should know that the gallery has asked me about the possibility of more," she said.

"More what?"

"More of your work."

"What?"

"There has been significant interest in these paintings, even before the exhibit opened. The gallery is quite confident that they would be able to sell additional works by this particular artist."

"What did you tell them?"

"That I would speak to the artist and let him decide. If and how many he would be willing to exhibit and sell." Lia caught his hand in hers, gently uncurling his fingers from the two cards that he still held. "The choice is yours," she said. "To be seen. Or not. I will not think more or less of you no matter what you decide."

Gabriel looked down to where their hands joined. "Make every day count," he murmured under his breath. Without hesitation, he approached the two canvases and replaced the cards beside each.

He stepped back, reaching for Lia's hand again.

"How does it feel?" she asked.

"Like I just jumped out of a plane."

Lia laughed and lifted their hands. "And you're going to take me with you?"

"If you're willing to jump."

"Try me," she said.

Gabriel caught his breath as he gazed down at her. He wondered how scandalous it might be if he hauled her up against him and kissed her senseless—

"Excuse me. Are you Aurelia Leclaire?"

CHAPTER

25

Lia

PARIS, FRANCE
10 NOVEMBER 2017

Lia turned to find a distinguished-looking man with deep-set brown eyes and hair liberally silvered at the temples. He was dressed in a severe charcoal suit, though his turquoise shirt was open at the throat. He held a brochure from the ex-hibit in his hands.

"I am," she replied.

"Allow me to introduce myself. I am Luca Adler. We've travelled here from Geneva."

"Welcome," Lia replied, shaking his hand. "Is there some-thing I can help you with?"

"I'm not sure." The man's eyes dropped, and his forehead creased. "Your necklace. May I ask where you got it?"

Lia put her hand to her throat. The little enameled pendant was warm against her skin.

Gabriel slid his arm over her shoulder. "May I ask what your interest is in Miss Leclaire's jewelry?" His voice was pleasant enough but there was an unmistakable steely tone beneath.

"I've seen it before," Adler said. "That pendant, that is."

"It was a gift from my grandmère," Lia told him, puzzled.

"And your grandmother was the Estelle Allard mentioned here?" He gestured to the brochure.

"Yes."

"Indeed." The man still looked distracted.

"Is there something else I can help you with?"

"I think that maybe we can help you." He held up the brochure. "My mother saw the advert for this exhibition on the news. Saw the story behind it and the photos of the paintings that were to be shown. She recognized three of them."

Lia glanced at Gabriel, her heart skipping.

Gabriel extended his hand. "Gabriel Seymour," he said. "I was hired by Miss Leclaire to curate and restore this collection."

Adler shook his hand. "A pleasure."

"May I ask which three paintings your mother believes she recognized?"

"The Degas paintings. At the risk of sounding insane, I think they may have, at one time, belonged to my mother."

"Extraordinary," Gabriel said politely. "Do you have any evidence to back such a claim?"

"I think so. But I also think," he said, glancing again at Lia's throat where her pendant rested, "that my mother should be the one to show you. She's here tonight," he added. "And I would be much obliged if you would speak with her."

"Of course," Lia replied. She realized that she was gripping Gabriel's arm hard enough to make her fingers ache and forced herself to relax her grip.

They followed Adler to the far end of the exhibit where the ballerinas still practiced and pliéd across a painted stage. There were bunches of people here, craning their heads to get a better view of the canvases. In the center of the crowds, noticeable if only for her solitary silhouette, an elderly woman stood, gazing at the dancers. She was dressed somberly in a long dress of deep wine, her white hair drawn up and twisted to the back of her head in a style similar to the dancers whom she gazed upon. One hand rested on a gleaming black cane, the other held a small packet of what looked like paper against her chest.

"Mama," Adler said quietly, "this is Aurelia Leclaire and Gabriel Seymour. Miss Leclaire, Mr. Seymour, my mother, Dr. Alina Adler."

The woman turned toward Lia, intelligent dark eyes meeting hers directly before dropping to the pendant at her throat, the same way her son's had.

She drew in a sharp breath and wobbled slightly before her son steadied her with his arm. She dropped her hand, the one holding the paper, and Lia wobbled as well. For nestled at the collar of the woman's dress was an exact replica of the pendant Lia wore.

Lia was aware that Gabriel had slid an arm around her waist, and she was inordinately grateful for that.

"Your necklace," Lia managed. "Where did you get it?"

"It was a gift when I was a child," Alina replied. "It was one of the few things I took with me when I fled France during the war."

"How old were you when you fled?" Gabriel asked.

"I was six, maybe seven. My memories of that journey are in little fragments. Pieces that I confess I tried to avoid dwelling on for most of my life."

"Did you leave with your family?" Lia was trying to understand what was happening here.

"No. My family was...gone. It was just me who was left. I fled France with a group of other children. I remember darkness and cold and hunger and fear. A child never forgets fear like that." She ran her fingers over the head of her cane.

"She was one of many children who found refuge in Switzerland," Luca said. "She was adopted by my grandparents. My aunt was also adopted."

"I was Jewish," Alina said. "And I was one of the lucky ones."

"Tell me about the paintings," Gabriel prompted gently.

Alina held out the paper she still had in her hand. Only now, Lia could see that it was an envelope. "What is this?"

"It's a photograph. Take a look."

Lia opened the envelope and extracted a worn black-and-white photo. It was a picture of a little girl with dark hair and dark eyes, sitting in the lap of a pretty woman with the same dark features. They were both laughing, the woman's arms wrapped tightly around the little girl.

And in the background, above their heads, the Degas ballerinas danced across the wall.

"That's me. And that was my aunt Rachel," Alina said. "The paintings, as you can see, are in that picture. But that's not where I remembered them. I remember them hanging someplace else."

Lia couldn't breathe. "Where?" she whispered.

"A little room. One where I had to be silent all the time. Looking back now, I know that I was hidden. That room saved my life." She looked up at Lia. "Your grandmère, Estelle Allard, saved my life."

"You're Aviva," Gabriel breathed.

"Yes," the woman agreed.

"What else do you remember?" Lia asked.

"I remember that the apartment where I was hidden had crystal chandeliers that made little rainbows across the floor and walls when the sun came in the windows. I remember that your grandmother would read to me, and often she would sing. She sang all the time."

Lia looked down at the photograph again and the laughing child. "La Chanteuse," she whispered to herself.

"You never went back after the war? To Paris?" Gabriel asked.

The doctor shook her head. "My parents told me that I didn't speak a word for fourteen months after I was placed with them," the woman continued. "That when I arrived at their house, I didn't laugh, I didn't cry. I couldn't even tell them my name. So they picked one for me. Alina."

"But that wasn't your name."

"It became my name. And I became their daughter. I became a sister. I became a dancer, a doctor, a wife, and a mother. My heart was full, and I tried to leave the past where it lay because I thought it was best to look only forward." She smiled sadly. "After the birth of my son, I tried to find your grandmother because, for the first time, I understood how hard it might have been for her to let me go. But I didn't know her last name or even the address where we had once lived. But I know she loved me. And I know she gave me this." She put a hand to the pendant.

"She looked for you too," Lia said, swallowing against the lump in her throat. The constant trips to Switzerland finally made sense. "She looked for a long time."

"You should know that your grandmother saved a lot

of people." Alina smiled. "I shared that little room more than once."

"We think she helped smuggle Allied airmen out of France," Lia replied.

"And women," Alina added.

"Women?"

"Well, one. I remember that she looked like a princess. I remember that she knew how to speak Hebrew. And French. And English. She knew how to open the trunk that your grand-mother always kept locked. And she was a terrible artist."

Lia laughed and wiped at the tears that had started down her cheeks. The mysterious threads of history contained in a Paris apartment were being woven back together, and Lia wanted to know more.

"My grandmother never talked about her time during the war," she told Alina. "What she did. Who she loved." Lia smiled and glanced up at Gabriel. "Would you tell me more? Anything you might remember?"

"Of course." The woman smiled.

★ ★ ★

The overhead lights in the gallery had been dimmed, only the spotlights that caught each painting still bright.

Lia leaned back on the bench that had been placed in the center of the room and gazed at the woman painted in a swirl of angry scarlets and oranges, her arms still flung over her head, her hands still outstretched. Only now her stare didn't seem as angry and accusing, merely defiant. A survivor instead of a victim.

"Alina doesn't want to take the Degas dancers home."

Gabriel sat down beside her. His voice echoed strangely in the empty room, the exhibit crowds long gone, almost all the staff departing not long after. "She said it would be a shame to have them hidden in a room again. She'd like them to remain part of the exhibit. She's inquired about museum loans after that."

"What about the rest of the collection?"

"She can't for certain say what belonged to her family. Though I have a last name now, which might help determine which pieces are rightfully hers."

Lia sighed. "What am I to do with the paintings in the meantime?"

"What you've already done." He put an arm over her shoulder. "Share them with the world. And share the story of your grandmère along with it. Because both are extraordinary."

"Yes." Lia leaned into his warmth.

"When do you return to Seville?" he asked.

"I don't."

"But what about—"

"I didn't take that job. I thought I'd stay here." She rested her head on his shoulder.

"Because of the exhibit?"

"No."

He was very still against her. "I see."

"I hoped you would," she whispered.

They sat like that for a long minute, neither moving, simply...together.

"I brought you something," Gabriel said eventually, reaching behind him.

Lia straightened and turned as Gabriel placed a violin case in her lap. She stared at it for a moment before opening it. The Collin-Mézin gleamed under the single light above their head.

"I had it restrung and restored properly," he told her.

"Why?"

"Because restoring things is kind of what I do."

"No, I mean why are you giving this to me?"

"Because I'm rather tired of hiding things in the attics of Millbrook."

"Ah. Yes, that seems to be a theme this evening."

"Was that a thank-you, then?"

"Thank you. It's beautiful. Shall I play it?"

"Yes, but not right now." Gabriel closed the case and latched it securely. He set the instrument on the bench and stood. "Right now, I have something else in mind."

"What are you doing?"

Gabriel looked around him at the deserted gallery, the lone light from above shining down on his head and turning his hair raven black, putting his features in stark contrast. He held out his hand. "I find myself in a moment when no one else in the world exists except a woman who has made me understand what it means to make every day count. Every moment count." He held out his hand. "Will you dance with me?"

Lia placed her hand in his.

"Yes."

AUTHOR'S NOTE

The Paris Apartment is a work of fiction. While a product of my imagination, the premises and characters I've chosen to create are inspired by real people and real events. The characters of Sophie Seymour and Estelle Allard were shaped by the experiences and courage of Virginia Hall, Pearl Witherington Cornioley, Christine Granville, Josephine Baker, Nancy Wake, and Andrée de Jongh. Their memoirs, interviews, and stories only give us an idea of how truly extraordinary each of these women was.

Sophie's work at Bletchley Park was based on the real men and women who worked tirelessly against time and almost impossible odds to decode Nazi encryption devices. Most of us have heard of the Enigma cipher and the remarkable work by Alan Turing and his team to break that cipher. Told less often seems to be the story of Tommy Flowers and Bill Tutte, who, together with their teams, developed Colossus—the machine that was able to break the Lorenz cipher, known as Tunny at Bletchley.

The Lorenz cipher was favoured by Hitler and used by High Command—and for good reason. It was far more powerful than the Enigma and capable of exceedingly complex encryptions. Additionally, unlike the Enigma, it did not depend on Morse code. Attached to a teleprinter, it automatically encrypted outgoing messages and decrypted incoming messages, allowing longer messages to be transmitted with greater ease. Each of the links between Nazi command posts was given a name by Bletchley—the Paris–Berlin link was referred to as Jellyfish.

There is no evidence that there was ever a Lorenz machine installed in the Ritz Hotel in Paris—that is pure imagination on my part. However, there is certainly evidence that the Nazis housed cipher machines in other hotels and buildings used as headquarters. An objective of the disastrous 1942 Dieppe assault may have been to capture coding/cipher technology at the Hotel Moderne, according to author David O'Keefe. Knowing that the Paris Ritz Hotel served as the headquarters of the Luftwaffe and was the residence of Hermann Göring (who was tapped as the successor to Hitler), a need for a direct, protected line of communication to the Führer seemed plausible for this work of fiction.

There is also no evidence that Bletchley Park ever received any intelligence from SOE operatives such as photos, code-books, or even sketches of the Lorenz machine. Declassified documents from the Target Intelligence Committee (TICOM), which was a joint operation between the U.K. and the U.S. targeting the capture of German signals intelligence organizations, provide the first Allied description of a captured, intact Tunny communications train, but not until 1945, long after D-Day. Nazi Field Marshal Albert Kesselring's captured "Fish Train" included six German trucks housing Tunny machines, radio transmitters, receivers, and encryption devices. Each truck contained two bunks for the driver and assistant, who operated the equipment. Tutte and his team did not have the benefit of this information at Bletchley. All the decryption work done was the product of an astonishing feat of reverse engineering.

The first Colossus machine, developed by Flowers, was operational by December 1943, allowing the Allies to intercept and decode critical information leading up to and after D-Day. For this story, however, I chose to imagine that Bletchley and its brilliant minds might have had a helping hand.

The Paris Ritz Hotel, with its socialites and industrialists, collaborators and spies (and, yes, hidden cupboards and stairways), remained the glamourous headquarters of the Luftwaffe throughout the war. The Charles Le Brun painting *The Sacrifice of Polyxena* (currently hanging in the Metropolitan Museum of Art, New York) that I have used in this book was, in fact, discovered hidden in plain sight in the luxurious Coco Chanel suite prior to the hotel's recent renovation. The provenance for this painting before its discovery in the hotel remains unknown. The current theory is that when César Ritz purchased the *hôtel particulier* at No. 15, Place Vendôme, once the home of princes and dukes, the Le Brun canvas was already hanging within. I chose a different history for this painting.

Other events that serve as a backdrop for this story that will be familiar are the bombing of Wieluń, Poland, in September of 1939, where I imagined Piotr was killed, and the Vél' d'Hiv' Roundup in July of 1942, when Rachel and her family members are taken. The objectives of the Luftwaffe bombing of the small and nonmilitary town of Wieluń, arguably the first major act of World War II, are not entirely clear. Some historians have suggested that the Germans received reports of the presence of Polish cavalry, like Piotr's character, in the vicinity of the town, but others disagree.

Regardless of motive, beginning in the early morning of September 1, the Luftwaffe dropped 46,000 kilograms of bombs on civilian targets, including the clearly marked hospital. There are also numerous accounts of the Luftwaffe strafing fleeing civilians. The timing of the initial bombing is a subject of debate, with Polish sources marking the first run at 4:30–4:40 a.m., while German records show the first run beginning at 5:40 a.m. For the purposes of this novel, I have used the German military records.

There is no debate, however, on the timing of the 1942 Vél' d'Hiv' Roundup, which began at 4:00 a.m. on July 16, 1942. Over 13,000 Jews were arrested by French police, more than 4,000 of them children. The majority of those arrested were held at the Vélodrome d'Hiver or other internment camps before being deported by cattle car to Auschwitz, though there are numerous stories of individuals hidden by friends or neighbours or who managed to escape arrest.

One of these courageous people who helped Jewish children escape occupied France altogether was the Frenchman Georges Loinger, whose creative methods of getting children out of France and into Switzerland included dressing up his charges as mourners and leading them through a cemetery located along the Swiss border. Aviva's journey out of France in this novel is based loosely on Loinger's efforts.

Lastly, the network of men and women that Estelle and Jerome were a part of was based on the very real Comet Line. This resistance organization operated in occupied

Belgium and France and helped Allied airmen and soldiers evade capture and return to Britain. An estimated 3,000 civilians assisted the Comet Line by hiding or escorting Allied airmen, and up to seventy percent of these helpers were women.

QUESTIONS FOR READERS

1. The theft and destruction of art is only one of many crimes perpetrated by the Nazis during World War II. What impact do you think this loss has on individual families who cannot rightfully claim or recover property? What significance does the loss of art have on society today? Do you understand why many people risked their lives during WWII to save artworks?

2. Was Lia right or wrong to display Gabriel's art in the exhibition without him knowing? What do you think convinced Gabriel to finally claim his work as his own?

3. Estelle had a very solitary childhood and adolescence, independent from her parents. Similarly, Lia lives a life separate from her immediate family. Do you think life-styles follow families through generations?

4. Many Parisians who patronized the Ritz, including Coco Chanel, collaborated in some manner with the occupy-ing Nazis. Were they right or wrong to do so? Do you

think it was a matter of survival? Or do you think it was the opportunity to further themselves that some took advantage of?

5. Why do you think Sophie told Estelle about some of her personal life? How isolated do you think both Sophie and Estelle felt when they met each other? What do you think drove their partnership?

6. Many characters hide their identities throughout the novel. Sophie hides that she is British, the airmen hide that they are American and Canadian, and even Estelle hides that she speaks German. Are there identities and opinions that you hide in your daily life? Why do you feel the need to do so? Do you think that many Jewish people still feel like they should hide their faith today?

7. So many of the characters appreciate art and art history: Estelle, of course, because she grew up with valuable paintings, but also Gabriel and his grandfather because they create art, and even young Aviva who loves Degas's ballerinas. Do you appreciate art? What kind and from what time period?

8. What does the attitude toward working women in the story tell us about gender norms in the 1930s and 1940s? Sophie's fellow spy Gerard is arguably the most overtly sexist character but what other characters discriminate against women? Were you at all surprised by the lack of or amount of freedom these women were granted?

9. As Estelle became more and more invested in her work with the French Resistance, did you feel that she changed in any way? How were those changes apparent through her interactions with others? Do you think these changes would make it harder for her to have a successful relationship with Jerome?

10. Did you feel that Estelle's violin was an important symbol in the book? How did Estelle feel about the damaged violin? Why did she keep it?

11. The historical WWII setting allows us to explore many themes such as race relations, political resistance, and struggling to survive. How are these themes relevant to current events today? Do you think there have been meaningful improvements since the 1930s and 1940s? Do you think there will be a future time when these issues will be resolved for most people?

12. Estelle and Sophie resist the Nazis in very different ways. Sophie reacts with anger and defiance, risking her life to spy for the British. Estelle proceeds with calm and caution, avoiding extreme risks for the sake of Aviva and the airmen she hides. Which one do you admire or relate to or sympathize with more? Who is more heroic in your opinion?

13. Did the book give you a better understanding of life during the Nazi occupation in Paris? Did you know that the Nazis took over the Ritz Hotel during the war? Have

you visited Paris? If not, would you like to go? And if so, what would you like to see while you are there?

14. Were you able to visualize the glamourous settings of Estelle's apartment and Millbrook Hall in lifelike detail? Would you prefer a life in Estelle's urban apartment or in Gabriel's ancestral home? In a film adaptation of the book, what actors would you cast as Estelle, Sophie, Gabriel, and Lia?

15. Did you cry while reading this book? Which scene moved you the most? Which character's fate would you say was the most tragic? What will you remember the most about *The Paris Apartment*?

FURTHER READING

Atwood, Kathryn. *Women Heroes of World War II* (Chicago Review Press, 2011).

Copeland, Jack. *Colossus: The Secrets of Bletchley Park's Code-Breaking Computers* (Oxford University Press, 2010).

Cragon, Harvey. *From Fish to Colossus: How the German Lorenz Cipher was Broken at Bletchley Park* (Cragon Books, 2003).

Edsel, Robert. *The Monuments Men: Allied Heroes, Nazi Thieves, and the Greatest Treasure Hunt in History* (Hachette Book Group, 2009).

Eisner, Peter. *The Freedom Line* (William Morrow, 2004).

Helm, Sarah. *A Life in Secrets: The Story of Vera Atkins and the Lost Agents of SOE* (Hachette UK Book Group, 2005).

Hodges, Andrew. *Alan Turing: The Enigma* (Random House UK, 2014).

Mazzeo, Tilar. *The Hotel on Place Vendôme: Life, Death, and Betrayal at the Hotel Ritz in Paris* (HarperCollins, 2015).

Mulley, Clare. *The Spy Who Loved: The Secrets and Lives of Christine Granville* (St. Martin's Press, 2012).

O'Keefe, David. *One Day in August: The Untold Story Behind Canada's Tragedy at Dieppe* (Knopf Canada, 2013).

Pearson, Judith. *The Wolves at the Door: The True Story of America's Greatest Female Spy* (Rowman & Littlefield, 2005).

Ronald, Susan. *Hitler's Art Thief* (St. Martin's Press, 2015).

Rosbottom, Ronald. *When Paris Went Dark: The City of Light Under German Occupation 1940–1944* (Hachette Book Group, 2014).

Sebba, Anne. *Les Parisiennes: How the Women of Paris Lived, Loved, and Died Under Nazi Occupation* (St. Martin's Press, 2016).

Stevenson, William. *Spymistress: The Life of Vera Atkins, the Greatest Female Secret Agent of World War II* (Arcade Publishing, 2007).

Vaughan, Hal. *Sleeping With the Enemy: Coco Chanel's Secret War* (Random House, Inc., 2011).

Witherington Cornioley, Pearl; edited by Atwood, Kathryn. *Code Name Pauline: Memoirs of a World War II Special Agent* (Chicago Review Press, 2015).

From the Combined Intelligence Objectives Subcommittee/Target Intelligence Committee (TICOM) Archives.

NW32823—*Demonstration of Kesselring's "Fish Train"* (TICOM/M-5, July 8, 1945).

NW32823/Appendix 7. *Transportation of O.B. West Non-Morse Station (Jellyfish) With Attached Personnel.* (TICOM/M-5, July 8, 1945).

ACKNOWLEDGEMENTS

I often hear comments that writing is a solitary endeavor, and certainly, at times, it can be. However, each book I have written has always been the result of a team effort. This one was no different, with many people making this book possible. Sincere thanks and gratitude to:

Dr. L. Storsley, doctor and violinist extraordinaire, for answering all my questions about morphine addiction and violins; Bletchley Park Trust and research historian David Kenyon, who answered my queries about the Lorenz and provided me directions to the TICOM archives and Oberbefehlshaberwest in Saint-Germain-en-Laye; the Monuments Men Foundation for offering guidance on recovery and restitution of stolen works; my agent, Stefanie Lieberman, who has been in my corner from the beginning; my editor, Alex Logan, who is brilliantly talented and makes each of my books better; and the entire Forever team, including Daniela Medina, who created the incredible art on the cover of this story.

Finally, a heartfelt thank-you to my family for all their love and support throughout this wonderful journey.

ABOUT THE AUTHOR

Award-winning author Kelly Bowen grew up in Manitoba, Canada, and attended the University of Manitoba, where she earned Bachelor of Science and Master of Science degrees in veterinary studies. She worked as a research scientist before realizing her dream to be a writer of historical fiction. Currently, Kelly lives in Winnipeg with her husband and two sons.

Learn more at:

www.kellybowen.net

Twitter @kellybowen09

Facebook.com/AuthorKellyBowen